nexis

A TRICKSTERS NOVEL

nexis

A TRICKSTERS NOVEL

A.L. DAVROE

ENTANGLED PUBLISHING, LLC

Entangled Publishing, LLC
2614 South Timberline Road
Suite 109
Fort Collins, CO 80525

Entangled Teen is an imprint of Entangled Publishing, LLC.

Visit our website at www.entangledpublishing.com.

Edited by Liz Pelletier
Cover design by Louisa Maggio
Interior design by Heather Howland and Jeremy Howland

Paperback ISBN 978-1-63375-017-3
Ebook ISBN 978-1-63375-122-4

Manufactured in the United States of America

First Edition December 2015

10 9 8 7 6 5 4 3 2 1

*To all the women and girls in this world who
have lost something precious but continue to fight.*

part one:

ELLANI DREXEL'S FUNERAL PYRE

chapter one

POST-AMERICAN DATE: 6/14/231

LONGITUDINAL TIMESTAMP: 8:05 P.M.

LOCATION: DOME 5: EVANESCENCE

I stand frozen, my arm intertwined with my father's and my body seized tight as a thermal coil, too frightened to step beneath the arched gate. G-Corp's grand ballroom is broad and high, like the orchestra halls of old, but this nano-glass bubble held high by steel girders and thick white columns is not a place where music is born. It's a place where futures are born—where my future begins. Breathless, I stare down, taking in the perfect features, exotic touches, pale skin, shimmering fabric, and delicate details of the inhabitants of my new realm: The Elite of the Aristocracy.

Dad leans in close. "What do you think?"

"Wow." I'm not sure he can hear the word over my thundering heart.

"I know," Dad says. "Can you imagine that The Broadcast was actually concerned about whether this place was an adequate location for this year's Executive Ball?"

This year the ball is being held on the hover-station—a

massive platform that hangs suspended between the city of Evanescence and the dome that protects her from the harsh world outside. I force myself to look away from the realm below and up at him, confused. "Why?"

He rolls his eyes as he guides me across the landing and toward the stairs. "Apparently they weren't certain if it would meet the expectations of Evanescence's most discerning Aristocrats. Though, I can't imagine something grander than this, can you?"

I give him an "are you kidding me" expression and turn back to the guests.

Dad clears his throat, touches the brass-colored plastic buttons on his lapel, and straightens his shoulders. "Ready?"

I pull up a cool, Aristocratic smile and paste it there. "As I'll ever be," I say through the fake expression. We descend the main staircase, the clicking of our hard plastic soles silenced by the thick pile of a green rug lining the chrome steps.

As we make our descent the spotlights swing wide and pin their heat upon us. For a mere instant, they blind me, making me feel like I've died and am walking into the light of mythical heaven—descending into the dream-realm of angels. But then my shoe clacks onto the hard white tile of the dance floor, and I'm reminded of my tangible, mortal world.

As if on cue, thousands of projected fireworks spring to life in midair—twinkling in and out of existence like vivid flowers—blooming and dying in time with the siren-song of GAGA 8.9, the cyberstar that G-Corp chose to sing for our entrance. I feel frozen again, drowned and unable to process my surroundings beyond the noise and light and all the confused emotion welling in my stomach.

As the fireworks sparkle out and I'm left standing under the bright lights, I remember where I am, and I swallow hard. Against the creamy tiles and columns hedging the staircase, against the emerald green carpet and reflective chrome, against all the clean perfection, I feel like an ugly scab. Logically, I know that no one is staring at me. My father is the one the spotlights are for, and there are so many other beautiful things to look at that the Elite couldn't possibly bother with me, but I still feel like they are glaring at me, accusing and unaccepting. I imagine the men and women are whispering to one another, their lips moving indiscernibly behind raised fans and champagne flutes, calling out and disowning my dark, imperfect Natural features.

Dad steps close and places a hand on my bare elbow. "Ellani, are you all right?"

I look up at him. My expression must tell him how I'm feeling, because his cool fingers tighten on my feverish skin and he smiles his reassurance. "It *is* a bit overwhelming at first. Isn't it?"

"They're staring at me," I mutter, hoping he can understand through my glued-on expression of congenial happiness.

Dad's face breaks into a broad grin as his hazel eyes flash across the throngs of Primped, Altered, and Modified Aristocrats. "As well they should."

I give a sidelong glance at Dad, uncertain if he's being cocky or honest. I can't tell. He has a right to be cocky. In less than a month, my father—a mere Programmer who once barely managed to scrape by on the fringes of the Aristocracy—has managed to climb to the top of Central Staffing's personnel list and is now one of the Elite.

President Cyr, the man who owns the whole of G-Corp, and thus all of Evanescence, steps up onto the platform centered in the middle of the vast circular room. His presence renders everyone still and quiet, as if he has the ability to control our behavior with a single thought. As expected of the President, he's perfect: tall and handsome, with hair that has been Altered to the color of sapphires and skin that glints under the spotlights. He's dressed in bright white, a color only the Presidential Family is allowed to wear. For a moment, his silvery eyes sweep over the crowd, his smile growing deeper and wider until I think that it must be painful for him to smile so enthusiastically.

Once he sees that everyone's eyes are upon him, he bends close to the sensors. "Ladies and gentlemen." As his voice blares throughout the room, he sweeps his arm wide, overtaking the crowd and holding his hand out in the direction of where my father and I are standing. The spotlights come back to us. "Warren Drexel."

The crowd explodes. As they clap and yell my father's name I ball my fists, trying to keep myself from shaking. All I can do is hope that no one notices how plain I am in comparison to my father—that my holo-mask does what I've programmed it to do: hide me in plain sight. Holding my breath, I dip into a well-practiced curtsy and say a secret prayer that I won't do something uncharacteristically stupid like bend over too far and land on my face.

As I straighten, the holo-screens hovering over the dance floor flash replays of this evening's awards ceremony where my father received Evanescence's most prestigious accolade: G-Corp's Civil Enrichment Award. He received that award for the development of Nexis, the most advanced and entertaining virtual-reality game in the known history of Post-America.

My father smiles and waves in appreciation, hamming it up for the crowd. But most of them are now focused on the screens, their internal programming telling them not to look away lest they miss something important. When The Broadcast shows a replay of the award being presented to my father, there is another round of applause and appreciative murmurs. Everyone listens to my father's acceptance speech, and they renew their appreciation when he exits the stage. Then the screens go still, their broad, flat expanses reflecting G-Corp's emblem—a silver *G* on a green triangle.

All eyes go back to the center of the room, but President Cyr is no longer at his podium. For a long moment, everyone seems at a loss as to what to do next. The cheering dies down and in the next instant it's as though Dad's sudden fame is forgotten. GAGA 8.9 gets back up onstage and begins another song. In a flurry of sharp brocade coattails and gossamer gowns cut in the Neo-Baroque fashion, the crowd turns back to their conversations, the perfect epitome of what all Aristocrats are like—bored and quickly dissatisfied with the latest trends.

"Sheep," my father mutters under his breath. He puts his hand to my back and urges me away from the stairs.

An android walks by, her chasis the typical service model— bland and forgettable—and her outfit a black uniform with the G-Corp emblem on the chest. She's guiding a hover-tray piled with plates of jewel-colored fruits, hearty vegetables, delicately cooked meats, and exotic cheeses.

My mouth waters as I reach out and snatch a plate.

My father does the same. "The only good part about these damned balls is the food." He turns to face me and grimaces. "Would you turn that ridiculous thing off? I want to see my daughter when I speak to her."

Annoyed and a little self-conscious, I turn my holo-mask off. Without the customized holographic projection that I've programmed into it, people will be able to see what I really look like.

"Much better."

I avoid looking at the people around me as I pop a grape into my mouth. With a small moan of pleasure, I close my eyes, relishing the sharp snap of the skin as my teeth clamp down and savoring the tart flavor oozing around my tongue. I chew it slowly, loving how refreshing and sweet such a small piece of food can be.

Dad picks up a piece of apple. "It's a crime how something that was once so common is now so rare," he reflects.

I nod. Most agricultural land outside has been destroyed, and hydroponic space within the dome is at a premium, making fresh produce expensive. Only synthetic and preservative laden foods are easy to come by now. "That's the case for lower-class Aristocrats, but that won't be an issue for us now, right?" I say, hopeful. "With the success of your game?"

"Perhaps."

He examines the apple, thoughtful. "You know, apples used to grow all over America. There's this fun little tale about a man named Johnny Appleseed."

I give him a pained expression. "Please Dad, not here."

He takes a deep breath and holds it, his intelligent eyes examining me. "You know, there was a time you liked my stories."

I roll my eyes. "I do, Dad. Just—not right now. It's embarrassing how you go off on these tangents about what was and used to be." I want to tell him that he sounds like a crazy man, the way he obsesses about the past, but I don't think he'd take that well.

"I'm trying to make a point, Ella."

"I know. It was *so* much better before the war. I get it, Dad. But..." I take a breath, trying to collect my thoughts. "Why bother? It's not like anyone complains about it. I mean, most people don't even know what it was like before the war. The Aristocrats only know Evanescence. It doesn't matter that a chasis was once an internal frame or that it was spelled differently. And no one cares that we didn't spell things with far fewer capitals," I say, using examples he gave at breakfast this morning when a lecture on my misuse of singular and plural pronouns (whatever those are) turned into him going on a tirade about how proper grammar has declined over the last few hundred years. "That was then, this is now. A chasis is an android overlay and it's spelled with only one *S* and random things are capitalized. Besides," I add, getting back on topic, "the Aristocracy prefers the taste of synthetic, preservative-laden food anyway. It's not like most of us can't afford to eat such unhealthy food."

Now it's Dad's turn to roll his eyes. "Oh yes, with the advent of Custom babies, most predispositions to disease, weight gain, and slow metabolisms have been removed from the Aristocratic genome. Besides, even if Aristocrats did manage to gain weight, they could just have the fatty tissue removed, couldn't they?" There's a strange, part-sarcastic, part-bitter tone to his voice that I don't quite understand.

I squint at him, unsure of what he's getting at. He takes a bite of the apple, chews it, and then frowns. "They taste better in Nexis."

I open my mouth to respond, but a shadow manifests in the corner of my vision, and a smooth, familiar voice interjects. "I completely agree."

Dad's eyes light up. "I figured you would, Zane."

Zane? I glance up at the newcomer just as he flashes a perfect grin that I've sighed over more than once when he shows up on The Broadcast. Zane Boyd. "Of course," he says, his posture angling so that he's now standing beside both me and my father. "Though I can't say I've been quiet about my support of the game. It's simply genius."

Dad lifts his hand and raises his brows at me. "You see?"

I sigh. All I ever hear from him is Nexis this and Nexis that. He's obsessed with that game. I mean, good for him, he developed a stupid game that won him the Civil Enrichment

Award. Other people feeding his obsession isn't helping. "It's just a game, Dad," I whisper.

His brows lift. "That game has done, and will do, a lot for you, young lady."

I look away, ashamed. It's not that I'm not grateful for what he's accomplished for me. The game has given me a higher social class. When it comes to arranging a marriage for me, it will be to a boy from an Elite family. With the extra credit Dad earns from the game, I can have things that I've always wanted. And, because his abilities as a Programmer are now well known, the likelihood of me getting a good job placement after school is much higher. It's everything I could ever want wrapped with a huge, silky bow.

But if time could be reversed and all those days he spent locked up in his workroom could be turned to days that he spent with me, I think I'd give up all the benefits. Even when he does spend time with me, all Dad seems to want to do is talk about programming and his game. I'm sure he thinks it's exciting for me. I am, after all, his daughter—his biological protégé—but I don't have as much interest in my abilities as a Programmer as Dad does. I'm good as a Programmer, I know that, and part of me *is* a little interested in the genius that is Nexis but, I don't want to be a Programmer. I want to be a Designer and my jealousy of the game is enough to keep me silent about any Programming questions I might have about it. I can't tell any of that to Dad, though; it would break his heart. So instead of saying what I really think, I say, "I know."

"Do you?" Dad asks. "Not just for you. For many people. Zane, why don't you tell my daughter about the story you're covering in the Outer Block?"

Zane Boyd looks down at me and I feel my face flush. I don't normally get attention from anyone who is Elite, let alone a Broadcast anchor. Avoiding his penetrating stare, I focus on his suit instead. Harley Dean, my favorite designer. I knew there was a reason I liked this guy—besides the fact that he's Custom stunning, has tasteful Mods, and covers his stories with admirable outspokenness.

"Well," he says, and I can't help but look back up into his Altered eyes—royal purple with luminescent flecks—"there's been talk that Lady Cyr will be funding gaming houses for the Disfavored."

I blink, stunned. I never would have expected Dad's game would be the thing that bridged the gap between us and them.

Zane continues. "I've gone out once already to do some preliminary coverage for a miniseries I'll be running later this year. I'm extremely interested in how the game will impact the Disfavored."

I cock my head, impressed. Zane isn't much older than I am. I remember passing him in the halls at school when I was transferred to Paramount Prep after my first set of aptitude tests. It's not only amazing how gifted and charismatic an anchor he is, but also how brave he is. "Aren't you frightened? Going out among them?"

He laughs at me, his whole face lighting up. "Frightened? Of what?" He sobers up. "They're just like you, Ellani."

I feel my jaw drop in shock. I'm not sure if I'm more moved that Zane Boyd actually knows my name or that he's bringing attention to my Natural features.

Dad reaches out and grasps Zane's shoulder. As if sensing my confusion, he says, "Considering the game's recent coverage on The Broadcast, Zane and I have been seeing a lot of each other lately. You've come up in conversation more than once."

Why? I don't factor into Nexis at all.

Zane narrows furtive eyes. "I've been looking forward to finally meeting the daughter of Cleo and Warren Drexel."

I hold out my hands. "Well, as you can see there isn't much to her."

He smirks. "I beg to differ."

Dad clears his throat. "I think I'm going to leave you two to—" but he is interrupted by a familiar voice. "Well, Warren, aren't you proud of yourself?"

I turn to see Uncle Simon, my father's brother and business partner, standing just behind me, a tall crystalline glass of champagne in one hand and the sleeve of an uncomfortable looking Bastian—his adopted son—in the other. Uncle Simon is dressed in a militaristic navy blue jacket that follows the Justaucorps design. The braided cord around his cuffs and lapels has been woven through with fiber-optic thread so that a constant waterfall of rainbows glistens at the slightest movement.

"Oh, I'm not sure they needed to make such a grand spectacle as all of this," Dad says. "They've never made such a big deal about the award before."

Uncle Simon drops Bastian's sleeve and claps my father on the shoulder. "Come now, this is no time to be bashful. Nexis is the most revolutionary game to hit Evanescence since the dawn of the Post-American Age. Bask in the glory, my brother." He tips his head back and downs his champagne.

"How many of those have you had, Simon?"

Bastian rolls his eyes and says, "Five since we arrived."

"You be quiet, Bastian," Uncle Simon scolds. "You're an awful son."

Looking like he's mentally searching for a reserve of patience which, being my Uncle's son, he does often, Bastian runs both his hands through his hair—onyx black with strands of silver woven throughout. Bastian is a Natural—a Disfavored actually. But Uncle Simon adopted him when he was very young and, unlike me, he's had the luxury of Altering and Modifying himself ever since. He looks almost Aristocratic. "You *did* ask me to count for you."

Uncle Simon glances down at the glass and, shrugging, grins to himself. "Well, stop counting. Ella, you look like you want to dance." He grabs my wrist, making me drop my plate, and practically tosses me at Bastian. "Bastian, dance with Ella. Isn't she lovely tonight?"

Bastian, despite the annoyance in his angular features, gently sets me back on both my feet and ignores the question. Instead, he says, "Honestly, you're making a ruckus. Look what you've done." He gestures at the shattered plate and then glances at the Elites close by who turned to stare at the commotion. Unlike most Aristocrats, Bastian is not the sort who likes to draw attention.

Dad clears his throat, breaking the tension. "Zane, I believe you and Bastian have met before."

Bastian bares his teeth in something that looks less like a friendly grin and more like a challenge. "Zane and I go way back."

Yes, if I remember correctly, they graduated together.

Zane leans close to my ear. "He's supposed to be almost as good at programming as you are, you must be competitive…"

I resist a shiver, whether it's Zane's whisper on the back of my neck or the way Bastian's fingers curl at my spine, I'm not sure.

Bastian smirks. "Ella and I have never been competitive. And I wouldn't say I'm half as good." His jet black eyes slide over me. "Not nearly. I've seen what she can do. She's her father's daughter."

"See?" Uncle Simon breathes, drawing the word out. "Warren, you should live it up." He looks at me while pointing at my father. "You agree with me, don't you, Ella?"

I nod, hoping that agreeing will save me from getting sucked into another one of Uncle Simon's lectures on the value of virtual reality on the psyche of the Post-American people. I love my Uncle Simon, he has a quick smile and excellent taste in clothing, but he bores the heck out of me, especially when he's drunk. "Yeah, Dad, live it up."

"Smart girl, our Ella." Uncle Simon punches Dad's arm. Another service android walks by and my uncle takes a moment to change out his empty glass for a full one before turning back to me. "You should be very proud of your father, Ellani. He's done a great thing for humanity."

Zane echoes the sentiment.

"And for our family," Uncle Simon adds.

I wince, hating that he brought the sudden skyrocket of our status into the conversation in front of a gorgeous Broadcast Anchor, who I'd rather not remind I'm from a lower-class household, but he seems to be watching me, gauging my reaction with an amused expression, and suddenly I feel a bit lighter.

"Oh, I know," I say, trying to sound as reverent as possible while all I want to do is laugh. "Just the fact that I'm here at the biggest social event in Evanescence speaks volumes."

Uncle Simon narrows tipsy eyes at me, as if he can hear my underlying sarcasm. "So, why are you standing here, girl? Shouldn't you be dancing or something?" He shoves Bastian, which makes him step in to me in what feels far too much like an embrace. "Dance with my niece, you oaf."

The muscles in Bastian's jaw clench as he steers me toward the dance floor. "Anything you wish, *Father*." Which is a jab because Uncle Simon hates being called that.

To my surprise Zane turns as well. "I hope you gentlemen don't mind me stepping away."

Confused, I turn to my uncle and my father who both look quite satisfied with themselves. Disgusted, I turn away. As I let Bastian lead me into the crowd, I hear Dad say, "Will you stop with those. You're making a fool out of yourself."

I slump my shoulders. "Is he ever going to learn?"

"I doubt it," Bastian reflects. He glances back over his shoulder.

I smirk at him. "I think it's safe."

Bastian must not believe me, because he doesn't let go or step away, so I do it for him. We walk side by side for an awkward moment before he glances at Zane. "Is there a reason you're following us?" Zane grins, making Bastian stop and turn on him. "I know what you're doing."

Zane's brow raises, he glances at me, then back at Bastian, then back at me before stepping up to me and offering his hand. "Would you like to dance?"

Stunned, I take his hand and let him lead me onto the dance floor. Zane is a good lead, which makes it easy for my mind to notice the people around us…watching.

"Are you enjoying yourself?" he asks.

I try not to look at him. "Yes. Now that I'm away from my father and uncle."

He scoffs. "They're both brilliant men."

I roll my eyes. "Don't remind me."

"You'll be like them one day. Someone great."

I lower my chin, rejecting the notion. Everyone wants to be great. To be great is to be noticed, and to be noticed for greatness is what everyone in Evanescence wants. But I don't want to be great in that way. "You're so certain?"

Zane stops mid-step in the middle of the dance floor and steps away from me. Uncertain what I've done to earn his rejection, I lower my head. But the next instant he catches my jaw with his fingers and raises my gaze to meet his. I have trouble meeting that gaze, but when I do, I can't turn away. He stares at me for a very long time before saying, "I am, actually." And then he stares some more. I feel my heart hammering and my face heating.

And then there's someone beside us, tapping his shoulder, and he looks away.

"May I cut in?"

Zane nods, melting away to allow Bastian to step in and take my hand. His fingers slide along my waist, and he presses me backward, making me dance although my feet feel heavy. After a few turns, I regain my focus and fall into step with him.

"What are you doing?" he mutters.

I frown at him. "What do you mean?"

He grumbles under his breath. "He's a playboy, Ella, you know that."

I ball my fist at his shoulder and look away. "I didn't ask him to come."

His muscle goes limp under my fingers, defeat. "Yeah, I know. Your father did, which is even worse. What is he thinking?" Before I can voice my suspicion, Bastian keeps talking. "I mean, that guy? As a suitor for you?" His body goes stiff. "Over my dead body."

I blink up at him, stunned by his sudden streak of protective-ness and by the news that Zane is apparently a suitor.

After a moment, he realizes I'm staring at him and looks back down at me. "What?"

I smirk at him, trying not to laugh. "I didn't know you cared."

He frowns at me. "I've known you since we were kids. I wouldn't let some scoundrel like that besmirch your reputation."

I want to laugh at him. "What reputation? Seriously, Bastian, you're overreacting. If Zane Boyd wanted to pursue anything with me, it would be a blessing. He's a good match."

Bastian clenches his jaw and looks away, fighting for patience again. "Just shut up and dance."

chapter two

Delia Haverfeld is not a difficult person to find. She, like me, was born a Natural—a child who wasn't genetically Customized to fit the golden ratio. Together, Delia and I are two of only a few teens in Evanescence who do not fit da Vinci's Canon of Bodily Proportions. But, unlike me, even though her parents chose to have a Natural child, they allow her to Alter and Modify herself; anything Delia doesn't like about her Natural body is easily changed. Since she was legally able, she has gone through various surgeries to make herself both blend in and stand out among the other Aristocrats.

She's had the base Modifications: she's been nipped and tucked to remove fatty tissue, she's had Rhinoplasty to make her nose more unique, and she's had a breast augmentation. She also has some Alterations: ocular inserts that change the holographic projection of makeup around her eyes, and she's had an epidermal injection of Argence to make her skin lighter and brighter. Her latest and most successful Alteration turned her once midnight black hair to an odd striped combination of red, yellow, green, and blue.

She claims she got the inspiration from seeing an old holograph of an extinct tropical bird called a macaw. While I find the color combination unseemly, it does make her easy to spot in a crowd—and that's all that matters among the Aristocrats.

While Bastian—who has designated himself my chaperone for the evening—is off finding me a glass of champagne, I slip away. I find Delia in a small group of fellow students and head toward her. When she sees me, her surgically perfected face lights up.

"NiNi," she yelps and comes skimming toward me.

Delia has a natural grace that no amount of Altering or Modifying could bestow upon an Aristocrat. Above all else, I think that's why the other girls pay her any mind.

I reach out and accept her outstretched hands. She pulls me close, and we exchange distant kisses to each other's cheeks. Then she steps away with a grin.

"You look ravishing, darling."

I fall easily into the over-affectionate, seemingly self-deprecating Neo-Aristocratic dialect that we've all spoken since first-year in school. "Not at all, love. What a splendid hairstyle you're wearing tonight. Have you a new Primper?"

She giggles, her laugh a Modified tinkling of bells that reminds me of something fizzy on the base of my tongue. Pretenses forgotten, I lift a brow. "That's new."

She bites her bottom lip and casts a sidelong glance toward the three other girls she's been standing with. I only recognize one of them. Carsai Sheldon. She's the most popular girl in school. Her father is President Cyr's oldest and most personal friend; she always has the latest Mods and Alts.

I like her about as much as I like lab-grown caviar: not at all. From the moment I began attending Paramount Preparatory High School for the Gifted, she has made it a point to give me grief. Delia claims it's because Carsai is jealous. It wasn't my family's wealth and social standing that got me into the prestigious school, it was my sheer academic aptitude.

But it's beauty, not brains, that make you stand out among the younger set of Aristocrats, so my proficiency as a Programmer means little to Carsai. Since Delia is also a scholarship case like me, she treats Delia just as horribly. So I'm a little confused as to why my best friend is socializing with her.

As if sensing my "she's gone traitor" thoughts, Delia tugs on my arm. "Uh, we'll be right back."

Carsai nods and turns back toward the other two girls who, I've decided, must attend a different Aristocratic preparatory school.

Once we're out of eye and earshot of Carsai and her Altered cronies, Delia spins me around and presses me into a little nook. I have trouble keeping my face from showing how hurt I feel. "What are you doing with Carsai?"

Delia's eyes dart out toward the people standing nearby, but no one seems to have heard. "Keep your voice down," she whispers.

I clamp my teeth together and glare at her until my face hurts.

"Okay," she says, throwing up her hands. "She likes my new Mod."

I scrunch my nose, unconvinced. Delia's new laugh is a pretty Modification but unlikely to draw Carsai's attention—especially since she just got a similar one.

Delia's shoulders drop, her face losing all pretense. "Okay, fine. She was asking about you."

I blink. "Me? What for?" That can't be good.

She shrugs. "She wanted to know about your dad's game. She was wondering if you had access to a cheat code to infiltrate another person's game."

I frown, confused. "She doesn't strike me as a gamer."

Delia shakes her head. "No. But…" Her eyes wander back out toward the crowd and land on a particular group that I, despite having two entertaining gentlemen in tow for the evening, have also been keeping a partial eye on since arriving. "*He's* been playing it."

I nod, suddenly understanding where Carsai is coming from. She's not interested in me. She's interested in Quentin Cyr, the son of the President. She wants me to get a cheat code so she can access his game. "Little sneak…"

"I wish I had thought of it," Delia says with a sigh. "Imagine how romantic playing a game with Quentin would be."

"Yeah. It would be pretty cracked." *Why didn't I think of that?* I glance around for Bastian, wondering if he could be convinced to reveal one, but I get distracted by Quentin.

Delia, fussing with the sleeve of my dress, draws my attention back to her soft brown gaze and away from the boy I've been in love with since the moment I set eyes on him. She wants to Modify her eyes, genetically splice them so that they look reptilian or get them injected with nanites so that they change color with her mood. But I think she'd lose something if she changed them. Eye Mods have always set me on edge. They seem to take the last vestiges of humanity away from a person.

"This is a beautiful dress, Ni."

I sigh and stare down at what was, up until an hour ago, my pride and joy. A lovely black satin and silk gown with a low square neckline; full, laced and ribboned sleeves; and a long stomacher that hides my Natural flaws. All of my dark brown,

Natural curls have been piled on top of my head and held in place with a fantastic comb with synthetic feathers, glass beads, and sequins. My shoes are three-inch heels made of a smoky plastic that looks like black glass decorated with delicate lace and ribbons, made to match my sleeves. In all, the outfit makes me feel like a mysterious, towering obelisk.

"I don't feel so beautiful wearing it."

"Is your reception off?" Delia's voice is shrill. "It's the most beautiful dress here. You always have the most beautiful dresses. And considering who I've seen you walking around with this evening, it's obviously doing what it's supposed to."

I blush. Since I can't use my allowance to buy Alterations and Modifications, I pour my heart and soul into the only option I have left—fashion. I have made it my life's mission to design the loveliest, most unique wardrobe in the entirety of Paramount Prep. I've had momentous failures as well as successes, but at least I manage to turn heads. It has become more than a life mission or a hobby. It's something that I truly love and I wish, almost as much as I wish I could kiss Quentin, that I had been born a Designer instead of a Programmer. I smile. "Thanks Dee."

She looks up and grins. "I like your mask, too. The simplicity of the demi-mask really emphasizes your dress."

My mask is the same type of generic holo-mask that everyone is wearing. The mask headpieces allow us to choose from a large variety of pre-programmed holographic projections; each is then tailored by our G-Chips to fit perfectly over our unique features, moving and adjusting as we speak and make expressions, but still meant to look like a true physical mask. However, being Ellani Drexel and having been born with a remarkable talent for programming, I've made a few adjustments to mine. "It gets better," I whisper.

Delia watches with wide, fascinated eyes as I reach up and

press a button on the side of the headband-like headpiece, calling up the mask my father told me to turn off not so long ago. Nothing in front of me changes, but I can tell the projection has by the astounded gasp she emits. "Oh my sparks," she breathes.

I stand still, proud of myself as she steps from side to side examining my face. What she's seeing is no longer a demi-mask over Natural features, but a perfect Aristocratic face—a face that I wish I had. "It's perfect. I can't tell the difference. Those look just like real Mods."

In almost comical timing, Bastian wanders by us, searching eyes skimming, lingering, but ultimately passing on, still looking. Delia hides her grin behind her hand until he looks away.

Smug, I cross my arms. "Feel free to bow before my genius."

She takes a dramatic step backward and curtsies. "I am unworthy."

We both break down in laughter, her new, Elite-worthy giggle making me feel like I've lost an old friend who I never truly knew.

chapter three

POST-AMERICAN DATE: 6/14/231

LONGITUDINAL TIMESTAMP: 9:43 P.M.

LOCATION: DOME 5: EVANESCENCE

We sit at a table close enough to Quentin Cyr that Delia and I can see him, but far enough away that no one will say anything to us. Sometimes it's as if the other Aristocrats think they'll catch some kind of Natural disease from us.

Dee puts down her glass of champagne and says, "So, how does it feel to be a celebrity?"

I smirk. "You mean being the only person left in Evanescence who still looks like a Natural?"

Dee's face falls, knowing that I'm subtly jabbing her for leaving me to be the only freak. "I was talking about your dad."

"I know."

There's an awkward moment of silence but eventually, she says, "He'll have to let you Mod and Alt now, right? I mean, you're both Elite now."

I stare at my hands. "I don't think so." It doesn't matter to Dad how out of place I am, he's *really* stubborn.

"Oh," she breathes. As if wanting to give herself something

more cheerful to think about, Delia's eyes dart toward where Quentin Cyr is sitting surrounded by Aristocratic friends and his slave Dolls.

He seems bored by all the attention, his eyes—like diamonds twinkling under the thousands of tiny LED lights—look glazed. When he shifts, his hair gleams—each strand like a fiber-optic ray of starlight and his silvery skin has a delicate pattern that shimmers mutely when he moves.

"He looks like an angel," Delia whispers, awed.

I nod, not bothering to remind her she's never actually seen an angel. But I do agree with her. Dressed in a slashed white doublet and white breeches, lounging on his throne like a prince, and looking so perfect, I swear I might see some wings manifesting behind his lovely, lace-swathed head. I smooth out the fabric of my dress, thinking of how we'd look so complementary on the dance floor together, a swirling black and white pair. "I've never seen a person with such an eye for Alteration and Modification. He should be a Designer."

"Yeah, it's like every surgery he undergoes only serves to intensify the aesthetic pleasure of staring at him."

I glance at Dee. She has got her chin propped on her fist and is doing the goo-goo eyed thing. "Careful, you might start drooling." She doesn't seem to hear me. I glance back at Quentin, the desire I have just to stand close to him hurting my chest.

Of course, such perfection comes with a price. As much as I want to only stare at Quentin, I can't help how my eyes wander to his collection of Dolls. Dolls aren't dolls at all, but Disfavored Naturals who have, for some reason or another, subjected themselves to allowing Aristocrats to experiment on them in the search of just the right Modification or Alteration. In Quentin's case, it's a group of boys who all seem about our age. Quentin always keeps his Dolls close to him. He dresses them in simple black, overly stiff outfits—like a troop of stoic masterpieces dressed in the unifying mark of a military uniform.

As gaudy as the whole troop of them look together, each is lovely in his own right. It seems Quentin puts some thought into who he will use for what experiments. It would do no good to begin Alting and Moding at random and letting all the Dolls you surround yourself with become so ugly you couldn't stand to even look at them. It's as if Quentin wants to make a point—a Doll is his master's marionette.

"I've never noticed how many Dolls Quentin actually has," I say quietly.

Delia shifts next to me. "What?"

"The Dolls. Do you think he drags all those Dolls around to brag?"

Delia's gaze drifts to the Dolls standing to Quentin's left. "Brag how?"

I roll my eyes. Delia, while sweet and wonderful and a genius with codes, lacks common sense. "A display of wealth. To show how many people he was willing to buy, to show how much he continues to put into each one. How many credits do you think all those people and all those Mods and Alts cost him?"

Delia nods to herself, her lips lifting at one corner. "He can give me one if he's looking to fatten his credit account. I'll take Shadow."

I glance at the Doll standing just behind Quentin's shoulder. That Doll is the most heavily used out of all of them, perhaps so much so that he may not qualify as beautiful any more. Out of all the Dolls, he seems like Quentin's favorite. Quentin even takes him to school with him. That Doll never speaks to anyone but Quentin and no one knows his name. We all just call him Shadow.

There are many lower-class Aristocratic girls who, knowing they'll never have a chance at even speaking to Quentin, begin obsessing over Shadow—as if that will somehow bring them closer to Quentin. They wonder who he is and why he's a Doll. Some fantasize that Quentin has yet to court a girl because he is secretly involved with Shadow—a scandal of secret love between such distinct classes.

Personally, I'm not interested in Shadow. His unnatural, Modified eyes and over-sharp features are predatory. Like a genetically spliced and puzzled-together toy soldier, he's always rigid—as if he can barely move in his starched uniform, and he stares at us in such a way that he looks as if he wants to strangle us all. He knows he's a sideshow freak, and he hates us for putting him there.

"You can have him," I say, turning my eyes back to Quentin. "I'm only interested in the best."

"What about Zane Boyd? I saw you dancing with him earlier. He's a total catch."

I shrug. "Bastian says I shouldn't."

"That's because Bastian wants you for himself." Her voice is sad and resigned. It's always been clear to me that Delia has always had a thing for Bastian.

"Does not."

She lifts her brows. "Oh come on, Ni, I've known you both for forever, and he likes you. It's obvious."

"He doesn't. He acts like I'm a giant burden that Uncle Simon constantly shoves on him. And he's my cousin—that's gross."

"He's not your real cousin."

I wave my hand dismissively. "That doesn't matter. He's like an annoying older brother. It won't happen. Besides," I say, turning away. "Bastian thinks Zane is talking to Dad about courting."

Delia gasps, her eyes wide. Eventually, she says. "I do hear things about Zane…"

I close my eyes and sigh. "Yeah. I know." He'd be the disloyal sort of husband, should this marriage come to fruition. For a moment, I toy with the idea of rejecting the concept. But, I remind myself that, in the Aristocracy, marriages are for convenience, not love. And Zane is a good choice for me, more than I deserve. I'd be lucky to get him.

"There are a lot of marriages like that, though," Delia says. "It doesn't mean you'd be unhappy. He's wealthy, has lots of power, and he's well liked."

I nod.

"Maybe it won't even happen, though. Maybe we're just speculating. Maybe you'll marry Quentin?" she offers.

I smile at her. I love this girl. "Maybe…"

She leans forward. "Maybe you should go show him your mask?"

I turn to her wide-eyed and can't help a scoff. "You're joking, right? I've never been within ten feet of Quentin. I doubt he even knows I exist. Besides, I don't have a high enough social standing to present myself."

Dee holds up a finger. "Correction. You *didn't* have a high enough social standing. Your father has been elevated to the Elite, which means you have as well. You're now eligible to present yourself to someone as high ranking as Quentin."

"I guess so." I bite the inside of my cheek. "Still, the prospect of actually calling attention to myself in front of him…"

"If you're good enough to attract Zane Boyd's attention, then you're good enough for Quentin Cyr." In the next instant, Delia's fingers are clamping around mine. "Come on, silly."

The hover-chair goes spinning as she hauls me out of my seat and drags me across the dance floor.

chapter four

POST-AMERICAN DATE: 6/14/231

LONGITUDINAL TIMESTAMP: 10:02 P.M.

LOCATION: DOME 5: EVANESCENCE

Delia squeezes my hand as we stand in the small crowd of girls lining the carpet. "Ohmysparks, I'm so nervous," she squeals.

"I can't believe I let you talk me into this," I mutter back.

Delia and I stand on the edge of the group of girls wanting Quentin's attention, practically hiding behind one of the massive columns supporting a ceiling painted with fat, naked children with fluffy wings. Delia's hand is shaking in mine. I know she's the one shaking and not me because, again, I've gone so stiff I can barely breathe. I have no idea if either of us is reacting out of excitement or fear.

Carsai glares at us from where she's standing with her two friends and some of the other Elite girls from Paramount. They're all standing closer to Quentin's inner circle, unafraid to get close and flaunt themselves for his inspection. She mutters something to the closest few; they glance toward us and start cackling. I turn away from them and look back at Quentin. His friends and his Dolls watch us girls with interest, though Quentin doesn't seem to be looking at all.

The crowd of Aristocratic boys and Dolls divides, giving us a clear view of Quentin as he stands. He stretches and yawns, showing a lazy carelessness about this whole affair while giving all of us a tempting glimpse of his abdominal enhancements. He glances sideways at Shadow, and some kind of silent message is exchanged between the two of them. Shadow picks up Quentin's untouched glass of champagne and follows him as he takes steps down the dais. I hold my breath as he walks toward us, Shadow haunting his footsteps and his friends from school and his Dolls trailing like the Halley's Comet that Dad once showed me a holograph of.

He slows as he comes closer to the girls gathered at the bottom of the dais, his eyes slicing to the side to examine each with half interest. Delia and I have watched this happen at other balls. This is always how it works. If a girl isn't astounding enough to catch his attention from the corner of his eye, he won't spare her a full glance. If he likes what he sees upon further examination, he'll ask that particular girl to dance. To my knowledge, only three girls have been asked to dance in the past. Carsai was one of them. Once. He never asked her to dance again.

Delia's fingers tighten so hard around mine that I want to cry out, but I try valiantly to keep my face serene as I watch his feet advance down the green carpet. He passes Carsai without a glance. Her two friends step forward to intercept him, and he brushes past them, too. He pauses as he comes flush with Delia. Stops.

I chance a glance up. He's staring at me.

I swallow, uncertain whether I should curtsy or remain still so that he can examine me. Should I look into his eyes?

Slowly, his brow—or, what remains of his brow—creases downward, and the sparkles in his eyes twinkle out until I'm looking at flat amber eyes. Suddenly he scowls, turns, and stomps away. For a long moment, we're all too stunned to move. Then, everyone begins tripping over each other in their effort to herd after him.

Everyone but Shadow. He's standing over me, tall and overbearing as a droid security officer, his eyes that frightening combination of something caught between animal and human: something made soulless by the machinations of a superior man. He stares at me with an expression that I can't read—his face is too badly Modified to properly relay emotion.

I stare back at him, unable to look away. I feel pain in my chest, and shame. My face is hot, and my eyes are tearing. Who else is staring at me like this beast?

He reaches out toward me. I try to step back, but I hit the pillar behind me, so I lift my hands to protect myself from his attack. Before I can stop him, before I can cry out, he snatches the holo-mask headband from off my head, throws it to the ground, and slams his heel down upon it, snapping the frame in half and leaving two twisted, silver crescents connected by wires on the floor.

I turn my gaze from the broken holo-mask to him, bewildered and confused. I had thought he was going to bring physical harm to me. But all he really wanted to harm was my mask. The thing that made me like the other Aristocrats. Why? Why does he care?

Shadow lifts his terrifying eyes, black as my dress, and a strange expression crosses his mutilated features. His face is so far gone that I can't tell what his features are saying to me. Satisfaction in the cast of his chin? Betrayal in those primal eyes? Disgust in his upturned nose? Disappointment in the cast of his thin lips? Apprehension in his stance? He looks like he both wants to pounce on me and run away from me at the same time. Kill me or flee from me. Are my Natural features that hideous to look at? The expression is there for a mere instant before he lets out a long sigh, shakes his head, then turns and walks away from me.

I feel like I'm standing on a pedestal, on display before everyone, and not in a good way. Carsai is laughing just to my left. I can't look up. I refuse. I know they are laughing at me. Know that I'm ruined. The blood is rushing too fast in my ears; the tears are blurring my vision. All I can do is stare at the destroyed pieces of what, three minutes ago, had been something that made me part of a world I longed for. I have been put in my place.

"Well," Delia breathes, her voice shaking. "That was just plain rude." She grabs my wrist and drags me to the nearest bathroom where we barricade ourselves away from society and the Aristocracy. Away from Shadow's cruelty, Quentin's rejection, and Carsai's mockery. Dee holds me, letting me cry on her shoulder until I have no tears left. Then she tries to put me back together again.

"They're all just jealous of you, NiNi."

I shake my head at the bare chrome wall of the stall door. "They hate me."

Her face scrunches in concern. "N-No, they don't. They just aren't used to it. I mean, I've never seen it. But it's smart."

I shake my head. "It was stupid. I was stupid. I'll never get anywhere now."

"You never know," she ventures. "You're still turning heads. And that's what it's all about, right?"

Laughing bitterly, I shake my head. She doesn't get it. I'm ruined. I've made a fool of myself in front of the most Elite people in school. Quentin hates me. And to top it all off, I let a Doll shame me. I wish I were dead.

chapter five

POST-AMERICAN DATE: 6/15/231

LONGITUDINAL TIMESTAMP: 12:04 A.M.

LOCATION: DOME 5: EVANESCENCE

After Delia leaves, I find an alcove and decide to hide in it until it's time to leave. A few minutes later, Bastian steps in and sits beside me. "Here." He offers the broken bits of my holomask.

I lower my chin. "I don't want it."

He's quiet for a long moment. "That was stupid."

I close my eyes. "I know."

"We're not like them."

Annoyed, I open my eyes and cut them toward him. "I know."

He stares at his hands. Modified hands that have been Altered, turning the Natural into something acceptable. I don't know where Bastian thinks he can get off even saying "us." "What's so special about Quentin Cyr anyway? I mean, he's just some stupid—"

"Don't," I breathe.

"But—"

"No, Bastian. I don't want to talk about it." I give him a desperate expression. "Just let it go, okay?"

His eyes examine mine for a long moment, then he says, "Finc." He gets up and lays the headband beside me. "You really do look beautiful tonight. I should have told you that earlier." He turns and walks away.

Sighing, I stare down at the headband until a shadow falls over me. "That's quite the contraption."

I close my eyes. It's Zane. Great, he saw the spectacle, too. Will my shame never cease? Well, there goes the courting. He'll never want to be with a pariah like me now. "It was a stupid idea to wear it."

He steps to the side and sits next to the headband. He picks it up, turns it over between his fingers. "Was it? I think it's pretty revolutionary, actually."

"That's my point. If I could do that with a simple holo-mask, then anyone could."

Zane purses his lips. He knows I'm right. If I was able to program a mask to make my face look just as Modified and Altered as any Aristocrat's, then what's to stop one of the Disfavored from doing it? A mask like that undermines the system. Eventually he smiles, apprehensive, and meets my eyes. "Well, they don't have Programmers as talented and ingenious as you out there. So it's a good thing you're on the side of the Aristocracy, isn't it?"

I snort and look away. "I'm a threat to them."

He places a hand on my knee, and it makes my stomach go aflutter, despite my bad mood. "It's good that you're aware of it."

My floating stomach sinks, and I shake my head with a bitter scoff. "Is that supposed to comfort me?"

His fingers tighten, drawing my leg open so that our knees touch and he leans closer to me. "Not at all," he whispers in a spine-tingling purr, eyes alight with secret sparkle. "It should scare you. It should scare you and enliven you. It should make you want to start a fire. Because you can."

Confused by his words and what he's doing to my body, I stare at him for a long time. He sounds like Dad, spouting nonsense like this all the time. But, unlike Dad, Zane has a wild and dangerous charisma on his side. His touch and tone stir my insides, make me want to get up and run, make me want to do what he asks me to do.

"Are you all ready to go?"

Zane and I both jump at my father's voice. He's standing at the mouth of the alcove. With a blush, I hop to my feet. "Yes," I blurt, somehow feeling guilty. "Yes, I'm ready."

Dad nods toward Zane. "I'll speak with you soon, Zane."

Zane beams, his smolder now buried under congenial innocence. "Of course."

I move to follow after my father, but Zane catches my hand. I turn back as his fingers whisper along my skin and he presses the broken pieces of the holo-mask into my hand. "Remember what I said," he purrs, his eyes meeting mine. They're flat plum-colored now, no sparkle, but they're so deep. Deep and mysterious and promising.

There is no way I could ever forget this moment, this feeling of impossibility within. How could I ever hope to live up to being this man's wife? How could I even think of being with him? Or Quentin Cyr? Or even Bastian, for that matter? There is nothing here for this man.

"Think about it."

Swallowing, I nod and, reluctantly pulling away, trot after my father.

As we walk along the hall, he looks down, his face contorted with concern. "You're being awfully quiet."

I shrug.

"What did you think of Zane?"

I shrug again.

"Did something happen?"

I bite my lip. He wouldn't understand.

"You want to talk about it?"

I shake my head and stay silent as we take the aerovator down to track level and stand at the station while the android valet scans us. Then we wait for the retrieval code to go through. A few minutes later, our G-Corp issued company pod comes skimming out of the garage.

As Dad approaches the pod, it recognizes his implanted G-Chip and the door springs upward with a pneumatic hiss. The valet helps me get in, his mechanical hands strong and sure in mine, his protocol expertly bundling my massive gown and petticoats in after me.

"Honestly," my father breathes, attempting to get in beside me, "the clothes you kids find fashionable these days. So illogical. Why did your female ancestors bother fighting for the right to wear pants if you're just going to wear such restrictive, foolish garments?"

I ignore his comment. I'm in no mood for another one of Dad's tangents about our cultural regression.

As soon as Dad's body clears the sensors, the door closes behind him with a click. We sit silent as Dad's G-Chip responds to his neural impulses and relays destination coordinates to the pod's navigation program. The engine hums to life and the pod, running on autopilot like every other transport in the city, begins skimming over the hover-track. A few long moments pass in the bright blue-white light of the pod's interior. It's obvious that Dad is waiting for me to say something, but I don't feel like talking.

Eventually, he pulls his flex-bracelet off his wrist, snaps it flat, and tunes into The Broadcast. For a few minutes, I watch with him, reviewing a recap of this evening's events until I see myself coming down the stairs to the main ballroom, my face hidden behind one that isn't my own. I turn away and stare at my reflection in the mirrored interior of the pod. My Natural face and body are hideous to look at. No amount of Mods and Alts could hide that I'm not a Custom baby like most of the other Aristocrats.

Disgusted with my Natural human appearance, I punch the button on the side of the door. Immediately, the chameleon nanos in the window screen shift unreflective translucent, showing me Evanescence by night. The central block is a jumble of high-rise towers laced in mirrored screens; colorful, illuminated advertisements; and neon hover-ways that seem to stretch forever into the smog clinging to the dome that stretches from one side of the enclosing wall to the other. It's as if a confluence of bright white waves crashed over the wall, slammed to the ground just inside, and then crested upward and into each other at the center.

Where our residential block is, you can look out the window screen and see through the dome to the Disfavored on the other side. Those people are Naturals, like myself. Their ugliness shunned and barred away, allowed in only when some benevolent Aristocrat takes pity on them. Like Uncle Simon did with Bastian. Like Quentin did with his Dolls… Like Zane is no doubt doing with me.

I know why Zane is showing any interest in me at all. Because he's rebellious, and taking a Natural wife would anger the Cyrs. Because he cares about his ratings, and they'll go up if people see him conducting a charity marriage to a pathetic Natural.

I know why Quentin didn't pick me. I'm not beautiful enough. Nothing natural is beautiful. Naturals are disgusting and unworthy of the touch of a Cyr.

I punch the button again, closing myself off from the world I live in but don't belong to. "I know what I want for my birthday."

Dad doesn't look away from the flex screen before him. "Oh? I was thinking we could go visit the Imperial Garden."

"No," I say quietly, picking at the edge of my own flex-bracelet. "I was thinking of something else. Something I've wanted for a long time."

Dad spares me a nervous sideways glance before turning his kind eyes back on the screen. "Like what?"

I take a deep breath, hold it, and then say, "I want a Mod."

Dad tenses, his handsome face going rigid. "Please, Ella, we've gone over this."

I continue, insistent. "How about an Alt? They're cheaper." Then as an afterthought I say, "Plus, they're less invasive—just topical cosmetics, completely reversible."

"That's not the point."

"But, Dad—"

"No buts, Ella. You know how I feel about Modifications and Alterations. It's vile to cut your body apart, to shoot it full of nanites."

"You don't seem to have any problem with anyone else getting Modifications."

He puts the flex screen down on his lap and turns to me entirely. "That's different."

"How?" I demand.

"Because they aren't my little girl." He reaches out and puts a hand on my arm, as if that could make everything better. "You're a Natural, Ella. A beautiful, healthy Natural and there is nothing to be ashamed of."

I feel my fingers ball into fists around the satin of my gown, crushing it. I try not to let my anger taint my voice, but I don't do a very good job. "You don't get it, Dad. *You're* a Custom baby; you've never had to deal with not being perfect. I'm ugly. I don't fit in. I don't look like my friends, boys don't like me."

"Don't even tell me boys don't like you, Ella, when I've got one of the most affluent eligible bachelors asking after you."

I'm fairly certain the only thing Zane Boyd is interested in is status, wealth, and having an exotic wife. And oh, won't I just be the object of awe at each party—the freak. "People make fun of me."

"They're just trying to intimidate you. They're all insecure in their own skin."

"Insecure?" I repeat, incredulous. "What could possibly make them feel insecure?"

Dad looks at me for a long, quiet moment. "Look at me, Ella. Look at me, and look at every other father out there."

"I don't follow."

"We all look the same. We're all perfect. Yes, we might have different colored hair or eyes, but there's only so much variation on perfection. And that uniformity makes people feel like they aren't unique. Why do you think we began developing Mods and Alts? Those kids at school are picking on you, not because you're ugly, but because you stand out without even trying. They hate themselves, and they take it out on people they feel threatened by."

I roll my eyes. "No one is threatened by me. Have you seen Delia? She has Rhinoplasty and Argence. And have you seen her hair? I've never seen hair that color. There's no way she's jealous."

Dad pulls his hand away and sighs in frustration. "Your mother would be furious to hear you talk like this."

I glare at him. He always has to bring her up. Whenever he feels like he can't win an argument with me, he brings her up, makes me feel guilty for shaming the memory of my mother. No more. "Yeah, well, she isn't here, Dad. Mom's dead. She's been dead for a long time."

He scowls, making his own Custom face look ugly. "I made a promise to her, Ella. She wanted you to stay a Natural. And damn it, I'm going to fulfill that promise if I have to lock you in your room for the rest of your life."

For a brief instant, I entertain the idea of hacking into Dad's credit account, stealing enough credits for a Modification, and altering my own citizen profile to make me old enough to get a Modification without parental consent. But the rebellious thoughts are quickly extinguished and replaced with a sharp headache, compliments of my G-Chip.

I wince in pain.

Every citizen in Evanescence has a G-Chip implanted at birth. The chip is wired into our frontal lobe, allows us to function with other technology, and grants us passage as citizens of Evanescence.

From a young age, we are taught that our chip is our life. Without the chip, we'd be unable to walk into our own housing units; enter and direct our own transportation pods; we would be barred from schools and work places; we couldn't interact with our flex-bracelets, robots, or habitat control systems. Without the chip, our medical records, our basic data, our credit accounts, our nutritional readouts, our very identities would be lost. We couldn't be found. We couldn't be monitored. We'd be no one. We might as well be Disfavored.

I put a hand to my head and wait for the pain to pass, hating that I can't control my thoughts enough to prevent the parental controls from punishing me when I think about breaking the rules. In return for the G-Chip, we are—to some degree—controlled within the confines of the law. I am underage. I legally can't get a Mod or Alt if my parent doesn't provide both the financial and legal support. My father has put these parameters into my chip's programming and the chip acts accordingly. If I even think of trying to do something rebellious, such as stealing credits or adjusting my age on my profile so that I can get a Mod on my own, the chip punishes me and eradicates these thoughts.

Pain mostly gone, I lower my hand and blink away tears. Sometimes I hate my chip. Sometimes the desire to cut it out of my body flits across my mind, but the chip corrects those impulses, too.

Dad places his hand on mine, this time in a gesture of empathy. He, too, was a child once; he must know what it's like to have to deal with the chip's punishments. "Ella," he says softly, as if speaking loud might be too much for my poor scrambled brain to handle. "Why can't you just accept who and what you are?"

I turn away from him and rub my pounding temples as tears of anguish begin pouring down my face. "Because I hate what I am," I squeak. Then, realizing what I'm truly trying to say, I turn back to him. "I hate you for making me be this way—for not Customizing me. I hate you," I growl.

He flinches as if I've slapped him, and his eyes go wide with surprise. "Ella, I—"

Whatever Dad is going to say is cut off as the pod suddenly beeps an alert, and the internal lighting begins flashing red. In the next instant all I hear is a horrible grating and then a loud, jarring bang.

Fire. Heat.

My own scream.

Nothing.

chapter six

Pain. Light.

I try to sit up, to turn my head. I can't move. I see a circle of white light. Someone is standing over me. He's speaking, but I can't hear what he's saying. All I can hear is a high-pitched ringing. I blink, trying to focus through the spots. A metallic face. Droid… A medical cap and gown. Doctor?

Something inside my ear pops and crackles. I wince in pain but open my eyes again when I hear a hollow, muffled voice. " — can't save it, Doctor."

I turn my head. *Can't save it?* The doctor nods.

The world goes black.

I dream of being at a ball. At this ball everyone looks at me and smiles at me. Delia is there, dancing with Shadow. She looks so very happy. I dance with my father and then Bastian cuts in. I dance with Bastian, then Zane cuts in. I dance with Zane and then, to my utter surprise, Quentin cuts in. We dance for a long time. More than one dance. I'm the first girl he's ever asked to dance with more than once. He's smiling and staring down at me, like I matter.

As we spin, I catch my reflection in one of the reflective surfaces and stop mid step. Quentin takes my hand and guides me to the full-length mirror mounted on the wall. I stare at myself. Custom, Modified, and Altered. I wouldn't know my own face except to know I'm staring at my reflection in a mirror. I grin huge and Quentin leans close, whispers in my ear. "You're so beautiful."

chapter seven

When I wake, I'm in Dad's workroom. I know the textured plastic walls, the clinical gray of the industrial rug, the massive panel of his supercomputer at the far end of the room, and the red sheen of the synthetic vinyl hover-chair parked before the desk.

The digital picture of my mother is on the desk like it has always been, her gray eyes peering out from unruly brown curls, her mouth soft, but the angle of her fine arched brows somehow critical. She died when I was young—so young that I don't even remember her. When I first ran to Dad, crying and frightened that I couldn't remember my mother's face, he uploaded this picture from his own G-Chip onto the digital frame. He'd stared at her for a long time, his eyes sad, and then he'd placed her on the top shelf of the desk so that we could both remember her face.

She has sat there ever since, watching, reminding me of my

faults. Dad says she was a staunch Naturalist—that she demanded to have a Natural baby. She didn't believe in Custom babies or Mods or Alts. It's because of her that I am what I am, that I'm a social reject. Sometimes I hate her even more because I look so much like her and less like my Custom father. It's not fair. Half of my genes are perfect. Why can't I look perfect? Why do I have to look like her?

Beside my mother's picture is a new picture of my father. It was never there before, but I'm glad it is. It's good to see him—his bright hazel eyes sparkling in the artificial sunlight, his matching brown hair mussed like he's just run his fingers through it. Handsome as ever a genetically altered person can be, as loving as a truly good person ever will be.

Why did I tell him I hated him? I didn't mean that. I have to apologize. I need to get up and tell my father that I love him more than anything. I reach up, but my arm feels like a ton of foundation steel. I moan, feeling terrible and numb at the same time.

"She's awake." The voice is Meems's.

I let out a long, relieved breath. Meems. Good old Meems. After my mother died, Dad purchased Meems. She's a domestic android that has dutifully raised me as her own since she was programmed. She is my first friend, my mother, and my confidant.

Her face appears before me, blurry around the edges. Her silicone chasis flexes as her artificial anatomy relays her emotional protocol.

She was made to be pleasing to look at, tall with short-cropped, bright blond hair and light blue eyes. Dad says she looks like a young Julie Andrews in a modern day version of *The Sound of Music*. I never bothered to ask what he meant by that. To me, Meems is Meems. That's all that matters.

She reaches out and puts a hand on my forehead, her synthetic skin soft and room temperature against my own. "How do you feel, Ellani?"

"Don't strain her, Meems." A stranger steps into view, her Altered and Modified body crowding out my nanny's. "Ellani? Can you hear me?" She leans in close, her perfume cloying and her face garish and tacky to my sensitive eyes. Her taste in Mods and Alts is directly opposite Quentin's more refined eye.

Her face looks like the painted, cherubic face of a child's festival doll. Her hair is a zigzag combination of red and white, her eyes a startling green. These colors were once Natural colors, but years of interbreeding has limited the Natural hair and eye colors to various shades of brown and black, and Natural skin is a basic light brown. Even my own gray eyes are considered exotic by Natural standards.

Unable to find my voice, I nod. But I try to give her an expression that asks, "Who are you?"

She smiles at me, though the gesture doesn't reach her eyes. "My name is Katrina. I'm going to be taking care of you for a while." Katrina glances over her shoulder to where a girl about my age is standing. "This is my other ward, Sadie." Unlike me, Sadie is a Custom baby, tailored to be—even before she was born—perfect. Sadie has hair the color of blood, eyes the color of holo-glass garden grass, and skin that is flawless and pale. She looks like she could be Katrina's real daughter.

"Call the doctor in," Katrina says. "She's awake."

Ignoring Katrina, Sadie stays and watches, her eyes as big as saucers. It's as if she can't take her eyes off me, as if I'm suddenly fascinating in a way that I never was before. "What's wrong with her?" Her voice is a chorus.

"Quiet," Katrina snaps.

I struggle to speak. The sounds I make seem dry and weak, foreign and hollow to my own ears. "Where's Dad?"

Meems and Katrina share an uneasy glance.

"Uh…" Meems makes a strange strangled noise. "He's uh, not here." Suddenly, she makes a horrible choked noise and runs from the room. I glance back at my father's picture. Strange that they've put his picture beside my mother's unofficial memorial; two chrome-encased souls on display. And why have they put my bed here in his workroom when I have my own room downstairs, and he needs to come in here and work?

And then I understand. The hollow expression in Katrina's eyes. Meems's uncertain, halting explanation and sudden display of programmed emotion. "He's—" My voice fails me. I struggle to swallow through the lump in my throat. I feel acidic, panicked blood coursing through my body, threatening to make me burst into flames. I tear at the covers, struggle to get up, to run screaming through the house for my father.

I try to leap up.

My legs don't catch me.

Too light and unbalanced, I tumble to the floor.

I struggle to sit up, my arms like rotten noodles under my Natural weight.

I struggle to stand, but I can't seem to get my legs underneath me.

Frustrated, I look down.

And everything goes still. Silent. Horrifying.

I scream.

chapter eight

POST-AMERICAN DATE: 6/17/231

LONGITUDINAL TIMESTAMP: 8:34 P.M.

LOCATION: DOME 5: EVANESCENCE

I can't stop staring at them. Or rather, the lack of them. The macabre reality is like watching someone pick away a bandage with sharp, Altered fingernails. Except there is no blood, no scab. No promise of rebirth. Only death and loss. Loss of life and limb. Literally.

A desperate giggle escapes my lips.

"She's been staring at them since we got her back into bed," Katrina is telling the doctor.

The doctor, a Custom Aristocrat in a long synthetic coat, doesn't look up from the digi-chart his android nursing assistant is displaying. From where I lie, the holographic projection of the chart covers the assistant's entire body, leaving nothing but a disembodied pair of legs attached to a shadow.

Legs? Are those my legs?

"She's in shock," I hear the doctor say.

When I look up, my hands reach down and touch the ends, as if they've been waiting for my eyes to look away so that they can prove I'm only seeing things. They only find what my eyes already know. There's nothing there. My fingers and my stumps both seem to recoil, frightened of each other's touch.

It's true. There's nothing there anymore. My bottom lip won't stop trembling. Words are coming out of my mouth. I can hear them, but I don't understand them.

Katrina gives me an uneasy glance, her fiery red lips turned down and her fake green eyes limpid. "She hasn't, you know…" Her fine, manicured fingers fly to her head in an absent, red-nailed gesture. "Gone crazy or anything? I'm not certified to handle those kinds of cases."

It's a dream. A nightmare. I'm going to wake up. They will be there. He will be here.

The doctor spares one last glance at the chart and dismisses it. It disappears, revealing the chasis of an assistant nurse, plain face, white uniform, foolish white hat. "No. It's most likely the medication. It should wear off soon." His voice is smooth and reassuring.

Like Dad's voice. Tears begin oozing down my cheeks.

"Have you told her about her father?"

Katrina shakes her head, a wave of false color and emotion. She doesn't care. She can't possibly. She didn't know my father, and she doesn't know me. Though she plays this role well for the doctor. "No. I didn't get a chance to. I think she knows, though. I think she senses it."

The shroud is falling over my world. Black shroud, white light. I'm not here. I'm dead. This is not me. I'm dreaming my death march. Legless death march.

"There are options," the doctor is saying. "Once she heals and gets her strength back. There are prosthetics or nanites. It doesn't have to be permanent."

Katrina remains silent for a long moment. "We'll see. I can't really deal with all of this right now. Walking into this? Well, it's a proper mess. It's not my decision. I'm just the caretaker."

"Understandable. Please keep an eye on the G-Chip's readings. Notify me if she experiences any pain or refuses to eat."

"Yes. Thank you doctor."

Yes, thank you doctor.

chapter nine

POST-AMERICAN DATE: 6/18/231

LONGITUDINAL TIMESTAMP: 2:49 A.M.

LOCATION: DOME 5: EVANESCENCE

I have to pee.

I have to pee, and the bathroom is so far away.

"Meems," I whisper. Not loud enough. "Meems." I try louder. It hurts, scratches, makes my throat feel raw.

No answer.

I have to go. "Meems!" I cry, as loud as I can. As hard as I can. "Please." My voice breaks.

Still no Meems. *Where is she? I have to GO. Now.*

I wrench the blankets aside. Refusing to look at the stumps, I grip the side of the bed and try my best to lower myself down gently. But I'm weak. I'm weak and tired, and I was never that strong in the first place.

My arms give out, and I collapse on the floor. Pain shoots up my back, makes my skin sting and my muscles spasm. I force myself onto my stomach and try to crawl. My fingers scrabble against the floor, but the low pile is stiff and unforgiving, offering little purchase. The stumps bump and thump, responding to brain impulses that demand my legs help propel me. But the signals are lost; there are no legs to make move. Only the stumps, and they hurt. They hurt when they thump against the floor.

I go limp, wanting them to be still, wanting to stop the thumping and the twitching and the pain. Hating it all.

I try to hold my bottom half still, try to pull with my arms, but I just don't have the strength. I try and try until there is nothing left in me. Nothing but the desperate need to be in the tiny room that now seems like a mirage to a drug-addled mind.

I can't hold it anymore. As I lose control of myself, feel the hot terrible stuff seep down what's left of my legs, soaking the bandages and puddling under my stomach, I finally realize that I will never wake up. This is not a dream.

I have no legs.

My father is dead.

My life and everything about me is uglier than ever.

I finally begin to cry.

chapter ten

POST-AMERICAN DATE: 7/2/231

LONGITUDINAL TIMESTAMP: 10:15 A.M.

LOCATION: DOME 5: EVANESCENCE

Meems comes in, all bright and cheerful. "Well, what would you like to do today?"

For a long moment, I just glare at her. She knows very well that I can't *do* anything. When her expectant gaze doesn't waver, I look away.

I don't feel comfortable with how reliant on her my new handicap makes me. I feel like the geriatrics of old—before nano-tech and assisted suicide made it so that you could either live forever or, like my grandparents, die before you were pickled.

From the corner of my eye I can see her plant her hands on her hips. "Are you going to lie there and mope for the rest of your life?" she demands.

I turn and blink at her, blurry-eyed and lost in my own misery. Without realizing it, the words, "Go to hell," escape in a raspy breath. It feels good to say it. Eloquent. Succinct. I've always loved that old line. Dad once explained that hell used to be some kind of religious person's version of the Outer Block, a place where the Disfavored were banished to so that the Aristocrats wouldn't have to see or interact with them.

Before I know what's happening, Meems is across the room, her hand coming hard across my cheek. I wrench back, pain blooming through a body that has halfway lost itself to oblivion. When the stinging subsides and I can see straight once more, I whip my head up and scowl, ready to scream and rage at her, but she speaks first. "You are still alive." Her words are a tight, low hiss. "Do you think maybe you should have died instead of your father? He certainly would not have sat around rotting like this."

Meems's affirmation of his death is like a knife to the chest. A choked exhale escapes my lips. While I had my suspicions, as long as no one said anything about him, I could have almost convinced myself that he was anything else but dead. I start crying again, the reality of it just as painful as the loss of my legs. Overcome with grief, I bury my face in my hands.

The bed shifts as Meems perches herself beside me. I feel her hands come around me, pulling me close to her and holding me there, like she did when I used to have nightmares as a child.

"He's gone." I sob into her shoulder.

"Yes," she says, smoothing my hair. "But you are still here. Make him proud of you, Ellani. Be strong. Do not let this beat you. You must persevere."

I pull away and blink up at Meems's face. "H-How?"

She closes her eyes and looks away. "He would not like you like this."

I bite my trembling lip, hot tears still falling. She's right. Dad wouldn't be happy to see me wasting away. It's been weeks since the accident, and I've been moping and feeling sorry for myself. Still. "It's not as if I don't have a reason for being this way."

She nods. "I know. Despite my suggestions that it might

speed your recovery, Katrina and her ward will not come up and see you."

Why would they? Katrina, my new Evanescence-issued guardian, and the other ward who the city placed into her care, have no reason to care about me. I'm a disabled Natural, someone who was shoved into their care, someone who came with unexpected problems that they most likely didn't sign up for. I look down at my stumps and grimace. "I have no legs, and Dad is gone." The words come out in a squeak.

"You have a right to be upset," Meems concedes. "But I will have none of this behavior, Ellani."

I lower my head and shake it, hiding a bitter half smile. She never has been a patient android.

"Come, I think it is high time you did something productive with your time."

I don't fight Meems as she practically drags me out of bed and dresses me, but I don't do much to help her, either. When she ties knots at the ends of each of my pant legs, I cry harder.

"Oh, honestly," she breathes. She picks me up and plops me in Dad's hover-chair. "Some of us have work to do. Go feel sorry for yourself over there." With that she shoves the hover-chair in the direction of the window.

With nothing else to do, I watch the security droids below until I realize that, from this window, I get a clear view of the Outer Block and the wastelands beyond. The vast system of Disfavored neighborhoods that border Evanescence on all sides is hidden from the Aristocrats by a huge maximum security wall, but my house is built close to the wall, and I can see over it.

Down below, the shanty huts are built one on top of another, as if some great Aristocratic giant dumped industrial waste in the cracks of the earth. The makeshift rope ladders and uneasy scaffolding allow for a city of plastic sheets, scrap steel, and precious wood to rise in and among the rickety concrete mortar shells and steel skeletons of a world lost in time. It's brown and gray and dirty, filled with poisonous gases, sludge water puddles, fractured culture, and a steadfast struggle for survival. Through the smog and steam, shafts of weak sunlight shine, teasing a glimpse of the creatures who made it all happen.

Zane's words echo in my head. 'They're just like you, Ellani.' I look down at my non-legs then back at the Disfavored below. We are alike. Natural, broken, forgotten, living a shattered existence. And just like that, I feel a strange kinship with the Disfavored, and I suddenly don't feel so alone. If they can go on, then so can I.

"The Disfavored are so tiny," I say, wiping away half dried tears.

Meems looks up from where she is making my bed but goes right back to watching her hands fold the rayon sheets. After all these years, she knows I'll explain myself when I've collected my thoughts.

But I don't know what else to say; I don't know what to think anymore. I have so much I want to express—more that I want to scream about—but it's all a bottled tempest, a jumble of computer coding that I can't untangle and execute.

I watch her make the bed.

Eventually she looks up again, her expectant face saying she's still waiting for me to explain my comment about the Disfavored being tiny.

"The Disfavored," I say, canting my head toward the window. "They're so small and helpless looking, but they must be very strong to live out there."

Straightening, she smiles, the synthetic skin of her chasis crinkling at the corners of her mouth and eyes. "Your father thought that as well. He liked watching them. He used to tell me that they were like ants—so small but capable of transforming the landscape. They inspired him." For a moment, she seems lost in thought, and then she continues speaking. "One of the reasons he made the game is because of the Disfavored. He said he could look out the window—at the Disfavored—and see what the world and humanity used to be like, and the fact that they still lived gave him hope."

"Hope," I repeat. *Hope for what?* I stare out the window, trying to see what Dad saw, trying to embrace something— anything—of his. At this distance, I can see as far as the domes of our sister cities, Cadence and Adagio. "Cadence looks so…blue."

Meems comes to stand beside me at the window. "The nano-glass on the domes, most likely," she explains. "I am sure they say the same about us."

Squinting, I try to focus on Cadence. I've never been to another city. I don't know anybody who has. I've heard there are tunnels connecting the cities, but no one uses them. In an effort to avoid another war, the cities avoid one another at all costs.

"Do you think they have Disfavored, too?"

Meems crosses her arms. "I suppose so."

Together, we watch the Disfavored in the street below. Most of the people on the street wear cumbersome masks that protect their lungs from the toxic smog of the wastelands. Their drab clothes are made of recycled cloth, cut more for function than fashionable form. As they hustle and limp along, they have the harried appearance of those being chased—as if an invisible droid officer follows them with a Taser.

Instead of hovering on tracks, their few broken-down pods lumber along on wheels over cracked, gray-black stretches of concrete, whatever merchandise they haul loaded up in rickety crates that threaten to topple into the street.

It all has the look of eminent collapse. An accident waiting to happen.

Accident…

"What happened, exactly?" I ask. "With the accident. Did anyone else get hurt?"

She glances down, distracted. "No."

"But it was such a bad crash."

"It was only the one pod."

"One pod?" That almost never happens.

At my confused tone she says, "Sensor malfunction. The pod failed to make a turn, flew off the track, and hit the security wall. The front of the pod was completely destroyed."

My stomach rolls over. "Did he…did he suffer?"

She refuses to look at me as she says, "He died instantly. Could not have been a swifter, more efficient death." Her voice has reverted to the same mechanical tone it gets when she recites supplemental lessons or repeats laws. She gets that way when she wishes to recoil from her emotions — which means she's lying.

I feel the blood drain from my face and, twisting my fingers together where they sit between my outspread half legs, I swallow the bilious taste in my mouth. "I yelled at him before he died," I confess. "I told him I hated him." I bite my lip and shake my head. "I'm a horrible person. I should be dead, not him."

"But you are not dead. You are the one who lived."

I let out a trembling breath. "It was such a stupid argument." Because I wanted a Mod, the last words to a father I loved more than anything were words of hate. And now look at me. I'm more hideous than ever. I glance up at her. "This was a punishment. A well-deserved one."

Meems glances down at me, her face unreadable.

"If I could have my father back, I'd be happy to be my Natural self forever. I'd never complain again."

She looks away. "Unfortunately, that is not a possibility."

I look back out the window. "What should I do now?"

"You are smart, Ellani. Too smart to let your brain rot." She walks toward the desk. When she comes back, she's holding my flex-bracelet. "Do something productive while I help Tasha with the chores. And…" She pauses in thought. "If you feel that you must escape this new life, I suggest other, more productive ways of doing so than feeling sorry for yourself."

I cock my head. "Like what?"

For a split second, her eyes flit toward the gaming console before settling on me. "Your father had much ambition for you."

I don't hide my sarcasm. "Yes, because playing games would be so useful."

"Just think about it." She places a hand on my shoulder and turns to leave, but then she pauses, reaches into her pocket, and places something on the desk. A small transparent data storage box.

"What's that?"

She doesn't turn to look at me as she says, "It is your father's G-Chip. It was removed before his body was laid to rest. Katrina told me to put it in the disposal unit, but I thought you might want to keep it. Perhaps you can find a bit of your father in its contents."

She has her hand on the door when I find words again. "I had a dream last night." I stare down at my trembling hands. "Not a nightmare, for once."

"Did you?" she remarks, no emotion in her voice. "If not another nightmare of the accident then perhaps you've gone back to dreaming of Quentin Cyr?" There is a note of hopefulness in her voice, like she thinks some part of old Ellani is in here somewhere. I'm not as convinced as she is.

"You know how Dad used to talk about those things called dogs?"

"Yes."

"I had a dream with dogs in it."

"Most likely you are mentally struggling to find your father via your dreams."

Ignoring her analysis of my mental state, I take a deep breath. "The dogs. They were wrong, I think. Not like he would have imaged them at all. They moved all wrong and, when I touched them, I couldn't feel anything."

"That's because you do not have the information you need to create a realistic experience."

I touch my chest, where it suddenly feels tight. "We've lost so much of our world, and we don't even bother to properly remember it." I close my eyes. "I wish I had asked Dad more about all of this. I'd give anything just to know what he thought a dog felt like." Feeling tears gather at the back of my throat, I shake my head. "I can't ask him that now. It's a part of him I'll never be able to have—or remember."

She's quiet for a long moment before saying, "Maybe you can."

Meems's words bring my attention back to her, and I blink. "What?"

"Your father once told me that the game has much of himself in it. You should play."

I scoff, trying to hide the fact that I've thought often about the game. As much as I hated it and wanted Dad to give it up and pay more attention to his own life, I couldn't help wondering what the excitement was all about. Still, there's a stubborn part of me that wants nothing to do with it. "I've always hated that stupid game. Why would I want to play it?"

Meems's eyes wander to the servers banked in the wall. "Because, next to you, this is what he loved most."

I look away. "He loved that game more than me, Meems. You

know it."

"Maybe," she says quietly, "but you have said yourself that you have nothing remaining of him but what he left behind. Nexis is his biggest legacy, your inheritance whether you choose to be a Programmer or not. He made the game for you, Ellani, so that you could see what he saw, experience something wonderful. Perhaps even become as devoted to sharing wonder with others as he was."

"I hadn't thought about it that way." I could learn about my father and his passions. I could know what he valued most by seeing what was important enough to include in the game. "But I've never played a game like his before."

Meems grins. "Nobody has. That's why it is so successful. Imagine, being able to create an entirely different life for yourself."

I can't help an anxious glance at my stumps. It's been weeks since my amputation—plenty of time for the nano-knit injections to run their course. Clinically, there's nothing wrong with me. I'm healed. But I still get phantom pain, and my stumps still twitch whenever I think of moving. I wish I could turn those brain signals off, tell my autonomic system that there are no legs to stand on anymore. "C-Could I have my legs back?" I wonder, feeling stupid and weak for even hoping.

Meems bites her lower lip. "I do not know. From what we have seen in The Broadcast it is as if you can have an entirely new life in Nexis. You can look different, sound different. You can have a different class and occupation. You can even have a new family in the game."

I frown, not liking the idea of a new Dad. "I wouldn't go that far."

"The point is that the virtual reality is so advanced in this game that you could if you wanted to. It is very addicting. That is why he integrated the time limit."

Deep in thought, I stare out the window. From what I can see of the sky beyond the artificial one projected against the dome, the true sky is yellow-gray and covered in slate and blue-black clouds.

When I was a child, Dad would tuck me in at night and tell me stories about what the world used to be like. "The sky was once blue," he would say. "Blue with white clouds. There used to be small winged animals called birds that flew across the world—so high that you couldn't even see them. They tasted clouds, Ella. Clouds that were cool, moist, and gentle. Clouds that were good. Even the rain was good."

Out there, the rain is acidic and if a cloud were to ever dip low enough for you to breath in its yellow-brown vapors, you'd be dead in less than a week from the radiation and biotoxins.

Humanity has destroyed the world, and now the only way we survive is by trying to take back just enough of what we destroyed to get by. Air filters and purifiers, sky scrubbers, water filtration. It's no longer healthy to walk outside; not even plants can live out there. Yet, the Disfavored do it every day. They have to.

Unlike Evanescence, the Outer Block is not covered by a nano-glass dome. The Disfavored roam the wastelands between the domes or pile their Disfavored cities up against the walls of the domes—as if their simple presence might ignite mass osmosis and provide them with what the Aristocracy has. But it doesn't. Out there it's just a desert of unfortunate human bodies, death, disease, pollution, and loss. They live off our waste, like parasites.

Without thinking about it, I turn and stare at the gaming console. We have everything we could desire here in Evanescence. We have everything that the Disfavored need, yet Dad made a game that everyone seems to want to escape into. Why? What could be in there that we don't have here? I think about Quentin, and I remember Carsai wanting a cheat code. I wonder if she ever found one. I wonder what it must be like to have everything you could possibly want—and more. What if I could have more than legs? What if I could be the perfect Aristocrat I've always wanted to be? What if I found the cheat code to play with Quentin Cyr?

The Broadcast says that President Cyr has sanctioned Lady Cyr's petition for gaming houses in the Outer Block. Will Zane Boyd discover what the Disfavored think of Dad's game? Will it give them more? Make them *want* more?

I squint at Dad's workstation. The wireless VR console is set up and ready to go, waiting for my father to re-immerse himself in the game he loved so much. I've looked at that console often, sometimes hating, sometimes curious, but I always told myself *no*. On stubborn principal I said no. But why say no anymore? Everything in the world is a *no* for me now; I'm the only one who will give me a *yes*.

"Meems," I say, my voice sounding like a whisper, a shameful secret. "Do you know how to connect to it?"

She grins, almost conspiratorially. "Of course I do. Are you ready to play the game?"

chapter eleven

POST-AMERICAN DATE: 7/2/231

LONGITUDINAL TIMESTAMP: 1:13 P.M.

LOCATION: DOME 5: EVANESCENCE

Meems moves around me like a nursing assistant android. I'm tucked into bed, the VR console remote clipped around my finger, the wire sensors adhered to my wrist. She hands me the blinder, and I slip it over my eyes, depriving myself of the artificial light. The soundproof caps come down and in the next instant I'm now deaf to the world as well. The sensory deprivation is made more frightening by the knowledge that I can't get up and run if something touches me. I have no legs, no eyes, no ears—and then no sense of lying down.

The bed and blankets disappear from behind me; I can't feel the synthetic silk of my pajamas against my skin. I'm sitting naked and alone in the dark.

A door opens somewhere off to my left, revealing a shadowy figure against the glaring white of an empty hallway. I squint-blink, trying to make out her features, but then the lights come on, blinding me.

I throw up my hands, defending my eyes against the searing

burn of light while still trying to keep her in focus. My eyes water, and I can't help blinking the tears down my cheeks. Eventually, she comes into focus: a beautiful young woman in a strange gray outfit with black skin and equally black cord-like hair. She grins, her teeth and the white of her eyes stark in contrast to her dark skin. "Welcome. You must be Ellani Drexel."

I gape at her. I've never seen anyone with such dark skin. From Dad's stories, I know her as a person of African descent, but people like her no longer exist. They, like people with true white skin, have been interbred out of existence. Every Natural has tan skin, like mine; and if you are a Custom baby like most Aristocrats you're Argent—a sort of glowing, pinkish pearly color. Many Aristocrats choose to Alter their skin so that it's pale—like Quentin's—but I had always assumed it was so that Alts and Mods showed up more clearly.

Realizing I still haven't acknowledged her, I say, "Uh, hello. H-how do you know my name?"

Still smiling, she walks toward me, her odd shoes—some sort of soft sole fused with what I can only assume is synthetic plant material—squeaking on the ugly, mottled brown tiles. "I know everybody, cher. Especially the Anansi Child."

I like the way she talks, a slow, soulful, and raspy voice with an interesting accent. It's a unique voice Alteration as well. I wonder if she's ever met Quentin. He could learn a thing or two from her. "Cher? Anansi Child? Who are they?"

She giggles, something that seems to come from deep in her stomach. A real giggle. "Aw, honey. That'd be you."

Confused, I say, "No, you had it right the first time, I'm Ellani Drexel."

Her full lips close over her teeth, toning the grin down to a smirk. "That so?"

I nod. "Yes. And who are you?"

"You can call me Dallas."

"Dallas…can you tell me where I am? I was supposed to be in a game, but I ended up here. Did something go wrong?"

"You're in the game, cher."

"Ellani," I correct. "What do you mean? This isn't a game, it's just a…" I glance around, trying to figure out exactly where I am. Glowing white walls, ugly brown tiled floor, no windows, only the one door, me sitting naked in a strange angular chair with what looks to be the same sort of wheels that were attached to that thing with the pedals Dad once showed me a picture of… What was that contraption called? A bicycle? I shake my head. "It's just a room."

"You're in the Epicenter," she says, walking around me. She places her hands on two protruding bars at the back of my chair and propels me, making the chair move forward. "The Oracle is waiting to see you."

She's pushing me toward the open door, toward the white hall, and I feel panic bubble in my stomach. "Wait a nano; I'm not dressed."

"You don't need clothes, cher."

I growl under my breath, annoyed that she can't seem to call me the correct name, as I attempt to cover my naked skin. Doesn't she understand that public indecency is against the law? I remind her. "Rule Number 23: Exposing oneself without the adequate coverage of clothing is both indecent and offensive. Exceptions are to be made only in the case of medical procedure, private reproductive and recreational activities, or in the privacy of one's bed or bathing chamber."

"Those rules don't apply here. This is Nexis, cher. Nothing applies here but live and be happy." She pushes me into the hall.

Being naked does not make me happy. Keeping my arms locked over my chest, I frown. "Don't you have laws?"

"Only the laws of nature."

I roll my eyes. "Thanks for the lesson in cryptology, *cher*."

"Don't mention it, honey."

I remain silent as she pushes me along a curved, white cylindrical hall. My nakedness forgotten, I reach out and touch the walls, flawless and cool yet unforgiving and a bit grainy. There are no seams or rivets. "What is this stuff?"

"Marble."

I glance back at her. "Marble?"

"Yes, it's a type of rock."

"You mean like the stuff the statues in the pictures are made of? That's supposed to be impossible to find in large quantities."

"Not here, sweet cakes. We've got hundreds of quarries worth of it here."

"Quarries? What's that?"

She reaches out and pats my shoulder. "All in good time, child. Look, we're here."

She stops in front of a massive wooden door. I long to reach out and touch it. I've always wanted to know what wood felt like. I imagine it would be rough yet somehow pleasant to touch. Two figures in billowing gray robes, their faces hidden by hoods, step forward from either side of the door and bow.

I glance at the woman with the black skin Alt. "Don't they have proper chasises?"

"Chasises?"

"You know, silicone covers for robots?" She looks clueless. "Android skin?"

She lifts a brow and glances at the figure bent closest to her. "Oh, she's not an android. She's an acolyte."

At my blank expression, she explains. "She serves the Oracle."

"Which makes her an android," I reason. "People don't serve

other people. We have robotic servants."

Dallas lifts her hand to cover a chuckle.

"What's so funny?" I demand.

"You have an interesting grasp of reality," she says, still laughing.

One of the acolytes stands and opens her arms wide, revealing pale white hands. She *does* have a chasis. So why is she covering it? How odd to hide one's androids under a sheet of wrinkled cloth. Worried, I ask, "Are you sure it's all right to go in there without clothes?"

"Perfectly fine," Dallas reassures me. The acolytes shove the door open, revealing a dark room with yellow and orange light dancing in it. "Have at it, girls." She shoves me forward, the momentum carrying me through the door and into the dark room.

Along the wall are torches with actual fire in them. They line the whole circumference of the room, tossing warm light on the lone figure sitting in the center. On a massive chair covered with blue velvet cloth sits a woman. Or rather, a ghost.

My heart jumps into my throat. "Mom?" I whisper.

She stares at me, her expression so much like the one she wears in the picture I know from Dad's workroom—my room— that I have to rub my fists in my eyes and reexamine her. No, she's definitely a carbon copy of my mom. She has to be a copy. Because Dad said Mom was dead. Is this what Meems meant? I can see what Dad truly valued by going into this game—a game that has brought my mother back from the dead.

"Welcome to Nexis, Ellani Drexel." Her voice is soft and soothing, a breath of oxygen fresh from an air scrubber.

I cock my head, uncertain if I'm mistaken or not. If she's Mom, shouldn't she get up and hug me? Shouldn't she call me daughter or Ella? Shouldn't she do or say something more personal than sitting and saying, "Welcome, Ellani Drexel"? Could this larger-than-life woman in pure white robes really be my mother?

Somewhat hurt that Mom seems to know exactly who I am but doesn't seem all that moved by my appearance, I fight to find my voice. "I-I thought you were dead."

"The Oracle is immortal."

Confused, I say, "But you're a Natural. You can't be immortal."

"I am the Oracle."

"So, you're not my mother?" I verify, somehow let down.

She remains still and silent.

I frown, now more annoyed than anything that this Oracle person stole my mother's face. "If you're not my mother, then why do you have her face?"

"I am how Anansi made me. The Oracle's face is the Oracle's face."

I have no idea what she's saying. "Um, and what exactly *is* an Oracle?"

"I'm here to prepare you for your path in life, Ellani. To guide you on the path Anansi has laid out for you."

"Anansi? Who is that?"

"What do you want out of this game?"

I blink, thrown off by her new train of thought. "What do I... want?"

She smiles, those soft lips gentle and her brows so sharp and well-executed. I can't help staring at her. She may not be my real mother, but she sure looks like her. I can imagine my mother's expressions looking much like this Oracle's. "You're here for a reason, aren't you?"

"Uh." I feel myself blush a little bit. "I came because of my father. He, um, he programmed this game and I was just..."

My voice trails off. I suddenly feel foolish for even being here. What do I expect to find in this game? It's not like I'm going to discover Dad lurking around some corner of his own virtual world. Still, it is *his* world. This is where he was happy. I want to know and understand him. I can't do that by just cracking the code or reading his personal files. I have to know Nexis.

She nods, the light catching her eyes and making them look like they glow red. "You wish to see what he accomplished here?"

I mirror her nod. "Something like that."

"Hmm," she breathes. "How best to frame your adventure, young spider?"

"Spider?"

"Yes, that is what you are. I have always known. The spider will find her comrades in trickery, she will weave her threads, and she will cast the net, and then, the Anansi Child will catch them all by surprise. She will inherit the earth."

I glance down at my stumps, my expression exuding meaningful sarcasm. "I doubt that. Dad says spiders have eight legs. I don't even have two."

Her eyes narrow at me, showing me a wrath that I never would have assumed my real mother carried. "Don't ever doubt me, Ellani Drexel. I know all."

I flinch at her acidic tone. "I'm sorry."

Indignant, she sniffs as she looks from me to one of her acolytes. "Bring me the chalice."

The acolyte seems to float toward a side table where she selects a tall silver cup from among its contents. Holding the chalice above her head, she ascends the steps and kneels before the Oracle. As she reaches into the chalice, the Oracle looks back at me. "I shall name and select your attributes, Spider Child."

From the corner of my eye, I see the other acolyte take a seat at a panel of computers that look mysteriously like the station in Dad's workroom. "Stamina." The Oracle withdraws a small piece of paper, looks at it, and tosses it back into the chalice. A series of holo-screens begin flashing in front of the acolyte. "Allure." She draws another slip with the same results. She goes through "Advantage," "Dexterity," "Acuity," "Perseverance," and "Sense" before she dismisses the kneeling acolyte with a wave of her hand.

"What was all that for?" I ask.

"We are assessing your character," she responds. The acolyte returns, this time with a small black box. "You may approach."

Without my mind or body to propel it, the chair begins rolling toward the massive chair where the Oracle is seated. Somehow, as if by a feat of magic, my chair climbs the stairs and stops the moment the wheels skim the hem of her white robes. This close I can see she's unique in a way that Aristocrats could only dream about. She opens the box and presents me with the contents.

There is a thick stack of hand-sized papers inside, the depiction on the back a simple black spider on a perfectly symmetrical web. "Divide the deck and select the center card."

I do as she requests, picking up half of the deck and pulling the center card from the bottom of the stack in my hand. I hold it up.

"Ace of Diamonds," she says. "I will grant you one bodily Modification wish."

The acolyte races up the stairs and presents me with a round red chip with little ridges along the edge. "Is this a coin?" I ask, taking the chip in reverence. Coins are so rare, a true gift from the past.

"Of course it's not a coin," the Oracle says. An acolyte appears at my side and drops a small bag into my lap. The Oracle points to it. "That is coin."

Openmouthed, I touch the little bag. "Is this leather?" I ask. "Actual, real animal skin?" Excited, I dig inside and pull out one of the coins. It's the color of the coin called a penny and it has the profile of a man wearing an odd hat engraved on it. I hold it up and compare it to the chip. One is cold etched metal while the other is smooth plastic. "If this is a coin then what is this?"

"It's a Modification chip," the Oracle says to me. "You may use it now or later. Whichever you prefer. You can change anything about your avatar—your voice, your hair or skin, your build. Just use it intelligently."

I stare at the chip in the palm of my hand. "I can do anything?"

She sighs. "Yes. What else would I mean?"

Excited, I look from her to the chip to the obvious use for my chip. I can use this chip to get the one thing I can't have. "Can I use it to get my legs back?"

Her eyes go a little wide, as if she's surprised by my request. "Well, of course." She pauses for a moment and stares at me, her gray eyes—so much like mine—calculating. "Is that what you want?"

Without hesitation, I extend the chip toward her. "Yes."

She looks at the chip, but doesn't take it. "You know," she begins, her voice low, "you *could* ask for something more general—to be perfect or whole or something of the sort. It may offer you more. You could be more beautiful—like an Aristocrat. Someone that beautiful is bound to turn heads and instill the love of another. Isn't that what you want? To be idolized and loved?"

I meet her eyes. She looks so much like Mom—a woman who attracted the attention, adoration, and love of my father. Dad didn't change her in the slightest. He could have done anything to improve my mother, but he didn't. I look down at the chip in my hand. I've only ever wanted to look like an Aristocrat—to attract the love of Quentin.

But really, all I needed was the love of my father. If I had died instead of Dad, would he put me in the game? What would I look like? How would he preserve me for all time?

I already know that answer. He wouldn't make me an Aristocrat. Dad loved me just the way I was.

Looking up, I shake my head. "I don't want that. I just want to be able to walk on my own two legs again. I should experience the world my father wanted me to see as the daughter he would want to remember. That's the only real way to honor his memory—to be who he wanted me to be."

Smiling, she takes the chip. "A wise choice. Good luck, Anansi Child."

I open my mouth to ask her why everyone keeps calling me that but, as she settles back, she snaps her fingers and the world goes dark.

chapter twelve

I wake up in an odd bed made of cool green threads and scratchy green sheets. For a moment, I struggle to free myself until realization makes me go still. Green.

Sticks. Dirt. Grass. Leaves—extinct things.

Eyes wide and hands shaking, I reach out and touch one of the leaves hanging around me. It's tender and delicate as pastry crust, but smooth as paper. It has tiny veins like the ones that run up my arm.

Overwhelmed, I reach out and touch every leaf in turn, gentle and reverent. The sudden desire to pick one and take it with me for keeps, to scratch at it and discover what the blood running through its veins looks like, makes me recoil my hand. How could I want to destroy something so beautiful? Just for the sake of possession and discovery? Swallowing, I clench my fists until the unwanted urges pass.

Awe dampened by fear of my own natural human tendencies,

I tentatively reach down and run my hands through the grass—hair-like leaves for the earth. I dig my fingers into the dirt, loving the moist grain of it under my fingernails. I've never touched dirt; all the dirt of the earth is covered in Evanescence. I've only seen it from my window, out where the Disfavored walk, and this dirt isn't like the hard, swirling dust of the wasteland on the other side of the dome. This is fertile, welcoming stuff, full of strange bits of dying things and…I pull my hand back with a start as something cold, wet, and slimy wriggles between my fingers. I stare at the slick, pink-brown creature with no eyes or legs as it wriggles in the dirt and wrinkle my nose.

What the heck is that thing? Not anything I want to touch again. Wanting to escape the foreign creature I get on my hands and knees and…I pause. Knees. I have knees. I look between my arms. Yes, they're there. Two wonderful, healthy legs. Not even scarred. And they're my legs. I'd know them anywhere. Legs that I always thought were knock-kneed and fat, not shapely at all. But, sparks, is it wonderful to see them.

I grin.

They're here. The joy of it is like an explosion of electricity, winging to every nerve in my body, making me want to dance.

With a cry of joy, I leap up and touch them, wanting to prove that I'm not seeing things. Yes, my skin. I feel my hands and I know my own flesh.

Overjoyed, I begin sobbing, hysterical. As I cry, I walk, then I jog, and then I run, twirling and shrieking with joy through what I'm understanding to be a mythical wood filled with trees and plants that in real life are extinct. I crash through an actual stream with water so clear and pure that I can see the rainbow-colored pebbles at the bottom. Shafts of true sunlight break through the bright green canopy, casting motes of dust and the tiny bodies of insects in golden relief against the woody undergrowth, warming my skin when I pass beneath them. I suck in air that is hot but moist and has a taste of something rich and secret—as if simply breathing it in might be a cure for all ailments.

My heart is hammering a frantic beat, my lungs want to pop, and my eyes threaten to dry out if I spill yet another tear, but I can't stop. I don't want to stop. I have to move and revel and worship the wonder around me. It's a dream, I'm sure of it. But it's the best dream I could ever have. The only thing that would make it better would be to have my father step out from beyond one of these massive trees and take me up into his arms.

This is what it's like to be alive.

I run and I run and I run until I trip on a root and face-plant into the dirt, abruptly ending my revelry. Wincing, I get to my feet. *Ouch.* That really hurt. And I'm bleeding. My brand new wonderful knee is bleeding down my perfect, chubby calf. I frown. *Can people bleed in dreams?*

For the first time, I really take stock of myself and where I am. I'm wearing leather. Some kind of soft black vest pulled tight over a black shirt made of fibers I've never felt before. I have on a pleated skirt, black and yellow and red stripes with stretchy black cutoffs underneath. I'm wearing knee-high black boots, a broad utility belt, and that little pouch with the coins at my hip. The Designer in me recoils. This outfit is ugly, and—even in one of my worst nightmares—I wouldn't be caught dead wearing any of it. I touch the skirt. "I hate stripes."

Spinning in a circle, I see sunlight seeping through the leaves and beyond it blue sky. I can hear the song of birds, the whisper of wind through the leaves, the creak of branches, and the hum of an insect. These are things that I wouldn't know or recognize the true sound of, even in my subconscious, so I can't be imagining or dreaming this place.

Smiling, I say to no one in particular, "I'm still in the game." I'm not with the Oracle anymore. I look back at my legs. "She granted my wish."

So now what? I look around. Play? Play what? I'm in the middle of the woods. Granted, I'm quite happy to be here, this is exactly what I wanted to see—what Dad did with his world, why everyone wanted to play this game so much. But where are the other players?

Circling again, I search for some sign of life. There's a small indentation in the ground. A path? I follow it, taking the time to marvel at this virtual paradise that my father created and left for me as a memory of himself.

Eventually, the path intersects with another that widens and gives way to broad, flat stones. Bending down, I touch the dusty white rock at my feet. Marble, like the stuff on the walls back at the temple—the stuff that Michelangelo carved those wondrous statues from. I look one way and then another. For as far as I can see in either direction there is only the marble road cut into the green-brown of the forest. I look up. Here, I can see the sky. The bright blue sky filled with fluffy clouds. Dad was right. The sun is a blood-red hex on the land back home, but the sun here is a tiny yellow-white orb—a distant onlooker.

Despite wanting to use my legs, I lie down on the road and stare up at the sky. I've never seen such a vibrant shade of blue, never known such pure smoke clouds. They look almost like Alterations for the sky. Gray, white, blue, and slightly gold tinged.

Lifting my hands, I reach out to the distant beyond, wanting to be part of it. This is true beauty. This is what people should be wearing on their skin; true clouds should glide over Custom blue eyes.

I frame the image between my fingers. Instead of finding new things to dazzle our eyes, we should have memorialized this thing of beauty, should have made it so that when I was born I could look at this and know that this is what we destroyed.

I lower my hands. It would be a good lesson.

I glance around once more. This whole place is a lesson. A lesson in what we lost.

A lesson from my father to the world: *look what you've done…and you don't even remember doing it.*

Recalling that strange urge I had to pick the plants for my own, to break the leaves so that I could have their hidden secrets, I put my hands over my face, hiding the tears of shame and the grimace of loss.

chapter thirteen

It takes me quite some time to convince myself to open my eyes once more. I almost don't want to see the beauty that I can no longer have. But what would be the point in coming here if I didn't play? Holding my breath, I scramble to my feet and stumble down the embankment. I glance in one direction and then the other. There's nothing to make one way different than the other and no indication as to where I should go.

"Hm," I breathe to myself. "Which way?"

A gentle breeze picks up. From somewhere above me, perhaps from an overhanging tree branch, a thin silver thread drifts down and lands on my shoulder. I bat at it, annoyed with it in the same way I get frustrated with strands of hair that get stuck to my clothes and taunt me with their phantom tickles until I find them and feed them to the disposal unit. Instead of tumbling from my shoulder, the strand just seems to get wrapped around my wrist.

The wind blows again, making the strand tighten and yank

at my skin. For a moment I just stand there, letting the warm air pull at the string that in turn tugs at me—as if it's trying to tell me to come along with it.

I bite my lip, curious. "What if I go this way?" I turn my body against the breeze and move to take a step. All at once, the silver strand tightens on my wrist and wrenches me so hard that I stagger backward and tumble onto my butt.

Wincing, I say, "Okay, maybe not." Wary of getting more tangled in the string, I struggle to my feet. Feeling like a fool, I lift my wrist and speak to the string. "So, we're going this way then?"

As if in response, the breeze buffets my back, and the string begins to tug once more as if there's an invisible balloon attached somewhere high above and it's caught in the breeze. "Well, okay then. We're going this way."

I head down the white marble road, all the while the sun warming my back, the breeze pushing me like the gentle hand of an invisible giant, and the silver strand tugging at me like an anxious child.

One moment I'm on the white road, surrounded by thick undergrowth and the next I'm stepping into a space that looks eerily similar to the wastelands beyond the Outer Block and feels as hot as the incinerator in the basement of my housing unit.

As I come to a halt on the cracked red-brown dirt, the wind whispers away and the silver strand unravels, dropping from my wrist. Lifting my hand, I rub my skin, the warm phantom feeling of the string still present on my flesh. I scan the sky, hoping that I can see the strand hanging above, but there's nothing there. I speak anyway. "What now?"

No answer.

I blink down into the valley below. For a good distance in any direction, there's only a blank white sky, a hot sun, and the yellow-red-brown of the gritty earth. There are walls of odd rock rising in the distance, looking like forgotten asymmetrical building blocks. I turn around. The cool, lush invitation of the forest stands before me and to either side of me—an impossible wall of wilderness stationed in the desert.

I spin back and squint harder against the wavy haze of heat drifting over the desert. "Why'd you bring me here?" I mumble. And then I see them—arms flailing against the wind blowing over the bald peaks. Wind turbines. And below the superstation, in the center of the vast nothingness of the valley below, is a town.

I nearly dive into the gurgling fountain at the edge of the city. Falling to my knees, I take heaping palmfuls of water, burying my face in the cool, clear liquid and then taking huge gulps of it until my thirst is slaked.

As I let myself sink back on my haunches I grow aware of the people around me. Suddenly embarrassed by my actions, I struggle to my feet and glance about. No one seems to have noticed. If they have, it's apparently normal for people to come staggering out of the desert and face-plant into the first instance of water.

The people here dress in plain, functional clothing. Thin white shirts, broad leather hats, sturdy brown pants, and pointed boots that clink when they walk. Here and there, I see a Modification or an Alteration, but most have hard, windblown faces, eyes that look permanently squinted against the sun, and skin that's sort of reddish-brown, but they don't look unfriendly. I swallow a thick ball of spit and scrub my hands against my cutoffs.

"Okay," I say to myself. "You've gotten yourself here, Ellani, now what?" I spin in a slow circle. This place, wherever it is, looks a little more promising than the Outer Block. There is a broad central road sprawled out before me and to either side rise brick and stucco buildings with real glass windows. There are no signs or road names posted anywhere, but there aren't any transport vehicles to direct, only people walking back and forth—some guiding huge four-legged animals that are larger and sleeker looking than dogs.

My stomach chooses this moment to growl. I cover my torso, embarrassed. I didn't think one could get hungry in a game. Though if I can sweat and get thirsty and feel like I'm being incinerated in the desert I guess I can get hungry, too. One would think the game would wake up a player if her body were demanding sustenance, but that doesn't make sense; I ate right before coming into the game.

Is it possible that my biological clock runs differently in the game? I have no idea. There's so much I don't understand. I wish I had paid more attention to Dad when he went off on his little tangents about Nexis.

My stomach growls again. Either way, I'm hungry now. Chewing a fingernail, I investigate the street before me. Normally our habitat control unit, Tasha, provides all my dietary needs, but I know that the Aristocrats sometimes go to eateries where high-end foods are served. I've never been to one. However, I remember Dad saying they were modeled on something called restaurants.

I touch the purse of coins at my hip. "Okay," I whisper to myself. "First things first." I walk up to a brown-eyed girl sitting on a bench outside of a building with a sign reading "Express."

"Excuse me?"

She puts her hand to her broad brim hat—probably to keep it from slipping off—and tips up her head. "Oh," she exclaims with a massive smile filled with yellowish pointed teeth.

Eyes going wide, I take a step back, heart suddenly in my throat—cutting off my breathing.

"I'm sorry," she continues. "I was off in another world." She laughs to herself, her teeth looking threatening in the harsh light. "What can I do for you?"

Swallowing hard, I glance over my shoulder, trying to decide if everyone here looks like she does. I've heard about the cannibals who live in the wastelands. They often raid the Outer Block, abducting unfortunate Disfavored and stealing valuable resources. They sharpen their teeth like this girl does. "Um, n-nothing," I mumble, holding up my hands. "I'm sorry."

Rushing away from the girl, I duck into a side street and press myself against the wall. I stay there for a long moment, heart pounding, trying to discern if she's following me. All I can hear are my own terrified gasps and the stamps and snorts of the four-legged creatures tied beside me. Fingers clutching the brick like I might need to climb it, I glance around the corner.

She's gone.

I duck back into the alley and swallow hard. Where'd she go? Is she following me? My eyes rove up, inspecting the roofs above. Nothing and no one standing on the flat rooftops or peeking through the sun-bleached canopy stretching between the two buildings. I inch along the wall, progressing toward the adjacent street. One of the massive animals seems to startle at my approach. He lets out a cry and stomps backward until the leather line tying him to a railing pulls taut.

Holding my breath, I slink in front of him, slide up against the other side of the building, and inspect the next street. I don't see the girl, but there are other people walking down the road. Should I go out? Are they all cannibals? Should I just go to a different city? Leave the game? My stomach grumbles again, choosing for me.

I take a deep breath, though my throat is tight with fear, and step out onto the street. For an intense minute, I stand there waiting for someone to notice me and raise a call. But, as it was near the fountain, no one seems to notice me or care. I begin walking briskly down the street, trying my best to remain in the long shadows of the building, because the merciless sun is beginning to make my skin feel tight and dry.

chapter fourteen

'm lost. I'm hungry. I'm thirsty again. I plop down on one of the wooden crates stacked against a wall and slump my shoulders. It feels good to sit down. Exhausted and overwhelmed, I pull my legs up toward my body, press myself against the wall, and bury my face against my knees.

I've never walked so much in my life or had to deal with being hungry and thirsty for so long. My throat feels like it's going to crumble inward. My stomach feels hollow. I wish I had one of those big animals to ride like everyone else seems to be doing. Those animals seem a little scary, but I'd chance a ride to give my legs a rest and cover more ground faster.

"You know, you can sell your Mod chips on the black market. Maybe get yourself another outfit or something."

I look up, confused by who would be talking to me. There's a boy standing above me. He's a Natural. At first, my brain starts to re-design him—nipping, tucking, implanting, and ornamenting. *Stop it.* I have to look.

I blink at him. He's maybe a little older than me, but something about his presence is as commanding as Quentin's. Interesting. I unfold my legs and straighten, my attention now fully diverted. "What?"

As if exhibiting some sort of patience, he smirks crookedly at me. "You're new here, right?"

I examine the people passing by then look back up at him. "How do you know?"

He props a foot on the crate and rests his elbows on his knee, leaning in and over like he's about to show me something he doesn't want anyone else to see. There's something so compelling about his dark, lean features and self-assured body language that I find myself instinctively heeding the cue. I hunch and lean a little toward him, curious about what his big secret is.

His deep brown eyes flash up and across the street, surveying and watching… Predatory. Something about that expression makes my stomach stir, and I find myself inching close to him, drawn. "You're not carrying any weapons," he whispers in the same sort of purring manner Zane uses.

I blink, forcing myself to break my trance and look around. "Weapons?"

Most of the people passing by are wearing some sort of utility belt, like mine, or a holster, like the boy standing over me. But, unlike me, their utilitarian accessory actually serves a purpose. Nearly everyone is indeed carrying a weapon. Whether it be some kind of gun, Taser, or bow, they've all got something. Even that girl had her teeth. Everyone except me. I blush. He must think I'm an idiot.

"It's a pretty sure sign of a newbie around here." There's a slight teasing humor in his tone. "It's not safe to wander the Wild West without a weapon."

Embarrassed, I give him a nervous sidelong glance. "I-I didn't know."

He rolls his eyes and makes a "figures" face. "Not knowing won't save you from getting attacked by a gang of marauding robbers. You learn pretty fast, though. You have to in Garibal."

"Garibal?" I repeat, trying to look as if his opinion that I'm a few circuits short of a switchboard doesn't matter to me. "That's where we are?"

He scoffs, revealing a deeper, more genuine boyish grin. Slightly crooked, a little bit mad, and all the way stirring. No sharpened teeth. I take that as a good sign. "You're joking, right? Have you even looked at your map?"

At my confused face he sighs and drops a pack from one of his shoulders. It hits the ground with a *thump*, leaving a cloud of dust. "Move over."

I stare at his dark, commanding face, wondering if it's normal for seasoned gamers to take to tutoring newbies in their spare time or if this one has some kind of trick up his sleeve. He doesn't look like a bad guy. In fact, I believe I might find him attractive, at least, for a Natural. But then, looks can be deceiving. Then again, I'm not certain if it's just his looks I'm drawn to.

Vowing to keep my guard up, I scoot over and allow him to sit beside me. While I know I should feel nervous about a stranger sitting next to me, his presence makes me feel safer from the other gamers. *He* has weapons, after all, and something about his large frame and earnest eyes tells me he's not going to hurt me.

"Okay," he breathes, shrugging out of a long leather over-coat. "Let's see it."

It takes me a minute to compute what he has requested of me. I'm too busy staring at him, half confused, half intrigued by his natural body—lean, well-muscled arms with tawny skin, a black shirt—sleeveless like mine—across his broad chest. "What?

Oh. Um…" I glance about my person wondering where one might find something called a map.

Reaching out, he puts his hand on mine, his warm, electric touch effectively bringing a cease to all physical movement and brain function. He touches like Zane does, in a dangerous too-intimate way, but I like it. In the time it takes me to find my senses, register that I should probably say or do something, and vow to do so, he is dragging my arm across his knee and flipping it over in front of him.

There, on the inside of my wrist, is some kind of circuit patch—like an ingrown version of my flex-bracelet.

"Let's see," he muses, his breath sending goose bumps up my arm as he hunches over the patch, poking at it with strong fingers. "You've got an updated version of the OS, but it should still be…" With a beep, the circuit patch lights up and a holo-map comes into focus a few inches above my arm. He turns to me and grins again, the map throwing sandy yellow and rich tan land features against his high cheekbones and square jaw. "See, easy as trans."

His smile makes me want to smile back, so I do.

He leans back so that we can both see the map clearly and releases my arm, but I don't move it. "This is you." He points to a bright green triangle sitting on the far edge of a deep brown depression marked "Garibal."

Fully expecting the patch to respond to my chip, I mentally request 30X magnification. Nothing seems to happen; there's still only a brown depression. "It's empty," I argue. "We're in a town, aren't we?"

He taps a series of gray bars on the side of the map. The image centers on me and zooms forward, the blurry brown smudges of Garibal rising up and coming into clarity as buildings.

"Oh," I breathe, feeling stupid. "You have to zoom in manually?"

"You've never played a game before, have you?" he asks, his voice softer now, somehow kinder and more intimate. It occurs to me that his face is very close to mine.

I shake my head. "First time. I've never felt the need until now."

Retreating from the odd magnetic pull that drew him close to me, he leans against the wall and crosses those well-muscled arms over that broad, equally muscled chest. If I were to see a boy like him in Real World, I'd say he was a Disfavored laborer. No one in the Aristocracy is built like him—there's no need with robotic service and labor. However, while I may not know much about games, I do know that inside *this* game, gamers can change their physical appearance to anything they wish with the use of Mod chips. Just look what I did with my legs. This boy could be from any class, could look completely different in Real World.

"If you haven't noticed yet, G-Chips don't work here," he explains. "You do things the old-fashioned way here. The game is modeled off of older technologies. The creator was a history buff, I think. There are a lot of arcane additions."

Hearing someone talk about my father makes my chest feel heavy, and heat slips up my throat. Wanting to change the subject, I say, "You know a lot about this game. Do you play often?"

He shrugs. "Yeah, I guess I do. It's my way of escaping."

I look down at my feet, moved by the quiet way he said those words and the sad expression in those bottomless, nearly black eyes. This escape means everything to him. Dad made this game for boys like this one, who have something they want to pretend doesn't exist in Real World. That's why this game won the Civil Enrichment Award. Suddenly I feel very proud of my father.

He clears his throat, the deep rumble of it sliding up my spine and drawing my attention back to the map. "You're going to want to go…" He zooms out and then traces a zigzag across the map, blazing a bright yellow dotted path toward a larger open space on the other side of town. "Here. This is the market. You can trade in your Mod chips and get a weapon there."

I frown at him. "Again about my Mod chips?" I'd forgotten about them in the sudden onslaught of his presence, but here he is, drawing attention to them again. "I don't have Mod chips."

He frowns back at me. "You don't?"

"No."

Cocking his head, he stares at me for a long period of time in which I begin to feel hot and squirmy. Not many people have looked at me in the open, appraising way this boy is currently doing. If he finds something particularly garish about what he's seeing, he's hiding it well. "You can't have used them."

I knit my brows, my stomach suddenly sinking. He doesn't think I'm pretty enough to have used a Mod chip. "What makes you think I haven't? You have no idea what I look like in Real World."

He reaches out and touches my forehead, making my eyes go wide.

"W-What are you…?" I stammer, my words liquid and ungraspable under his touch.

He runs his finger over a long thin scar that I got in the accident with Dad. I'd almost forgotten it was there. I don't bother trying to look in the mirror anymore; I can't see over the counter without my legs. "The world outside has a nasty habit of seeping in here. A newbie girl never arrives with a blemish. It's unsightly."

I feel my cheeks flare hot under his touch. Putting my hand to my forehead to hide the scar, I pull away, ashamed. "Pardon my unsightliness," I mutter.

"I didn't mean it that way," he growls back, his voice suddenly defensive. "I was being sarcastic."

Glaring sideways at him, I try to find the truth in his words, but all I feel is hurt. Hurt that even here, in a world meant to be an escape from judgment, I am still found lacking; hurt that while I gave his Natural body the benefit of the doubt and found positive things about it, he won't do the same for me.

He rolls his eyes again, frustrated. "Look, I just meant that when given a chance to Modify themselves, most girls choose to do so, because that's how they are programmed to think in Real World. They use Nexis to be what they can't be in real life."

Forcing my hand away from my face, I cross my arms, wanting to prove myself strong enough to deal with my blemishes but also wanting to cut myself off from this boy because he speaks the truth, and I find myself not liking that I'm so easily pegged. I came here to have the legs I don't have in real life, to be closer to a father who I can no longer see or ask questions of. "Yeah, well, maybe I just want to be myself. There's nothing wrong with being different. Or for being how nature intended you to be. Natural things are wonderful. I mean, just look at the trees," I reason, trying to argue this to myself as much as him.

He leans forward and places his elbows on his knees. I can feel his eyes on my face, staring at my scar. How can someone stare for so long at someone else?

Nervous, I glance at him again. "What?"

Smirking so that a deep dimple appears on his lean cheek, he gives me an endearing sort of expression. "Personally, I think the scar adds something. It makes you look very mysterious."

Again with that spine-tingling purr talk. I look away, embarrassed, and clear away the hot lump in my throat. "So, um, yeah, where were we?" I fumble with my wrist, trying to call up the map that dissolved at some point during the discussion.

He chuckles to himself as he waits for me to figure out my patch, and his chuckle just makes me even more scattered. I hit a random button and a different screen pops up. There is a column of words with numbers beside them, and I grasp at the opportunity to lessen the intensity between us. "What's this?"

"That's your stat grid. Your attributes are here." He points to a descending row of words that begin with "Stamina" and end with "Sense" then points to the numbers. "These are your ratings."

"Ratings?"

"The game assesses your personality traits and assigns numbers to them. See the green ones? Those are ones you are currently using and the ones that are flashing are the ones you are currently building."

I seem to be using everything but my Strength right now, but the ones I'm building are my Dexterity, Acuity, and Perseverance. "But what do they mean?"

He shifts beside me, his leg brushing mine, and I almost jump out of my skin. "It's a little complicated."

Eager to prove to him that I'm worth his time in training me, I point to the number associated with my level of Acuity. "Somehow, I get the impression that I'm not an idiot."

"Yes, you've got a number of fine qualities," I feel my jaw drop, but he moves on like he didn't just compliment me. "Let's take 'Strength'; it's a measure of your physical strength. The higher the number, the greater your ability to lift something or push yourself physically. But," he says, leaning close and pressing an arrow on the screen, making everything shift to the left to reveal another set of words and numbers, "there are a lot of other associated aspects of strength. Your ability to heal, for one, and an association with your Dexterity for another. It's not entirely important in VR games, because we're actually in our bodies and can read them much more clearly. However, it does help if you want to examine exactly where your strengths and weaknesses are, and it helps you assess what will improve your abilities."

Nodding, I suddenly find myself staring at his close features. "So," I breathe, groping for words though they seem so evasive all of the sudden, "all these numbers are pretty useless?"

His eyes swing to meet mine. They're big and framed with long, thick eyelashes. He is, quite literally, pretty. Then he grins, and I'm glad I'm sitting. "Yeah, I guess. But they are fun for the hardcore gamers."

I turn away, unnerved and confused by what's going on. "Well, that's not me." I scoot away, trying to find the brain that I know Ellani possesses. "On to something else." I push another button, and a different screen comes up.

"That's your skill sheet." He leans over, purposely re-invading my space again, and reads a set of random words like "sneak" and "thief" and "repair" and "science." "No weapons skills, hardly any physical or battle training, but you're pretty promising in the brains department."

Feeling both bold and embarrassed at his compliment, I roll my eyes and sass him. "I told you I wasn't an idiot."

He continues scrolling. "And a healthy dose of beauty to go with those brains," he notes offhandedly, making me look away from the screen and back to him. He continues staring at the screen. "But how will you get by with those?"

"Same way you do." It takes him going still and turning to look at me for me to realize I just said that. Eyes wide, I sit upright and try to recover from my slip. "I-I mean… What do I need to fight for?"

Smirking in a different sort of way—one that just reveals the dimple on his pinkening cheek—he turns away and clears his throat. "Everything about being alive is a fight."

I open my mouth, but nothing comes out. He's taken my words, my breath... What a beautiful person. My mind begins to race, searching for something to say that's just as profound, something that will make him think the same thing about me, because I suddenly want him to feel that way about me, as well. I want to be beautiful too...and for once there's nothing a Mod or an Alt could do to fix it. "I—" But my stomach growls again, making his eyes go wide.

He blinks, obviously amused. "Are you hungry?"

Blushing, I cover my stomach. "N-No."

Knowing I'm lying, he narrows his eyes at me.

"Yes," I admit.

Standing, he offers his hand. "Come on."

For a long moment, I stare up at him. I know that taking his hand might mean something, that this is an offering for more than just a tutorial on how to function in this game. He's inviting me along with him. At least for a short time. Accepting me when so few have done it in the past. Telling me that, for now, I'm beautiful enough to look at.

Eager to belong, eager to touch, I reach up and take his hand.

chapter fifteen

POST-AMERICAN DATE: 7/2/231

LONGITUDINAL TIMESTAMP: 7:18 P.M.

LOCATION: DOME 5: EVANESCENCE

I sit up with a start and blink into the darkness. I can't see or hear anything. Frightened, I lift my hands to my face only to find that I'm wearing a pair of caps and a blinder. I pull them off and squint at my surroundings. I'm back in Dad's office.

Meems leans forward, her face both curious and cautious. "Well?"

I stare at her, bewildered. "What happened? Why'd I come back?"

She nods toward the VR set on the bedside table. "Your time ran out. The game disconnects you after six hours."

I lift the blanket away from my stomach. I don't have to look to know they're gone, but I do anyway. Yup, gone. I drop the blanket and slump my shoulders. "I had legs." I look to Meems with urgency. "I had legs, and I saw my mother, and there were trees and grass." I flop back down on the bed. "Quick, send me back."

Meems smiles even though she's shaking her head. "I cannot."

Knitting my brow, I frown. "Why not?"

"You have to wait."

I frown harder. "Why?"

"He built in a safety. You cannot stay for too long, and you have to spend a certain amount of time outside of the game. G-Corp would not have accepted it otherwise. You still need to be a productive citizen, Ellani. Spending too much time dwelling in the past will not build the future."

I puff out my cheeks, annoyed. "But I was being productive," I mutter. "I was learning what my father wanted me to see."

She gestures toward the workstation. "You still have the files. That, too, is learning through your father."

"You're right," I sigh. I stare dreamily through the window as Meems disconnects the sensors from my arm. "The sky used to be so beautiful, Meems."

"So I have heard."

I watch her place the sensors back into the small drawer in the VR set. "You should go in and see."

Straightening, she wipes her hands on her apron. "I cannot do that. Virtual reality is not for robots."

I look away. "I know. Sorry. It was stupid of me to have suggested it." I know that VR doesn't work on artificial intelligence. "Sometimes I forget."

Meems sniffs. "I do not."

Domestic androids are programmed with a vast spectrum of emotional and cognitive functions. They can be everything from maids to nannies to foster parents to mail-order brides to sexual or emotional companions. When it comes to self-perception, identity, and the full gamut of human capability, they are just like humans.

But they aren't real humans. If I wanted to, I could turn Meems off with one master command. I could take off her skin, exposing her inner mechanics to the cold, cruel eyes of the world. I could disassemble her in less than a day. I could reprogram her to be a stone-hearted warrior like the security droids patrolling the wall. I could make her forget those she loves, make her be someone different than she is.

I'd never do that, of course. I love Meems. There are days when I wish Dad had never felt it necessary for me to understand at such a young age that she wasn't a real person. Most days, if I don't think hard about it, it feels like Meems is my real mother. Even now, though Katrina is supposed to be my guardian, it's Meems who is my caretaker.

When Dad was alive, part of me wished that she and Dad had loved each other—that we were a real family. There were days when I'd walk in on Meems and Dad talking in hushed voices, their eyes intent on each other's, and I swore that they did. That gave me hope, but I know it was a pretty lie I told myself.

The bottom line is that Meems is not a human. She is not my mother. She was not my father's lover. She's a creation of humans, forever to live with the knowledge that she can never be one of us and will always be subject to our whims. Even her skin is not her own.

And I can see that she hates that about herself.

A long time ago, Dad offered to purchase Meems an updated chasis. Meems was horrified by the prospect. She said, "Why would I change my own skin? This is who I am. This is what I look like, this is how my family knows me." Back then I agreed with her. I thought it would be horrifying to wake up to someone I loved looking like someone else.

But as I aged, I realized that I did it every day. My schoolmates and neighbors, my family members, my best friend and the boy I had a crush on, they all changed on a day-to-day basis. People changing skin became so normal to me that I no longer felt like change was horrifying. It was good to change what you were into something better. I even wanted that for myself.

Like androids, we humans change our bodies. Often, we do it so much that some of us are more machine than human. Which makes me wonder: what is a human, really? What makes me more worthy of experiencing a blue sky with voluptuous clouds than Meems? She has value. She's more valuable to society than I am at this point. Yet I still enjoy an aspect of society that she does not.

Disturbed, I puzzle over this as Meems lifts me off the bed and places me back in the hover-chair. I can't help but glance back at the VR set. "When can I go back?"

She spins the chair toward the workstation. "Six hours in, eighteen hours out. That is the law."

I scrunch my nose. "I won't be able to concentrate after that." I glance over my shoulder. "Maybe I can just go to bed?" Sleep and dream about green forests, blue skies, white marble roads… and a dark-eyed boy with an amazing smile.

Meems lifts my hand off the armrest and places it on the desk. "If I put you back in that bed, you would not sleep. You have just slept six hours; your body will not want rest."

I sigh. "I know." VR sets put the body in a sleep-like state, relaxing it in such a way that the body achieves a R.E.M. cycle while the mind is still deeply engrossed in the system. That's why there are so many monitors and sensors associated with going under VR. The set monitors the external environment for the subject and will withdraw him or her from the game if there is an abnormality.

As Meems perches in the chair beside me, I place my elbows on the desk, and I pick up the chip she left me. Glancing at her, I see that she's sitting ramrod straight and staring off into the corner. It's obvious she's in her own little world and doesn't want to talk, so I insert the disk into the workstation and begin clicking through files.

Dad had a huge collection of encyclopedias, history books, and personal notes. Like the game, it's like finding another part of my father that I never knew. I try to find something that looks as interesting as what I've just experienced. But it's no use; nothing could be as incredible as actually seeing the real thing. Dad must have known that. I turn back to her. "I can't concentrate."

She doesn't look up. "What did you do?"

I shift my gaze down to the desk top. "I ran," I admit, sheepish. "And I watched the sky."

Her brow wrinkles. "That is it?"

Feeling like an idiot, I shrug. "If the sky really looked like that here, then maybe it wouldn't be so strange to spend hours staring at it," I reason, looking back up at her. "They move, you know. The clouds. I didn't know that. I thought the clouds always stayed the same. Like how they look on the nano-dome. Or, maybe that they just sort of hung low and clung around things like the poisonous clouds in the wasteland." Frowning, I shake my head, desperate to understand. "How could we destroy it, Meems? The sky? And the trees?"

Meems stares at me for a long moment then says, "Why do you want to destroy your face with Modifications and Alterations?"

I blink at her, incredulous. "That's different."

"How?"

"Mods and Alts are for improvement, to make people beautiful."

Meems stands and points at the picture on the screen in front of me. I follow her direction. It's a picture of a large, gangly, four-legged creature with a hump on its back. It's standing beside a leathery-faced man with an odd scruffy thing on his jaw. "That man had facial hair. Do you think his wife thought he was not beautiful?"

I scoff. "Obviously she hated it. Body hair is useless and silly. That's why we engineered it out of the human genome." Bodily hairlessness is, thankfully, something that I retained from my father's Customized genes.

"And you do not think that making one's skin sparkle is also useless and silly?" Meems counters. "I am certain that humans evolved to possess body hair because it was once advantageous. However, I do not see how sparkling skin could be advantageous."

Biting my lip, I think about her words for a few seconds, then I say, "It's to help us progress in society. Being beautiful makes you stand out."

"And who decided that sparkling skin was beautiful and beards were not?" she wonders. "From what I can see of humans, you often destroy wonderful things in the pursuit of something that your delusions make you think is more wonderful."

I look away. I think of Delia and how she wants to destroy her lovely eyes. I think of Quentin and all his desecrated Dolls. I think of pictures I've seen of old cities like the one called New York and compare it against the forest in Nexis. I remember my childhood horror at the idea of Meems changing her skin... because her body and face made her who she was, and I didn't want her to be anybody else.

Meems straightens and turns away. "What you humans need to do is find beauty in the fact that something is naturally the way it is. Perhaps then you wouldn't be so destructive."

Blushing a little bit, I say, "I did find something there that I found kind of beautiful."

Her brows quirk. "Oh?"

"There was a boy there."

Her eyes seem to dance. "And?"

I look away, feeling stupid. "We started to talk…and then I got pulled out."

Meems's mechanical chuckle makes me look up. "No wonder you want to return so bad."

chapter sixteen

When Meems leaves, I keep mentally going back to the game and that boy. I hope he's still there when I go back in. I hope he'll wait for me. Anxious to fill the hours until I'm able to play again, I pick up my flex-bracelet. I snap open the bracelet, letting the nano shingles realign and snap back together so that the once cylindrical bracelet is now a flat screen. Bending the lower half to a sixty degree angle, I set it on the windowsill and sit back.

I am able to navigate the applications inside my flex-bracelet using the G-Chip neuro-link. I turn it on, call up holo-projection mode, and open the puzzle program Dad uploaded onto my G-Chip. Dad gave me a puzzle to work on the night he died. Ever since I was a little girl, he gave me complicated encoded puzzles to decode, each one more difficult than the last. This one, it seems, is the puzzle to shame all puzzles. The image manifests in what looks like a massive knot of fiber-optic string, each string representing a line of code that I have to unravel and realign. If the pattern behind these puzzles holds true, once I've written a program to decode this puzzle, a private message that he left for me will appear.

It's extracurricular activities like this that make me the best Programmer in Paramount Prep. I used to hate them, but now this puzzle is the only thing I have left of my father. I'm going to solve it, going to read that message.

As I puzzle through the code, one of Tasha's automated vacuums wanders into the room, drawing my attention back to the insular world of my father's workroom. I open a neuro-link to Tasha, letting my G-Chip read my active thought processes and send them to the habitat control computer.

"Not now, I'm doing work."

The vacuum pauses in the center of the room, the light on the top flashing red. Tasha's response appears as a thought in my mind, her computer-generated voice halting. *"Are you studying?"*

I frown, wondering if she's teasing me. She must know that I have not left my room in weeks. How could I be doing schoolwork? I cock my head at the camera in the corner of the room. Her sensors watch me, observe my movement, and constantly monitor my chip. *"So, what if I am?"*

"You do not need ears to watch the wall."

With a beep, the vacuum continues to hum across the floor, the light now flashing green. Smiling, I give up my fight with Tasha and look back to my flex-bracelet.

As I demystify the complex jumble, a message pops up on the bottom of the screen. It's Delia. My heart leaps and I grin, stupid with happiness.

Today was a bad day. I miss you.

A flush of shame heats my face. I haven't spoken to her in weeks; I've been too busy wallowing in my own self-pity and embarrassment. Poor Delia, she must be worried sick about me.

I sit forward, ready to write back, but I don't know what to say. A massive wall has gone up between what was and what is. I'm not the same person anymore and, even if I could climb that wall and peek over to see her, I wouldn't know what to say to her.

But I have to say something. She's been sending me messages since the night of the ball, sometimes three or four a day. Sparks, why didn't I even bother to pick up my flex-bracelet and check my messages? I can't ignore her any longer than I already inadvertently have. I open the first one, an old vis-call from the night of the ball.

Wanted to let you know how beautiful you were in your dress tonight. I thought your mask was super cracked, so what if Quentin didn't? He's so Passé. Love you most. Dee

I smile to myself, thinking how very much I love seeing Dee's smiling face right now. And Quentin... If he thought I was atrocious then, I can only imagine how disgusted he'd be of me now. He'd probably have Shadow stomp my face in like he did my holo-mask. Still, I miss seeing him.

The messages continue from there, vis-calls and text messages. Dee thinking that I'm not coming to school because I'm ashamed and telling me not to be silly, and then Dee getting concerned when I don't respond, then her suddenly leaving morbid, awful messages like: *I miss you so much. It hurts and I can't stop crying, I can't believe it. I feel so alone. I wish you were here. Make it stop.* On a daily, sometimes hourly, basis.

I sit back, heartsick. Doesn't she know about the accident? Why hasn't she just come to see me? She must know I've been injured and that my father is dead. Wouldn't Uncle Simon or Bastian have told her? Wasn't it part of The Broadcast?

One would think that the recent winner of the Civil Enrichment Award getting in a fatal accident might make the news. Baffled, I pull up archived copies of The Broadcast from the days following the ball. There are pictures of the ball, of the awards ceremony, of me and my father. Tiny pixelated gems of the pride and joy in my father's face, of him holding my arm and posing with me. Of our last few moments. I save each one to my personal files and keep searching.

Finally, I find the file that I'm looking for.

Zane is the one reporting. He looks grim, and his voice holds none of the charismatic cadence it normally does. "It is with a heavy heart that I join Evanescence's Elite as we say good-bye to one of our most gifted citizens. Late Saturday night, just hours after receiving the prestigious Civil Enrichment Award for his development of the groundbreaking virtual-reality game, Nexis, Warren Drexel was killed in a freak pod accident. After extensive investigation funded by none other than President Cyr himself, it has been concluded that the accident was caused by a sensor malfunction within the pod. Joining Citizen Drexel in death is his daughter, Ellani Drexel—who was removed from life support after it was determined that there was no hope for revival. Sources claim Ellani had shown incredibly promising aptitude scores which, in time, would have surpassed her father's. In light of the loss of not one, but two of the city's most valuable Programmers, the Cyrs themselves have shown up to say good-bye to Warren and Ellani."

I stare in mute horror as the camera pans out, revealing an astounding number of Aristocrats lined up along Citizen's Way as two memorial pods drift down the main hover-way. Following after them in gleaming open-air pods are the hollow-looking Uncle Simon and Bastian, the tearful Delia and her family, a few other people who worked with my father, and of course, the Cyrs. Lady Cyr, for all her statuesque beauty, looks particularly distressed. And then there is Quentin…

The boy I love, the boy that I'd do anything to make look at me. The boy who now believes I'm dead. And for once, he doesn't look bored. For once, there's emotion on Quentin's face. He actually looks grieved. So does Shadow.

The pods stop at Central Square, and everyone begins to disembark. Delia is suddenly streaking across the square. She throws herself at Shadow—punching and kicking, screaming, but I can't hear what she's saying in the commotion. All I hear is my thundering heart as Bastian pulls her from Shadow. She struggles away from him and collapses into a sobbing mess next to one of the memorial pods. Her frightened little sister, Nina, attempts to go up to her, comfort her, but Delia pushes her away, making her land on her rear end. Nina starts to cry, too, and their parents look mortified. I feel mortified. Delia would never push Nina like that. Nina means the world to Delia. Tears begin spilling down my face. "No," I whimper.

Before I know what I'm doing, I'm screaming, "I'm not dead. I'm not dead. I'm not in there. I'm right here, Dee. It's empty. It's a lie. Look at me! Look. At. Me."

I scream until I'm panting, and then I settle down, realizing that there is no point in screaming at a Broadcast that is long past. Sparks. Everyone thinks I'm dead. But how? Why? Why am I here? Why am I still alive? What's going on? Why on earth would someone lie about my death?

I have to tell Delia I'm not dead. She's been mourning me, worrying her poor little macaw-inspired head. I have to see her and make her understand why I haven't been around, why I've been hiding away. I can't let her think I'm dead. How awful.

Both nervous and eager, I attempt to dial Dee for a vis-call. The line abruptly goes silent, which means that Tasha is blocking me.

"Why are you blocking me from visual calls?"

In the instant before she responds I worry that she's been

hacked or has picked up some kind of malware, but then she says, *"The parental controls on your G-Chip have been adjusted."*

"What? But why?"

She doesn't answer; she's not programmed to ruminate on possibilities. I frown, dread pooling in my stomach. Confused, I link up with the hover-chair and maneuver it toward the door. I need to talk with Katrina, figure out why I'm being blocked, and if she won't come to me, then I'll go to her. I need to contact Dee, and Uncle Simon, and Bastian. I need to be able to call out.

The door closes before I can get within ten feet of it. Frowning, I command it to open. It doesn't respond.

"Tasha?" Even in my mind, my voice sounds strangled and a little frightened. *"Why are you locking me inside?"*

"I have been forbidden to let you leave this room."

"What? For how long?"

"Indefinitely."

Sudden panic rises in my stomach. *"I'm a prisoner?"* Being held by someone who is a complete stranger. A stranger living in *my* house and changing *my* G-Chip? This cannot be happening.

Tasha doesn't answer.

Gnawing my lip, I sit and stare at the door. Can I break out? The sharp, earsplitting headache I get in response answers me. Circuits, there is no way out. Which means I can't hack my way, either; my chip will turn my brain to goo long before I get past the first firewall.

The chair gravitates back toward the window. Whether Tasha or some subconscious part of me guides it that way, I don't know.

I pull up Dee's latest message and reread it.

The respond button has been locked—as has every other social networking option on my flex-bracelet. I'm completely cut off. I blink at my bracelet in disbelief.

Then it hits me like a ton of scrap metal. "She's really keeping me prisoner," I whisper out loud. But why?

A few moments of deliberation leaves me with one option. She must be trying to steal my inheritance. And that means she's never going to let me have restorative surgery on my legs.

If there was ever a time for me to get restorative treatment for my legs, now would be best, when Dad's trust fund for me is large enough to cover it. But if Katrina is keeping me prisoner, making people think I'm dead, that means she's intending to use the power of guardianship over me and my estate to use Dad's credits for her own devices. Without legs, I can't get out. If I can't get out or call out then I can't go to anyone for help or fight her for ownership of my home and inheritance. I could be held like this until one of us dies.

Feeling sick again, I propel the chair forward once more and slam the door with my fist. "Katrina," I scream. "Katrina. Let me out. You can't keep me like this." I slam again. No one comes. I keep slamming and screaming. "Let me out. Let me out. You can't just lock me up and steal away my life. Let me out!" I pound one last time, then collapse to the side of the chair, panting and heart hammering.

Eventually, Tasha says, *This room is soundproofed.*

"Right," I breathe. "I'd forgotten that." Dad had the room soundproofed so he could focus. She stuck me up here so she didn't have to hear me scream for vengeance. Or for mercy.

Overwhelmed with the prospect of being trapped for the rest of my life, the chair glides back to the window, which would be my only means of escape...if I had legs to climb out of it.

I stare at Dee's words, over and over. I'm trapped. I will never be able to get out. Even if I could get the door to open, the hover-chair would get me maybe ten, fifteen feet from the house before the remote power connection with Tasha snapped. And then what? Crawl on my belly among the droids? Even if

I screamed, would someone honestly come to me? A legless Natural girl sprawled in the street? They would think I was a discarded Doll.

My best friend thinks I'm dead. My family thinks I'm dead. For all intents and purposes…I am dead.

part two:

FLOWERS GROW ON ELLA'S GRAVE

Unsent Letters to Delia

Dee,

This has been the fifth letter I've attempted to write you in almost the same number of hours. I'm overcome with so much anger, guilt, and betrayal that I can't seem to focus my thoughts enough to get it all down in a note to you, but each attempt seems to get a little clearer so I'll keep trying. Even though I know these words will never get to you, I feel it's important to write you. You need to know that I love you so very much and I think of you often, even if my silence has not and will continue not to reflect that. I still want you in my life, even though I am no longer allowed to be in yours.

I'm horrified by your grief at my death. The notes you have sent trouble me—as did your behavior at the memorial service. You've never been a violent person, nor have you ever been cross to Nina. You have to try to stay strong, to not lose sight of what makes you a caring, wonderful person. Please don't push away the people who love you. Yes, they sometimes leave us—I know that more than anyone—but that doesn't mean we shouldn't continue to love. As Meems keeps telling me, you need to persevere. Stay strong and I shall try my hardest to do the same.

Also, please forgive me...

As I've said in my previous notes, I'm sorry I didn't try to contact you sooner. I can only blame my state of mind for not thinking to even reach out to you. Perhaps I was ashamed. I don't really know the reason. Please don't take it personally, as I didn't reach out to anyone. Not Uncle Simon or Bastian... You were the first one I tried to contact.

In some ways I'm glad I did not try sooner. If I had tried to talk to you any earlier, I would have discovered my false death and this imprisonment weeks ago. Feeling the weight of this reality—I fear what depression I might have fallen into so close to learning of my father's death and dealing with my new injury. Finding out so late that I am imprisoned and dead to the world outside is a terrible blow, yes, but after dealing with what I have recently endured, I feel much stronger and better up to the challenge. Losing the people on the outside is not like losing Dad was. You're still alive, after all, and that means more to me than you being with me. I only hope you find happiness. In return, I shall do the same. I've already started. I finally went into Nexis, Dee. You'd be proud of me for finally swallowing my pride and doing it. It's wonderful in there, and I hope you go in soon as well, if you haven't already. I've even met a new friend. Well, perhaps a friend...

To be honest, I'm a little frightened. I don't want to replace you, but I'm already growing lonely with only Meems to talk to. You know I love her, but she's so matronly sometimes. I don't feel like I can talk to her about some things like I can with you.

I'm going to be trapped here for a long time it seems—why else fake my death? I hope you'll forgive me making a new friend, allowing someone new into my life when it has always been just you and me.

This boy...he doesn't make me feel the same way I do when I'm with you, so I don't think you need to worry. I don't know if what exists between him and me is even friendship at all. It's all so intense. And I've never wanted to please someone more. Not even with Quentin. He makes me feel strange, Dee. The way he looks at me... I can't stop thinking about him and I want to go back into the game. Even though I feel so drawn down and low after learning everything I have today, I just want to go back in. I'm anxious to see him, to see him grin again. Is that a good thing?

Forever Your Best Friend,
Ella

chapter seventeen

I'm already walking, my hand in the dry, callused palm of the boy I haven't been able to stop thinking about since yesterday. I smile at the back of his head as he leads me toward a squat building with a neon red sign that says DINER.

"You're still here," I say.

He glances over his shoulder. "So are you." He looks away. "Must be my charm." His hand twitches in mine, squeezing a little tighter, and I can't help the breathlessness that suddenly overcomes me. I want to laugh. I want to vis-call Dee and tell her. But I can't do that. Not anymore. And that makes my heart suddenly heavy. So I squeeze his hand back, promising myself that I'll be a better friend to this boy.

As we enter, I'm accosted out of my malaise with cold blowing air, all sorts of strange smells and noises, and the odd sight of someone standing in the center of the room singing into a stick-like thing that seems to be projecting her voice.

Cocking my head, I stare at the tall woman wearing a sparkling red dress that spreads at her high-heeled feet. She's got jet-black hair and very pale skin.

Another woman, this one older and more run-down looking, comes around the kiosk with a meaningful expression on her face. I hold my breath, but when she smiles her teeth look relatively normal, so I smile back.

I look from her to the singer and then back again, uncertain if she's part of the show. This one is wearing a bright white shirt and black shorts that reveal much of her shapely, bare legs. She plants a hand on her hip. "Well, here comes trouble." She's talking to the boy.

He grins. "Hi Patty."

She nods toward me. "You got yerself a little friend?"

Lifting our intertwined hands, he shrugs. "She's hungry."

"Ain't we all?" She reaches into the kiosk, pulls out some kind of portfolio, and tucks it under a tan, muscular arm. "Come on."

We follow her to the end of the aisle. I slide into the seat, and he sits beside me. My attention goes back to the woman singing near the front door.

"You want the specials?"

I glance up. "Hm?"

Patty glances over her shoulders. "Ain't you ever seen a say-lon singer before?"

I blink at Patty. "Say-lon singer?" I wonder if this is another one of those terms that Dad would say got "lost in translation" over the years. "What's she doing?"

Patty plants a fist on her hip. "What's it look like she's doing? Kiara's entertaining the customers."

"Entertaining?" I cock my head and listen to the raw noise coming out of Kiara's lungs. "She's terrible."

As the boy starts giggling, Patty rolls her eyes. "Not compared to everyone else who auditioned. You're an Outsider, ain't ya?"

"Well, I'm certainly not from around here."

"Probably an Aristocrat, too, by how clueless ya look."

I straighten, indignant.

A good-natured light ignites in Patty's watery blue eyes. "Don't get yer panties in a twist, short stuff. Look." She points toward Kiara. "That girl there, she's singing for real with her natural voice. She ain't Customized nor Modified or whatever else you people do to the people who entertain you. Do you even have people entertaining you anymore? Or is it all synthesizers and electronics?"

I frown. "We have cyberstars, of course."

She scoffs. "Cyberstars, she says." She glances at the boy and shakes her head. "What's that then? Androids?"

He nods. "They're the most efficient form of entertainment. Twice the vocal range of a human and you don't need to worry about sore throats or drug addictions."

She throws her hands up in the air. "Shame it is. Absolute shame." Then she draws a sharp breath. "Soups for today are chicken noodle and clam chowder. Waldo'll be around for your order in a bit."

As she walks away, I look to the boy, uncertain of what I'm supposed to do. He leans over, taking the portfolio, and opens it in front of me. "This is a menu. You look through it and decide what you want to eat."

"Um, okay."

I hunch down and stare at the meaningless lists and pictures before me. I turn one page. And then another and another.

Overwhelmed, I glance at the other customers. They're all bent over plates and glasses. I look back at the menu. Caesar Salad. Tuna Sandwich. Roast Turkey with Stuffing. Spaghetti and

Meatballs. Nothing makes sense. Not the numbers or titles, though I can at least understand some of the vegetables. I know that tomatoes and lettuce are grown in hydroponics. Though I've never tasted either.

A boy with a name tag reading "Waldo" comes to the table. "You ready to order?"

"The usual," the boy with me says.

Waldo looks to me, expectant. I bite my lip, uncertain, and turn to my new companion. "I don't know what to get."

He gives me a gentle smile then looks back to Waldo. "Make that two."

As Waldo walks away, I scroll through the screens on my bracelet, trying to find something else to talk about with this boy. The screen flips to a new map—a series of concentric circles. "What's this?"

"That's Nexis. The whole thing." He points at the first layer. "This bit here is called Utopia Zone. It's the primary drop point for new players. Players have their own private immersion area where they can acclimate themselves."

"That's the forest area I woke up in?"

"Yeah. Pretty cracked, right?"

I sit back. "So, why aren't you all living there instead of here? Seems like it would be way nicer to live there."

He closes his eyes. "We can't. Utopia Zone is literally a Virgin Earth area. You could remain there, but you can't change the land in any way. We wouldn't be able to develop at all if we all stayed in the forest. Besides, no other players can go into your square of the forest, so we'd never meet anyone else."

I scrunch my brow. "Why'd he make it like that?" I ask, more wondering to myself than anyone else. "It's like a tease."

"I suppose it is. But it's nice having somewhere to just get back to the basics—somewhere that will never change, right?"

I nod. Utopia Zone is Dad's way of making an eternal natural world—something the players in the game could enjoy but not destroy. "Okay I get it. So, what's this one?" I point to the second, larger sphere.

"That's the Free Zone. It's the area where all the gaming takes place. No matter what kind of game you're playing there is a place for you in the Free Zone."

I narrow my eyes. "It can't have everything."

His grin is a slow thing that ignites his eyes and makes me squirm. "You wanna bet?" He lets his low words and his expression sink in, making me sweat a little under my vest before moving on like it didn't happen. "This system mutates every millisecond, creating new characters, new scenarios, and new story lines. There are over one hundred thousand individual playing fields in Free Zone and more or less can be added as needed."

I blink at him. "That would allow for infinite gaming possibilities."

He nods. "It's necessary to make sure every player gets to play exactly the type of game that would appeal to them."

"Then how are you and I here? How are those people here?" I point to the other people in the diner. "We can't all be playing the same game; it's statistically impossible that we'd all desire the same gaming experience."

He scoffs. "Is it? Who is to say that that woman right there," he points at Kiara, "isn't playing a very different game than you or I? She could just be living the dream of being a say-lon singer, or maybe she's a spy or an assassin. Just because she's in the same setting as we are doesn't mean she's playing what we are. Take me." He points at his chest. "I'm playing a quest game; that waiter, Waldo, could be playing a simulation game; Patty, the owner, could be playing a strategy game. And those people there," he points at three men in a booth on the far wall. "They might not even be real. The AI simulations in this game are topnotch—populated from the personality programming we use in our androids back home, except here they have no limits; you can't tell the difference between a person the game created and a real person's avatar."

I twirl a curl, thoughtful. "So what happens when someone wanting to play a first-person shooter game lands in a simulation town? Are they just allowed to blow other gamers' heads off?"

He rolls his eyes. "No. Don't you get what I'm saying? The game wouldn't let that happen. If shooting random townspeople was the kind of game someone wanted to play, the game would put them in a sphere with only AI. Another gamer's avatar wouldn't end up on that level unless they *wanted* to be there, maybe as a law enforcement agent or something."

I lower my brow. "It sounds kind of sick to me that someone would be able to just go around killing as they pleased."

He looks away. "Some people really like that kind of thing."

"It's cruel."

"It's just AI. The people in there aren't real."

I think of Meems. She's not a real person, she's AI driving a mechanical body. It wouldn't be okay if someone just shot her. "Still," I say. "It's not right."

He's quiet for a long time; I can feel his eyes on me. Eventually, he reaches out and taps the map out of existence. "Hey," he says, trying to get my attention. I give him a sidelong glance. His pinched eyes and quirked lips indicate that he has picked up on my mood. "Are you upset?"

I fidget under his intense stare. "I'm not sure if upset is the right word." I don't know how to feel right now. "Maybe just a little overwhelmed. And confused." Why would Dad create a game where people could realize sick fantasies?

Waldo comes to the end of the counter across the aisle and places two tall glasses filled with dark liquid on the polished red countertop. "Order up."

"Got it." The boy stands and heads across the aisle. For a moment, I stare at his broad shoulders, admiring how the shirt he's wearing emphasizes the lean muscles in his back just as well as it does his chest and shoulders. I sort of want to touch those tempting bits of him.

He has an early Alteration—I think it's called a taboo... no, a tattoo—easing from the top of one shoulder and coiling around one bicep. It's a red and white dog-like creature with dark, intelligent eyes like his. My companion roots in one of the pouches hanging off his leather belt and hands a couple of coins to Waldo. As he turns back with the glasses, I look away and make a point of staring out the window, though there is nothing happening in the dry, empty street. I don't want him to know I've been staring—how embarrassing.

He leans close, placing the glass filled with dark bubbly liquid in front of me. I pretend to be startled and immediately give the drink more attention that I actually feel toward it. Pulling it close, I sniff it. It smells sweet, and the little bubbles tickle my nose. "What is it?"

"Dr Pepper."

"Doctor?" I lower my chin to the table and squint at the drink. "How can a drink be a doctor? Is it medicinal?"

He scoffs at me.

I look up. "And pepper...that's a spice, isn't it?" I cock my head. "I read that people used to believe that some spices have medicinal qualities." I poke at the bubbles. "What ailment does this Dr Pepper cure?"

He rolls his eyes in endearment. "Thirst, I surmise." He reaches out and gently pulls my finger out of the liquid. "Perhaps boredom as well."

I frown at the drink, annoyed that such a simple beverage could stump me so easily.

"You really need to lighten up. Stop overanalyzing. It's just a drink with a silly name. Here." He takes a long plastic tube out of its white paper packaging and places it in the drink.

Confused, I pick up the tube and stare at it. "Is this to administer the medicine?" It drips on the table.

"No." He reaches out and takes my hand again, his voice amused. "It's a straw. You use it to suck the Dr Pepper out of the glass." He guides my hand back down so that the straw is in the Dr Pepper once more, then he tugs it away and holds it.

"So it is an instrument meant to administer the medicine. It has red and white stripes, like the barber poles I've read about," I reason.

"No. It's an apparatus to drink," he says. "Nothing more, nothing less. I doubt any doctor anywhere utilized these in the administration of medicine." His voice is exhibiting waning patience. Perhaps he's annoyed that I'm paying more attention to the drink than my hand in his. But, I can't pay too much attention to it, I'll start to panic and do something foolish. Besides, what if the hand-holding is something very simple, like he doesn't want me to play with the straw anymore?

I scrunch my nose, trying to stay on topic. "What is the point of this 'straw' then?"

"Maybe to keep the bubbles out of your face when you drink?" he says with a shrug. "Or maybe just for fun? You know, sometimes we do things because they are completely pointless and just fun." He leans over and puts his mouth on his own straw. I can see the level of the liquid in his glass dropping; it must be disappearing into his mouth.

I lean forward and try my best to emulate his gesture, sucking on the end of the straw closest to me. I feel like an idiot doing it. The medicine tingles at first. Then there's the cold and the sweet and an odd bite. I pull away and touch my lips with my free hand. "It's good."

He stops drinking and smiles, the straw easing out of his lips. "It's my favorite."

"If not medicine, then what is this stuff?"

"Soda, pop, bubbly—depends who you're talking to. I guess there were a lot of names for it back then. It's carbonated and comes in many flavors and colors."

I stare at the glass, reverent. "Soda," I repeat. "It's great."

Black and white movement in the aisle catches his attention, and he pulls his hand away. I turn in time to see Waldo place two orange plates piled with tannish sticks on the table.

"Excellent." The boy leans over and grabs a bottle filled with red sludge. "Can't have fries without catsup."

"What'sup?" I ask.

He glops a huge pile of it on the edge of his plate, dips one of the sticks in it, and then thrusts it toward my mouth. I flinch backward.

He lifts a brow. "Eat it."

I focus on the stick with the "sup" stuff on it, making myself go cross-eyed, and grimace. "It looks unappetizing."

He draws the stick back and bites his lip. "Sometimes things don't look as good as they really are," he says, serious. He looks almost hurt.

I give him a pained expression. I know all too well where he is coming from. "You sure?"

He nods. "Oh yes, quite sure."

He holds it out again, and I reach out and touch his wrist to steady the fry as I lean forward and take a bite. It crunches under my teeth, but it's soft and sort of chewy on the inside. The 'sup gives it a salty-savory moist quality.

He watches, eyes expectant and heart beating under my fingers as I chew. "Well?"

Smiling around my food, I nod and force myself to swallow. "You're right."

He makes a satisfied expression and pulls his hand back. "I told you." He pops the other half of the fry I just bit into his mouth. I can't help watching him as he chews.

After a few minutes of eating, he says, "Are you ever going to ask my name?"

I nearly choke on the sip of soda I'm drawing into my mouth. I gape at him horrified, my face burning with embarrassment. "Oh my sparks, I'm so sorry. I completely forgot."

He shrugs. "No big deal, I have this amazing habit of taking words right out of girls' mouths." I can't tell if he's being sarcastic or not. "My name is Guster."

"Guster," I repeat, committing it to memory. "I'm Ella—"

"Uh oh," he breathes, cutting me off.

The warning in his voice makes me frown. "What?"

He doesn't meet my questioning eyes, instead he gestures toward the front door with his chin. "Trouble."

I follow his eyes in time to see three huge, black-armored men walk into the diner. Before I can examine them further, he grabs my arm and drags me under the table, pulling me inappropriately close and hunching over me as if he expects the ceiling to collapse on us.

"What—" I yelp, but he shushes me and makes a meaningful point of peeking out from under the table. I lean with him, searching and finding the black-clad men.

"Who are they?" I whisper.

"Damascus Knights," he responds. "They're from the Central Dominion."

I watch them a moment longer, their helmeted heads searching back and forth among the diner patrons. "They look like beetles."

He breathes a scoff of agreement, the exhalation brushing over my ear and sending shivers down my spine. "If only they were as harmless. Don't take them lightly."

"What are they looking for?"

He pushes away from me and props himself against the wall. "Considering we're the only ones hiding? I'll give you three guesses."

Great. I turn away from the Knights so that I can glare at him. "What? Why?"

He grins to himself, cocky. "Let's just say I found something they want."

"So," I urge, "just give it to them."

He begins rummaging through the bag he's been carrying with him. "Nah, I kind of like it. They'll have to fight me for it." He pulls out a small metal weapon that I can only assume is some sort of antique gun, then leans forward once more, collapsing the space around us.

He pushes the gun into my hands. "You know how to use this?"

I give him a horrified look. "No."

"Oh right, I forgot. Useless in a fight." He spares a glance back toward the Knights, who have now taken to accosting Waldo, then back at me. Before I can figure out what he's doing, he loops a hand around the back of my neck and drags me forward. His lips brush mine, trapping my breath in a hiccup of heat and confusion. His fingers tighten on my neck and all of a sudden he's full-on kissing me, his lips firm and commanding in a way that makes my skin ignite and my bones feel like rubber.

He pulls away and stares at me for a split second. In that

moment I know I should be yelling at him, telling him he shouldn't take advantage of me in such a way, but I'm too preoccupied with staring back at him, drinking in his handsome face and quirky grin.

"If I die, cry for me?"

I feel my eyes go wide, and I'm not quite sure how to answer. His fingers trail down my neck, lingering and teasing before he draws them away entirely and punches at the circuit patch on his wrist. In a split second a set of armor similar to that of the Damascus Knights seems to materialize across his chest and stomach, up and down his body, encasing him in glistening black enamel.

He lifts his hand, and the armor around his wrist retracts and buckles downward, allowing for a larger, more modern gun to unclip and land in his waiting palm. "Stay here," he commands, his voice oddly distorted by the helmet that hides his face. "If one of those things comes near you, shoot it."

I open my mouth to retort, but he's already stepping out of the shelter of the table. The white, dog-like creature on the back of his armor looks like it's bounding along as he crawls. He rises tall, a tower of courage and cunning, drawing attention to himself in the small crowded diner. The Knights see him instantly and go silent. One drops Waldo's collar.

"You boys looking for me?" Guster asks, his tone playfully suicidal.

One Knight looks to another. "It's that fox kid." The other nods.

And then all hell breaks loose.

A gun goes off. I don't know if it's Guster's or one of the Knights', but that's all that is needed to bring everyone's weapons out and firing. The Knights scatter in three different directions, their movements quick as a blur. The mirror over the counter explodes under the impact of a laser strike, spraying outward in a glimmering halo as Guster leaps to one side and dives behind the counter. He joins Patty and the man behind the counter, shooting out over my head.

In the deafening thunder of guns releasing round after round, I scream with countless others as glasses and dishes shatter. The things called fries, chunks of ice, soda, and eating utensils go skittering across the tiles, napkins and straw wrappers go fluttering. A table slams to the floor; a chair careens over my booth and lands with a clanking thud in front of me.

A bullet flies by my head—and then another. In the instant between the second and the third bullet, I see tiny shafts of wood and tufts of fluff go flying past my eye. They're shooting through the booth.

Realizing I'm going to get hit, I throw myself down and roll away from the booth. As I roll, I can see that one of the Knights is coming around my booth. The patrons have set up a barricade of tables and are driving him in my direction, though the bullets don't seem to be affecting him. In fact, the bullets seem to be bouncing off the gleaming black carapace he wears as armor.

He shoots back, the beams from the laser rifle he's carrying piercing everything he shoots at. In a flash of glittering crimson, Kiara falls among the patrons. Dead. I stare at her, her eyes wide open in surprised horror as my father's mythical Grim Reaper appears before her. The Reaper, a cloaked figure in billowing black, raises his weapon—something that looks like a crescent moon on a stick.

Shink.

"Ella."

Guster's voice pierces my horror, brings my senses snapping back in time for me to see the Knight now heading toward me. I yell as I roll again, avoiding a shot from his laser rifle. The glass on the floor bites into my arms as I rumble through it and launch myself to my feet.

Everything goes into slow motion. The sounds are like the long, drawn-out wails of the recorded whales of old—as if calling from some unfathomable depth. I can see each and every bullet screaming by me, every particle of this world swirling among the others. The Knight's movements come in incremental, jarring motions in this macabre ballet. The sights of the laser rifle are coming to rest on me. There's only a moment before I join Kiara on the floor.

There is no time to think, only to react.

I raise the revolver and hold it with both hands. For a brief moment, terror overcomes me as I realize I have no idea what to do with it. But then I do. In a lightning-fast motion that might indicate years of familiarity, my thumb releases the safety, I take aim, and squeeze the trigger. The gun resounds, the rebound shooting up my arms, making me flinch; but I've braced myself well. I stay on my feet, able to watch as my bullet takes the Knight right through the reflective silver of his eye socket.

Unlike my opponent's laser rifle, my bullet draws blood— shooting a geyser of it out of the back of the Knight's helmet and driving itself into the wall. The Reaper swoops out of thin air, not even bothering to fully manifest before swinging his blade.

Shink.

The crescent passes through the Knight and then the very fabric of what makes the Knight seems to pixelate. For an instant, he's a real, palpable thing and then, like the mirror, he explodes into a million tiny pieces and disappears in a cloud of glittering dust—a human supernova. All he leaves behind is a gleaming black diamond that just spins on a fixed axis overhead.

The world speeds up again. Shaking, I stare at the spot where the Knight once stood, at the smear of blood on the back wall and the gun I still hold raised against him.

He disappeared.

I killed him. I destroyed. I'm no better than all the humans who destroyed the world before me.

"Ella."

I reach out, touching the air, wanting to verify what I've done. My fingers find the diamond and, as they brush it, it bursts into thin air—just like the Knight. I flinch backward, feeling a sudden sting up my arm.

"Ella." Someone grabs my arm. "Snap out of it."

I glance up, wanting to find Guster's wild, dark eyes, but all I see is the face of another Knight. Fear grips me, and I try to pull away, try to raise the gun again. He slams his fist into his forearm, making the armor dissolve while he struggles to keep me under control. After a moment, logic returns to me. I recognize Guster and stop fighting.

More Knights burst through the door, making him whip around and shove me toward a back hall. "Run."

I run with Guster. I run because I have no idea what I've done or how I've done it. I run because I feel weak and vulnerable, and something about Guster's presence feels protective. I run because I feel cold, and his hot hands on my clammy skin are the only thing I can feel.

Out the back door, through an alley, down a street, and into another alley where a strange vehicle awaits.

"Get on," he commands.

The utter confusion of how I'm supposed to follow his command seems to kick-start my mind, alerting me to the world around me. I'm suddenly aware of the lasers striking near us, jumping off the alley walls, sending chunks of brick and cement flying, fogging the air with dust, and choking each breath with the scent of promised incineration.

I don't fight Guster's hands as he lifts me and sits me on the vehicle. In the next moment, his body encases mine, spreading warmth along my body as the vehicle rumbles to life between my legs and we shoot out of the alley…into a whole troop of Knights waiting on the main road.

"Hang on," he screams.

I duck down low, whimpering as he leans even harder against me. Laser beams ping off the vehicle. I glance up, confused as to why we haven't been blown sky-high and realize there's some kind of hard shell around us. He accelerates through the line of Knights and zooms off through the choked and jagged street, all the while laughing like a madman.

chapter eighteen

POST-AMERICAN DATE: 7/3/231

LONGITUDINAL TIMESTAMP: 6:33 P.M.

LOCATION: FREE ZONE, GARIBAL; NEXIS

We ride for what feels like forever, though Garibal doesn't seem to disappear despite that. I see little fountains here and there, flashes of brightly colored cloth and the claustrophobic walls of narrow streets, but we're going so fast that I can't really focus on anything as we zoom past the panicked and leaping creatures that Guster called horses. Finally, he skids to a halt near a fountain at the center of a wide-open, empty square. As soon as he lifts his weight off me, I launch myself off the strange vehicle and stumble away from him.

I feel wild and terrified. I just killed someone. I just killed someone and he gave me the gun to do it and now there are people chasing me.

"Ella," he says, holding his hands out to me like he's trying to calm me. He takes a step toward me.

Almost without my thinking about it, I lift the gun and aim it at him. "Don't come near me."

He freezes, his eyes trained on the gun, which is shaking so badly in my hand that I wouldn't be able to hit him even at such a close distance. *What am I doing? Do I want to shoot him?* He lifts his eyes to mine and holds my gaze. "Drop the gun, Ella."

"No," I spit. I cock the gun for good measure. I glance down at my hands. They don't feel like mine. My hands wouldn't know how to cock a gun or pull a trigger. My hands don't want to kill this boy, they want to touch him. "How do I know how to use this thing?" I demand, horrified at my own familiarity with it.

His eyes focus on the gun, on my arms, and then back up into my eyes. "Stop aiming at me, and I'll tell you."

"Tell me and I'll think about not aiming it at you."

Sighing, he lowers his hands, shoving them into his pockets. I glance from one hand to the other, uncertain if he's going to pull something out of his pocket to use against me. Would he? After kissing me like that? He looks away from me, walks to the edge of the fountain, and sits down.

I toss a stray curl out of my eye. "Isn't it kind of dumb to turn your back on someone who has a gun on you?"

Crossing his arms, he gives me a cool expression. "Isn't it kind of dumb to pull a gun on someone you don't want to shoot?"

I narrow my eyes at him. Am I that obvious? "Who says I don't want to shoot you?"

He lifts a brow, gives me a long, weighted glare, and then looks off over the square. "You don't. Besides, seems to me like you and I now have the same enemies. Shouldn't that make us allies?"

Allies? With him? The idea makes my stomach feel warm. But he almost got me killed back there. Pretty and tingly and purr-voiced...he could be the death of me. I lift the gun from where I've inadvertently lowered it and aim it back at the space between his long-lashed, pretty eyes. "That's your fault."

"It's the game's fault."

I don't know what to say to that, and suddenly I don't feel so sure of what I'm doing. Feeling sick, I back away from him and lower the gun. He's right; I really shouldn't point it at him, especially when I'm so wound up. I might accidentally shoot him, and that's the last thing I want to do. Damn him for knowing it, too. I stare at the gun in my trembling hands.

"I shot someone," I whisper. In my mind I can hear the gunshot, see the blood and brain spattering out of the back of the Knight's head.

The gun slips out of my fingers, hits the ground, and goes off. *BAM.* Screaming, I jump back, startled, as the bullet ricochets off to one side. In the next instant I'm sinking to my feet, sobbing. "I killed someone."

Guster's hand clamps around my shoulder. I don't acknowledge him, even though I feel his hand all the way to my very last nerve, only continue sobbing harder, my tears stinging skin that has gone dry in the harsh desert climate of Garibal.

"Hey," he says gently, grasping my other shoulder and trying to get me to look at him. "Hey, you didn't kill anyone. No one got hurt."

I shake my head, disbelieving. "I saw him die," I whimper. "I saw the blood. I saw it. And then he just…" I pause, recalling the horrible vision of the Knight dying before me. "…exploded."

"His avatar got killed, that's all. That's all we are here, just avatars. Our real bodies are outside in Real World."

I try to let his words sink in, but my brain wants to deny those precious words. "But," I say, shaking my head, "it felt so real."

He grasps my chin, tilting my face so that I'll look at him. "It's *supposed* to be like that, right?" He smiles his reassurance. "It wouldn't be the best virtual-reality game around if it didn't."

Again, he's right. Logically, no one should be able to die

playing a VR game. So no matter what my eyes tell me, my brain has to win this battle. Sniffling, I try drying my eyes with the back of my hands, but strange stringy stuff just gets caught on my face. I blink and pull my hands away. There's silver string like the kind that came out of the sky and guided me to Garibal wound around my hands. Grimacing, I rub my hands on my thighs.

"Here." He leans forward and places a clean white cloth against my cheek, gently wiping away the dirt and tears. Or perhaps my heating cheeks are burning them away. Then he sets out on my arms, pulling away silver fibers and wiping away blood. "Look at your arms," he mutters, his eyes examining the cuts I got from rolling through the glass.

They do look pretty bad, though I can hardly feel them. All I feel are his warm hands. He searches in one of his pockets and pulls out a vial filled with vibrant green liquid.

"What's that?"

"Healing potion." He pulls the stopper out with his teeth and spits it to one side. He puts it in my shaking hands, holding them around the vial so I don't drop it. "Drink."

I lift the vial to my lips and then pause, my eyes going to his again. The cautious, don't-talk-to-strangers part of me is still wary enough of Guster that it thinks I should question a strange drink from a strange boy. But when I look into his eyes and I feel his hands around me…I feel safe—like he could never hurt me. Logically, if he wanted to hurt me, he would have done it already, right?

I take a sip. It's colder than it feels in the vial and has a horrible, salty flavor.

"The whole thing."

"I would prefer it if medicine actually did taste like Dr Pepper." Grimacing, I down the rest in a single gulp and cough. I can feel it in my body, like something cold and alive climbing through my veins, seeping into my skin from the inside out. Any moment, I expect my pores to start oozing green slime but, as I watch my arms, the cuts disappear, leaving nothing but healthy tawny skin. Amazed, I glance up at him.

Guster frowns at the empty vial and sticks it back in his pocket. "That stuff is expensive. You owe me. First you try to shoot me and then you put me a hundred pennies in the hole. You're lucky you have a high Allure rating."

I feel heat prickle up my spine and look away, embarrassed.

Reaching out, he picks up his gun. "Don't ever drop an early revolver like this; you could have killed someone." He puts it back in my hands.

I stare at the gun, hating it for how it makes me feel so weak and stupid. I turn it over in my hands, examining it. "I shouldn't even know how to fire something like this," I reason. "What the heck happened?"

He stands, examines one of the silver strands that is now tangled in the cloth he used to wipe my face and arms. "Spider silk."

I let the words sink in. "Spider?"

He chuckles, deep and low, sending a shiver along my thighs. I whip my head up, confused. Planting his fists on his hips, he stares down at me. "You can keep that revolver if you promise not to point it at me again. You're going to need a weapon, at least until we can find something more suitable for you."

"We?"

He cocks his head. "You wanna fight those Knights on your own? Especially after you killed one of their buddies and looted his armor?"

I struggle to my feet. "I didn't loot anything," I growl. "And I thought you said I didn't kill anyone."

"Not a real person, no." He reaches out and takes my hand,

flipping my arm downward and slapping my patch.

"Ouch." A millisecond later, my body is encased and everything has a rose-colored digital overlay on it. I look down at myself. I'm wearing armor like that of the Knight's, but this one seems smaller, better fitted to my frame. "What the…"

He drops my arm. "You didn't kill a real person. But you killed that guy's avatar, and you got this as your reward. Pretty cracked spoils."

I fumble with the raised patch on my skin—dismissing the armor. Taking a deep breath, I go back to the more pressing topic of why the other Knights would think I killed their friend if Guster claims I didn't. "Can't he just start at the beginning of this level or something?"

He shakes his head. "It doesn't work like that. You die in the game, you can't come back and play the same character ever again. Everything you did as your character, everyone you knew, you can't come back to it. It's gone."

I scrunch my brow. "You don't remember it or something?"

"Oh, you remember. But the game just won't tolerate it. You can't come back as the same character; you have to be someone else, play a whole new game. And if you try to make contact with the same people or places you knew as your previous character, the game will try everything possible to prevent you."

"That seems stupid. So what if you want to come back to the same thing you knew? What's the big deal?"

Guster bites his lip in thought. "Come here." He holds out his hand indicating that I take it.

Wary, I outstretch my fingers then draw them back. "You going to slap me again?"

He rolls his eyes and quicker than I can see, his hand lashes out and grabs my outstretched fingers. I blink at him, astonished, but he just grins at me and leads me to the edge of the square.

Beyond the square with the fountain there's a dusty street with dozens of people. Against the walls of brick and whitewashed stucco buildings, strange tents and booths have been set up. In each tent there is something different. Bolts of brightly colored cloth with intricate patterns, crates of fruit and vegetables, cages of strange animals, odd bundles of plants, stacks of baskets, twinkling bits of jewelry, weapons. Everyone is shouting and milling about. No one seems interested in what's being shouted at them, but their eyes scan back and forth, obviously looking for something.

"There." Guster points to a couple standing next to a stall filled with baskets of spices. The man has his arm around the waist of a woman holding a baby.

"Okay…" I don't get why he pointed them out.

"That baby isn't a real person."

Startled, I blink at him. "What?"

He glances at them. "Those two people have a life together here, have a baby here, but for all we know one could be the wife of a wealthy Aristocrat and the other could be a Disfavored man destined to rot in a jail cell for the rest of his wretched life. Yet here they are. And there is the result of their happiness."

"You mean, you can have a baby here? The game makes one for you?" Meems had said people could have a new family, but I hadn't thought about marriage or babies.

Guster nods. "You can have anything here. That's why the game is so wonderful. I dare say it's probably destroying a life or two in Real World, but people should be allowed to be happy, don't you think? If that man really is Disfavored then he'd never have the opportunity to fall in love and marry a woman so beautiful. All the pretty girls are sold to brothels and Doll Houses in the Outer Block. Likewise that woman would probably never know real love. Everyone knows Aristocrats don't marry for love."

I stare at the couple and their baby, understanding exactly what he means. I would never be able to walk again if it weren't for this game. Circuits, with the way Katrina keeps me locked up I'd never be able to do anything if it weren't for this game. I think about all the experiences I've had since coming here. This place is a dream come true. "So, if it does all this awesome stuff, why can't you go back to it if your avatar is killed?"

Guster smiles to himself. "That baby will never know about the outside world. She'll grow up and maybe fall in love with someone who came from Real World. Maybe they'll have their own children. How would that child's perception of her world crumble if her father, who she saw killed, suddenly reappeared? There have to be rules, Ella. Even here, there are rules. It's a game. You play it. If you win, well, bully for you. But if you lose, you lose. Not even a game created to make everyone happy will reward sore losers."

I shake my head, marveling at my father's world. "This game is crazy."

"The game has no limits. It will create whatever is needed to maintain the illusion. The dead remain so, and the game has no problem creating people who don't exist just to enrich someone's gaming experience."

I turn away from the market and look back at the empty square. "Including making a quiet, undisturbed place to talk?"

He shifts beside me; I can sense the heat of him standing close to me. I step away, turning back toward him. "What about you? Are you real or just some piece of AI the game created to guide me?"

He meets my questioning eyes, his own sparkling in the late afternoon light. He looks and feels real, but then so does everything else here. "What do *you* think?"

I stare at him for a long moment. He's too good to be true,

but I don't say that. "I think you're too convenient."

The corner of his lip twitches. "Well then, that makes two of us." He brushes past me and heads back toward where his machine is parked beside the fountain.

I follow after him. "I'm serious."

He spins around, pinning me with a hard expression. "So am I. How do I know *you're* real? Just because one of us tells the other we're real, does it really mean anything? Could one demand the other tells about what life's really like in Real World? What's to keep us from lying about that? What's to make the other believe it when we tell a truth that the other can't or won't believe?"

I stare at him, handsome even in his anger. Can I really believe that someone so intelligent and earnest is a phantom a game made up? What's to keep me from believing exactly that? It seems too strange and exhilarating that he randomly found me and so readily wants me as an ally. I swallow, hating that I'm even asking it. "Why did you start talking to me? Why'd you just pick me up and take me under your wing like you did?"

The skin under the bottom of his eye twitches and he looks away from me. "You're a side quest."

chapter nineteen

POST-AMERICAN DATE: 7/3/231

LONGITUDINAL TIMESTAMP: 7:18 P.M.

LOCATION: DOME 5: EVANESCENCE

Shooting upright, I tear the blinder and caps off. "What?" I growl.

Meems blinks at me, frightened by my outburst. "Ellani?"

Tears burn on the brims of my eyelids, but I refuse to let them fall. I bite the inside of my cheek until I taste blood and try to even out my breathing.

Meems puts a hand on my arm. "Are you all right?"

I don't look at her; I know I'll burst out crying otherwise. I knew it was too good to be true. Why would any guy want anything to do with me unless it was part of some kind of side quest? What does he want from me? And what am I supposed to do about it?

"Ella?" Meems is shaking me.

I put my hands out, trying to get her to stop. "I'm fine," I hiss. "Just leave me alone."

Her hands recoil as though I've suddenly become white hot, and she drops them at her side. I hunch my shoulders. "Sorry. I didn't mean that."

"Is the game not going well?" She's using the mechanical voice, letting me know that she's hurt and doesn't want to forgive me so easily.

I grimace. "I don't know."

"Would you like to talk about it?"

I shake my head.

"Well," she breathes. "I am here should you need me." She moves off to the corner and stares out into space, withdrawing from me.

Sighing, I plop back down on the pillow and try to figure out what to do about Guster and Garibal and this game that my father created.

chapter twenty

POST-AMERICAN DATE: 7/4/231

LONGITUDINAL TIMESTAMP: 1:15 P.M.

LOCATION: DOME 5, GARIBAL; NEXIS

"A spider is, first and foremost, a builder. However, it is also a destroyer—a killer. Within men, there is an innate fear of the spider. But to some, (the wise ones in my opinion), the spider is a symbol of luck, illusion, wisdom, rebirth, and creation. My favorite saying from these wise people is, *If you wish to live and thrive, let the spider run alive.*"

Meems looks up. "What is that?"

"Dad wrote it here." I point to the main holo-screen on his work computer. "It's one of the files in his G-Chip."

Reading these files, I feel closer to him—knowing what he knew, learning his secrets. At times, I feel nearer now than I did when he was alive. The files have consumed me since yesterday, given me a reason to stop thinking too closely about Guster.

"He's got all this spider stuff in this file he calls 'Anansi Program,'" I say. "I don't get it."

"Have you tried looking them up?"

"I remember learning from Dad that a spider is a kind of

eight-legged insect that catches its prey in some kind of woven silk net and, according to the Archive, Anansi is supposed to be a storybook character or something—a trickster who takes the form of a spider, but the things he talks about don't always fit those definitions. I've tried looking for more information about it, but I can't find anything else. It seems that many of the Anansi stories were lost in the war. I'd ask on the Internetwork but, one, I can't get on and, two, I doubt anyone would know. It's not like they teach this stuff in school anymore."

Meems tips her head to one side. "I am aware of this. You are only taught Post-American history—the time after the Bio-Nuclear War, the resulting collapse of civilization, and the glorious history of Evanescence."

The VR timer goes off, but I ignore it, choosing instead to pay more attention to the files.

"Your alarm just went off," Meems says.

"I know. I heard it."

"That means you can go back in the game now."

Trying to seem indifferent, I lift a shoulder. "So?"

Forehead crinkled with concern, she leans forward. "Do you not want to go back in? You wanted to before. You were so eager yesterday."

I prompt a mind-to-text note to open. I'm intending on telling Delia about reading about television—which I'm assuming is the ancestor to The Broadcast. She'd like to know that Anchors like Zane have been around forever, but he seems like the best one. "Not anymore."

"What changed your mind?"

I puff out my cheeks. I don't want to talk to Meems about this. She's just an android; she'll think I'm silly. I glance at the message forming in front of me. I could write Delia a letter about Guster. But would that help anything? Without a response, I still won't have any input. I *have* to talk to someone about Guster or I'll burst. "I'm his side quest," I mutter.

"Is that what this is all about? You factor into this boy's game?" Straightening, Meems clasps her hands in front of her. "Well, maybe he's part of your game? Did you consider that? Maybe, whomever it is you just met in there will be a new friend, someone *they* cannot take away from you."

She lets that sink in for a moment. And I can't help but pick out that she says "they." We talked yesterday about my strange captivity, about Katrina, about the fact that Meems seems unable to execute any method to save me. Someone reprogrammed her. And Katrina, I'm certain, isn't smart enough to do it. Someone else is behind this. But why? To what end? Meems continues, cutting off my thoughts. "Do you not want to play with him? You seemed to enjoy his company."

I sigh. I do want to play with Guster. I liked being with him. "I want him to want to be with me because he likes being with me, not because he's forced to be with me or because he wants something from me. That's not how friendship should be."

She unclasps her hands and plants them on her hips. "That may be, but are you willing to tell me you do not ever want to see the sky again? No grass or trees, either? I thought you were going in there to *live*. Being forced to be with people and learning to like them is part of life."

And really? I don't ever not want to see Guster again, either. "Point taken." I bite my lip. "But what am I going to say to him?"

She shrugs. "Who cares about him? Do what *you* want."

I jerk a nod. "All right, let me just write Delia a quick note." I need to tell Delia about the thing called reality television. She would have loved it.

Guster is waiting for me when I materialize back in the empty square. He's sitting on the edge of the fountain. When he sees me he stands and opens his mouth, but something in my expression gives him pause. For a moment I stare at him, daring him to move an inch closer to me. I can't do this. I don't have the courage to rail and fuss that he's a terrible Prince Charming. I'm not ready to admit that I might actually like him as more than a friend. I turn on my heel and stalk away from him.

"Ella," he yells after me.

"Leave me alone," I growl. I can hear his footsteps behind me, following me. I quicken my pace until I'm running down the street. People are staring at us, trying to decide whether they should intervene.

"No," he says back. "I'm not going to leave you alone. Look, would you just stop and talk to me for a minute?" he demands, his voice straining over the noise of the market.

I run harder, my feet pounding out a rhythm against the road, my heart thudding and my breaths coming in quick gasps. I know I can't outrun him. His stats are probably higher than mine. He's probably got way better physical strength and stamina. I'll tire out faster than him. Maybe I should stop and let him talk, if only to catch my breath? As if on cue, he tackles me from behind, making both of us tumble limb over head into a pile of crunchy yellow stuff.

I immediately start trying to fight him, punching and kicking, but he wrestles my arms down and sits on me, pinning me. I lay under him huffing, trying my best to struggle, but he can easily hold me down without even hurting me. His eyes are bright, and his breath is sweet on my face. Despite the heat of Garibal, the warmth of his body is a thrilling comfort.

"Circuits, you're one hardheaded girl," he breathes. "It's a damn good thing you're cute."

I go still. "D-Do you really think I'm cute?" My cheeks heat.

He grins at me. "I don't chase ugly girls. You mind explaining what I did to get your sparks flying?"

I turn my head, not wanting to look into his eyes, and mumble, "I don't want to be a side quest."

"Is that what you're freaking out about?" His tone has that *women are so dramatic* quality to it.

Frowning, I blush harder, not liking how he isn't taking me seriously or how painful the idea of him not wanting to be with me is. It's silly to have gotten so attached to him so fast, but I can't really help it. I guess I had just hoped everything in the game would be perfect, and when I saw him and he seemed interested (and he kissed me), I foolishly assumed he was part of that perfection.

A long silence passes between us. He's watching me; I can feel his eyes on me. Sensing that I'm not going to struggle, his muscles ease up, his fingers unhinging and brushing along my arms.

Finally, he says, "I was told that you could help me in my quest, so I came looking for you." He reaches out and hooks a finger under my chin, turning my face toward him. "I didn't know what to expect. You're a pleasant surprise."

I scowl, trying not to show how good his words make me feel. "Right. And how am I supposed to believe a word coming out of your mouth? You might do or say anything to get me to do what you want from me."

One corner of his mouth curls up, giving him a crooked, dimpled smirk. "Except, I don't know what to say or do to get you to believe me."

"Why should I believe you?"

His brow creases, confused. "You know, I have no idea. It's not like I'm a terribly trustworthy person. Even in real life I'm nothing but a fakc and a liar—and I'm a thicf in this game, you know? I'm on a quest to get to the Central Dominion, break into the Anansi Chamber, and steal the Dominion's treasures. I'm sure you're not at all interested in something like that."

Despite his admissions, he just seems more intriguing. And Anansi? I lift my head. "Anansi Chamber? What's that?"

He sits back, allowing me to sit up and squirm out from under him if I wanted to, but I don't move. "I don't know. All I know is that's my quest and the Oracle told me to keep an eye out for people with the mark."

"Mark?"

He shifts slightly and shows me the tattoo on his shoulder. Upon seeing my own clueless face he reaches down and tugs at the leather vest I'm wearing. "You've got it on your back."

Not quite believing him, I sit up and unlace the vest. I can see it before I even pull the whole thing from my body. A giant white spider sewn into the black leather of the vest. "What does that have to do with a-a?" I point at his shoulder, uncertain of what the dog-thing even is.

"A fox? They're both Tricksters," Guster says matter-of-factly. "We're all Tricksters. The Oracle said to find those with the marks. Spider, fox, coyote, crow, rabbit. Together, we'll be able to get to the Chamber."

I shrug the vest back on and give him a long hard look. "You just want me to come with you so I can help you get into this chamber, is that it?"

He gnaws his lip, thoughtful. "You probably wouldn't believe me if I told you that I had no idea you were the person I was looking for until you got up off that crate, would you?"

I narrow my eyes at him. "Probably not."

He sits down next to me. "Whether you believe it or not, it's the truth. How could I see your back while you were sitting?" he asks. "I started talking to you because I thought you were beautiful and looked like you needed someone to talk to. I wouldn't do that in real life; it's not my style. But well, this is a game. I figure getting rejected here wouldn't be as bad as in Real World. Plus," he adds a little shyly, "I've probably got a better chance with someone like you here than out there."

I stare at him for a long, dizzying minute. He's way too good to be true. "Boy, you sure do know how to sugarcoat something, don't you? No wonder you call yourself a trickster."

He laughs to himself and shakes his head. "I'm inclined to say whether or not you were the person I was looking for, I'd still ask you to come with me. Every knight needs his lady, every thief needs his reason not to get his hands cut off." He reaches out and brushes his fingers up my arm. "Getting to touch you is pretty damn good incentive."

Now it's my turn to laugh. I smack his hand away. "Okay, Shakespeare, lay it on any thicker and you'll drown us both in poetic goo."

"Who's that?"

"Some dead guy who wrote poems and plays, though I can't seem to find any in the Archive."

"Hmm," he breathes. "Shame. I like poems."

For a moment the reminder of everything humanity lost of itself, leaving us with so little to remember, keeps us silent. Then Guster turns his head toward me. "So, you going to come with me?"

I lay back in the bristly yellow stuff—I think it's dried grass or something—and look up at the sky. If what Guster says is true—that the Oracle told him what he is and what his quest is, that means that I don't have a quest. Or perhaps that means my quest is Guster's quest. The strings did lead me here. *The spider will find her comrades in trickery.* The Oracle said that. I have a spider on my back. Guster calls himself a trickster, so maybe that *does* mean I'm supposed to go with him.

Guster lies down beside me. I look over at him; he's staring at the sky, the clouds sliding over his eyes. I can think of worse things than being a thief's reason not to get his hands cut off. But I say, "I suppose being a trickster isn't the worst."

He closes his eyes and grins. "Is that a reluctant yes?"

Is it? If I say no, then he'll probably go on his quest and leave me behind. I'm not ready to say good-bye to the mystery of this boy with a fox tattoo. "If I go, it's not as a pawn," I say, trying to sound reasonable. "For my own reasons, I want to see and experience this game. A quest would be perfect for that. And I'm curious about this Anansi Chamber thing." Very curious. Anansi. The spider. The trickster. The Oracle named me. She called me spider, she called me Anansi Child... So, does that make me a trickster, too? Does that link me to the Chamber? Isn't that why Guster wants me to come?

I look back up at the sky and close my eyes, savoring this moment of certainty. "Yeah," I say. "I'll go with you."

His hand finds mine in the dried grass and squeezes it. "I was hoping you'd say that."

chapter twenty-one

Guster keeps his hand in mine as we walk back down the street, as if he needs to reassure me that I'm not just some object. Either that, or he's afraid I'm going to run away again.

"I didn't realize we'd gone so far," I say, feeling like an idiot for running like I did. I don't know what I wanted to accomplish by running from him. Escape, obviously, but I knew he'd catch me. *Maybe I wanted to see if he'd follow me?*

He looks up at the sky. "It's too late in the day to leave now. We can stay the night at my place and leave tomorrow."

I stop short, my hand tugging out of his. "Stay the night? Together?"

He glances back at me and smirks that devilish smirk of his. "Yeah. You didn't really think it through all the way when you said yes, did you?"

I avoid his eyes by fussing with the pleats of my skirt. "Sleeping hadn't really crossed my mind, no."

"It should have. You have to sleep here, too; your avatar

doesn't just keep going. You have to feed and take care of yourself here just like you do in Real World. Granted, you don't need as much of either food or sleep, but you *do* still need it."

I bite the inside of my lip. "But I don't feel tired," I reason. It's not entirely a lie. I feel pretty wired, especially now that he just suggested spending the night at his place.

He bends down, catching my gaze, and narrows an eye at me. "How many times have you come in so far?"

"Three," I say slowly, double checking in my mind. "Yeah, three."

"So, about thirteen hours. Usually your first time in you can go for about twenty-four before your health points start to drop." He glances at his wrist, checking his own stats. "I'm not that lucky, mine are already starting to drop, so you're going to have to at least take a nap. We need to align our bio clocks."

I make a clueless expression.

He takes my hand and starts walking again. "If you and I are going to play together, we're going to have to synchronize ourselves. Eat and sleep at the same time, log into the game at the same time. It won't do for one of us to pop out early. It's annoying and could completely destroy a job."

"Oh, okay."

"I tried to pop in when I thought you'd be back today, but apparently you weren't exactly waiting on the alarm."

I scrunch my shoulders. "Sorry."

He nods once. "That can't happen anymore. You need to log in right when the alarm goes off. Does your schedule in Real World allow you to do that regularly?"

"Yeah, I'm pretty free." I say with a half laugh. "So, um, how do we synchronize?"

"Oh, that's easy," he says. "Let's get someplace safe first."

I nod at his back as we reenter the empty square.

"Hop on." He gestures to the two-wheeled vehicle.

I swing an awkward leg over the seat, hunch over the body, and grab the lower set of handholds. He gets on behind me and mirrors my position, cupping my body and placing his hands on the control levers above mine. Trying not to think about his hard form against mine, I hyper-focus as his thumb flicks a switch and the vehicle springs to life, the strange shield shooting out and around us so that we're enclosed in an egg-shaped bubble.

Guster lifts a foot and taps my calf, letting me know I can put my feet up. I do so, allowing my weight to lean against the body rest and the handles as I plant my toes into the lower set of footholds. He twists his wrist, easing the vehicle forward, and lifts his own legs, his body resting heavily against mine for a brief moment while he finds the footholds, and then his body goes back to gently molding against mine. He twists his wrist farther, demanding more speed. For a moment, the engine just hums, gaining momentum. And then, we shoot forward—so fast that the back end skids—but Guster shifts his weight to one side, his body guiding mine to follow, and tipping the vehicle against the fall.

We zip across the square and between two buildings. Guster guides it expertly, hugging corners and urging it through tiny cobbled alleys with the ease of someone well practiced, his body training mine on how to ride the strange contraption. In less than ten minutes we blast through a narrow underpass, and we're suddenly on an open dirt road. Guster lets her open up, the distance between Garibal and our unknown destination growing by the nanosecond.

When I finally catch my breath, certain we're not going to crash and comfortable enough with his body held so intimately around mine to speak, I yell, "What is this thing?"

"It's a vivacycle, modeled after a futuristic version of a cartoon motorcycle," he yells back. "I designed it myself—you like it?"

"I don't understand a word you just said, but yes, I like it." Then I say, "It's a little loud."

Guster chuckles in my ear, the feel of it rumbling down my spine and the back of my thighs. "It's how you know you're alive."

He shifts his weight—I assume adjusting his foot in the holder—pressing himself against my backside. I blush harder. *Oh, I'm definitely alive.* I clear my throat. "Where are we going?"

He settles back down, and he somehow feels even closer now, his face close to my ear. "Base camp. The others will want to meet you." His voice rumbles along my ribs, sending electricity back and forth until my toes curl.

Others? And here I thought it was just going to be us. "What others?"

"There's more than just us wanting to get into the Anansi Chamber. They've all got their reasons. You'll like them, I think."

Time passes, the ground disappearing beneath us, though it seems darker now. Everything does. Curious, I lift my head and gasp. Above us is a vast emptiness filled with black silk and tiny white lights. Guster slows the vivacycle and comes to a halt. As the shield opens, letting the cool air touch our sweaty bodies, he sits up and draws in a giant breath.

I sit up, too, my eyes still on the sky. "What happened?" I ask, turning to him.

"Hmm?" He looks at me, eyes bright as those lights above. I'd forgotten how beautiful he is to look at, especially now in the gentle dark-light. Meems was right, natural things can be very beautiful, you just need to open your eyes and look.

I point upward. "Where'd the sun go? And why'd the sky get so dark? I thought there weren't radiation clouds here."

He smiles and looks up. "It's the night sky, Elle. The real one.

Not at all what we see on the nano-dome, is it?"

I stare at him, now certain that he can't be an AI created for my game. He's a real person. Someone from inside the dome, like me. Someone who chose to be a Natural inside this game. He's a Naturalist sympathizer. Someone who might actually love me for me in real life, and that makes my heart pound harder.

A strange noise sounds off to my left; I turn to it, confused as to why it seems so familiar. It takes me a moment to realize that it reminds me of a sound clip I heard from Dad's encyclopedia file on dogs. In the distance is a small cottage, a black outline against the deep blue horizon, the windows ablaze with yellow light. The door opens, and the figure of a female steps into view. A large furry creature blasts past her and comes hurtling toward us, disappearing in the deep darkness before leaping up again and coming to lay both its paws on Guster's thigh.

I stare at it, amazed. "Is that a-a-"

Guster laughs and scrubs his fingers through the animal's sandy coat. "This is Dune."

Tentative, I reach out, wanting to touch it, but the creature turns its head at the last minute and bastes me with a broad pink tongue. "Ugh," I wail, pulling my hand away and scrubbing it against my leg.

"Aw," Guster teases. "He likes you. Don't you Dune Boy?" He makes a stupid voice when he says this, his tone going all foolish and kissy faced. Dune whines and licks at Guster's throat, his whole body wiggling because he can't seem to control his tail.

I scrunch my nose. "That's disgusting."

He laughs to himself. "He's just saying hello. It's like a hello kiss, doggie style."

"I'm glad no one ever said hello like that to me."

His hands are suddenly around me as he grins. "Maybe some- one should." He wags his eyebrows.

I stumble off the vivacycle and back away from him, grinning and raising my hands. "Oh no. Don't you dare." But he's already getting off the vivacycle, arms outstretched toward me.

Laughing, I shriek and flee from him, Dunc barking and romping at my heels. Again, I know he'll catch me, so there's not really a point in running. But I do it anyway, because having someone care enough to come after me means something important. I just hope he doesn't really intend on salivating all over me…at least, not like Dune did.

When he finally does catch me, he grabs me around the waist. His momentum spins us around in a circle and downs us both in a patch of scratchy weeds. I can feel things crawling out from under me, making me wriggle underneath him as I giggle wildly, but he doesn't seem to notice the bugs. He's staring at me, his eyes twinkling in the darkness. In the next moment, he smoothes his fingers along my brow, brushing hair from my face, and smiles a soft, contemplative smile that makes my squirms turn from the outside in.

I take a deep breath, trying to center myself and focus on something other than the light feeling he gives me. "Why do you smile so much?"

"I'm happy," he says, shifting so that he can rest his weight on one elbow. "I like it here."

I cock my head. "You don't like it out there?"

His bottom lip disappears into his mouth, canceling his smile as his brow furrows in thought. "Do you run as much out there?"

"What?" I say with an exhaled laugh.

"You like running. You run when you don't need to, just to run."

I look off to the side, avoiding his eyes. I could say that I like running because I now have legs to run on, but it goes deeper than that. "Running here," I whisper, not quite knowing what

I'm saying, "It's not like being on the treadmills at home. It's different." I shake my head, feeling stupid. "I don't know, it's like I'm more alive here, bursting with energy. I used to hate running; it used to be a chore. It's not like that here. I get tired and I can't breathe, but it's a good tired breathlessness." I look back at him. "I guess that sounds sort of silly."

His smile returns. "I'm not sure I could explain it any better myself." Dark eyes wander out and over the landscape, drinking in the sky and the land. "Every time I come here, it's like being reborn. And, no matter how bad it gets here, I know there are more ways to solve my problems here than there are out there. The world is still alive here, people have potential, you're still allowed to dream."

Unable to help myself, I reach up and touch his face, drawing his attention back to me. "What do you dream of?"

His fingers twitch at my temple. "I dream of a lot of things," he admits, his fingers wandering through my curls. "I can imagine endless possibilities, have infinite wants."

I feel my cheeks warm as I say, "Do you want to know what I want right now?"

The grin quirks to the side. "Yeah, I do."

I hold my breath for a long moment before exhaling. "I want you to kiss me again."

Guster's eyes widen, as if this request surprises him. I can't imagine why it should, I don't feel as though I've hidden my attraction to him, but then his expression deepens into something soft and affectionate. When he does lean in to kiss me, it's long and hot, his firm lips smiling even as they travel along my jaw and down my neck. The intense feelings his attention arouses in me makes me sweat despite the cool night air, makes me want to jump up and run again despite how much I want to stay where I am. I want more than just a kiss. I want so much more from this boy. It scares me and it thrills me and, because I can't have anything in Real World, I want it all here—damned be the consequences. He doesn't stop until something close to my ear beeps in urgency.

Breathing heavy, he lifts his face and glances down at his wrist. He lets out an annoyed growl and runs his hand through his dark hair. "Final health bar."

I blink, not entirely in the moment. My mind and body feel stretched too tight—tight to bursting. "What does that mean?"

He rolls off of me and gets to his feet. "I have to sleep. We can do this another time."

I give him a disappointed pout.

He smiles and offers me his hand. "Trust me. There's going to be another time."

I lift a coy brow as I put my hand in his. "Who says I want another one?"

He hauls me to unsteady feet, pulling me close once more. "Keep running, Elle," he whispers in my ear. "I'll always catch you." He steps away and spins around, his attention falling on Dune who's sniffing around a clump of tall grass a couple of yards away. He lets out a shrill whistle. "Dune, come."

Dune comes bounding over, tongue lolling.

As we walk back toward the cottage, I totter on shaking legs and attempt to pull strands of dried plant life out of my hair.

"You're beautiful, even with weeds in your hair," Guster says without looking at me.

I let my hands drop to my side and stare at the ground. How does this boy know exactly what to say to me? "You're too good to be true."

"Didn't we have this conversation already?"

"Sort of," I say. "I accept that you're not an AI, and I understand you're from inside the city. What I don't understand is why you look like a Natural, and you think I'm beautiful."

He shrugs. "Matter of taste, I guess. We're both Aristocrats who chose to be Naturals here in the game. How much of that choice is biological and how much is social? Who cares? You and I hardly know each other, yet neither of us denies an incredible attraction to the other. I could be a murderer for all you know, but you still wanted me to kiss you."

When he sees the horror on my face, he quickly adds, "I'm not a murderer, though. At least, not in the murderous sense of the word."

Horror becomes confusion. "What do you mean, sense of the word?"

"I mean what I mean. You know I took out those two Knights this afternoon. But then, you killed one, too. But that wasn't my point. I was just using the murdering thing to draw attention to the fact that we're total strangers who just had an awesome make-out session based entirely on sexual attraction, and things would have gotten pretty heavy back there if I hadn't stopped," he muses, grinning again. He sounds both pleased with himself and entirely happy about it, and that just makes me want to knock him back to the ground and demand he finish what he started.

Disturbed, I stop and pinch my lips tight. "I feel like maybe…" My voice trails off, uncertain of the right thing to say. His words were meant to soothe my insecurity, but they seem to have the opposite effect. What am I doing? He's right, I was totally going to go all the way back there. With this boy I hardly even know. Does the fact that this is a game make that okay with me? Am I just using him for some kind of release? Rebelliousness? No, I'm not using this boy. I honestly have intense feelings when it comes to Guster. But what if this initial attraction wears off and we're left with nothing real between us?

"You know, back home, they'd call us idiots for doing what you and I were just doing. People don't just have random make-out sessions based on sexual attraction."

Guster makes an exasperated noise somewhere between a sigh and a growl and looks up at the sky. "Don't bring that Dome stuff here. This is a game; we can do what we want, and there are no repercussions."

I frown at him, insistent. "It's not that easy to just pretend that the rules no longer exist."

His head snaps to the side, his expression suddenly fiery with annoyance. "It's not a rule. It's a stupid social norm. Interpersonal relationships should be based on real love and real friendship, not social status and reputation. And what two people decide to do with their relationship should be no one's business but their own. I'm attracted to you, I want to kiss you, then damn it, I'm going to kiss you. It's human nature to act like this."

"That's how it should be," I agree. "But it's not. Look," I say, drawing a long breath. "It's not that I'm perma-freezing anything, I'm just saying that I think we should get to know each other better. You know, before things, um…go too far?"

Guster cocks his head in thought, his dark eyes tight. "Out of curiosity, what's too far when you're only playing a game? Anything you do here isn't real life. There aren't any rules here, no one to judge you for doing what you want, and no one out there will ever know what you've done here. That's the point of this game."

"Maybe I *want* to go slower," I growl, suddenly feeling like I'm been pushed in a corner. When his expression turns to one of astonishment, I remember I'm the one who asked *him* to kiss *me* and I cross my arms, feeling ashamed. "I'm really not that kind of girl. Though you wouldn't know it with the way I've been acting with you." I can't really help it, Guster just feels natural and right.

I'm attracted to him in a way I've never felt before. He makes my mind and body want things they've never wanted before. And he makes me feel smart and beautiful and capable, despite being Natural.

"Don't sound so ashamed of yourself," Guster says, his voice defensive again. "It was just a simple question. If it's what you want, then you can have it. You can have anything you want, within reason. I don't want you to think that I'm trying to force you into anything. I'm just trying to understand you better— much as you seem to think I'm only out to satisfy my socially unacceptable desires," he adds sarcastically.

A scoff escapes me. "I feel like an overemotional, over-analytical idiot." I roll my eyes at myself, my voice also sarcastic. "There's a combination I never thought possible."

Guster chuckles, then his wrist beeps again. "Half a life-point," he breathes. "Come on, let's go inside." He places a wary hand on my back. When I don't flinch, he slips it across my shoulder, guiding me forward once more.

When we get to the door, Guster turns me to face him. "We should synchronize; I'm going to get pulled out soon."

He looks at his wrist, then at mine, and then fiddles with my circuit patch, his breath and the fluttery movements of his fingers on my skin making me squirm. "All done."

He lowers my wrist and moves to drop my hand, but I snatch his back up. "This is okay," I say, wanting to reassure him that I haven't put insurmountable walls between us.

Grinning, he nods. "Ready?"

He shoves open the door before I can answer. It's a common room with a table, a fireplace, and chairs. A small hall leads to two more rooms in the back. There's a stairwell to the left, leading up to an open loft with a few visible beds. Everything is made of rough-cut, gnarly wood.

There's a pretty girl by the fire. She's leaning over the flames, the cropped cords of her red hair hanging over her face. There's a dark, leathery old man sitting in a chair by the window, his clothes black and gray and made of rough fabric, his eyes closed as though sleeping. A young man, maybe in his early twenties, is at the table. He's bent low over some kind of gizmo with wheels, his green eyes intent behind a shock of blond hair.

Dune brushes past us and thumps toward the redheaded girl. He nuzzles her arm, demanding her attention and causing her to spill a spoonful of whatever she's cooking into the fire, making it hiss and spit. "Dune, you big dummy," she squawks.

The old man's eyes flash open, glance toward the fire—black and beady—and then shut again. "Should just shoot that damn mutt."

Guster hustles me inside as he says, "You kill my dog, I kill you, Opus."

Opus grunts but doesn't open his eyes. The girl looks up, revealing her bright blue eyes. She's a Natural, I'm fairly certain. At least she looks like one in the game, but she's a darn pretty one. Prettier than me, that's for certain, and I can't help but wonder why, if Guster is so into Naturals, he's pursuing me and not her. "Gus, did you find what you were looking for?"

Guster smiles and glances at me. "Sure did."

"Hmm," Opus mumbles. "Always bringing home strays."

Guster drops his pack on the floor. "Good thing that I do, otherwise you'd still be panhandling back in Akri. Wouldn't you, you bloody codger?"

Opus waves his hand and wrinkles his face like he has just tasted something sour, eyes still closed. "I'm trying to sleep, boy, can't you see that?"

Guster rolls his eyes. "Guys this is Ella. She's our spider."

Opus's eyes open then. "What?"

Guster turns to him and pins him with a dark glare. "You don't like it you hitchhike right back to where I found you. Her inclusion is not up for discussion." For a moment, the tension in the room is palpable.

The redhead clears her throat and raises a pale hand. "Hi Ella, I'm Nadine."

I lift a timid hand and greet her back.

She looks to Guster. "You're just in time. Dinner's ready."

"Awesome," the blond guy finally says. "I'm starving. What is it today?"

"Uh," Nadine glances back into the pot and frowns at it. "Well, it was prairie rill stew."

The blond guy's face crunches, confused. "But?"

Reaching out, she pats Dune on the head and grins. "But Dune ate the rill you caught yesterday so it's vulcare stew…again."

Opus throws his hands up over his wiry gray hair. "Again. Grief, Nadine, you're going to kill us. It's the third time this week we've had vulcare stew."

Nadine glares at him. "If you don't like it, you don't have to eat it, old man." She turns to me. "Some people have no gratitude."

"Well, if Opus isn't gonna eat, clear the pot, woman," the blond stands and moves toward a cupboard set against the wall and comes back with a handful of bowls. "I, unlike some people, love your vulcare stew."

Nadine accepts a bowl from him, ladles some of the stew into it, and then slaps his hand away when he grabs for it. "Guest first." She holds it out to me. "I hope you're hungry."

Stepping forward, I accept the bowl. "I am, actually."

She smiles at me. "I'm not the best cook, but I'm better than these idiots."

I try to mirror her smile back. "I can't cook at all."

"None of us could," she replies, turning back to ladle out

more stew, "but we learned. You will too. I'll teach you."

Cooking. Never thought I'd learn that at all. Tasha does all of that. "That would be fun."

Gus leans against the door and crosses his arms. I glance up at him. Though he's got that satisfied half smile he always seems to be wearing, he looks exhausted. I hadn't noticed it until now. I touch his elbow. "Shouldn't you be getting some sleep?"

He looks down at me, and the smile lazily deepens. "Yeah." He moves to step around me and stops. "You can sleep with Nadine, if you want." He points up toward the loft. "Morden and Opus sleep to the room on the right and, um, I'm on the left." There's an awkward invitation in his voice that makes me blush again, but the others don't seem to notice it.

"Brat thinks he should have a room all to himself," Opus mutters from where he's crouched with an empty bowl.

Morden, the blond, ladles stew into Opus' bowl. "That's 'cause it's his house."

I give Gus a questioning look. He shrugs. "I stole it." He leans over and kisses my forehead. "Don't let them intimidate you. They're harmless if a little eccentric or grumpy."

"Speak for yourself," Opus growls, plopping back down in his chair by the window.

Gus lifts a warning finger at him as he walks through the room. Dune gets up and follows, squeezing through the door to Gus's room right as it closes.

Morden shoves his contraptions into a little basket he had by his feet and scoots over. "Here, doll, you can sit next to me for now. We'll have Opus make you a chair tomorrow."

Opus grunts around a mouthful of stew, juice dribbling down his chin.

Nadine sits in the one remaining chair by the fireplace. "He grumbles a lot, but he's an excellent carpenter. Aren't you, Opi?"

"Don't call me that. I ain't your Opi."

She grins at him and wiggles her fingers. Smiling to myself I lift the spoon and take my first bite of home-cooked food. "Wow," I breathe, "this is really good."

Morden leans close to me. "Nadine is modest about her talent." He nods toward Opus, who is shoveling spoonfuls of stew into his mouth. "He complains, but he likes it."

I smile and continue eating. After a few minutes I say, "Nadine, how did you learn to cook like this?"

She lowers her spoon. "I used one of my mod chips to buy five experience points in the culinary arts."

I cock my head. "You can buy experience points?"

She scoffs. "Well, yeah. I mean, it's not like I'd know it otherwise, right? After a few days with these idiots and the crap they cook, it became pretty obvious it would be a mod chip well spent. I mean, I could have used it for something stupid, but things are different here—valued differently. And it's a useful skill. I decided to be smart with my mod chips. Culinary arts, hunting and trapping, and textile arts."

I find myself wishing I'd had better luck with the cards and gotten more mod chips. "If you chose not to use your mod chips to gain experience points, how else can you get them?"

Morden says, "The old-fashioned way, of course. You actually do them. Hence 'experience.'"

"You can get them faster, though," Nadine says. "You can read training manuals or take tutorials. That's how Gus learned a lot of things in the beginning."

"The beginning?" I ask.

"Yeah," Nadine replies with smirk. "Gus and I have been playing together since the beginning."

"Oh." I look away, an uncharacteristic tinge of jealousy yanking at my chest, and finish my stew in silence.

chapter twenty-two

POST-AMERICAN DATE: 7/4/231

LONGITUDINAL TIMESTAMP: 6:30 P.M.

LOCATION: FREE ZONE, GARIBAL; NEXIS

Not long after we finish eating, Nadine, Opus, and Morden go to sleep, leaving me alone in the cottage. For a long time, I just wander around the room, touching things I've never touched before, lifting jars of spices and holding them to my nose, staring at the massive star-spangled blanket of midnight sky and the blue-gray desert of moon-washed earth. And I listen. The fire crackles low in the hearth, the flames having died down to glowing embers. The cottage seems to sigh, settling itself into sleep as the alternating heat from the fire and the cold night air make the wooden timbers groan and creek. Outside, wild dogs are howling, the breeze makes the tall grass rustle, the wind turbines squeak, and the insects chirp and chitter.

I'm aware of a gaping openness. The world is so large and wonderful. Despite it all, I feel empty and alone. I turn from the window and move back toward the bench. There I sit and wait to be pulled back into Real World—a world that I know and understand, a place where I'm never left alone with just my thoughts and the vast mystery of creation.

A door creaks open behind me. I turn to see Dune sticking his head out of Guster's bedroom. When he sees me he whines low, and his whole body begins to wriggle.

"Hi Dune," I whisper, happy to see someone in the vast loneliness.

He whines again and prances foot to foot as if uncertain whether to come to me or stay with Guster. Smiling, I get to my feet and go to him, relieving him of the hard choice. I go down on one knee—it seems right to meet him on his own level—and offer my hand. He doesn't lick me this time. Instead, he gives me a cursory inspection with a wet black nose and nudges my hand with his snout. I scratch him like I saw Guster and Nadine doing earlier, right behind his ears and then down his neck and shoulders.

He opens his mouth, his tongue dribbling absently onto the hewn wooden floorboards as he smiles at me, content. He leans against my hands, directing my attention to places that must itch or feel better. As he moves, his tail smacks against the door, opening it wider.

The air in Guster's room is cooler, and the only light is the phantasmal square of moonlight leaking through the window. Guster isn't here. His bed is mussed, as though someone were sleeping in it, but the game must have drawn him out already. I glance behind me, wondering if the others are gone as well. Made bolder by the certainty that Guster is no longer in the room, I stand and creep in.

Curious about him and everything there is to know about him, I turn a circuit around the room. It's a sparse arrangement. One window, a door to the outside, a large bed, some kind of box at the foot of the bed, a narrow closet, a bank of drawers. There are no pictures or adornments. I slide a drawer open. It's filled with weapons and vials and purses. I run my hands along the clothing hanging in the closet, press my face into the shirts. They smell like grass and wind. Today's clothes are thrown over the box at the foot of the bed. I pick up his shirt. It smells faintly like sweat, but more like wind and sand and something that seems like a scent meant only for him. I hold it as I go to the side of the bed where he must have slept. Touching the sheet reveals a warm memory of his presence.

Dune hops up on the bed and stares at me, expectant.

Confused, I cock my head. "This isn't my bed."

He whines and lifts his paw as if reaching out for me.

I frown, unable to understand why my ancestors would have thought a companion incapable of speech to be a good idea. "Are you afraid? Of being alone?"

He barks at me, his body language now indicating agitation.

"Shhh." I hold out my hands to shush him, afraid he'll wake everyone else even though I'm sure they've been pulled out as well. He starts pawing at the blankets, his upper body bounding down and his legs splaying out as if he's dodging something, and then buries his face in the sheets.

I look back down at where Guster's body once was and move to the other side of the bed. "Okay," I say to Dune. "But only until you fall asleep." I pull off my boots and unfasten the utility belt, leaving them in a heap on the floor. Then I slip out of my vest and my skirt, leaving the shirt and the cutoffs to protect me against the chilled air. Dune prances back and forth behind me, nudging a cold, wet nose under my arm every so often.

When I'm done, I slip between the sheet and the blanket, determined that this isn't where I'm going to stay but too chilled to remain entirely outside of the promise of the blankets. Dune settles down beside me, his big body snuggling up to mine, giving more warmth. He puts his head on my arm, his eyes intent and staring in a way that I don't recall ever being looked at before. I smile at him and put my hand on his head.

"Robots don't get afraid of being alone in the dark."

He whines low and leans forward, his tongue lapping at my face, but missing because he seems too comfortable to get up all the way.

I scratch him, slow and methodic, working a rhythm that makes his lids droop over his limpid dark eyes, and I think of the song Kiara sang this afternoon in the diner. In memory, her voice isn't as bad as I thought. It's as beautiful as she is. Or was. I close my eyes against the idea that her songs and beauty are no longer part of this game, no longer part of the world.

Unsent Letters to Delia

Dee,

His name is Guster. And I still can't stop thinking about him. I could probably write you ten pages telling you all about how he looks and makes me feel, but there's part of me that doesn't want to share that with you. Is that selfish of me? We always liked Quentin together and, as much as you told me you'd take Shadow, sometimes I wonder what would have happened if one of us ended up with Quentin.

That's nothing to worry about now, of course. Since Quentin thinks I'm dead, I guess it's up to you entirely to catch his eye. Certainly, punching Shadow did that. I wish I could ask you what you were thinking when you did that…

I'm on a different path than you, destined to love a different boy who will be mine and mine alone. Perhaps it will be Guster who is that boy for me. Even then it's a bittersweet love, because I can only have him in a dream realm.

When I got pulled out of the game, my stomach sank and I felt this awful depression come upon me, because I knew he wasn't part of this world. Whoever Guster is in real life, he's not for me in this world. We're both a lie. I wish you better luck. I hope you find Real World love, the kind that you can wake up to in both dream and awake.

Forever Yours,
Ella

chapter twenty-three

The breeze is cool and gentle, teasing strands of hair over my cheeks and tempting me out of my dreamless sleep with the scent of adventure. I blink, trying to adjust my eyes to the low, gray light of early morning. Through the open door I can see the world is still not quite awake. Guster is standing in the doorway leading to the outside, his arms crossed against his chest, a steaming cup of something cradled between the crook of his elbow and his large callused hand.

I make an effort to remain still. I don't want to disturb whatever far-off place his half asleep eyes are visiting in the middle distance, don't want to break the perfection of his peace, or the low timbre of the song he's humming to himself. He stays like that for a long time, longer than the warmth of the blankets and the dog curled beside me will allow. Longer than his lullaby voice will allow. I drift back to sleep, dreaming of mysterious, handsome boys standing in the white-light of dawn, watching over the world like angelic sentinels who vibrate with heavenly song.

When I wake again, it's to the sound of drawers being opened and closed and things being packed away into bags. I sit up, lethargic and slow, realizing that Dune is no longer asleep beside me and that Guster is rummaging through his bank of drawers, looking for something.

"What's going on?" I ask, my voice heavy with sleep and confusion.

Lifting his head, Guster glances over his shoulder, his eyes examining me and his mouth relaxing in a gentle smile of reassurance. "I'm sorry; I didn't mean to wake you up."

I glance down, the puzzle pieces finally clicking into place and my brain finally waking up. I slept in Guster's bed. Which means that at some point, Guster woke up and found me next to him…after I told him I wanted to go slow. I feel my cheeks go warm as I try to look at him again.

"I uh, didn't mean to, um…it was Dune's fault."

His smile broadens into a grin, but he turns back to his drawer before speaking. "It's fine." He pulls out a small pouch and dumps it on the top of the bank of drawers; coins and small glinting jewels spill across the polished wood. "I'd be lying if I said it didn't please me to roll over and find you beside me. I was hard-pressed not to wake you up and tell you all about it, but I'm a gentleman. For now, at least," he teases.

I sit up entirely and wrap my arms around my legs, dismissing the coiling feeling between them. Sparks, that tone, that smirk, that glint in his eye… It's going to be hard to hold off on what my body is practically screaming for me to do.

Guster begins sorting the contents of his pile into smaller "like" piles. "Morden made breakfast if you want something to eat. We'll be leaving soon."

I tip my head at his back and then, realizing he can't see me, I say, "Leaving? For where?"

He swipes a pile of silver coins into the pouch and tucks it back into the drawer. "We're going to head out toward the jump pad."

"Jump pad?"

He turns back to me and tosses something at me. I catch it with both hands and when I open my fingers, there's a small red stone sitting between my palms. "What's this?"

He leans against the wall, watching me in the heavy way that he does, and shoves his hands in his pockets. "That's a jump stone. You use it to pay passage through the jump pad. One stone will pay for one jump for you and your party from your current level to any other Free Zone playing field within range."

I look back at the stone. "You mean this lets you get into other games?"

He steps forward, his movement bringing my eyes up as he comes toward me and sits on the edge of the bed. Reaching out, he takes the stone from me and holds it up so that the light catches the facets and reflects tiny rainbows all over the room. "That's exactly what it does."

Confused, I knit my brow. "But how can that be? I thought the game made an effort to prevent gamers from getting into one another's games."

He closes his hand around the gem. "Oh, it does. But only the games that we're not supposed to go to. We have to go to other places. We're on a quest. How would we solve the mysteries, collect the required magic items, or get to our place of destination without being able to move freely?"

"Good point." I breathe. I hadn't really thought about all that. "So, where are we going to tell the jump pad to take us?

And why are we going there?"

Guster looks down at the floor, his expression grave. "That, I don't know."

"So," I say, "You're just going to shoot in the dark until you hit something?"

He shrugs. "Seems to me that the Oracle will take care of it. She's been good about it thus far, bringing us all together."

I stare at Guster for a long minute, then back at his dresser where most of the coins and gems are still piled, unsorted. "Why do you want to go to the Anansi Chamber? I mean, it seems like you already have so much wealth. What's inside that you want so bad?"

His eyes slide sideways, and he reaches out his free hand and traces the outline of my leg, so that shivers run up my spine. "What's inside that chamber isn't gold or jewels. It's a different kind of treasure. Something a little less tangible, but no less valuable."

I lean forward, and grasp his wrist so that we can both focus. "What is it?"

He looks up then, his face so close to mine that he could kiss me. And I secretly want him to, but he doesn't. I've drawn a line and he's respecting it—despite my inability to stay out of his bed. He looks into my eyes for what seems like eternity. Then he says, "Look, the Oracle told me to go there, so that's what I'm doing. I have faith that what I'll find there will be worth it."

I draw away. "You mean, you could be on a wild-goose chase and not even know it?" I mentally score a point for myself. I've been wanting to say "wild-goose chase" since I read about it.

He smirks.

I look down at the blanket, at my legs underneath. "What's 'worth it'? I don't get it. Just last night you were talking about how wonderful this game made you feel. Now you want more?"

"Yes, I want more."

I look up and glance around the room. "What else could you possibly want?"

He reaches out, and his palm opens against my cheek, his fingers curling around my hair, and he smiles at me, mischievous and teasing. "Everyone has their secrets, Elle, especially thieves."

I twist my mouth, annoyed, but I don't say anything. This is, after all, only a game. I don't need to know everyone's deepest desires or secrets; I just need to win. That's the point, right? That, and seeing my father's game. If moving from playing field to playing field in search of a sign from the Oracle is what Guster is planning, then I shouldn't complain. It gives me an excellent chance to explore. But I'd be lying to myself if I thought that Guster didn't factor into all of this as well. Part of why I'm here—playing this particular game, going on this particular quest—is because I want to be with him. The mere possibility of a future with him is enough to make me follow him.

So, yes, I at least need to know some things about him. "I'm just trying to understand you, Guster."

"I know. And you will. In time. You were right about yesterday; we should take time and get to know each other. Back home…we don't get that, do we? We can't choose."

He's right, of course. If the accident hadn't happened maybe I would have been married to Zane whether I liked him or not. He was lovely, of course, but what if I found him lacking in character? That means something. But then, everything I've seen of Guster's personality so far, I've liked. "Just tell me one thing," I say, trying not to sound desperate or frustrated.

Giving me an indulgent expression, he fiddles with the strands of hair, twirling one curl around his forefinger. "If I can."

I hold my breath, trying to think of the best way to frame what I want to ask him. "Are you lying? Is this some kind of ruse to get what you want and then you're going to end up betraying us all in the end?" *Betraying me? Lying to me about your feelings?*

His hand stills and his brow knits down hard, shocked. "What?"

I look away, feeling like an idiot. "Well, it happens in the stories. Someone always plays a trick, betrays the others in order to get what they want," I reason. "It's always the mysterious one who won't answer questions, won't explain himself," I add, trying to avoid the confusion in his expression. "I just want you to know that I don't want what's in that chamber, so there's no reason to betray me to have it all for yourself."

His bitter chuckle makes me jerk my head up where I meet his eyes, which have gone hard with hurt. He pulls back, shaking his head. "I'm glad you think me capable of such a thing." He stands and moves to turn away.

Suddenly aware that I've struck a very tender nerve, I grab his hand to prevent him from leaving me. "I don't," I blurt out. "It's just...oh, I don't know. I'm just being suspicious. I—" I don't know what to say. I want to say that I wish to stay with him, that I don't want him to ever leave me, that I feel safe and satisfied with him in a way that I've never felt before. But that would be foolish. I just met him. I barely know him. And I really don't know anything about these kinds of feelings. Instead, I say, "I don't think you'd betray me. I'm just scared. I've learned I can't trust things in Real World, and I'm used to losing people. I'm sorry." It sounds stupid and weak, but I don't know how to communicate with this boy who makes me feel like I've spun around in a circle for three days straight. "I *really* want to trust you, and I'm scared of that."

I can see the muscles in his back relax under the cream-colored fabric of his shirt. He drops my hand. "I won't betray you," he says finally. "I want to trust you, too. I want more than that, honestly, and that kind of scares me, too. And I'm not keeping secrets. I just want to do things in my own time. For once. All I want is to be in control of my own life, just once."

We've both just revealed so much. My insecurities, his inability to avoid the vortex of duty that exists within Evanescence. I slip out from under the sheets and move toward him, touching his shoulder with nervous fingers. "Okay. You can have that. Just like you said, you can have anything you want, within reason. And, just so you know, I don't intend on betraying you, either."

He nods once but doesn't turn toward me. "Whatever is in that chamber, I bet it's something for all of us. I can't imagine the Oracle sending people who wouldn't want it."

I bite my lip. "Maybe some of us are just here for the journey, not the destination."

He lowers his head and, for a long moment, he doesn't respond. Then he reaches up, and his hand closes over mine, squeezes. "This journey is turning into more than I bargained for." He lifts my hand, kisses my knuckles.

I feel a warm sort of cocoon closing over us. Over this moment. And then my stomach growls again.

A breath escapes Guster. "You should go eat. I need to finish packing." He glances over his shoulder, the fire back in his eyes and the quirk of a smirk back in his cheek. "But you should probably get dressed first. Call me prematurely possessive, but I don't care to share that with anyone."

I pull my hand away and glance down at myself. It occurs to me that the clothing I've left on my person is quite tight, which, like his, leaves little to the imagination. Blushing, I bend to collect my clothes and redress myself.

Guster goes back to sorting his wealth. "We'll stop and get you some more clothes. I'm sure you hate that outfit. The Oracle must have a sense of humor."

I step into the skirt and pull it over my hips. "Oh, I don't know. It's actually quite utilitarian, despite being ugly."

He scoffs.

"Though…" I breathe as I lift my arms to push them through the armholes in the vest and smell my armpits. "I wouldn't mind a couple of changes." I sit back on the bed and work on struggling into my boots. "So, we're just going to go to the jump pad and get spit out wherever it sends us."

Guster slides the remaining stack of gems into a final pouch. "Yes. And, Oracle willing, we'll end up someplace useful. We'll need to collect a couple of things before trying to infiltrate the chamber. Maps, magical items, supplies. And we'll need to build our skill sets, train—that's usually how games like this work. Once we get to the Central Dominion we're going to have to bust through a number of secured areas and find our way to the chamber. I'm assuming we'll be fighting a large number of Knights, and who knows what else the game has defending the Dominion."

I stomp into my boot and look up. "What is the Central Dominion?"

He turns to me, face serious. "Honestly?"

I nod.

"It's home," he says flatly. "But worse."

"Worse?"

"Yeah." He places the purse into his satchel and comes back toward me. He drops his weight on the bed, making me bounce. "Most of the Aristocracy just wants what they already have, plus more. Central Dominion is like Evanescence, but worse. Aristocratic players can have everything they want there. There are no G-Chips, no credit limits, no regulations for Mods and Alts; security is unbelievably tight because they've become paranoid that someone will take what they've got."

I wonder if that's where Quentin is. And I wonder if Carsai ever found him there. "So," I say, my voice sounding calmer than it should. "This is basically a suicide mission." It's not a question, just a certainty. And I'm not afraid. Why should I be? It's just a game, and I can always come back and see the beauty of this world as a completely new player.

Guster grins. "Yeah, basically. But we'll have a hell of a time playing until the end."

Dune pushes into the room, and I hear Nadine call after him. He jumps onto the bed, ignoring her and nudging my hands for attention. I scratch his ears as I watch Guster fiddle with more purses. "What are you gonna do about Dune?"

"Well, I can't very well take him on the vivacycle," Guster reasons. "He'll stay here, keep the vandals away. Just in case we manage to come back in one piece."

I grimace. "You're gonna abandon him? Don't pets need to be cared for?"

Guster glances over his shoulder. "If they're real, yeah. But, Dune's just a piece of AI. He doesn't actually need to be cared for. Players disappear out of the arena, and he just goes back to being code. If another player wanders in, his code will execute and he'll perform his protocol as a guard dog to protect the base, but other than that he's just in sleeper mode. I've left him plenty of times and he's fine. Even if he was real, Kathy at the diner knows him, and she'd take care of him."

I stare at Dune. He stares at me, panting gross-smelling breath into my face. "It's really creepy how real this stuff is."

"Yeah," Guster says. "It's pretty damn great."

part three:

ELLA PLAYS THE GAME

chapter twenty-four

Guster grabs my arm and steadies me against his solid body as the jump pad powers down. The world is spinning and my stomach is doing flip-flops. "First time's always the worst," he reassures.

Feeling nauseous, I grimace as Nadine and Opus step off the low platform and turn in slow opposite circles. Guster looks to Morden, who is standing closest to the navigation grid. "This place looks familiar. Where are we?"

Morden looks down, checks against the holo-map displayed over his wrist, and frowns. "I think we're in Canal Town, but I'm not entirely sure."

Guster turns away and rolls his eyes. "Thank you, Mister Navigator." He steps off the platform and walks past Nadine. Pausing at the confluence of two streets, he looks both ways, nods to himself, and then walks back toward us. He steps back up onto the platform and moves to guide his vivacycle down the ramp.

Morden takes a step after him. "Are we staying?"

Guster glances over his shoulder, his eyes mischievous. "No Mord, I just thought my vivacycle needed a walk. You know how antsy she gets."

I chuckle to myself as I struggle into the arm straps of my pack. Much as I don't relish the additional labor, carrying a light pack will help me build my strength. Behind us, Nadine and Opus collect the two remaining vivacycles, each a little different than the other. I'm under the impression that the vivacycles will be our main mode of transportation across the different playing fields. That's fine with me; I don't relish walking across countless realms.

"So, explain to me why we can't just tell the jump pad to take us to the Central Dominion?" I ask.

"It's too big of a jump," Guster explains. "You need to move from place to place, like a piece on a game board."

"Like hopping squares?"

He nods. "You can't just pick up your piece and send it across the board; you need to follow the rules. Jump pads only move a certain number of fields at once. Though no one knows how many or in what direction their destination field is."

"What about the map?" I ask. "Can't you just check where you are and where you are going against the holo-map?"

"Unfortunately, no," Guster says. "The map doesn't show where the fields are in relation to one another, only what each field looks like once you get there."

I frown. "That's an awful design flaw."

He shrugs. "I suppose Drexel thought it would be too easy that way."

I stare at him, momentarily derailed by his use of my last name.

Morden says, "We could try to get there by randomly saying various field titles we know and hoping one of them is close enough to the Dominion to hop to it, but the odds of that happening are very low."

Guster nods his agreement. "I've only collected about thirty maps from fields I've been to, and even then, I may not be able to get to one from the other because there might be too big of a jump between. Statistically speaking, the likelihood of just letting the game randomly send you somewhere and then trying the Dominion from there is more likely to work, which is why we're here."

A little confused, I refrain from asking more questions until I puzzle out the answers to the ones I've already asked.

Once the jump pad is cleared, Guster pulls off to the side and waits for all of us to join him. "So," he says, "it looks like the game sent us to Canal Town. We've already tried getting to the Dominion from here and it didn't work, so the next place we go will also be game's choice."

Nadine looks up from strapping her pack on the back of her vivacycle. "But if we've been here already, why stay? Shouldn't we just move on?"

Guster glances at me. "Ella hasn't been here before."

"Huh?" I breathe.

"So what?" Opus demands. "What's she got to do with it?"

I turn questioning eyes on Guster, wondering the same thing. He meets my gaze, gives me a wink, and jerks his head toward the vivacycle, indicating I get on. As I turn to do so, I hear him say, "Don't know until we know. Must be a reason we're here, right? I don't believe the game does anything by chance."

Opus grumbles to himself, but Guster talks over him. "We've got another three hours before pullout. Hit the taverns and the market; try to find some useful information, or search for a special item that may be of use to us."

Nadine mounts her bike behind Morden. They look awkward,

her body barely able to reach around his. "Yeah, and what are you two going to be doing?" she asks.

Guster gets on behind me. "Mind your own business."

She and Morden exchange a furtive glance that makes me blush because they both saw me trailing Guster out of his room earlier.

"You taking the tavern?" Morden asks Opus.

Opus grunts and rumbles out of the court. Nadine and Morden follow for a short distance and then angle off a few blocks down. Turning, I look at Guster. "Where *are* we going? Or is that not my business, either?" I ask, my voice a nervous challenge.

The skin at one edge of his mouth crinkles. "You want to go clothes shopping or not?"

I lift a brow, shocked that he'd guess my weakness so easily. "What about the quest?"

He lifts his legs and accelerates out onto the street, turning around a high-wheeled carriage being pulled by two boys in bright blue linen uniforms and then darting between two white buildings with high columns. "You can get answers anywhere, Elle. You want gossip, you go ask a woman. Where do you find women? Around clothes."

I roll my eyes at the road ahead. "Spoken like a man," I mutter.

G uster follows behind me, a silent shadow with a self-satisfied smirk, as I walk between aisle upon aisle of bolts of exquisite fabric, lace, and drawers full of delicate buttons. Wide-eyed and overwhelmed by the sheer beauty of it all, I run my fingers over the cloth, only half listening to what the woman leading me through the shop is saying.

With a bounce of a voluminous satin bustle, she stops at the end of the last row and spins to face me. "So, do you see something you like?"

Unable to decide on just one beautiful thing, I glance at Guster, who gives me a smug expression. It's as if he knew this would short-circuit my pleasure center and is silently gloating. He may not be able to do what he wants to me with his own fingers and lips, but he's smart enough to know there are ways around that—other ways to please the person you've got your eye on. Seeing that he's not going to be much help, I turn back to the woman. She's dressed in a deep ruby dress that frames the milky white of her shoulders, emphasizes a waist drawn in tight by something she's explained is a corset, and hugs her hips. She steps toward a bank of shelves and reaches for a booklet full of patterns.

On the drive through Canal Town, Guster explained to me that the time period reflected here is that of the late Victorian era. I've made a mental note to learn more about the era because it seems entirely like something the Aristocrats back home would like—all perfection and design—and, maybe one day, I might be able to recognize my dream of becoming a Designer.

Suddenly humbled by the thought of never being able to do something as simple as attending another fashion show, I turn toward the large window beneath the seamstress's workbench. The shop is built on top of one of the many bright red bridges arching over the deep water canals that crisscross the city.

The buildings on either side of the canal are grand and ornate, their symmetry astounding. The water below is a clear bright blue that reveals the white sand and brightly colored fish that dart between the stone pylons. In the middle distance, a great clock tower shoots high into the sky, a lance aiming toward the sun. To the left of that, and nearly as high, are the glimmering golden dome, minarets, and flying buttresses of a great cathedral.

I look down at the people milling through the streets. They're dressed in bright clashing colors, the cuts of their luxurious fabric ornate and silly. They wear large hats with odd bobbles and feathers. They ride in high-wheeled carts pulled by workers who dress in matching costumes, or they take long sweeping boats down the canals—the dashing men at the helms poling through the waters and singing in sweet, falsetto voices that I can hear despite being indoors. Some people ride bicycles along the roads bordering the canals, others walk little dogs on brightly colored twists of ribbon, and some picnic on the causeways between the main canals.

It's all so much that I can't take it in. To come from such a stark and barren place like Garibal or the plains where Guster lives to this lively, luscious place is like waking up in the Utopia Zone all over again. I want to laugh and cry and run around. I want to pull the rainbow bunches of flowers and aromatic roasted nuts out of the carts on the corners and toss them all around me. I want to dive into the water, touch the sand, and swim with the motley assortment of fish schooling around the thin hulls of the boats.

Someone pushes something into my hands. I blink, realizing I'm back in the dress shop with the woman in the bustle. "How about this? It's iridescent silk taffeta from Durfrey." She lifts it to my face and touches my cheek with it. "It brings out the gray in your eyes. She'd be stunning in this, don't you agree?" She turns to Guster for the answer. All he does is stare at me in a way that makes me lift a hand to my throat. Is it legal to stare at someone like they're the newest Harley Dean jacket?

Bolstered, the woman turns back to me. "This will make a

lovely pleat, it will catch the light—make you twinkle like a star. And that swan neck of yours, we must frame that—something low, but not too risqué." She opens the fabric up and drapes it across my shoulder. "I'll put buttons down the front of the bodice...mother of pearl? No, onyx." she adds, building the dress around me with her eyes. "Oh, and a shawl here—along the shoulder—Chantilly lace, I think. And you'll do best with bell sleeves—"

I gently reach out and pull her hands away. "This is all lovely," I say. And I mean it. "I'd be fawning over this if I were back home and deciding on something to wear to a ball." I have to look away from her bright, expectant eyes. I used to be that enthusiastic about brocade and silk, used to be just as torn over what width of ribbon or size of button. Looking at her is like looking at a future me—a me who was able to grow up and follow a foolish, halfhearted dream to be a Designer and not the Programmer I was born to be. Part of me wants to stop right now, ask this woman to take me on as an apprentice. I glance back at Guster then swallow hard. "But we're going to be doing a lot of traveling. Do you have something a little more...functional? And durable?"

She frowns. "Another Quester?"

I nod, a little sheepish.

Sighing, she hugs the fabric to her chest. "Seems we only get Questers these days."

Guster seems to perk up at that. He steps forward and puts his arm across my shoulders. "We're looking for her father."

My chest tightens at his words. I want to turn around and punch him in the stomach for being so insensitive, but there's no way he could know about my father.

The woman's thin, plucked eyebrows lift. "Oh? Where's he gone?"

Guster's hand slides up the side of my neck and pets my hair, as if trying to comfort me. "We're told he was captured by the Damascus Knights and taken as a slave for those in the Dominion." I try my best to look tragic and abashed. It's not that hard.

The woman's eyes go sad, and she shakes her head. "Horrible," she breathes. "That's a terrible fate."

Guster's fingers tighten against my neck, pulling me close. I glance up at him, narrowing the eye this poor woman can't see. He fixes me with a deep saccharine stare that is too intense for me to take anything but seriously, then touches my face, tracing my features as he speaks. "We're trying to rescue him. We want to be married, you see. And we couldn't possibly go forward without his consent. It wouldn't be right. And we want him there. He has to give her away, of course." He throws an endearing little smirk in before pulling me close and kissing me.

I don't deny him the kiss. I sense what he's trying to do, and I've been aching to lean in and do the same all day. It's just as good as I remember. Better. I don't want him to stop.

When he pulls away I feel my jaw drop in astonishment. Where did this boy learn to kiss the way he does? And talk about icing the cake of this ridiculous yarn he's spun. But it works. The woman throws her hands up and drops the silk in a blue-gray-purple flutter. "Oh, you poor dears," she wails. "Oh, that's just beyond terrible. Poor star-crossed lovers. And you." She comes forward and clasps my hands in hers, dragging me out of Guster's grasp. "You brave, brave girl. Here, you come with me. I know just what you need."

She begins dragging me toward the back room. Guster moves to follow, but she holds up her hand. "Not you, young man. Save your eyes for the wedding night."

She hustles me through the back room, making sure to lock

the door behind her and then herds me down a pair of darkly lit steps in the back. At the bottom we walk through a dry, windowless room stocked with barrels and crates. There is more fabric down here; judging by its quality and the exotic color palate, these are her true gems. I stop to offer them the reverence they deserve, but she rushes past them, and I have to reluctantly drag myself away. She heads to the very back and shoves some old brown paper off a large black box with a rusty lock on it.

Reaching between her bosom, she pulls out a grizzled key then crouches over the lock. "I've been waiting for a very long time to give this to someone who is worthy, and if it isn't you, young lady, then I don't know who is," she whispers, her voice urgent.

I can't resist glancing around the cellar in search of someone from whom she might need to hide her voice. I can hear carriages rumbling through the covered bridge below, but I can't imagine anyone could hear us down there.

She opens the box and rummages down to the very bottom. When she comes back up her perfect coiffed hair is mussed, and there's dust all over the front of her, but she doesn't seem to notice. Instead, she sits back and unwraps the package she rescued with deft, certain movements.

When the paper falls away and I see what's inside I don't know what it is or how to react. It's a patched-together bit of cloth made with rough-spuns and crude, faded fabric, not at all something I'd expect from a woman selling such fine cloth. "Uh," I breathe as she presses the musty, water-stained thing into my hands. "What is it?"

She looks up at me, her eyes bright despite the dimness. "It's a freedom quilt."

"Freedom quilt?" I repeat. I hold it up, trying to see what sort of properties a freedom quilt carries, but all I can see are the rough patches, tattered threads, and uneven decoration. "What does it do?"

She pushes my hands out of the way and smoothes the fabric over my lap. I can feel the rough seams and mistakes even through my cutoffs. Whoever made it was a terrible seamstress and had no eye for color. It's as if a child created it, the images crude and blocky, the stitches large and irregular, the beading and designs asymmetrical. "It's a map," she whispers and points at the quilt between us. "This will take you to the Central Dominion."

A few minutes later, I'm hustled back upstairs, my "map" carefully folded and encased in a swath of fine red-and-white striped cloth with a fleur-de-lis pattern along the white strips.

Guster straightens from where he was leaning, looking casual and sexy, by the bank of windows. "Find something you liked?"

I give him a wide-eyed expression that doesn't even begin to convey my feelings in this moment and glance back at the woman who smiles conspiratorially and pats down a strand of dusty hair. I turn back to him and nod.

He loops his hand under my elbow and, grinning, turns me around. "Excellent. Let's go make that marriage happen."

When we get a couple of blocks away from the shop, Guster powers down the vivacycle and turns into a grassy area under a tree.

"Why did we stop?" I ask as he dismounts and moves toward a wrought iron bench under the tree.

He sits down, settling his elbows on his knees, and then gives me a long, heavy look. Finally he smirks. "You gonna sit there and stare at me all day, Elle, or are you going to come sit with me and tell me all about that thing you're carrying?"

I glance at the striped fabric I'd tucked under my body for the ride. "Fabric?"

He props his chin on a fist and puts on theatrical airs. "Oh really? Never would have guessed that one." He sobers. "What's *inside* the fabric?"

Catching the playful note, I lift a brow and try to look like I have no idea what he's talking about. "What makes you think there's something inside?"

"Because you'd *never* pick out that fabric. Besides the fact that it's just not sensible for what you need, you wouldn't wear stripes if your life depended on it. At least, not willingly."

I cock my head. He's right. I hate stripes, but how does he know that? I glance down at my skirt, which is striped. I *had* said it was ugly...hadn't I? Had I mentioned it was ugly because it was striped? I must have.

"We also both know you're an Aristocrat and can't sew for shit. So? What is it?"

Sighing, I get off the vivacycle and move to sit beside him. I don't put distance between us. I can't, because I don't want to, and I'm not certain that any distance between us wouldn't get hastily closed anyway. Personal boundaries all but evaporate when riding with someone on a vivacycle, and it feels like I'm used to his large body beside mine. I hand him the package, and he unravels the fabric and squints at the quilt. "Wow, it's uh, it's great. You'll look amazing in it," he says, voice strained.

I slap his arm, offended. "I didn't pick it out, you ass. She gave it to me."

As if he can see the use of it, Guster nods. Then he gets to his feet and opens it. Holding both ends, he cocks his head one way and then the next. "I guess it will be an okay disguise. They'd definitely take you as a beggar if you wear this."

I give him a flat look. "I wouldn't be caught dead in that thing."

He spins it around and puts it over his head, cloaking himself like the acolytes in the Oracle's temple had been. "No? It's a cracked burial shroud, don't you think? It's so ugly I don't think I'd even have to rot much to scare the pulse out of someone."

Crossing my arms, I look away, trying not to laugh. "Hell wouldn't even want you."

He leans in close. "You would, though."

Holding back a grin, I push him away. "You stink like a corpse."

He pulls the fabric off his head and wrinkles his nose. "Yeah, could use a good scrub."

"Could use an incinerator, more like."

Guster yanks it off his shoulders, spreads it over the grass, and stares at it for a long minute. He moves to a corner, then to another, examining.

I try to ignore him, watching the beautiful people ride and walk by in the street beyond, but his lean form moving back and forth and his dark eyes tracing invisible shapes on the ground becomes more engrossing. I could stare at him for hours. And maybe I do, because I don't come back to my senses until a large clock tower to my left starts chiming. Shaking myself out of my Guster-induced trance, I pretend to have been staring elsewhere and say, "Have you found the meaning of life yet?"

Out of the corner of my eye he sits down on the grass. "Well, this part here is Canal Town."

My eyes snap back to him. He has his elbow propped on his knee and his chin propped on the respective fist, his dark eyes intent on the corner piece. "What?"

He points to the corner square with his free hand. At the center is a jumble of blue strings crisscrossing one another in a geometric pattern. I move off the bench and sit beside him. Closer, I can see that colorful beads have been strung along the blue thread. In one area there is a gold disk and in another a pair of black arrows that have been sewn in opposing directions, one shorter, one longer.

I glance up at the city around us. Blue canals frequented by colorful fish and people. A golden dome. A clock tower.

He lowers his hand and grunts to himself. "I don't get it."

"Get what?"

"I don't understand how to read it."

I scrunch my brow. "Read it?"

"Yeah," he reasons. "I mean, this is obviously a map. Here's Canal Town and that square over there…" He points at a sandy yellow square with tiny Xs clustered along one edge, "is Garibal."

"Garibal?"

"Yeah, can't you see the wind turbines on the ridges?"

"All I see are black Xs on a yellow square." I give him a strained expression. "I think maybe you need to recalibrate or something, Gus."

He shakes his head, his eyes never leaving the blanket of squares and shapes. "It's a map," he insists. He reaches out and puts his hand on the center square, covering the silver and gold threads. "And it leads to the Central Dominion."

I feel my face fall in surprise. "Yeah," I say. "That's exactly what she said. How can you tell?"

Guster's forehead scrunches. "But it doesn't make sense.

Everything I know about Nexis indicates that Nexis is an orb, playing fields overlapping playing fields, like a..." He pauses, looking for a good analogy.

"Onion?" I offer, annoyed that he's brushing off my question and hoping I can stump his uncanny intelligence by using some of my own.

He nods once. "Onion." Then he shifts and indicates the quilt. "These are squares, organized in a rectangular pattern, not a circle. So, I don't understand the arrangement. If I did, if I could see how the fields are lain on top of one another then we might be able to see what order to go in to get to the center."

I reach out and touch the fabric, marveling at the sudden tiny details of each of the patches. There are hundreds of squares. The fact that Guster found Canal Town and Garibal so quickly—plus the fact that he knows what an onion is—are key indicators that he's smarter than I originally gave him credit for. I think about how he talked to that woman in the shop. It's like he knew exactly what to say to get what he wanted out of her.

What *had* he wanted out of her? Did he know she had this map? I lift my eyes and narrow them at him.

He glances up and smiles, confused. "What?"

"You're completely unreal."

"What?"

"How'd you know she'd give me this? How do you know it's a freedom quilt?"

He glances back down at the quilt. "Is that what she called it?"

"Don't dodge the question. How'd you know what to say to get her to give this up?" I demand.

He levels his eyes at me, the tightness in them saying he doesn't like my tone. "I didn't know."

I frown at him. "I don't believe that. You knew exactly what to say to get her to gush, just like you know exactly what to say to me. It's like you've got some kind of cheat code to see what you shouldn't see and say what you shouldn't be intelligent enough to say."

His brow lifts again, amusement clear on his face. "A cheat code?"

I blush a little. "Well, yeah."

"That's brilliant," he exclaims with a laugh. "You're such a Programmer."

I feel my jaw drop. "How do you know I'm a Programmer?"

He smirks. "Eugenics, Elle. It's hard not to be yourself when you've been bred to be that way. You're Programming stock; it's obvious by the way you interpret the world. You see the patterns, and you see what's wrong, but you can't see the true anomalies for what they are." He points at the quilt to make his point.

I don't understand a word coming out of his mouth, but he continues talking, relieving me of responding.

"And I'm no different. I know how to read people, know how to say things in just a way to get what I want. I manipulate, I manage, I lead. It's not something to be especially proud of, but it's useful. Wouldn't you agree?"

There's only one kind of Aristocrat with those kinds of traits. He's a Manager. And Managers are Elite. All of them. I suddenly want to run away from Guster, because he's so big and I'm so little. Loving a Manager is just as impossible as loving someone like Quentin Cyr. I try to shrug it off. "So, you're a thief *and* a liar."

He shrugs. "I've already admitted these things, but I'm charismatic and loveable, nonetheless." He grins at me, trying to ease me. He's aware that he's just spooked me. If he's as good at reading people as he claims to be, then he has to realize it. When my expression doesn't change, his becomes serious. "Are you going to be afraid of me now? Because you can leave if you want. I haven't chained you to my side, have I?"

I bite my lip. In some ways he has. Not physical chains, but if not chains that keep me thinking of him throughout the day, then what? "No."

"Good. Then stop with the drama, Elle. Either decide you're going to trust me, or go off on your own. I don't want to do this every time you learn that I'm a little more like every other human being and not as perfect as you think I should be."

I look away, feeling ashamed. He's right. I'm judging him for something he hasn't even done yet. And what girl wouldn't be interested in a man who can read someone as well as he can? Someone like that can understand you, is aware of how to help you.

"Fine," I huff, crossing my arms. "I'll try."

Unconvinced that I'm being sincere, he narrows his eyes at me. "It's kind of sick how mistrusting being Aristocrats has made us."

I blink. I've never considered myself to be a mistrusting person. But...I look down, thoughtful. Maybe I should have been. Just look at what happened with Katrina. "The Aristocracy is a backstabbing lot of social climbers. Their only concerns in life are that of themselves and their advancements." He knows it, I know it. "So," I say, looking back up. "If eugenics are to prevail, then we will be just like the society that made us."

The skin under Guster's eyes tightens as he tips his head to one side. "Do you ever wonder why our ancestors destroyed Real World?"

I furrow my brow. "The Bio-Nuclear War was an accident."

He looks away, his eyes trailing a boat on the canal. "That's what they tell us. They say it was terrorists who started it, and maybe it was. But there were a lot of other factors that were working against humanity even before the war. Economic downturn, environmental degradation, political strife, globalization, the growing reliance on technology, allowing the wrong people to take positions of power, and allowing these things to continue to spiral out of control because people were too selfish to give up the convenience it offered."

"What are you getting at?"

"Seems strange that *our* ancestors—out of so many millions—were allowed in the dome. Why them and not someone else?"

"G-Corp chose the best and the brightest; we all know that."

"Who decided they were the best?" he demands. "Back then cities were being leveled, pandemics were running rampant, neighbors turned against neighbors, infrastructures were crumbling. Society was imploding. Who took the time to conduct these tests? How were they funded and controlled? Where was the data stored? How did they reach out from coast to blacked-out coast in search of humanity's best hope?" He shakes his head, his expression weary. "It was those with the power, those with the wealth and the right connections who lived through the terror of nuclear winter, radiation poisoning, and the drift of biological weaponry. The same people who caused it in the first place are the ones who rose out of it, barely scathed."

A long moment of silence passes in which the horrible reality of my existence becomes clear. The original inhabitants of the dome weren't the best and brightest at all. They were the most ruthless and cunning—the ones who were most willing to sacrifice others so that they might live. And I am a part of them, part of a mass eugenics program where society strives to produce "the best"…from a base stock of cheats and liars.

As I realize just how horrible the thought of being like those in the dome is, inexplicable tears sting my eyes. "I don't want to be like that." I whip my head back and forth, rejecting his words. I've seen the world. This game has shown me what we once had. I can't bear knowing the blood in my veins is the blood of someone so heartless—that the likelihood of those living around me doing it all over again is beyond inevitable. "I don't want to be like them."

He shifts in the grass beside me, coming close and putting an arm around me. I shrug him off. I don't want his intoxicating closeness. I don't want his wild scent and tempting lips beckoning and making me forget what's important. This is a time for me and my own thoughts.

Seeming to understand my need for control, he resigns himself to just sitting close by, offering his presence and comfort should I need it.

A long time later, I lie with Guster on the quilt, waiting for the game to pull us out. Now that the fresh air and sunshine and grass have touched the squares of the map, it no longer smells so foul or looks so ugly. I trace the squares with my sore, bloodshot eyes, searching for something to connect everything, and frown to myself. Guster is right. I have a Programmer's brain. I'm looking for the coded pattern, searching for the algorithm to crack this mystery. Trying to find the logic in all the chaos.

The knowledge that these traits are probably so keen within me because I have the mind of a criminal sours the glory of the chase, and I grimace. *Tricksters. We're all tricksters.*

Guster rolls onto his stomach and brushes his fingers against my forearm. "You okay?"

I shrug and look up at him. "I'm sorry I freaked out. I didn't mean to be cold with you."

He smiles, gentle, and instead of speaking he says *I know* by leaning in and kissing me softly. I roll back a little, beckoning him closer, because right now all I want is to lose myself in the goodness of what exists between the two of us.

He follows willingly, pulling his weight halfway over me and caging me in with his arms. After a few seconds the soft kiss becomes more intense and, squirming, I run my hands along his sides and back. Wanting more of him, I slip them under his jacket, allowing myself to finally touch the muscles under his tight shirt. I feel him groan against my lips and, smiling, he speaks in a teasing whisper. "Elle, have you forgotten we're in public?"

I had, and the embarrassment of it is enough to break the kiss and have me rolling back onto my stomach in mortification.

He touches my spine, a warm reminder of no hard feelings between either of us. "What do you see?"

I don't bother hiding what he already knows I've been doing. Trying not to look ashamed of myself, I say, "We can assume that all of these squares represent an actual playing field in Nexis. These can't be all the fields, so this sample must represent some key relationship to getting to Central Dominion. That in mind, we have to think about *what* makes each one unique to the map. All the squares are exactly alike in size and shape. But," I emphasize, "each square has a shape inside of it—some have a circle, some have a geometric shape, some have an irregular shape. To top that off, the shapes inside the squares have pieces taken out of them."

"So." Guster breathes. "For now, we assume that the shapes inside each square have relevance."

"But *what* relevance?" And then I see it. "Oh…"

He sits up on his elbows. "What?"

"This is a giant math problem. A differential equation."

He looks back at the quilt, his eyes wide and a little confused. "Okay," he says slowly. "I don't get it."

I smirk at him. "I thought you saw the big picture of everything?"

He rolls his eyes. "Just explain it."

I get on my hands and knees and point to the four squares in the corner closest to me. "Take these four squares. Each has a different shape inside. Canal Town has a square, this green bit here has a triangle, this blue one has a weird blobbish thing, and this one has one that looks like a dog head."

Guster chuckles at me, but I ignore him. "Four shapes out of hundreds of random shapes, all with additional pieces taken out of them, further changing their shape. But what if the shapes aren't what matters at all? What if it's the space inside the shapes that does?"

Interested, Guster gets on his knees. "You mean, you think each one of these shapes has a different area?"

I nod. "I wasn't sure at first, but even the squares that have the same shapes inside them have different-sized bits taken out of them. Like this one." I point at the dog head, which is missing a triangular bit where the dog's eye should be. "There's another sort of dog-head shape on the other side; I saw it earlier. It's the same size, but it has a square, not a triangle, taken out of it. The difference in the two eye shapes taken out of the dog-head shape would change the amount of space the two dog-head shapes take up."

Guster nods. "I see what you mean. The shapes inside each of the squares represent land mass. So, if we find out the exact size of each of these shapes, we can order them from largest to smallest and assume that the land mass correlates to the particular field that the decoration on the square indicates."

"Yes. If your onion theory is correct, then the gaming levels with the smallest land mass should be closer to the Central Dominion." I look down at the quilt, suddenly anxious to get to calculating.

"Stack them one on top of another, just like that stacking rings game we played with as kids."

"Once the squares are in order, all we'd have to do is match one square with a level we recognize and, using the order, move straight on to the Central Dominion."

He grins at me. "You're brilliant."

Blushing, I look away. "It's just a theory."

"A really good one. We've already got Canal Town as a point of origin. All we have to do is put them in order."

I bite my lip. *The mind of a criminal. Trickster.* "I might have some points in the brain area, but I don't have the kind of brain power necessary to do these kinds of computations." I actually feel a little relieved by this. I'm not an evil genius after all.

Brows drawn low, he frowns. "Can't you write a program to do it?"

I scoff. "Well yeah, that's easy as trans. But…" I pause and look down at the quilt. "These are tiny squares, and there are hundreds of them; the slightest miscalculation could mess it up. There's no way that I could memorize the exact size and shape of these and run the computations at home."

"So write the program and run it here," Guster suggests.

"With what?" I ask, sweeping my eyes around meaningfully. "Steam power?"

He grins. "No. We just need to find a playing field with high enough technology for you, right?"

I cock my head. "Right. But," I say, pointedly, "that would mean leaving Canal Town, which means losing our point of origin. How easy is it to retrace your steps through the jump pads?"

The grin fades, telling me the answer. "We'll figure out

something."

"And we're going to do it without destroying anything, right?"

Guster gives me a long hard starc. "What did I just say that implied destruction?"

I bite my lip. "Nothing. You didn't, I just…" *Feel like an idiot?* I lift a shoulder, uncomfortable with his weighted glower.

"This is a *good* thing, Elle."

I roll my eyes. "That's what evil geniuses are for."

He glances sideways at me. "That's what beautiful brainiacs are for. There's a big difference."

"Oh? What's that?"

"Intent and conscience. Always look at what you are doing, and ask yourself if you are doing the right thing. Look at who is being affected and who is gaining from your endeavor."

"So, our infiltration of the Anansi Chamber accomplishes this how?"

"Ever hear of Robin Hood?"

I shake my head.

Guster smiles his insane, wonderful smile. "Inspirational man."

Unsent Letters to Delia

Dee,

My letters have been short lately and I apologize. I have so much that I'm doing, I keep busy almost all day. I spend most of the time reading Dad's files. Who would have ever thought history would be so exciting. Meems is having me do all of these awful exercises, and I ache all the time, but I feel stronger and I think I might actually be losing fat without getting liposuction. What a strange concept.

Then, of course, I watch The Broadcast daily. Have you been keeping up on Zane Boyd lately? What do you think of the Gaming Houses? I often wonder if you've started playing the game yet. It's been a few months since I started playing, and I can't imagine life without Nexis at this point.

Have you made a move on one of your crushes yet? Quentin or Shadow? Perhaps you've finally reigned in Bastian. I've got Guster, and I couldn't be happier. Oh Dee, when he kisses me or when he touches me, it's like magic. It's like all the things inside of me get up and dance and squirm. And he understands me. He's so intelligent and compassionate. He sees the big picture in everything. I wonder who he is in Real World. I don't ask him ever; it's clear he hates talking about life in Real World. I can't help hoping he's not married or in love with another girl out here. It's entirely possible, right? I don't know why I care. It's not like I could be with him out here. I'm not even alive anymore, let alone viable. Still, it's hard to deal with the idea of sharing the person you love with someone else.

Yours,
Ella

chapter twenty-five

Meems places a bowl at my elbow. I don't take my eyes away from the Wright Brothers until they return to the place called Kitty Hawk in 1908.

I check the digital readout of the clock suspended near the edge of the holo-screen—two more hours. Anxious for something else to distract me, I look to the bowl that Meems has provided me and then at her. "What's this stuff?"

"I believe the historic term for it is gruel," Meems says flatly. I can tell she's a little flustered.

I lean over and sniff it. "It doesn't smell appetizing."

She crosses her arms. "I doubt it is. From what I can tell it is what the Disfavored are eating."

I frown. "Why did you give it to me?"

"Because that is what Tasha gave me to feed you."

Reaching out, I push it away. "I'm not eating this stuff."

She lowers her arms in partial exaggeration. "It is all we can give you."

"What does that mean?"

"The nutrition rationing in Tasha's system has been altered. This is all that she is allowed to provide to you."

I stare at Meems for a long horrified minute, then back down at my gruel. There's maybe six ounces lumped down at the bottom of the stainless steel bowl. "Who changed it? Katrina?"

"I don't know."

Of course it is. Who else would it be? Everyone else thinks I'm dead. But why? "Is she trying to starve me to death?"

Meems doesn't answer, but her expression seems to say just that.

My fists ball in my lap as anger and frustration fill me. "Circuits, I just wish I understood what is going on."

"But you cannot."

A scoff escapes my lips. "No. I can't." I shake my head. "I don't know what to do." Since Tasha won't allow me out of the room, and I can't send messages, I've asked Meems to carry notes down to Katrina on a number of occasions. I've requested audiences with her. Was denied. Demanded an explanation. Was given nothing. I wanted to move back into my room. She'd already given it to Sadie. I wanted to go outside. She claimed I was too unwell to go out. I asked for a tutor. She wanted to know what good an education would do me now. I begged for a pair of cybernetic legs. I had reasoned that cybernetics are cheaper than the combination of stem cell and nanotechnology necessary to regrow a new pair of legs, so I had thought she'd at least give me that. But she claimed it wasn't in her power. Which confused me because if she's a normal court-appointed guardian she should have that power.

I look away from Meems. "If I say anything to her about my food, I'll be given an excuse." I knead my forehead. "I wish I could access Dad's accounts. By rights they should be mine now, right? I bet they're brimming." I could have ten new pairs grown for me.

"Most likely," Meems says slowly. "The Broadcast says that your father's game is growing in popularity. Lady Cyr has petitioned the installation of more Gaming Houses in the Outer Block."

I nod. I've been keeping up with The Broadcast. Not only is the game incredibly popular within the city, but Zane Boyd's reports claim it's revolutionary in the Outer Block, that there have been gang wars over control of the Gaming Houses, riots to gain access to the terminals, and gaming tokens have become the prime form of currency with the Disfavored. From my window, I've watched the Disfavored stand for hours just to get through the door of the Gaming House near my residential unit. "What that means is that Dad's game is banking ten times the sales. The royalties from all these Disfavored gaming installations are going somewhere."

Meems nods furtively at the floor, not indicating the industrial carpeting but the people who live in the rooms below mine. "I suspect one need not look far."

I nod. From my window, I've seen Katrina and Sadie walking in and out of the house. I've seen deliveries and people coming and going. If the steady mutation of my household is any indication, then a large sum of credit is going into Mods and Alts for my new speckled and bedazzled pseudo family members, into expensive food and furniture, into lavish parties, into designer clothing, into the new Chimera pod that drives Sadie off to school every morning. "But does that mean that she's taking it or being paid off?"

"I do not know the answer. Does it matter?"

I stare at the floor for a long moment. Does it? Whether I knew who was keeping me captive or not, would it change anything? I still can't escape. I still can't communicate with the outside world. All it does is give me a person to direct my hate toward. And what good does hating do when you can't do anything about that, either? It just makes you miserable. "I suppose not."

I reach out and drag the bowl back toward myself. A thick crust has formed over the stuff, and it has gone cold. Cringing, I take up a spoonful and shove it in my mouth. It's like mud on my tongue, tasting like what I imagine a Disfavored shanty wall must taste like: smoke, rocks, and anguish. My gag reflex tells me to spit it out, but I force it down. I'm hungry, and if I don't eat I can't focus.

I want to finish reading Dad's files. I want to decode the last puzzle and read his last secret message. I want to figure out why he's obsessed with spiders. I want to go back into his game and be with Guster. And I definitely don't want to give Katrina, or whomever she works for, the satisfaction of silently offing me so they can live on my fortune indefinitely.

As I force myself to eat the terrible stuff, Meems watches, her mouth pulled down in displeasure and her eyes scrunched in sympathy. When I finish I drop the spoon into the bowl like I've just completed a marathon and push it away from me.

My stomach feels swollen and heavy despite the small amount of food in it, but I turn back to the holo and lose my discomfort in a world of men who dreamed of flying. Men who saw birds soaring and wished to touch the blue of the sky. Men who might have had pet dogs and touched the bark of trees. Men who knew what real air tasted like and felt the sun on their skin. Men who, like me, probably loved running.

chapter twenty-six

When I manifest into Nexis I collapse in relief. Nadine gives me a strange look. "Um, are you all right?"

I giggle. "Yeah." I take her hand as she offers it to me, and stand. "I'm just relieved to be here."

"Yeah," she says, pulling away and planting her fists on her hips. "I know what you mean."

I cock my head. As a rule, the people in our group don't talk much of their outside lives, but Nadine often slips up and alludes to hers. I've decided for certain that both she and Gus are Aristocrats, like me. Morden and Opus I'm still not sure about.

I glance around. We're in a heavily forested area, something that looks and feels like the tropical jungles in Dad's files. Gus, Morden, and Opus all went to explore, leaving Nadine to supervise my cooking. Though after five months of her teaching me, I'm perfectly fine on my own. I think she just wants an excuse to hang out and have girl time.

"Nadine," I venture. She doesn't look up from pulling the

feathers off some weird bird-thing she shot yesterday, but she grunts. "What's it like for you? In Evanescence?"

Her fingers go still, and her blue eyes flash up. For a moment, I think I've misstepped, so I start to explain myself. "I mean, you don't have to talk about it if you don't—"

"It's all right," she cuts in. She shrugs a halfhearted smile. "I don't care."

"Oh," I breathe. "I just figured, since we've been friends here for so long...it would be nice to know something about each other." Why am I saying this? It's not like I'm willing to tell her about me... It's not like I could ever be friends with her in Real World. Could I tell her I'm a prisoner? Would she save me? Would she even care? Would anyone believe her if she told the authorities?

She rips out a chunk of feathers, and it makes an awful noise. "I'm a Developer. I'm married to a man I hate and I have a five-year-old little boy. That's about it. It's boring. Every day I do the same thing. See the same people. Act the same as I did yesterday—which isn't really me at all. I try to make the same people happy even though I never can."

I blink at the candid bitterness in her voice. "I thought most Aristocrats were happy."

A scoff escapes her. "Are you? You think Gus is?" She shakes her head. "Not that he ever talks about himself. But I see it in both of you. You just did it. Same thing I do. You breathe here; it's a relief being here. We suffocate in that little dome."

I focus on the fruit. Pineapple, mango, papaya. Some villagers taught us the names, and I found some recipes in Dad's files that Nadine is helping me with. Lately all I can do is think about food back in Real World, so I've been reading a lot of recipes. "Do you think we all hate it?"

After a long moment, her shoulders relax and she sits back

from the fire. "No. I don't. I think there are very few people who even know what unhappiness is. They just follow the crowd, follow the rules, and get what they want. That's how it goes, right?"

Maybe if you're a normal Custom, but not for me. "I suppose."

"For the rest of us? Well, we're just prisoners."

I blink at her. A bitter part of me wants to tell her she doesn't know at all what it's like to be a prisoner, but she looks away and continues speaking. "It's not like we're bound or locked up or anything like that. But, when you think about it, living under a dome, being part of our society, it's a prison in its own right. We can't escape. Even before we are born, it is decided who and what we will be. We are assessed and corralled into what Central Staffing wants us to be. Our parents decide who we should marry, we have to look and act and be what is expected of us. Sometimes…sometimes I just wish I could climb into a refuse bin and get ejected out into the wasteland, to run away, be one of the Disfavored."

"Have you ever seen what the Outer Block looks like, Nadine?"

She frowns. "On The Broadcast."

I shake my head. "Zane only shows us the nicest parts. I wouldn't want to be out there. They're sick and hungry and cold. It's violent and cruel." I look away, remembering seeing a man beat another to death with a rock the day before yesterday. So much blood in the dry dust.

"Yeah," she breathes, "but they're free."

I have nothing to say to that. Being held prisoner and being treated the way I have makes you think. It makes you wonder what's worse, makes you consider what you'd sacrifice just to go to sleep knowing that you'd wake up free.

"Let's not talk about Evanescence here, though, okay?" she says. "I'd rather talk about anything else."

I give her a gentle smile. I know exactly how she feels. We're only given a few hours to be free of Evanescence, why bother bringing it here, too? "Okay, fine. You tell me what's going on with you and Morden."

Chuckling, she stirs the pot. "Only if you tell me what's going on with you and Gus."

"I have no idea what you're talking about," I lie, pulling a false innocent face.

"Uh-huh." She rolls her eyes. "You two are disgustingly obvious."

"We're not disgusting." I yell in mock chagrin. I throw a mango pit at her in emphasis, and she nearly falls over laughing. We devolve into tossing rinds, seeds, and husks at each other until we hear yelling coming toward us.

Startled, Nadine and I both straighten and stare toward the noise, our grins slowly melting to concerned frowns as we both realize that the voices are Guster, Morden, and Opus. However, theirs aren't the only voices in the chaos—there's a whole chorus of additional screams and hoots and howls.

A moment later the boys come bursting through the clearing, running at top speed, but with giant grins on their faces. "Run," Gus yells, even though he's laugh-gasping.

I turn to comply, but I'm caught mid turn by the herd of screaming little creatures that are chasing the boys. They're like furry little people with beady black eyes and sharp yellow teeth. Just as I realize that they're throwing berries at me, Gus grabs my hand and drags me after him. We leap through the underbrush, and I soon lose track of the others.

"What are those things?" I gasp, frightened even though he doesn't seem all that bothered.

He ducks as one of the creatures flies at him. "Flying monkeys."

I spare a glance behind me. They look very angry but, at the same time, they're so cute and fluffy it's sort of hard to be scared of them. A berry hits me on the shoulder and, as soon as it does, it explodes into sparkles and bubbles.

Grinning, I slow, tugging Guster to a halt. The monkeys stop, too. Surround us. Stare at us. I glance around, at the tiny faces and unblinking eyes. "I-I don't think they're dangerous."

"No," Guster says simply as he brushes glitter out of his hair. "Just annoying."

I touch the glitter on my arm and finally take him in. He's covered head to toe in silver glitter and pink and purple paint. In some strange way, he looks like he's been Altered. "Why were they chasing you?"

"Mord dared me to try and catch one. I got close, grabbed it by the tail, but I think I made them angry."

A laugh explodes out of me before I can help it. When I can breathe again, I say, "You idiot," and give him a playful slap, which sends up a little puff of glitter.

Blushing, he rolls his eyes and playfully shoves into me, invading my space, and I relish it. Every hour of every day spent with him, the slow slope of falling for this boy in more than just a carnal fashion has been like slowly pulling the strings on some great tapestry. Every day the weave becomes tighter, the picture clearer, everything more complete. I love him close to me in more than just body. I lift my arms and pull him into a hug, which he returns without a moment's hesitation.

"Seriously, though," I say into his shoulder, "all three of you are idiots. Didn't you guys learn anything from practicing your shooting skills on the trees back in Oz?"

"How could I?" he mutters, touching his backside. "My butt is still bruised from the smack that one apple tree gave me."

I try to look sympathetic, but I can't stop smirking. "Well, you deserved that smack…and the string of profanities she threw at you, you idiot."

"Yeah, well…" He seems at a loss for how to respond so kisses me instead. When he's satisfied, he draws away and says, "I'm a handsome idiot." His hands wander up my back, he pecks the corner of my mouth. "And you'll kiss me no matter how much glitter I have in my hair or how bruised my ass is." He kisses me again.

I smirk against his lips. "True." I pull away and put my finger to his lips, halting him. "But we should probably clean off."

He stares at me, holds my gaze as he moves to evade my finger, kisses my jaw. "Should we?"

"Yes."

He makes a noise of agreement against my neck as he trails kisses and explores with his hands. "Baths are good," he murmurs against my skin.

"Gus," I giggle, trying to squirm away from the tickling feeling he's giving me.

Displeased with my feigned attempts at escape, he growls into my neck and presses me against the nearest tree, startling the monkeys perched there so that they retreat into the leaves and out of sight. I can't help laughing some more. I feel so light and airy, as if the glitter bombs were actually filled with laughing gas. It takes me a moment to calm down, to realize that Guster isn't smiling—not his normal grin, anyway. This is a very quiet, content expression, his eyes deep and bottomless. He looks at me like this more and more and, every time he does, it takes my breath away. I've never seen anyone look at anyone like this before. It makes my heart pound and my blood pulse and a warmth spread throughout my chest.

"You okay?" Though I know he's more than okay.

His eyes slide sideways, survey the quiet forest around us.

"We're alone."

I reach out, touch his face with the tips of my fingers, let them wander through his hair, down his neck. "Yeah. It's nice."

He looks back at me. The distance is closing between us. "It's been a long time since we've been alone. I've been waiting for a moment like this." Suddenly I know where this is going. And we're kissing again. Not the wild crazy kisses that he steals in his madman bouts of play. This kiss is long and slow and hungry. It's hot and tingly and determined. It's the kind of kiss that involves the whole body, the kind that makes you forget where you are and exactly what's happening.

I touch him, tracing his muscles through his shirt, and then I get bold and slide my fingers under his shirt. His skin is warm and smooth and hard. I want it against my own. I pull the jacket from his shoulders and hear it fall to the ground. His neck free of his high collar, I pull away from his lips and move to his neck, kissing his tendons and prominent Adam's apple. He growls under his breath, his fist bunching the fabric at the small of my back, pulling my shirt tight against my chest and stomach as he hitches his pelvis against mine.

I'm filled with a need like I've never had for any boy in my life, more even than Quentin. I want him so bad it's physically uncomfortable. I've been wanting since the beginning, but managed to hold it off. Held it for a good long time, until I was certain there was more than just lust for Guster and even longer because we've not been alone or had the chance to take a moment's breath. "Gus," I plead against his skin. Because I don't know what else to say or how to say it. I want things, I need things, I'm scared of these feelings—yet there is nothing I want more. And I want them with him. No one else. Just Guster.

His hands find my wrists, and he pulls away and fixes me with heady, molasses deep eyes. "Where?"

Rolling my eyes at his sudden romantic need to make this right, I shake my head and say, "I don't care." Not anymore. Delia and I used to talk about the right moment and location for this sort of thing. But really, to me, it seems it's the person, not the setting, that makes it special.

He lifts a brow, shrugs, and just like that his leg is gently kicking my legs out from under me. He holds me so I don't fall; instead he lowers me against his jacket. "Here, then," he informs, voice thick and edgy as he gets to his knees and kisses me again.

His fingers grip my thighs, dragging me under him. His mouth strays and finds bare skin as his body brushes mine. He keeps the goal fresh in my mind—and I play the game, doing the same to him. Giving him promising expressions, letting my touch slide under his clothing, nibbling his ear, creating friction and desperation between us.

Intermittently, I yank off his clothes, drinking in the perfect planes of his body with my lips and fingers and eyes and tongue. He's gentler with my clothes—treating them reverently like they're extensions of me. And maybe he thinks they are since, after taking a number of tutorials he bought for me on textile arts, I made them myself. If he sees something about my Natural body that displeases, he doesn't reveal it. Instead, he treats me like the goddesses I've read about in Dad's files. Slow, gentle, reverent—like there's all the time in the world, and my pleasure is the only thing he cares about. I try to do the same, to show him my feelings in a physical sense.

Eventually we're so wound up that any apprehension I normally would have is gone. I'm blinded by want and need and the desire to be everything all at once. And it's freeing. Like running. But I'm not running alone. I have Gus with me—the whole way. In tentative touch, in bare skin, in gasping breath, and that final union that we've been seeking, dancing around for months. And it's so much better than I could have imagined.

And then we're coming down from some place I'll never be able to describe or grasp, and I'm lying beneath him, bodies sticky with humid air and covered in sparkles, my heart beating against his throat, and the late afternoon sun peeking through bare spots in the canopy. Stroking his hair, I take a deep breath—the best I can, considering his weight on my stomach—and let it out. I could stay like this forever. In this moment. It's perfect.

I want this to be Real Life. I want to feel safe and loved like this all the time. I want to be with Guster, wake up to him here *and* there.

And just like that, I'm suddenly crying.

Guster looks up, bewildered. "Elle?"

I try to wipe my eyes, to hide the sudden well of emotion in me. "It's nothing. It's fine."

"Hey. Hey," he whispers, rolling off of me and grasping at my hands. "It's not fine. What's going on?"

I take deep breaths, trying to calm myself, center my thoughts. "I don't know."

"People don't start crying for no reason." He brushes his fingers against my cheek, banishing tears, then pulls me close again, stroking my back. He's quiet for a long moment while I sniffle and hiccup myself out. Then, he finally says, "Tell me."

I shrug. "I was thinking about how life isn't fair."

His arm tenses around me, and he presses his face into my hair. "About us?"

I nod. "Not just us. In general. My life out there…I wish I could stay here forever."

Sensing the delicate subject, Guster's tone becomes apprehensive. He knows we don't talk about this. We've both forbade it, but at the same time we're both far too curious about the other to respect the boundaries. "Is everything all right? You know that

I'll help you in any way I can."

I remain quiet. Driven to moments of desperation from my gnawing stomach, I have thought a lot lately about telling Gus what's going on with me in Real World. Knowing who I am or not, being able to be with me or not, I know he wouldn't tolerate me being mistreated. One way or another, the boy at the other end of this avatar would try and free me from captivity. And that would be beautiful—like the stories in Dad's files. Except I don't know who is holding me captive. I don't know who or how powerful. Most importantly, I don't know how dangerous. And that's something I can't risk. Harming Guster would be worse than starving to death, and I remind myself of that every time I come back into the game and feel myself on the verge of confessing. "I'm fine," I whisper, kissing his chest—right over his heart. "I'm just being emotional, that's all."

"Promise me?" he says, his fingers curling in my hair. "I know something's wrong; you've been acting funny. I couldn't live with myself if you came to any harm."

I close my eyes and say, "That makes two of us." I trace circles on his pectoral muscle and take a clue from what Nadine told me earlier. "I'm not happy there. A lot of us aren't. You're not."

I wait for him to admit this to me. To tell me what makes him stare off into the distance when he thinks no one is watching him, but a long quiet falls upon us. I feel both of us suddenly drifting away from this subject—closing it down and forgetting about it for another few days. And that's okay. At this point, I don't want him to know that I'm suffering out there. It would kill him.

"Do that thing you do," I whisper into his shoulder. "With your voice."

I feel his chin lift. "What?"

I try to emulate what he sometimes absentmindedly does.

"Humming?"

I nod. "It makes me happy when you do that."

His head lowers, and he takes a deep breath. And then he hums me something, low and slow. And it lulls me into the false sense of security that I need when I'm here, because it's the only thing that gets me by.

A long time later, when Gus has fallen silent and I think he might even be asleep, I finally take a moment to take a look at where we are. I move to sit up.

"Don't," Guster whispers, tensing his arm around me.

I put my hand on his chest. "I'm not going anywhere. I just wanna see."

He rolls over, trapping me between the leather of his jacket and the hardness of his body. He shifts, nudging closer, so we fit on the outside the way we fit on the inside. "It's not important." He buries his face in my neck, holds me for a long moment.

"Shouldn't we get back?"

"Eventually." He shifts, pulling away far enough to steeple himself on his elbows, then spends a long minute staring down at me. Long enough for me to start to feel exposed and a little nervous that he'll find something he doesn't like on my bare Natural body. He's an Aristocrat, after all. When he does finally look back into my frightened eyes, he simply touches my cheek and says, "Did you know you have a beautiful blush?"

I blink, shocked. "What?"

His little smirk dimples his cheek. "I like that I put it there."

That blush he loves so much deepens, and I look away, flustered by that thing he does with his voice and the words he chooses.

Knowing he's an infuriating tease, Gus shifts, letting me know just how much he likes to make me blush. I squeak, and he instantly goes still. His brow knits. "You all right?"

I shake my head. "I'm just," I pause, uncertain of what I even am. I shake my head. "I don't know. I'm just…just, really happy, I guess. It's overwhelming. I just want to pop. Everything you do, you make me want to explode, there's so much goodness happening inside of me."

Smiling, Gus leans in and kisses me. "I love you, too."

Before I can respond, he pulls away and gets to his feet. He disappears behind one of the high tree roots we collapsed among hours ago, and a moment later I hear a splash.

I get up to find him wading across a crystalline pool. Even though we're in the middle of the jungle, this pool is lined with decorative tile, depicting a winged banana. I roll my eyes at my father. At this point, I know he can't possibly have programmed everything into this world, but the fact that silly things like banana pools and glitter-bomb-toting flying monkeys even exist make me love him more.

"Are you coming?"

In answer I jump in on top of him.

A little while later, the surface of the water glinting like a mirror from all the glitter floating in it, Gus and I finally decide we should get back to the camp before we're pulled out of the game, so we swim back to shore and get out. When he goes still and starts looking around, I glance over his shoulder to find out what's wrong.

"What?"

Confused, he bites his lip and continues scanning the area. One of the flying monkeys hops up onto a root and waggles his eyebrows.

Gus's shoulders drop. "Oh no."

"What?"

He leans forward and squints at the monkey. "Tell me you didn't."

The monkey grins in a malicious sort of way. Then points up. Thoroughly confused at this point, I decide to ignore them both and step around Gus. But… "Um, Gus, where are our clothes?"

He doesn't look away from where the monkey pointed. "How are you at climbing trees?"

chapter twenty-seven

Gus opens the door and steps back, letting me see what he's found. "Great, huh?"

I stare at the bulky, ugly pieces of technology in front of me. "What are they?"

"Computers," Gus says, walking into the room and hefting a giant squarish box off a laminate counter. "At least, that's what I hope they'll be."

I give him my best "I am not impressed" expression.

His smile droops. "It's all I could find, Elle. It's worth a try."

Turning away, I cross my arms. "Sparks, I hate this place."

We've landed in a strange time period where geometric shapes and odd colors rule. The women have huge hair, big synthetic boots, and bigger dark glasses. The men wear angular pants and shirts that seem to emphasize a long stretch.

Morden opens the kitchen door, making us both jump. "Far out."

Gus rolls his eyes. "You've embraced the lingo—be still my

psychedelic heart.'"

Morden pouts, his full lips looking ridiculous with the orange lipstick he's found. "I'm not entirely sure if that's the right use of the word."

Gus puts a fist on his narrow hip. "I'm not entirely sure that I care. What the heck is on your head?"

Morden touches the fluffy yellow thing on his head and the oversized peace symbol earrings in his ears glinting in the late afternoon sunlight. "It's a fro."

Gus scrunches his nose and glances at me. "Is that thing legal?"

I grin. "I dunno, maybe not in combination with that thing around his neck. Might stop traffic."

As Gus laughs, a self-conscious Morden touches his neck. "What's wrong with my ascot?"

I make a point of critically circling him before saying, "There are at least forty hexadecimal colors that *shouldn't* be in combination on that thing."

Morden sniffs, the mustache he's grown out bristling. "You have no taste in fashion."

I lift a brow.

"Well, there's something I never thought I'd hear someone say to you," Gus says, his tone serious.

Nadine comes in the next moment. She's wearing a wig, too, one that matches her natural hair color but gives her long, pin-straight hair that reaches past her backside. And a good thing, too; I'm not sure if her skintight mini-dress could do the job of covering her rear end on its own. Her long legs are covered up to the knees in shiny white plastic boots, she's got huge white plastic hoops in her ears, and a broad white headband in her hair.

"What do you think?" She strikes a pose.

I stare at her. "I think I'm regretting sending you to go shopping for me."

She grins. "Oh, I didn't get this for you. This one is mine. She bends and rummages in a shopping bag, then pulls out a white ruffled top with ribbons and a pair of what I've read are called jeans—only these are ponderously flared around the bottom of the leg. Finally, she pulls out a thick leather belt and a small vest. "These are yours."

I take the vest and hold it away from me like the betassled, plague-ridden thing it is. "Nadine, you've just reiterated why Developers are Developers and Designers are Designers." Turning, I hold up my new vest and give Gus a pleading look.

He grins at me. "Soon as we have those calculations, we're out of here. Promise."

A new fire of determination flaring up in me, I turn back to the heap of junk he has brought home to the house we're renting. Realizing that they're being ignored, Morden and Nadine disappear. A few seconds later I hear the television blasting the theme to the show I've come to learn is called *Schoolhouse Rock*. I stare harder at the mess, trying to see how this could possibly become what I need it to be. I let my head droop, overwhelmed.

Gus comes close to me, puts an arm around my waist, and presses his face close to my ear. "What's wrong?"

"Are you sure these will work? I mean, can't we at least try for something more modern? Maybe the twenty-first century?"

"I'm not sure if there is anything more modern, Elle. We could go for years and never find what we need. Besides, we're running out of jump stones."

Sighing, I drop into the chair—a chrome-legged thing with a vinyl orange seat. It matches the orange laminate tabletop, the yellow counter, and the black-and-white checkered floor. Oh, and the green box called the refrigerator, and the stupid cat clock with the tail and eyes that tick with the time. I don't even want to think about the shaggy brown rug or the thick, brown-orange-green tartan-patterned upholstery on the parlor furniture, or the wood paneling. All of it has one matching quality: it's ugly. The Designer in me is in constant crisis mode. I can't even go outside. It's worse out there. Row upon row of the same ugly houses... and those pink flamingos...

I shiver, dismissing the thought, then bury my face against my arm. "We've been in Discoland for too long. I want out."

Gus sits next to me and puts a hand on my knee. "Look, it's not that bad. According to what I've been reading about this era, this kind of technology shouldn't exist yet. They've got the integrated circuit, but the PC isn't available yet. I don't know how this got here, but be thankful it did. I can help you rebuild it; I've got training as an Engineer."

I glance at him. "You're an Engineer?"

He makes a hesitant expression. "N-No, I'm not an Engineer. I just have some additional training."

I give him a wry look and point a finger into his chest. "Real World you is a code I'd like to crack, Gus, I really would."

He takes my hand, kisses it, and grinning, presses it against his heart. "You already have the most important code."

I roll my eyes. "You are a cheese sphere."

He cocks his head. "I think you mean cheeseball."

"Same difference."

He looks around the room, his face more determined than I think I've ever seen it. "We'll make something out of this mess if I have to disembowel the toaster and the refrigerator to do it."

I laugh. "It shall be our Frankenstein."

"Franken-what?"

"Frankenstein. It's a book about a mad scientist who created a monster out of the parts of other humans."

"Ah, a man after my own heart," Gus muses.

I flex my brow. "So, by Engineer you mean Genetic Engineer

then?" I tease. "Besides, the person who wrote the book is a woman. Give her the credit." I reach out and pick up a flat board with crude alphabetical buttons. "Is this thing a keyboard?"

He smirks. "Yeah, I think so."

"Ugh, this stuff is arcane," I whine, my eyes rolling skyward. "It's going to take me forever to design the program without a G-Chip. Do you know how slow typing it is going to be?"

He shrugs. "As soon as we get the numbers in hand, we'll leave." Gus slips out of his chair and kneels in front of me, a hand grasping mine while the other escapes into his jeans pocket.

For a brief moment, my heart skips a beat, thinking he's going to do the wonderful custom I read about—proposing with a ring. But instead of a ring, Gus pulls out a jump stone and presses it into my palm.

Confused, I look up at him. "What's this?"

He smiles at my closed fingers. "Our last jump stone."

I cock my head.

He closes both his hands around mine. "Elle, when this is all over, I want to stay with you. This stone is a promise that once we reach the Central Dominion and fulfill our quest, we will start a different kind of game. We'll use this stone, go wherever you want. You can maybe design things and sell them like that lady at the shop in Canal Town. It doesn't matter to me, where we go or what we do, as long as you're happy, as long as we're together." Finally he looks up at me, expectant and shy.

I stare at him, mouth open. Perhaps this is something like the proposal and engagement ring. More than I initially thought.

He swallows. "Say we can do that? Say you'll stay with me, continue playing with me?"

Unable to find words to describe the welling pulse of emotion in my chest and stomach, I nod.

Relieved, he smiles and pulls me into a hug.

chapter twenty-eight

"I can't get this stupid thing to work," I growl. Frustrated, I throw my flex-bracelet on the ground and attempt to storm away from it. My mixed emotions just cause the hover-chair to spin in a confused circle and then bump against the wall.

Meems giggles at me. "You will figure it out. You just need a break."

"I can't concentrate. I'm too hungry."

I've been on Tasha's gruel diet for almost a month now. I've lost that natural curvature I once tried so hard to hide. Now I wish I had it back. I wish I couldn't see my bones, wish I weren't slowly starving to death. Every day I see Guster's smiling face, his love for me, and I'm consumed with guilt. I may not live to fulfill my promise to him, yet I can't tell him why, and I can't ask for help. I could never put him in danger like that.

So, every day I stare at the clock, wishing for my time in Nexis. At first, it was a need to see my father's world, to have my legs, to be with Gus, and to feel like there was a point to my existence.

Now, more than anything, I just want to escape the gnawing emptiness in my core. I want to get back into the game so I can taste real food and see my body as it should look. I want to escape my prison, not just these four walls, but Evanescence and this time of no hope. I want the world as it should be. I want possibility and the safety of Gus's embrace.

Meems looks away, hiding her face behind a curtain of short-cropped sunny hair. "I have tried to ask Katrina to increase your portions, but she claims it's out of her control. She says if you keep asking me to bother her, she will sell your father's workstation."

The chair backs up so that I'm hovering protectively before the workstation. "Over my dead body," I hiss.

"At this rate," Meems reflects, "you will be dead." Her face contorts as if she's in pain. "I feel that I am not fulfilling my duty to you."

The chair drops a little, reacting to my low mood. "Oh Meems. It's not your fault."

"I would cry for you if I had tear ducts."

I try my best to smile for her. "I'll be okay. It's enough that you're here with me. If not for you, I would have gone nuts a long time ago."

She nods but still looks depressed.

I prop my chin on my fist and glare at the bracelet on the floor. I'd like to pick it up and try working on the puzzle again. I want something else to think about, something I can control. But, it's out of reach until Meems decides to be nice and pick it up for me. It's little things like this that make me hate my handicap most.

"You know," I venture, wishing I had magical powers like those I've read about in old stories. "There used to be these people called superheroes. They used their minds to make things move."

"Those were stories made for entertainment."

"I know, but it's still a novel idea." Then, after a moment, I add, "It might come true. Androids were once fictional."

Meems cuts her icy eyes at me. "There is a difference between science and magic."

My stomach chooses this moment to growl. I blush at her expression and bite my lower lip. "There was also this superhero who was a regular man. He used to steal from the rich and give to the poor."

Meems's brow lifts, interested despite herself.

"Gus told me about him. They called him Robin Hood."

I'd like to do that. I'd like to steal the food right off Katrina's plate and give it to people who need it. I wince, expecting my G-Chip to zap me for the rebellious thought. But my punishment doesn't come. Frightened, I straighten. "Meems?" My voice comes out in a shaking whisper.

"Yes?"

"I-I just…" I pause, uncertain if I should admit it. I think of a few other illegal ideas. Changing my age in my files so that I can receive Mods. Nothing happens. Hacking into the Main Frame. Nothing. Stealing the credits out of Katrina's account, breaking out of the house, picking up a rock and bashing someone's brains in like the Disfavored man did.

The G-Chip doesn't do a thing. It's not punishing me for thinking illegal thoughts like it always has in the past.

Heart pounding in my ears, my eyes fly around the room. I can't breathe. *Is this a test? A mistake? What's happening?* I've never heard of someone's G-Chip not working. No, wait. It does work—at least partially. I can still interact with Tasha and my bracelet. So, either it's not sensing my rebellious and illegal thoughts, or the messages it's sending me to stop thinking these things are no longer getting to where they need to be. It's damaged. I touch the scar on my head. Was it damaged in the crash? No, it corrected me in the beginning, when I was first imprisoned and I had dark thoughts of killing Katrina to escape. Why not now? Did it...did it get turned off? Adjusted?

I turn to the desk with new urgency.

"What?" Meems demands. "What's happening?"

"Shhh." The screen begins blinking through the various security levels on Tasha's system. I can't have Tasha overhearing what's going on and reporting my G-Chip malfunction. I need to understand what's wrong first. Maybe I can fix it on my own.

Wait. Do I want to fix it? The screens begin to slow. *Of course I do.* They speed up again. *Do I?* Slow down. *It's for my own safety. The chips are to help maintain civil order.* Stop. Civil order? Is my falsified death, my captivity, my torture civil order?

Tasha's securities screen is in front of me, asking for the access code for the Inhabitants section. What happens if I don't fix it? All I'd have to do to get some food is hack and reprogram Tasha's Nutritional Allocations section. If I am able to hack the securities section, then that will mean that I am able to do something that no one else without G-Corp's clearance is able to do. It would mean the civil controls aspect of my G-Chip are completely offline. It would mean I am lawless, that I can move without being seen.

Like a spider.

Swallowing, I begin hacking the code.

Meems sets the plate down in front of me. "Are you sure about this?" she asks, her voice unsteady. She's worried. I'm mortified.

I did it. I hacked into Tasha. No one except an adult in a household should be able to adjust Nutritional Allocations, but I did. And the G-Chip didn't punish me. It let me do it. I expected security droids to crash through the doors and windows. But I waited. An hour. Two. Nothing happened. Eventually my hunger drove me forward, and I couldn't wait any longer.

I look down at the brushed steel plate. Genetically altered broccoli never looked so green, synthetic beef never looked so tender, hydroponically grown potatoes never looked so fluffy and light. I wipe the drool off my chin and begin tucking in.

"I cannot believe you did that," Meems reflects. "It is illegal."

I swallow and take a gulp of fructose bubbly, a sad version of what I assume used to be soda. "So is imprisoning someone and starving them to death."

She remains quiet for a long time. The broccoli disappears, so does the steak. "How did you do it?"

I shrug. "I thought about being like Robin Hood and stealing food from that fat, horrible Katrina. Stealing is illegal, so the chip should have stopped me, but it didn't. I hacked the security system, changed Tasha's coding so that she wouldn't report me and made it so that she'd feed me like normal. Still, nothing happened."

"How?"

I shrug. "I don't know. I don't care."

She narrows her eyes. "Does this not seem suspicious to you?"

I grimace at her. "What it seems like is a blessing. I have control now, that's all I care about."

"You know I am required to report you, Ellani," Meems says

in her mechanical voice.

I glower at her. "Go ahead. At least they'd get me out of Katrina's clutches."

Meems purses her lips. "I do not want to report you."

"Then don't."

"I have to. It is in my programming."

"Funny," I say. "You seem to be having a lot of trouble following your protocol lately. Why haven't you reported me already, Meems?"

She seems confused by this. "I-I do not know."

"Sometimes, I wonder how you do it. It's supposed to be impossible for a robot to go against its programming. In fact," I say, setting my fork down. "You shouldn't be as humanlike as you are, either. Sometimes I really want to take a peek inside your head and see exactly what Dad did in there."

She puts her hands on her head. "You would not dare."

I laugh. It feels good to laugh. I haven't done it in so long. At least, not in Real World. "I'm not going to touch your head, Meems. That would be wrong." I respect her too much for that.

She gives me a suspicious look, but I just go back to shoveling mashed potatoes into my mouth.

After a long time she says, "You say it would be wrong to tamper with my brain, but what you have done is also wrong. Illegal."

"And my captivity and torture isn't?"

Meems frowns at me. "Those chips are put there for a reason. Our society will not operate properly if people start breaking the rules."

"I know," I say with a sigh and then I laugh to myself. "A society full of rules placed on rule breakers."

"What does that mean?"

"Nothing." I shake my head. "Look, I'm not going to do

anything." Much as I want to take what is mine, liberate myself, exact vengeance—I'm not a criminal. And I still have no idea what I'm up against. Not, for the first time, I worry that G-Corp—maybe even the President himself—is behind my captivity. I have no idea why, and perhaps that's a paranoid thought on my part, but fighting something that large would be foolish—so would drawing attention to myself. "The food thing is the only rule I'll break, okay?"

She doesn't look convinced.

"Oh come on, you can't tell me you're honestly okay with me just lying down and accepting my death."

A slight headshake is the only gesture she gives me before the alarm goes off, telling us that it's time to go back into the game.

chapter twenty-nine

The last sheet falls from the printer, landing in a neat stack. Guster collects the stack and taps it to smooth the edges. "So now all we have to do is collate the data, right?"

"Right." I turn back toward Frankie—the name we've given the massive room-sized super computer that Gus and I had to build in order to execute this one complicated differential math equation. "Oh joy, another program."

Guster steps close to me and steals a quick kiss. I lean in to him, wanting more. I want him all the time, but he pulls away, grinning. "You've done well, Elle. Don't act like you don't enjoy this."

"Maybe, but—" My words are broken off by a crash in the front hall. A moment later, Nadine screams and then shots are fired.

Gus and I run toward the door. I hear him say, "What the—"

Opus bursts through the door, Morden on his heels carrying a limp Nadine. Her eyes are open, wide and blank. My heart goes still, terrified that she's dead.

Out of the corner of my eye I see a flash of black as Guster manifests his armor. He raises his gun. "Get behind me, all of you."

"Yeah, right." Morden lowers Nadine safely behind the counter and dons his own armor. A similar set to Guster's but portraying a rabid-looking animal with long front teeth and ears on the back.

Through the open door burst more Damascus Knights. My mouth goes dry. They found us.

As they begin firing, I drop to the floor and crawl behind the counter with Nadine. Opus is crouched beside her. He's got armor on, too. A large bird with outspread wings on the back. He's muttering to himself. His words don't make sense as he holds his hands over Nadine's puckered burn wound.

I stare at her stomach and then meet her eyes, which look less vacant now. She smiles tightly at me. "It's not so bad," she seems to be saying. But it looks bad. It all looks bad. It's like the diner all over again. Dishes shattering, shouts, explosions as laser pulses hit, the deep hum-thrum of laser rifles charging after each discharge, and the louder resounding *bangs* of real guns. The red liquid of a spilled glass of juice seeps along the black-and-white tiled floor. The green-gold of circuits scatter across the puddle, leaving tracks leading under the refrigerator. The scents of burned flesh and ozone lie heavy on a tongue already bitter with my own fear.

Gus yells out in anguish.

Before I understand what I'm doing, I slap my wrist and leap to my feet. In an instant the antique revolver is in my armor-clad hand, and the world is slowing again. I see the laser pulses rotating in lazy arcs in the air, can see the heat waves spinning away like ripples in water, resounding against the silver threads stretching from me to them to everything else in the world—the ties that bind us. The ties I can see and feel and manipulate like a spider weaves her silken threads.

There are five Damascus Knights, two at the front, two behind, and one coming through the back door. Frankie is shattered, his carapace split wide and his innards spitting ominous black smoke and sparks. Gus is caught in a backward somersault. The gelatinous wreck of sound waves caught in reverberation against his chest tells me that he's been hit. Behind him, Morden's face is turned partway to him, arms outstretched and face contorted with alarm.

My brain makes a few simple calculations. The threads move, slipping along limbs and tipping the odds. My thumb releases the safety. I take aim at my first target and brace myself.

The world speeds up.

I squeeze the trigger. *Bam.* Recoil. My recoil tugs a thread, knocking the arm of the nearest Knight so that his shot hits the wall to my left, showering my back with chunks of tile.

The chamber rotates as I pivot to avoid the tile while also shifting the threads so that they knock another Knight's arm backward as he takes aim at Morden. *Bam.* Recoil.

The Reaper appears.

Shink, shink. Two quick strokes and the two Knights shatter and disappear, leaving rotating jewels spinning in the air. Jump stones. My spoils.

A shot comes my way. I leap backward, calling on the threads to aid me, and land on the counter with a huff. The shot goes through the bottom cabinet of the island in the kitchen, making wood splinter and snap. I brace my feet wide and shoot blindly, trusting my instincts to guide my aim. *Bam.*

Shink.

A laser pulse flashes, hitting me hard on the hip, knocking me to the floor, but I feel no pain. I roll, yanking all the threads, dragging the remaining Knights down with me, tangling them together in a tight little cocoon. My prey. Little black bugs in my web. I roll up onto one knee, take aim one last time. *Bam. Shink. Bam. Shink.*

The Reaper disappears.

The threads recede.

I draw a breath and blink.

Sounds return. Spitting sparks, a fire alarm screaming, a groan of pain.

"Gus." I tumble forward, dropping the revolver and dismissing the armor. Morden's already at his side, yanking off Gus's helmet. I punch his wrist, dismissing the armor so I can see where he's been shot. His eyes are wild and dazed as my hands grasp at his chest, searching and desperate. I shove up his shirt, run my hands along his stomach.

"I-I'm okay," he grunts. "I'm okay. The armor absorbed it."

It takes another moment for my brain to calculate his words, to realize that I see no burn wound. I throw myself at him, wrapping him in shaking arms and sobbing into his neck. "I thought you were dead," I wail.

He puts his arms around me, holding me. "I'm okay. I'm okay," he keeps saying.

"Holy Hell, *they* aren't, though," Morden breathes. "I've never seen anything like that."

I look up, smiling despite my tears because I'm so glad that no one is dead, but when I see Morden's expression, my face falls. There's fear in his eyes. Fear and awe and respect. I straighten and look around the room. There's a fine layer of silken fiber everywhere, draped over the furniture and around our bodies and smoldering over Frankie's exposed innards.

When I realize what I've done, I sit down hard and stare in wonder.

"How'd you do that?" Morden whispers, his voice an accusing hiss.

I shake my head. "I-I don't know."

Gus grunts as he sits up. His dark eyes survey the damage. "Along came a spider," he muses, turning his bright gaze on me.

chapter thirty

POST-AMERICAN DATE: 2/22/232

LONGITUDINAL TIMESTAMP: 2:02 P.M.

LOCATION: FREE ZONE, NEO-NAPLES; NEXIS

"Right," Opus breathes as he struggles to keep the list from falling off the table. "So, this bit goes here."

We've moved on, gone to what seems to be an earlier period of human civilization. I think it's mostly Roman, but the upright walking, talking black-and-white striped horses who wear powdered wigs and colonial clothing, are throwing me off. Hundreds of paper squares—representatives of the squares on the quilt—are spread out around us with the small numbers that Nadine wrote on them facing up.

"And this one here?" Nadine asks, her face uncertain as she leans over Opus and puts her square on top of his. She's good as new, nothing a little healing potion and some rest couldn't cure.

"Yes," I say, standing on a chair among the paper quilt pieces. "Now, piece 356 goes on top of that. Who has that piece?"

Everyone looks around them, searching. Guster bends down and holds it up. "Here."

"78?"

"Got it." Morden doesn't meet my eyes as he comes forward and puts the piece on the stack. He hasn't looked me in the eyes since what happened in the kitchen.

Two hours later, the list is complete. All of the squares have been stacked in ascending order, looking like a fine obelisk in the center of the table.

"We should have stayed in Discoland," Morden mutters into his goblet. "We could have gotten Frankie to do this for us."

Nadine throws herself into a chair with a huff and airs herself with a feathered fan. "Frankie, if you remember dear Mord, was blown to bitty smithereens by the Damascus Knights."

"Oh yeah, I forgot about that," Morden says lightly. "Must have been too busy fighting for my life."

Nadine flashes a false smile. "Don't you mean too busy hiding behind Ella?"

As Nadine and Mord devolve into a fight about his manhood, Gus's eyes search over the rim of his goblet and find mine, their expression meaningful, and I look down at my hands.

We've jumped four times since Discoland. Each time the Knights have found us. Each time it seems I emerge the victor. It's always the silken threads. Yet I can't seem to figure out how I am able to manipulate them or even what they really are. I'd spend more time trying to puzzle out my strange, almost magical talent, but we have greater problems. The Knights' attacks are becoming more frequent, more frantic, and each time, the numbers are greater. They're following us, more deft and efficient than the mechanical hands of a sorting machine. The time between landing on a new gaming level and them finding us seems to be shrinking exponentially. It's only a matter of hours before we'll be attacked again. We all know it, and it's frightening.

Gus sets down the goblet and crosses his arms over the back of the chair he has his foot planted on. "Well," he says, his voice bringing everyone back on task, "we have our onion. Now we must peel it and inspect the layers."

"Excellent," Opus mutters. "Since we're talking about food, why don't you go get us some? Meanwhile the rest of us can abandon ship before another batch of Knights comes along."

"You're not helping anything," Nadine says, scowling. She signals the waitress, a young filly with bright pink hair, to the table.

Gus turns to me as Nadine begins to order. "We've got to examine the squares on the quilt and try to find a level we recognize—"

"What do you mean you don't have meat?" Nadine exclaims.

Gus clears his throat. "If we can find a level we recognize, then we can move from there."

Nadine's voice cuts in again. "Vegetarian? What's that?"

This time Gus waits for the waitress to explain the dietary preferences in Neo-Naples. "Fine," Nadine grunts. "I'll have these oat things here."

Gus takes a breath. "As I was saying, now that we know the order of the levels we should be able to jump from one to the other."

"So, basically," Nadine adds, handing her menu to the waitress, "We now have stepping stones? If we can just get to one of the fields represented on the quilt then we'll be able to go straight to the Dominion?"

I blink at her. It always amazes me how she can manage to do two things at once. I make a mental note to ask her if she's like me. If she ever questions the occupation assigned to her by

Central Staffing. I'm sure she's a fine Developer, but I bet she'd be an even better Tasker. I reach out and pick up the first paper tile. Number 503, the Central Dominion. I turn to the quilt where we've laid out numbers that correspond to the tiles. The center square, with silver mountains embroidered with gold thread and crystal beads. "The number of tiles represented in this quilt are only a fraction of the existing levels in Nexis, right?"

"Yeah," Gus says.

I go to the table and pick up the tile that was just under 503. Tile 284. A green, triangular shape with a black infinity sign over it. "So, that would mean this one here is the last stepping stone before the Dominion, right? And the one after that…" I go back to the table and pick up the next tile. 45. "Is the second to last." I take it to the quilt and find the corresponding quilt square. This quilt square is cut into quarters, black-and-white, respectively, with a small golden crown on one of the white quarters.

"Makes sense," Opus concedes.

"Okay," I say. "So if each of these quilt squares has some kind of clue indicating what level it is, then all we have to do is find a level that matches a square. That will give us a jump point to advance from."

"But we don't know where *here* is in relation to any of those tiles. There could be a hundred fields between each of those tiles," Morden reminds. "Plus, I don't know about you, but I don't know the names of half the places I've been to let alone those I haven't."

I slump back in my chair, making Morden jump. "We're in a bind."

"It's not so bad," Morden says, smiling for the first time in a long while. "Remember that time we tried playing Twister? Now *that* was a bind."

We all start laughing.

part four:

ELLA'S WORLDS COLLIDE

chapter thirty-one

For a long moment, all I can do is stare at Meems. She stares back at me, her blue eyes too large and bulging without the protection of her synthetic skin.

"W-What happened to your chasis?" I demand, incredulous.

Meems looks down as if seeing herself for the first time. Then she shakes her head and moves into the room, her domestic uniform hanging limp without supple synthetic skin and muscle to fill it out. As she comes forward, I can hear the whine of the motorized actuators and pistons in her legs; can see the fragmented movements of each segment of her body as it works to keep her upright; can feel the heat of her power cell; can smell the hydraulic fluid, grease, and oil in her joints; can see the glint of her internal processors and mechanical parts beneath the white plastic panels of her standard body.

I follow her with my eyes as she walks toward the bed and begins making it like she does every day at this time.

"You got out of bed on your own this morning," she notes.

While her jaw moves, her wide-open mouth looks garish and frightening without the facial and dental features of her chasis. She has no lips or cheeks, no teeth or tongue. She's like a chattering skull with glass eyes and no teeth.

Still confused and horrified by what I'm seeing, I swallow hard. "Yeah, I guess all those exercises you've been insisting I do are actually paying off." Now that I'm getting enough food to actually build muscle.

The bare mechanics on each side of her face move, a gear swirling on each side and a number of attachments hinging upward. I can't tell what expression they are meant to be making without her face over them. I hope it's a smile. "I told you they would be beneficial. You must keep yourself strong so that your body will take to your new legs when you get them."

I ignore her. While Meems has hope that I will one day get legs, I know that I'm trapped forever. In this body. In this room. I've accepted it. "Meems," I breathe, barely able to keep my skin from crawling away and leaving me looking like a biological copy of her. "What happened? Where's your chasis?"

"I have given it up," she answers simply. Too simply, her mechanical voice is there again. The one without emotion.

I crunch my eyebrows. "But you'd never willingly give up your chasis. That's who you are."

Her shoulders flex upward, with a *tzzt, tzzt* sound, and she tips her head to one side, the stainless steel bones of her spine clicking. I swallow hard and try not to grimace. Like this, I'm barely able to recognize Meems as the same being I've always known. No wonder we started putting encasements on our robots. Not only do they shield the sound, but they really help to maintain the illusion of some semblance of humanity. As she is now, she's nothing but an animated skeleton with a clockwork face and an internal processor.

My fists ball in my lap. "Why'd you give up your chasis?" I demand, my grotesque horror turning now to abject anger at having to endure her in this state. This is not the Meems I know. This is not my surrogate mother.

Straightening from the now-made bed, she crosses her arms over the plastic shield of her chest. Her pistons hiss, and her fingers move in ways that remind me of spiders as she clasps her elbow joints. "I gave it to Katrina."

For a moment I don't speak. I'm not entirely sure that I heard her correctly. "Katrina?" I repeat, my voice choked.

"Katrina," she assures.

"What for?"

"For you."

I can't help urging the hover-chair closer to Meems, compelled by her gentle tone of voice. "Me?"

She nods. "To pay for prosthetics. My chasis is older, but it is a custom model, so the materials that went into its design are far superior to most available. They are still worth many credits."

I don't understand. And yet I do. Tears fill my eyes, and I cover my mouth with my hands. "Oh, Meems," I whisper through my fingers. "You didn't need to do that."

"I wanted to. It is my choice. My body for your legs."

I want to argue with her, want to tell her that she's not allowed to make her own choices—that I technically own her, and I don't condone what she's done. I can't live with knowing she sacrificed everything that made her who she was so that I could walk among the living once more. But I will—because I respect that Meems wants to make her own decisions. More than her chasis, her independence and self-sacrifice maintain her own impression of her humanity. I bite my lips to keep them from trembling, but the tears start anyway, slow and hot.

"Katrina says that she will order the prosthetics this afternoon, and I can help attach them tomorrow."

I nod, not trusting myself to look at or speak to her. News of my finally getting legs should make me happy, but I only feel like I've lost another piece of myself.

chapter thirty-two

"How about this one?" I point at the picture of a middle-aged man with a bulbous nose and no front teeth.

Gus looks at him and wrinkles his nose. "That guy is small-time. We want a big one. Like this." He points at a picture that has been on the board for what looks like eternity. "Five thousand gold crowns to anyone who kills Glockmock the Terrible."

"Glockmock the Terrible?" I repeat with a scoff. "What kind of 'strikes fear into the hearts of many' name is that?"

"Come on, Elle, you should know by now that nothing is what it seems here. Remember the gummy bears?"

I grimace at the reminder. "That was a misnomer."

"Well, let's hope that Glockmock the Terrible is, too." Gus unpins the wanted poster from the bounty board and hops off the step, sending up a cloud of dust. "It doesn't matter what he's called, just that he is the most valuable kill."

I step down and join him in the street. "There's probably a

reason he's valuable. Like maybe the fact that he might not be easy to kill, for one."

He turns and heads toward the sheriff's office. "Well, you're the one who insisted we get our money the legitimate way."

I roll my eyes at his back as I trudge after him. "Killing an outlaw wasn't what I had in mind."

He climbs the steps. "It's the fastest and easiest way to get a lot of cash fast. Well, next to prostitution, but you didn't want to share," he says with a grin. "So, here we are."

I put my hands on my hips, stubborn. "I'm not joking, Gus. We could all get killed. We're not bounty hunters. We can't do this kind of stuff."

He turns and puts his back against the door. "Sure you can. How many Damascus Knights have you killed by now? You're great with a gun. I've seen you do it. Just do your spidey thing and tie him up for us, okay?"

I scowl at him, but he just gives me a kissy face and leans against the door, opening it with his weight. I follow him in. "Look, we don't have to put our lives in danger just for money."

"Yes, we do. We're out of jump stones, remember?"

"But," I reason, "I have a jump stone in my pocket."

Guster turns on his toe, making me nearly collide with his chest. He grasps my jaw in both hands, expression angry. "Don't you dare, Elle. Don't even think about it."

I slump my shoulders. "But—"

"But nothing," he says, forcing himself to calm down by lowering his hands to my shoulders. "That stone is ours. Yours and mine and we're not using it until the end of the journey. It means something. It's important."

I lower my eyes, feeling guilty that I even suggested it. The stone I carry in my pocket isn't just a jump stone. It's a promise, and using it would be breaking that promise. "I'm sorry."

"Look," he breathes, pulling me against him and pressing his mouth against my hair, "I know you're scared, but we'll get through this. Together. We always have, and we always will. You and I are an amazing team, right?"

Smiling, I nod, knowing he's right. Gus and I? We're invincible.

Gus puts the poster down on the table between Opus, Morden, and Nadine. Nadine's eyes scan the paper and then lift to Gus's, two deep pools of calculation. "What's this?"

Slapping his hand against the pitted yellow parchment, Opus gets to his feet. "Foolishness is what this is."

Gus doesn't seem to hear either of them. "He's been ravaging the countryside, killing cattle, burning farmhouses. He's a menace."

Morden doesn't take his eyes off a pewter plate filled with mushy gray-green vegetables. "So," he says, his voice soft and his expression hidden under his lanky blond hair. "We're on to performing public services. Tricksters to philanthropists?"

Gus shrugs and glances at me, looking for support. For a moment, I remain stubbornly silent. He already knows I feel the same as the others do. But his pleading expression makes me drop my shoulders with a sigh. We are, after all, partners (in more than just crime) and he's relying on me to back him up. He knows that the others value my opinion. He may be the leader, but I've become the brains and voice of logic. "We're out of jump stones," I reason, trying not to look guilty about the one in my pocket. "And if we can't make quick money to jump out of this level, the Knights will find us."

"So what if they do?" Morden demands. "We'll just fight them like always."

"You mean, Ella will fight them," Opus says. "You practically jump behind her at the first sign of trouble. Luckily she's a nice girl, saving your sorry rear after how badly you treated her the first time."

Morden has the good graces to blush. "I-I do not."

"Yes you do, you big baby," Nadine scolds.

I look down at my feet. "I could fight," I reason. "But this wouldn't be like all the other times. The other times I fought and we ran. We can't do that now. Once the Knights find us we'll be stuck in an endless loop of fight with no flight and no advancement to our cause." I shake my head. "That's no way to conduct a quest. It's bad enough that we've been traveling for months and we still can't seem to find an identifiable square. Without that square we'll never be able to orient ourselves on the freedom quilt."

Gus sits at the table and puts his hands out before him, examining them. "It would be good to know we can do *something* right." He seems to say this more to himself than to any of us.

Nadine picks up the sheet of parchment and holds it in front of her face. "Is that why you picked this, Gus? You're trying to prove yourself?"

Opus makes a strange noise in his throat, something between a grunt and a scoff, and smiles. "Prove himself? To who? What's to prove to any of us?"

I step closer to Gus and splay my hand over his, covering his callused palm with mine. When he looks up, I see my answer. Only himself. He needs to know he can do this, because he's starting to lose faith. He's starting to question what he's doing. I give his hand a reassuring squeeze. "This is Nexis, Gus. You can do anything you want."

He squeezes back. "That's why I'm doing it." He lifts his chin and meets the eyes of everyone in the party. "I'm fighting monsters here because I can't fight them there…and I want to. More than anything, I want to fight the monsters."

chapter thirty-three

POST-AMERICAN DATE: 6/21/232

LONGITUDINAL TIMESTAMP: 5:07 P.M.

LOCATION: DOME 5: EVANESCENCE

I command the door to open and urge the hover-chair out onto the landing. I haven't left my father's workroom in months, and it seems like I'm entering an entirely different world. Sights and sounds that should be familiar to me—the whir of the air scrubbers, the harshness of the LED lights, the low hum of Tasha working beneath the house—somehow seem foreign to me. I feel like a stranger, an interloper in my own home.

Through the big nano-window at the end of the landing I can see all of Evanescence sprawled out beneath the dome, her Aristocrats nestled in the protective bowl of her walls. It's late afternoon; the nano-panes mounted to the dome reflect a digital sunset. Red and orange bathe the high silver-white spires of the city, washing out the holographic gardens and the communal projectors airing The Broadcast, and making every window in the city reflect the sky. Pods of all shapes and sizes zip over the hover-ways that slip over and between the buildings like glowing aerial ribbons. The hover-station looms overhead, casting a black square of shadow over the lower reaches of the city. But that's fine; hardly anyone walks on the ground. The ground is for the service vehicles and robots. Aristocrats don't look down, they look up and ahead. That way they don't see who, and what, they're trampling on their way to the top.

But I see. I'm like Dad's spiders. I sit in my tiny nest, shoved into a corner and forgotten. I see up and out. I see down. I see beyond the wall. I see what was, and I dream about what could be. A legless creature with one foot in the past, one foot in the present, and one foot in a reality that doesn't exist.

I turn away from the window and direct the hover-chair toward the stairwell leading down into the main living area of our residential block. My shadow descends the stairwell before me, investigating the deep ominous reaches where the glowing white orbs of the LED lights don't cast their light. I can hear Sadie in my old room, babbling over the vis-com unit. And as I pass the doorway I can see her fussing with her newly Altered hair as she talks; apparently she can't get the Primper to execute a program that will make her golden highlights stand up straight enough.

I descend down to the common area and take a long hard look at what once used to be my home. It isn't my home anymore. Katrina has completely redecorated. Everything is far more opulent than it used to be, and there is no hint of the home that used to belong to my mother and father. The holos in the frames and alcoves—once gardens and fruits and family— are gone, replaced with replicas of modern art. Odd twisting statues—like live things caught in a disposal unit—and angular, hideous pictures that seem nothing but swaths of primary color and irregular shapes rise up around me as I guide the chair through the hall.

The comfortable upholstered furniture and soft carpeting

have been replaced with the hard bowl-like lines of plastic chairs, chrome end tables, synthetic stone floors. I recognize the Designer. Cassel. Expensive.

The voice on The Broadcast draws my attention, and I stop my advancement to watch. "It has been exactly one year since control and further development of Nexis was transferred over to you after the untimely deaths of your brother and niece. Can you tell me about the improvements you've been making?" On screen Zane is sitting forward, his expression intent. Across from him sits Uncle Simon, Bastian beside him. My heart starts beating hard, pulsing in my throat.

"Well," Uncle Simon begins to say, "I can't possibly fill Warren's shoes. But I can say that Bastian, the team, and I have been working hard, and we have something special planned for all of you very soon."

Zane grins. "I'm excited to see it."

Uncle Simon smiles. "As am I."

Zane's face grows somber. "Can you share with us what you're feeling right now? Do you feel like Warren would approve of your new developments?"

Uncle Simon sits back, exchanges a glance with Bastian— who looks uncomfortable as always. "I hope so. If he were alive, I would hope he'd be able to see and approve of my vision."

"And what about Ellani?" I perk up, giddy that Zane is still thinking about me. "If she had survived, what would you say to her right now?"

A slow smile creeps onto Uncle Simon's face, and he looks straight at the hovering camera. "That I am proud of her. That life hasn't been easy for her, but I'm proud of her for fighting on."

Tears burn at my eyes. It's so good to see him, to hear his voice.

Zane says, "You talk as if she's still alive."

Bastian's eyes cut at Zane, and he scowls. But Uncle Simon doesn't seem phased. "I like to think that she is."

I blink at the screen. Bastian's glare has shifted to Uncle Simon, but Zane just looks on, expectant. Uncle Simon explains himself. "I think of both of them often, you know? So, in that way, they aren't really dead, right? They're right here, right now. Watching us."

Yes. Yes, I'm watching.

Zane says, "Are you talking about ghosts, Mr. Drexel?"

Uncle Simon laughs. "Of course. Of course."

Zane begins to say something else, but the sound of glass shattering behind me sends me spinning the hover-chair around to face a wide-eyed, more hideous than ever, Katrina.

For a moment, the only sign of life between us is the automated housecleaning unit as it whispers out of its storage niche and begins to pick up Katrina's dropped glass of whatever she had been drinking before seeing me.

As soon as she manages to collect herself, she scowls. "What are you doing out of your room?"

I swallow at her icy tone. Part of me wants to gloat that I have bypassed her efforts to imprison and kill me, but another part of me is now terrified of her. I hardly know her, yet she has become like a storybook villain to my fractured psyche. But that just makes her even more like the monster I need to fight. I take a deep breath, think of Gus, let it out. "I-I came to talk to you."

She scrunches up one nostril as if perhaps she suddenly smells something foul, though I know it can't be me; Meems bathed me this morning. I try not to take offense. "It's about Meems."

Katrina rolls her eyes and turns away from me, heading back toward the newly remodeled kitchen. She pauses before bare, nano-glass counters and stainless steel panels and runs her hand down Tasha's main screen. "What do you think of this, Ellani? I thought we needed more counter space."

I flex my jaw, frustrated that she's ignoring my reason for being here, but I try to be civil. "Dad used to say there was no point in even having counters, since Tasha prepares all our food internally. He said that in this day and age, we didn't even need a kitchen," I say. Invoking the memory of my father within these walls seems to make the house mine again. Then I add, "Just a dining room. A place where a family can eat...together." I can't help the bitterness in my voice. Bitterness at his loss, bitterness that this woman who volunteered to care for me has opted to cut me out of her life.

She sighs as she steps close to one of the stainless steel panels and admires her reflection. "Yes, but they're so pretty," she whines as she pokes at her face, examining. "Do you think I'm getting wrinkles?"

Now it's my turn to roll my eyes. None of what she has done to this house is pretty. It's like she has sucked the soul right out of it.

"Momma." Sadie screams. The word cuts deep. Sadie calls her Momma. She's more than just a guardian to one girl who is not hers, but she's evil to me. Why? Why was I rejected?

She steps forward. "What?" she squawks back.

"This forsaken Primper is just making it worse. I want a better one."

"Fine. Order a new one." Katrina smiles to herself and shakes her head as she glances back down at me. "She's preparing for tomorrow's Senior Banquet."

Senior Banquet...a final rite of passage. If this were the life I should have, I'd be designing a dress to outdo all my previous dresses. Perhaps I'd be making it to match Zane's suit, because that would be where our engagement was announced. And then I would graduate from Paramount, be a Programmer, maybe work beside my father and my uncle and Bastian.

But I'm not doing any of those things. Because I'm not going to Senior Banquet. I'm not moving forward with everyone else, I'm staying behind. Legless, unwanted. Useless. No, not useless. Fight, Ella.

I clear my throat, put my head back into the game. "You're letting her get a new Primper?" With *my* credits, no doubt.

"Sure," Katrina says, turning away. One of the gold-plated panels flashes, indicating that it's responding to some internal command she has just given it. "I let her have whatever she wants." A moment later another panel slides back, and a tray with another glass of champagne slides out. Katrina picks it up, sips it, and then with a moan closes her eyes and smiles to herself. "Mmm. Vintage Perrier-Jouët. They say only about a hundred bottles survived the war. Did you know that?"

"But Primpers are expensive," I reason. "And I just passed the dressing room; there's nothing wrong with the Primper we have. In fact, it's not even the same one I remember."

She rests one hand in the crook of her arm and nurses her glass. "It's not. We've had two since that model. Have to keep up with the latest."

I blink at her. "Two?" That's enough for one prosthetic leg. Add in the new pod she bought Sadie and I could have skipped the prosthetics and gone right to having another pair grown for me. My frustration deepens, making me bolder. "I thought we were having credit problems."

She lifts her hand and waves it in the air, the pot-lights making her fiber-optic inlays glitter. "That's just something I told Meems to make her leave me alone."

"So you're using up all my wealth, not even bothering to feed me in the process?" I wonder, silently making a note of how

Katrina doesn't seem to have protruding cheekbones or ribs like a certain yours truly. While I've reprogrammed Tasha to feed me properly, I haven't regained the weight.

Slowly, Katrina straightens and cuts her eyes down at me. When she speaks, her words are tight and clipped, like she's searching for a reserve of patience while holding back a scream. "How dare you accuse me of cruelty and theft, Ellani Drexel. Be thankful you're even alive." She turns, braces her hand against the wall, and visibly takes a number of breaths.

"Now," she says, turning back to me with a false smile. "What did you say you came down here for? In fact, I distinctly remember Tasha being programmed not to let you come down here." She turns, looking intently at Tasha's main screen.

"I came about Meems," I remind her, trying to derail her from looking into Tasha's protocol. The last thing I need is for Katrina to discover that I've hacked Tasha. Not once, but twice. The second hack is a recent thing. I had to unlock my door. Which is something that I'm going to go right back to my room and restore before Meems finds out I did it. I hate that I had to break my promise to her, that I did another illegal thing, but this is for her.

"What about her?" Katrina demands, agitated. "She's downstairs at the docking station—recharging like she always is at this time." She flashes a dark grin and chuckles to herself. "Don't you even know what time it is? Did that accident fry your brain that bad?"

Self-consciously, I touch the scar on my forehead, thinking about my malfunctioning G-Chip. I take a deep breath, trying to steel myself against her words. "Katrina, where's her chasis? I know you haven't sold it yet because my legs aren't here," I reason. And then I cut my eyes at her. "Or did you conveniently forget why she gave it to you?" I don't hide my sarcastic, bitter tone. "Did all those Mods fry *your* brain that bad?"

She whips around, splashing the floor with half the contents of her glass, and charges me. *Clack-clack-clack* go her shoes, up comes her hand. I wince and lift my hands. But she stops herself mid-swing, hovers there. I peek between my fingers, meet her eyes. She's shaking, looks like she's surprised by herself. She takes a few deep breaths, lowers her hands and smoothes out her dress. "Watch what you say to me, young lady," she growls. "You have no right to speak to me like that. In fact," she says with a breathy little exhale. "You have no rights at all, so I'd be more careful if I were you."

The words I've wanted to say to Katrina for the past few months bubble up into my throat, but I swallow them down. I didn't come here to get myself thrown out on the street or sold to a Doll House. I need to stay here so that I can still access Dad's files, be with Meems, and go into the game. Yes, she's why I'm down here. I can't leave her alone with these horrible people; they'd probably sell her for scrap metal.

I ball my fists, take a deep breath, and hold it till the count of ten. "Look," I huff. "I didn't come down here to pick a fight. I just want to know if you're going to do what you told Meems you were going to do."

Katrina purses her lips and lifts her already half-empty glass. "I don't know what she thinks I'm going to do."

"Okay," I say, trying to keep myself from screaming. My shoulders feel so tight I could pop. "She gave you her chasis so that you could buy me prosthetic legs. If you're not going to do that, at least give her back her chasis. Please."

Katrina stares at me for a long moment, her face blank. "Meems and I never agreed that the chasis would go to your legs. Meems simply came to me, said that she understood that we were having some financial issues, and offered to provide her chasis to help pay the bills. She asked that it go to help you, and I agreed. She never said anything about your legs."

I frown, confused. Perhaps Meems had just assumed that the only logical use for credits allocated to help me would go toward the only obvious need that I had. "What did you use the credits for?"

Katrina shrugs. "I don't know."

"You don't know?" I repeat, shocked.

She lifts her hand and runs her fingers through her hair. "I'm not the one doing the selling, Ellani."

For a moment, I think she's joking. But her face is serious. So is her tone. Confused, I say, "But, I-I don't understand. She gave the chasis to you, didn't she?"

Smiling bitterly, she stares down at the cleaning unit as it again cleans up her mess. "You really don't know, do you?" She crosses her arms, as if holding herself against a cool breeze. "Well, why would you? They say you're a genius, but honestly, I just don't see it. Do you even know who I am?"

I stare at her for a long moment, too confused even to breathe.

"Your father and I, we were engaged to be married once."

I open my mouth, stunned, and for a moment I can't speak. "What?"

"Before *her*." She says "her" like the word is poisonous, spitting on it and mentally stomping all over it. Her eyes go wistful. "Before Cleo, Warren and I were engaged. It was a good match, and we liked each other. Loved each other, even. He called me beautiful, used to love the way I'd Alter and Modify myself, said no one was more beautiful." She draws a sharp breath and her voice goes dark. "But then *Cleo* came along. I'm sure I don't need to tell you what happened from there."

No, she doesn't. Dad once told me that the chemistry

between him and Mom was almost instant, that she'd come into his world and completely unraveled him. I assume it was much like how it is with Gus and me. They were married just days after meeting. It must have devastated Katrina. It must have been a social scandal—to break an arranged marriage like that. How embarrassing it must have been.

"One day he was there by my side and the next he was gone. I moved on, of course. Became a guardian for the city, took in Sadie, but I never stopped loving him." She laughs to herself, shaking her head. "When Cleo died, I thought that he'd finally realize that he'd always loved me more, but when I came back to him, he was distant and cold. No matter what I did to try to catch his eye. He only ever saw you. You, a Natural abomination that looks so much like *her*. It hurt."

I swallow, uncertain how to interpret what's going on, unsure if I should turn and run from the knife-like quality of her voice. Is she going to lose control, try to hit me again? She's already keeping me prisoner, trying to starve me; it doesn't seem like such a far-flung idea to take to beating me—the spitting image of a woman she loathes. But should I even believe her?

She turns away. "He never stopped loving her. He worshipped you as if you were a relic, his only remaining connection to her. And now he's gone," she breathes, her voice false and light. "And here you are. Her spawn with her face and all his love, living in what should have been my house with all the credits that should be mine. And now you're down here making demands of me." She turns and flashes me a slightly manic grin. "Honestly, Ellani, you're lucky I haven't choked you in your sleep."

For a horrifying moment, I just stare at her, wide-eyed. I'm too afraid to even breathe.

She turns away. "But killing you would cut off my paychecks.

And I'm not that stupid."

I blink at her. "Paychecks?" Why does she need the tiny city-issued checks for guardians when she has my entire fortune to spend?

Katrina turns and smiles at me, all mockery. "Stupid, stupid, Ellani. If you were anyone else, I'd feel bad for you. I'd feel bad about what they are doing to you, I'd stand up for you, try to help you. In the beginning I fought with myself. I'd think about this situation and say to myself, 'She's just an orphaned little girl, scared and alone.' But then I'd look at you on Tasha's screen and I'd just see *her*, writhing. And it made me laugh." A little giggle escapes her. "So maybe that makes me a little cruel, huh? But it's not like I'm the one doing it to you. I'm just taking glee in it. And theft? Well, we both know who the real thief is, don't we? And isn't it poetic justice? That you suffer for their sins? In many ways, it's not even cruel of me to relish your pain."

Her frigid hatred of my mother and her crazed grin send needles in my spine. I fight not to tremble, not to run away from the maniacal pleasure she gets out of my pain. I think past the surface of her words. She's not the one who is causing all this, she's just allowing it to go on, because she's a sadist. I knit my brow. "Who? Who is it that is keeping me here? Who pays you?"

Katrina opens her mouth, but we're both interrupted by a shrill squeak of dismay. I look up to see Sadie standing at the top of the stairs, fists planted on her hips. "Oh my sparks, Momma. What's *she* doing down here?" she demands, her expression very similar to one Nadine once had when a small rodent went running over her bare foot.

"I-I'm just-" I stammer.

Sadie ignores me and turns pleading eyes on her "mother." "Momma," she whines in her high-pitched voice. "Bastian will be here any moment. She can't be down here. I'll be ruined."

"I know, baby," Katrina says, holding out her hands, placating. "She was just leaving." She looks down at me, her expression snake-like. "Weren't you?"

"Bastian?" I squeak. "My Bastian?"

"Ugh," Sadie breathes. "He's not yours. He's mine."

Katrina sucks in a long breath. "Of course he is. Bastian Drexel is not *your* Bastian, Ellani. You're dead—therefore nothing is yours anymore. He's Sadie's fiancé now; you should congratulate her."

Head reeling, I stare at the still-scowling Sadie. Before I can think, I say, "Can I see him?"

"No, you can't see him," Sadie howls. "Momma," she practically screams. She's near tears now, and I don't really understand why.

Katrina holds up her hands. "Okay, okay. She's going upstairs. Aren't you?" She doesn't wait for me to respond. Instead she lurches forward and grabs the back of the hover-chair. She must have hit the manual override button on the back of the chair because, as much as I mentally slam on the brakes, the chair continues to skim back down the hall and up the stairs, Katrina behind me.

On the landing, Katrina releases the chair and it continues on its own, back into my room, then spins and faces the door. Katrina is standing in the doorway, arms crossed and frowning at me. "I know you're some kind of gifted Programmer. I know you let yourself out, and you'll somehow manage to do it again. How you managed to bypass your G-Chip, I don't know, but I don't recommend you do it again. I'll be watching you more closely now. If I see anything strange in Tasha's history, if I see any messages coming in or going out, if I see you outside of this room, I swear I'll report you, and they will not be merciful with you. People who can do what you do are a security risk, not worth keeping around, if you get my meaning. If you wish to live, you'll do as you're told. Is that clear?"

Stiff, I nod.

"Good."

Once the door slides shut between us, I let the shakes overtake me. And then I cry. And when I'm done crying I sit and think for a long, hard time. When Meems comes in to bring me dinner, I don't look at her. I've gotten into the habit of avoiding her face. It hurts to see someone I love walk around scarred and broken because of me. Especially since it seems her sacrifice was entirely in vain. Seeing that I don't want to talk, she leaves me with my untouched food.

When the alarm for Nexis goes off, I don't go in. Gus and the others are expecting me; we're going to go forward with our mission to capture and collect a bounty on Glockmock the Terrible, but I can't go. While that mission is calling me, I have a bigger, more important one here.

Unsent Letters to Delia

Dee,

I need your help, your strength. I feel like I'm in a dark place again. Confused and lost. Who is keeping me here and why? It's clear to me that Katrina isn't the one in charge here. Someone is pulling her strings— like the ones I use in Nexis. She's an awful person, but perhaps not evil. Not if she loves Sadie as much as she does. Yet her hatred of Mom and Dad blind her, make her complacent in my captivity and mistreatment. What do I do about it? And what about Meems?

I wish you were here. I need your big, beautiful brain to help me work through this puzzle like you've always helped me see clearly in the past. I hope things are well with you… Sadie is marrying Bastian, which means that I guess you're not. She's prepping for Senior Banquet, which means you are, too. I hope you have a beautiful-enough outfit. I would have designed yours for you—you need a special outfit for a night like that. I wonder who you're going to be announced to… Perhaps you've stolen a suitor right out from under Carsai. Hmm… stealing…yes, that might be it. I can still be Robin Hood. Oh, Dee, I knew you'd help me!

—Ella

I t isn't hard to find Meems's chasis. With the combination of the G-Chip and the Main Frame working together to glean exactly what you're looking for, Internetwork shopping is incredibly easy. Hacking Katrina's credit account isn't as easy, but it's certainly not as difficult as one might think it would be.

Part of me feels bad for Katrina and her history with my father. But the logical part of me says that none of Katrina's bitter feelings are my fault, thus I shouldn't have to suffer because Dad jilted her. The other part of me feels guilty because I promised Meems I wouldn't do any more illegal hacking and here I am, two hacks in one day. But this is a good cause.

"Now," I whisper to myself, "how to pull it off." I have access to the credits, and I know where the chasis is, but *how* do I make the purchase without it being obvious I've stolen from Katrina? I mean, I'm not really stealing; these credits are truly mine. Right? But still, the amount of credit in her account is nowhere near what I assumed it would be. So maybe she's right? Maybe she's just being paid, and she doesn't see any of my inheritance credits. There's no way I can take from her account without her realizing it.

And, if she notices the theft, she'll know it was me. Besides the fact that I have skill and motive, she can see exactly what I'm doing if she looks into Tasha's systems. Plus, if Meems suddenly has her chasis returned, that would be a dead giveaway.

I lean back in the chair. I could easily steal from the rich to help the poor like Robin Hood, but at what price? I remember what Gus told me. Assess the situation, look at who is being hurt and who is gaining. Meems and I are both gaining. Katrina will not suffer horribly. But what happens if Katrina does find out? I think about what would happen if I did get arrested for hacking. I've never heard of a trial where someone managed to bypass their G-Chip. So they are either dealt with without a trial, or it's so rare a thing that I'm the first person in history to experience this, and the significance of that is not lost on me. Either way, the resulting outcome doesn't look promising. I'd end up far worse than my current handicapped prisoner state. I have to keep myself safe, for Dad's sake.

I look up at the screen, my eyes tracing the scarlet numbers displaying Katrina's credit balance. With a blink, I close out of the account. A moment later, I pull up the account that Dad once put my allowance in. I don't have many credits. While I had been saving up for a Day-I-Turn-Eighteen-Mod, I never did save all that much. I always spent a good amount of my weekly allowance on the clothes that I once loved so much and now can't even wear. All those credits spent on frivolity, and I only wore some of those outfits once. Some not at all. "Such a waste," I breathe.

I look up at my account again, an idea blooming in my mind. "Maybe not."

Fifteen minutes later, Tasha pings into my mind. *"Inventory of Ellani Drexel's wardrobe complete."*

I sit up and mentally command her. *"Sell it."*

"Please repeat command."

I roll my eyes at the ceiling. *"Put the entirety of the inventory up for auction on the Internetwork."*

"Request acknowledged."

I sit back and wait. I consider it a gift from some benevolent superior being that Katrina hasn't sold all my belongings yet.

Within the first ten minutes, the first bid blips up on the screen. It's a fair sum, but not enough. I reject it. Three more bids, each higher than the next. I reject those. Then the fifth bid. Twice as high as the last, and exactly what I need.

"Done." I accept the bid and listen as the entirety of my wardrobe, carefully packed into a large shipping container by Tasha and her sub-unit minions, drops out of the lower storage deck, slams onto a shipping belt, and disappears behind the heavy doors of a pressure tube. A moment later, the container begins its journey through the vast robot-run network that, from the ground up, rules everything in Evanescence.

A moment later, the digits on the screen change, my credit account reflecting the new deposit. I stare at the numbers. Such a large sum. Enough to buy myself new legs. Enough to buy back Meems's chasis.

But not enough to do both.

I could have legs. If I had legs I could run away. I could meet up with Gus, here in Evanescence, as the girl he knows and loves, and live with him forever.

I glance at the adjacent screen, the one displaying the hollowed-out shell of the one mother I've ever known. She's being sold by a third-party dispenser; there's no way of knowing if the seller is Katrina or someone else, or if she's even changed hands since initially being sold. *Assess the benefactors and the victims.* Giving one last longing glance toward the outside world, I mentally press the purchase button under the chasis and watch the credit numbers run back down.

I have sold the clothes off my back to save the skin of another. I did it without lying, cheating, stealing, or tricking. I did it simply, by letting go of my Aristocratic frivolity, by accepting who and what I am. My father would be proud of me.

I am proud of me. "My name is Ellani Drexel," I whisper in the dark-light of my father's workroom. "I am, and always will be, a Natural." I grin to myself. "I can't step on anyone if I have no legs to stand on."

chapter thirty-four

POST-AMERICAN DATE: 6/22/232

LONGITUDINAL TIMESTAMP: 1:18 P.M.

LOCATION: FREE ZONE, FIEF OF LAU; NEXIS

As I materialize in the common room, Gus glances up from a tankard of cider. "Elle," he breathes. He's on his feet and coming toward me before I can even get my bearings. His arms are around me and his lips on mine in the next instant.

When he's satisfied that he has given a warm enough welcome, he releases my lips and presses his forehead against mine, holding me close.

"Hey," I say.

"You didn't make the last jump," he says, his voice a condemnation, yet there is a waver in it that lets me know he was worried.

I put my hands on his chest and urge him away, enough that I can look into his eyes without straining my neck. "I'm sorry. I had some complications back home."

The skin around his mouth pinches as something stormy darkens his eyes. "What's wrong?" His voice is deep and defensive, a sign of his protective nature. "Are you okay?"

I smile at him and kiss his neck, which is bare and available in the new outfit he has picked for himself. It's some kind of rough woven shirt that hangs loosely from his shoulders and laces across his chest, revealing more bare skin than the mandarin collars we've been wearing since Chinatown. "Nothing," I say into his skin. "It's fixed. Thanks for waiting for me."

He touches my cheek. "We wouldn't get far without you. *I* wouldn't get far without you."

I turn away, shy.

His arm tightens around me, and his fingers curl around my neck. "Are you sure you're okay? If you're in trouble in Real World, I'll help you."

I wrap my arms around his waist, wishing that I could take him up on that offer. But it's more dangerous than ever for him now. "Yeah." I bury my face against his shoulder, hold him close. "I just…had to take care of my android."

I feel his head cock against mine. "Android?"

A little laugh escapes me. "You sound surprised."

He's quiet for a long time. "What was wrong with it?"

"Her," I correct. "Meems. She's my nanny droid, or was; I guess I'm too old for that now, but she's family. At least to me she is." I pause, realizing I sound stupid. "I know that sounds odd. She's just a robot, after all. But Meems is special. It's like she's human. You know?"

"I do know, actually," he whispers. "I've got one like that at home." He laughs into my hair, a rough chuckle, releases his hold on me, then takes a step backward and looks into my eyes. "It's amazing how we've managed to blur the lines between man and machine. I mean, just look at us." He holds out his hand, indicating the room.

I glance around with him. "Speaking of, where is everyone?"

"Opus is in town. Nadine and Morden went up to the fort to talk with King Lau."

"King Lau?"

"He's the ruling body of this playing field. Hence the name, Fief of Lau. Nadine thinks he'll be able to give us a pin on Glockmock the Terrible." He reaches down and picks up his tankard. I watch him take a swig and place it back down. "I'm glad you came back. I was…" He pauses, looking for the right word. "Worried." His face reveals just how worried.

I reach out and ease the frown line out of his cheek. "I wouldn't just leave you, Gus."

He stares at the floor. "I know. It's just…sometimes I realize how fragile this reality is. The idea of never seeing you again…" He touches his stomach and I understand what he means. I feel that nausea, too.

Eager to change the subject, I cant my head to one side, taking in all of him. He's wearing tight brown breeches that emphasize the musculature in his legs. I'm anxious to see what he looks like from behind. "I like that outfit."

He glances down at himself and smirks absently. Then something dawns on him. "Oh, I got something for you."

I lift my brows, curious.

He shrugs. "Well, I needed something to do while I waited for you to come back into the game." He turns away, showing just how good his butt looks in his tight new pants, and begins digging in his sack. He draws out a big package wrapped in brown paper and gut string and hands it to me.

It rumples in my hand. Whatever is inside is soft and formless. "What is it?"

"Open it," he urges.

I untie the string, letting it fall to the wooden floorboards, and unwrap the paper. As I pull away the sheets of paper, Gus takes them from me and places them on the table beside his cider. As he takes the last piece from my fingers, billowing green fabric tumbles to the floor, revealing a beautiful crushed-satin gown with gold trim.

"Oh," I breathe, unable to say anything else.

"Do you like it?" He sounds anxious.

"I love it." I lift big eyes to him, trying to focus through the tears. "It's for me?"

He scoffs. "Of course it's for you."

"But we have no money. How did you afford it?"

He shrugs. "I did some manual labor for the guy at the general store. Too bad the man at the magic shop wasn't as keen on the offer, otherwise I'd have gotten a jump stone, too. Will you put it on?"

Eager to try on the beautiful outfit, I nod, my curls bouncing around my face.

He steps forward and takes my face in his hands, kissing me once more. I melt into his lips, savoring the taste and feel of him. It seems like a thousand years have passed since I've seen him and even longer since we've had a few precious moments to ourselves. He pulls me away, gently. "Good," he says with a nod. He turns me by my shoulders and gives me a playful shove toward the stairwell at the back of the common room. "Go put it on."

Washed and dressed in a gown that proves Gus has every curve of my body memorized, I go back downstairs. The rest of the crew is there, sitting at the table with Gus, talking in hushed voices though the only other person in the room is the serving girl sitting on a stool in the corner. As much as I'm happy to see everyone, my heart sinks at not being able to have more time alone with Gus.

I tiptoe toward the table and stand near a broad wooden column supporting the upstairs dining area. The fire in the squat hearth is warm on my back, making me linger in the shadows, though Gus notices my approach immediately. It's like he has radar. He lifts his eyes and stares at me, his expression moving to one of pleasure at the sight of me.

I bite my lip to keep from grinning as I reach down and hold my skirt out in a silent gesture of questioning. I turn, letting him see the way the dress laces up the back and hugs my hips and backside, then I toss my hair to one side, letting him see how the portrait neckline displays my throat and shoulders.

When I turn back to see what he thinks, he's smirking at me, flirtatious promise in his eyes.

Noticing that he's no longer paying attention to the conversation, heads slowly raise and turn in the direction of his very obvious gaze. I feel myself blush, knowing that the others are privy to this silent conversation between us.

Nadine stands abruptly, upsetting her chair, and rockets toward me. "Ella," she screeches, and throws her arms around me. "You're okay. We thought you died or something."

I pat her back. "Okay, Nadine, you're choking me," I wheeze.

Releasing me, she steps back and gives me a light cuff on the arm. "Don't do that again. You scared the nanos out of me."

I give her a reassuring smile, and we head back toward the table. Opus moves over, making room for me on the bench so that I can sit between him and Guster. Nadine goes back to her place beside Morden who says, "We were just talking about what King Lau said."

Nadine sits forward, her chest heaving against a baby blue

dress that is similar but not as fine as mine. "He says Glockmock the Terrible lives up on the mountain, but he's likely to come down soon because he hasn't eaten in quite some time."

"Eaten?" I ask.

Opus scoffs. "Glockmock is a dragon, Ella. Do you know what a dragon is?"

I purse my lips. "It sounds familiar," I muse. "But, no. I don't think so."

"Ha," he barks, his face breaking into a toothy grin. "The Spider Child doesn't even know what she's fighting."

Morden rolls his green eyes. "Leave it alone, old man, none of us do."

"I looked it up," Nadine says quietly. We all turn to her. "When I went home last time, I looked it up. It's a mythical fire-breathing lizard."

"Say that again?" Gus chokes out.

"A lizard."

"No, that bit about breathing fire?"

Nadine nods, her ruddy braids brushing her freckled forehead. "In the myths, dragons were massive lizards. The size of houses. They can fly and they have teeth and nails the size of droid-blades. And they breathe fire. They used to kidnap fair maidens, and princes used to have to fight them on quests." She looks up and grins, her blue eyes bright, and lets out a breathy little giggle. "You know, like the one we're on."

"What's his weakness?" Opus demands.

Nadine knits her brows. "Nothing really. It's supposed to be covered in an impenetrable armor of scales."

Morden plants his elbows on the table and puts his face in his hands. "Circuits," he mumbles, running his hands through his hair. "How are we gonna fight something like that?"

I glance at Gus who looks at me in the same instant. I can

feel the eyes of everyone else on me, expectant. "I-I don't know if the threads will work on something like that." As much as I feel their eyes, I feel their disappointment. "But it has to have some weakness," I say, trying to sound hopeful. "Maybe a weakness under the joints?"

Gus nods, though he looks a little distracted.

"Well," Nadine adds, "I read something about this one dragon, Smaug. This Tolkien guy wrote that this dragon had one weak spot in its scales. He claims that this one man, Bard, shot a black arrow into it after a thrush told him about it. But, none of us know how to use a black arrow, do we? And I don't even know what a thrush is."

The others continue talking, theorizing on how best to defeat the dragon when it finally does appear over the small town. I try my best to add to the conversation, but Gus's silence weighs on me. I need to get him alone so that I can talk to him and see what's bothering him.

When the conversation eventually devolves into Morden teasing Nadine and Opus reverting back to his grumbly old man self, Gus puts his hand on mine underneath the table. "Can you guys excuse us for a little while?"

Nadine and Morden exchange a meaningful glance, and Opus rolls his eyes. "Yeah, sure, go on," he growls. "We'll save the world without you."

Gus doesn't humor him with a response. Instead, he grabs my hand and practically drags me down a side hall. He gets to the end of the hall, glances around, and then hustles me through a door. Inside, it's dim, the only light coming from a dirty window on the far side of the room.

"A supply closet?" I say, incredulous. Gus grabs me by the hips and presses me against the back of the door, kissing me once more.

I attempt to kiss him back, but I can't keep from giggling

so he takes to trailing kisses down my jaw and neck instead. I squirm under the onslaught. "Oh, honestly, Gus. Did you miss me that bad?"

He looks up then, his face serious. "Yes," he growls. "I *did* miss you." He has his hands planted to either side of my head, the muscles of his body coiled under the rough gray fabric of his shirt. All at once, I'm struck all over again by how utterly powerful and beautiful Gus is, both mind and body. I have revelations like this on a daily basis, and they still amaze me.

I reach out and touch his jaw. "You're so serious today. What's wrong?"

He shifts his weight to one arm and takes the other away from the door, running his knuckles along my temple. "It felt like eternity waiting and not knowing if you were ever coming back."

I lean in to his hand, nuzzling and kissing his palm. "Why would you suddenly think I'd leave you?"

He lets out a long sigh. "It's not that I think you'd leave me, Elle. It's just that…" He searches for the right words. "I'm afraid you'll be *taken* away from me." He shifts his feet so that he can free up both hands and cups my face in his gentle grasp, drinking in my eyes. "We take this for granted."

I smile at him. "I don't. This place is a gift. So are you. I know that."

His brow dips low, framing his eyes. "And what happens when the gift goes away? What happens if one of us is killed here and never able to get back to the other? What if something happens with the game?"

I shake my head. "Nothing's going to happen with the game."

"How do you know? And beyond the game? What happens if something happens to one of us in Real World?"

I reach out both hands and cup his face. "Stop this," I say, pulling him close. I can't bear to even think about what he's suggesting. I don't want this to end. I can't even entertain the thought. Katrina's threats clatter around in my mind, making me close my eyes in shame. If I had pushed any harder yesterday, if things had gone any differently... As a hacker, as a threat to societal order, I might have been killed. Gus would have never known. I need to be more careful. I lace my fingers through his hair, tug at him.

Understanding the cue, he steps in to me, a pleasant crowding of body and breath, and takes my lips once more. Gus kisses me with the desperation of a man who can't seem to suck enough air into his lungs, his body hot and demanding in a way that my body can't refuse. He reaches down and pulls me against him, his hands sliding down my back so he can grip my bottom and lift me up into his arms. I cling to him, letting him guide me to the preparation counter and lower me there so I can sit with him comfortably pressed between my legs.

His lips wander across my jaw, down my neck, over my shoulders, his fingers clutching against the neckline of my dress, trying to free up more flesh for his exploration. He growls into my neck. "Why did I buy this damn thing for you?"

I smile at the ceiling. "'Cause you wanted to see me in it?"

His fingers slide down my back, finding the lacings for my bodice. "Well, I've seen you in it." He breathes into my neck. "Now, I want to see you out of it."

I groan to myself and reach back, staying his fingers. "You know, Gus, it has never been a goal of mine to make love shoved against a shelf in a food storage closet."

He smiles against my bare shoulder, his teeth white on my tawny skin, and his eyes dart up to meet mine. "There's a first time for everything."

I stare down at him. "You planned this, didn't you?" I accuse.

His fingers slip from beneath mine, coming to rest on my

thighs, and he straightens, meeting my gaze. "To have some time alone with you? Yes. We haven't had a chance to be alone with each other in days and longer since we've made love. Is it a crime to make love to the woman I love?"

I close my eyes, savoring the feeling of his hands on me, of this moment with him, and that one magical word, "love."

"Though," he says, kissing me on the cheek, "I did bring you in here to talk, not to do this." One hand releases my thigh, and he uses it to smooth the fabric down my stomach. "You look so lovely in this dress. I knew you would."

I grasp his hand and pull it against my heart. "Thank you," I say, meaning it. Gus couldn't know that I've just given up all my lovely Real World dresses, doesn't know how much this means to me. "You're too good to me."

He smiles. "Anything for you." He kisses me again, reminding me that we have more pressing business.

A few moments later, there's a sudden pounding at the door. "Oy, love birds." It's Opus.

Gus growls into my mouth. He pulls his lips away from mine and glances at the door, but he doesn't release me. "What?" He doesn't bother to hide his annoyance.

"Dragon's been spotted circling the peak. Innkeeper's saying that means a hunt's in store. You want to go for a hunt, or are you gonna bow out for another week in favor of different sport?"

Gus lets out a long frustrated sigh and drops his head against my clavicle. "Well, when you put it that way, how could anyone refuse?" he mutters.

"You coming then?"

Gus lifts his head and rolls his eyes. "Not in the way I'd like, but yeah, I'm coming," he grumbles so low, Opus couldn't possibly hear, but then, it's not meant for his ears, anyway.

I giggle, enjoying the joke. He smirks at me, gives me one last kiss, and pulls away. I slide off the table, straighten my dress, and follow him out of the storage room.

Nadine and Morden are standing in the doorway, their eyes focused on the distant peaks that border the Fief to the east. I can see the dragon, even from this distance, an oblong dot blazing a black line across the sky.

"Is that its tail?" Morden asks.

Nadine steps back and squints. "I think it's smoke."

We all glance back at the dragon in an attempt to discern the deep black trail it leaves from the thicker body it heaves over the jagged icy peaks.

Something occurs to me. "Doesn't that image look kind of familiar?"

It takes a minute for someone else to see it. "Yeah, it does," Gus says.

"What?" Morden asks. "I don't get it."

"That figure eight pattern over the mountains." Gus gestures toward the dragon. "That's on the last square." A crazy grin breaks across his face. "One more jump and we're there."

Shocked silence overtakes us until, with a great belch of flame, the dragon bugles a thunderous call that sounds like the very last gasp of a dying animal. A shiver runs down my spine.

"Well," Gus says, his voice steely and determined. I glance back in time to see him hit the defensive mode button on his wrist. A split second later, he's covered head to toe in armor. His visor lifts with a small pneumatic hiss, and he grins at me. "Trickster versus lizard, round one. The hunt is on."

"Great." Opus throws his hands up in the air. "The whelp's off to kill himself. Boy, let me tell you, if I was a betting man, I'd wager all my worth on your inevitable loss."

Gus grins again, broader and more mischievous than ever. "Excellent. I'll hold you to it, old man." He stabs a finger into

Opus's chest, his voice dropping. "That jump stone you've been hiding from us. That's mine the moment that terrible dragon heaves its last breath. That's our ticket out of here."

For an instant, Opus just seems to sputter, his deep, aged eyes disbelieving. "What?" he finally manages. "How'd you know about that?" he demands.

Gus just steps back, wiggles his eyebrows, and motions to his eyes. "X-ray vision." He turns on the ball of his foot and disappears through the open door.

Questioning eyes turn to me. I smile and try to shrug it off in a "yeah well" kind of way as I engage my own defenses. Morden and Nadine follow, as if programmed to react to my lead.

Morden turns to Nadine and says, "I always did like barbecue."

Nadine gives him a frown. "It always kind of gave me indigestion."

We wait for Opus who, after muttering to himself about being too old for this sort of thing, armors up as well.

I watch Gus, Opus, Nadine, and Morden walk single file across the stable yard. The fox. The raven. The rabbit. The coyote.

"Along came a spider," I whisper.

Smiling, I step out the door and join them.

part five:

ELLA DANCES THE TARANTELLA

chapter thirty-five

The closer we get to Glockmock, the more pronounced his stench becomes. It's not just his smell—a briny putrid stink—but also the choking scent of things burning. Wood, hay, and flesh. A horse rushes by the vivacycle, screaming. I glance back at it as it charges past Nadine. There's a vicious gash in its flank, blood streaming across its rump and tail.

I glance up at Gus. "If this is the last quilt square then we can just leave now. We don't have to fight this thing." I yell, wanting to be heard over the dragon's trumpeting and the howling and screaming of man and animal.

"Yes, we do."

"No," I argue, amazed that he hasn't put two and two together yet. "If Opus has a jump stone we can jump right to the Dominion. We don't need the reward money."

"It's not about the money," Gus says, so low I can hardly hear him. "It's about doing what's right. These people need our help, Elle. We can do this; they can't."

I turn away and search the sky for Glockmock the Terrible. Overhead, the sky is choked with gray ash and black smoke, a thick ring of it tumbling forth from the head of the dragon as it hisses and lunges. It has landed now and even though we're still a bit of a distance away, I can see its shoulders and long neck above the trees. In an instant, its neck arches downward and its head comes into view. Everything about it is elongated and angular. Its head is a wedge adorned with blades of black spike, greenish scale, and yellow teeth that are taller than I am. When it opens its mouth and belches a storm of flames, they whip overhead, stealing the air and searing my lungs with sulfurous poison. I cough, despite the distance and my armor, surprised that the protective bubble around the vivacycle can withstand the toxic stuff.

Gus leans into the vivacycle and guides it under the thick canopy of a tree. I hear the others follow and kill their engines. We all gather in a cluster, protected by the trees, and survey the situation.

Glockmock is half perched on the collapsed roof of a barn; the only things holding up the building are the flaming supports. For a moment, the beast leans backward on his haunches as if taking a large breath. I can see its black underbelly glinting greenish in the firelight as it fills with air. Then it shoots forward, belching another spout of flames. A house goes up in an orange-white explosion. I can hear the people within howling in agony as they are instantly incinerated. The door bursts outward and a woman, her dress and hair alight, comes spilling out. Her frantic shrieks draw the monster's attention, and Glockmock lurches forward again, its massive claws crumbling the edge of the barn.

Its head darts into view, an arrowhead built from nightmares, and its powerful jaws snap down on the woman, silencing her cries and dousing the flames. When it draws back, the only thing remaining of the woman is half a bare leg and a slippered foot.

I feel Nadine's fingers digging into my arm. "I'm going to be sick."

Me too, I think. I glance at Gus. He's staring hard at Glock-mock, the dragon's fire gleaming in his predatory eyes. When the dragon moves, his eyes move with it. Following the monster's thick tail as it thrashes back and forth; upsetting carts and barrels; knocking children to the ground and smothering them under its weight; tracing the wings as they open, creaking like old leather and beating against the smoke and the fire, spreading it faster; raining ash upon the world. He flinches when the jaws snap, turns his head away when the fire becomes too hot to stare at, cowers only slightly when the dragon bugles in triumph, making the world tremble and deafening us all.

I take deep panicked breaths, trying to think through the ringing in my ears. I have no idea what to do with this thing. "What are you planning?" I demand, dread in my distant voice.

Gus glances down at me, his face hard and determined. "We're going to kill that thing if it's the last thing we do."

I turn away from him, take in the monster once more, and swallow. "How?"

I feel his hand land on my shoulder and give it a squeeze. "Like we always do. Together."

I bite my lip to keep it from trembling and nod. "Okay."

"We can do this. Just think about the consequences if we don't." With that he drops his hand from my shoulder and strides out from under the trees. The flames catch in the reflective material of his armor; the fox on his back seems to writhe in delight, dancing in its own fox fire.

If we don't kill this creature, who will? How long will it terrorize this playing field? He's right. We have to do this. I hold my breath and step out behind him. I can feel the others do the same. "Okay. Let's do this."

Gus stops in the clearing. He's about a hundred paces farther ahead than any of us, and it's him the dragon sees first. A massive clawed hand disengages itself from the smoking rubble of the barn, causing the rest of the structure to collapse with an implosion of creaking wood and sparks.

Woomph.

Talons open wide and the dragon's hand darts toward Gus, whistling as it comes. I scream, but Gus ducks and rolls leaving the creature to slap the earth with a rumble. Gus comes up on one knee and fires at the arm, taking a sizable chunk out of a spike. A small dribble of black blood oozes from the stump where the spike used to be. The dragon lets out a howl of annoyance and sweeps the arm forward, bowling Gus over.

My breath goes icy in my lungs. Chaos ensues. Someone shoots from the left. *Bang.* Then Opus's machine gun comes from the right. *Ratta-tat-a-tat.* The dragon is distracted, its body twitching one way and then the next as if trying to decide who to attack first. It rears back on its haunches and bellows, belching fire across the town square, sending another building up in flames. Gus gets up and runs to my left, shooting rapid-fire as he goes.

I can't move. The world did not slow. Gus was in danger, and the world did not slow. Everyone is in danger. I am in danger. The world is not slowing. There are no threads. I'm paralyzed, too terrified by what this means. There are no threads. I am alone.

Something in the distance whips forward. I see it, but my mind is moving too slowly to register. It hits me hard, knocking me onto my butt and pinning me down, dragging me through the mud and ash. Spikes crack into my armor, pierce my skin. I cry out because they sting worse than anything I've ever felt.

Someone yells my name. Bullets begin raining down on the

dragon's tail. It lifts the muscular thing and moves to swipe it at the one firing at it, but he ducks under it, careens into me, and knocks me into a roll before the tail can backlash at me. I know Gus's body above mine just by the feel, and I know he's putting himself in danger to keep me out of it.

Come on, Ella get in the game. He sits up to shoot once more, and I stumble away from him, holding my ribs because they still burn from the spikes, but needing to distance myself until I can get my bearings. I lean against a small outbuilding that, even among the terrible smells Glockmock is raising, still stinks of sewage. Morden is behind the dragon, firing up into its vital regions. Opus is in the trees, firing at his chest. Guster is expertly taking out row after row of spikes, making the dragon bleed and thrash in pain, but it doesn't seem like enough damage. I can't see Nadine, but every so often I can hear a fresh explosion of bullets rain upon the dragon's impenetrable flank. Useless.

The dragon is thrashing and gnashing, stomping on buildings and digging ravines into the earth, spouting flame and roaring into the smoke-filled afternoon. In the few seconds I watch, it knocks down Morden, one spike going deep into his thigh. He cries out in pain. Nadine screams. Gus shoots to cover him as he crab-walks backward into the relative cover of the forest and Nadine's arms. The tail thrashes out, slamming hard into the trees, breaking them, snapping them down upon my friends. I can hear Nadine and Morden crying out.

I call for the threads. Demand them to come. Plead with desperation, but I get nothing. I have to do this without them. I *can* do this without them. I hope. But what am I going to do? All this is useless. We're doing nothing but making the dragon even angrier.

Gus screams. Screams for me and for him and for everyone. He gives up ducking and rolling. Instead, he stands tall and proud, firing like a madman at one generalized spot, hoping he can break through.

The dragon goes relatively still, as if noticing what Gus is trying to do. The head arcs away from the trees where Morden and Nadine are trapped, and he turns a narrowed eye on Gus. In the moment that its dark, abysmal eye catches sight of Gus, I get an idea.

I run at it. And as I run the revolver manifests in my hand. I come up behind Gus who holds the monster's attention so well that even as its head advances forward, jaws opening wide to snap the man I love in half, it doesn't see me streaking toward it, doesn't see me lift my arms and take aim.

Bang.

For a moment, I think the world has gone slow motion—that the threads have finally come. But no. The dragon's eye explodes on impact, showering Gus and me with thick, gross-smelling fluid. The dragon screams in pain, and a white membrane wobbles over the wrecked mess of the eye but, before it can raise its head to escape, I shoot it again in the same spot.

Bang.

And again.

Bang.

I empty the barrel in rapid succession, not hearing or registering or caring. I just know I have to make the shots count because the threads aren't there. And I'm not losing. I can't die. Gus can't die. I can't lose what I have here. I refuse.

Someone grabs my arm. I flinch away and continue squeezing the trigger even though I have no more bullets.

"It's dead."

The words are far away, distant. I can hardly hear them over the thundering of my heart, of my own panicked yelling, of the memory of screams and bullets and dragon howls. It will not kill

Gus. It will not kill my friends. I've come too far to let this stupid dragon ruin my quest. Someone kicks my legs out from under me, and I land hard on the ground. Gus's body is on top of mine, wrestling the gun out of my hand, trapping my arms down. He slaps my wrist. The armor goes, the revolver goes. There's only us and the blood and the tears I didn't know I was crying.

Gus touches my face. "He's dead, Elle. He's dead. It's okay. We're okay."

I'm shaking even with his body holding mine. Sobbing. Scared. My wide, panicked eyes jerk back and forth, searching. I find the beast's head just beyond Gus's concerned face, its yellow brain and black blood oozing out of the empty hole that had once been its eye and dribbling down its cheek. The Reaper appears.

Shink.

He's dead. I killed Glockmock the Terrible without the threads. I let out a nervous breath of relief and then I roll over onto my stomach and throw up.

chapter thirty-six

POST-AMERICAN DATE: 6/23/232

LONGITUDINAL TIMESTAMP: 2:37 P.M.

LOCATION: FREE ZONE, CENTRAL DOMINION; NEXIS

Just as the Damascus Knights leap at us, we disintegrate. As we reappear, huffing and sweating on the jump pad in the Central Dominion, we all collapse with a collective sigh.

I bend over, gasping for breath and trying to calm my slamming heart. "That was too close."

Nadine says, "Let's not stay to collect the reward next time."

"Oh, but it's so worth it," Morden says breathlessly, giggling to himself. "We're friggin' rich."

I lift my eyes and look at Gus. He coughs out a laugh and shakes his head. "You tired of running yet?" he asks.

I scoff. "Yeah, I'm getting there."

He stands up and looks around. "I vote that when we're done we spend all that reward money on an early retirement. I'm done questing."

"Amen to that." Opus mutters. "After this, I'm going off on my own."

Opus's bold declaration hangs in the air for a long, tense

minute before Nadine forces a smile and says, "You don't mean that."

"I do," Opus says flatly. "I'm done with all of you. Especially him." He points into Gus's face. "All he does is lead us into unnecessary danger. And for what? His own ego. I'm done."

Gus's expression remains stoic. He doesn't say a word, just turns and prowls away from the platform. Morden steps after him, but I hold out a hand. "Give him a minute."

"That was unnecessary," Nadine growls.

"I only said what we're all thinking," Opus hisses.

I cross my arms. "I wasn't thinking it."

Opus's snarling expression turns on me. "You're just as bad as he is. You enable him by humoring his fancies when you're supposed to be the voice of reason, supposed to be sousing out the danger to us. It's you who will really lead us all to our deaths, Ellani, mark my words."

His comment is like a slap in the face. "That's not true." I glance at Nadine and Morden. "Is it?"

Both avoid my eyes, but Morden is brave enough to say, "You can be very blind when it comes to Guster, Ella." Then he quickly adds, "Not that I blame you." He touches Nadine's arm. "I understand."

"Oh," I say, voice tight. "Well. It's good to know how everyone feels." I try to force myself not to feel their judgment, but it's hard. I had always assumed we were all on equal ground, all loved and accepted one another. "Why did you follow us then?"

Nadine steps forward and takes my hand. "Because this is your quest, Ella." I look into her eyes, confused. Smiling, she nods. "And we trust you to keep us safe."

I slump my shoulders. That's such a heavy responsibility.

Morden steps in front of me and pokes his face in mine. "You okay? You ain't gonna start bawling like a woman, are you?"

I lower my hand, balling it into a fist, and frown at him. "No, I'm not. But I might punch you."

He grins at me. "Yeah, you're gonna be okay." He crosses his arms and glances over to where Gus has slumped down beside a wide open expanse of concrete. "Better go lick your man's wounds."

I roll my eyes. "He just needs some time to collect himself." I know Gus well enough by now to give him space when he needs it.

"Well, we don't have that kind of time, so don't wait too long." Morden turns away. "So, we're here. Now what?"

"I don't know," Opus says. "I'm not sure where to look for the Chamber."

"If I had a treasure," Nadine says, sitting down on the edge of the platform. "I'd put it in the most secure place possible."

I nod. "So instead of running from the Knights we're going to look for them. Is that it?"

"Excellent," Opus muses. "It's an excellent day to die."

"We won't die," Nadine says. "Ella will use her threads to get us through and save us all."

My stomach drops, and I give her an uneasy expression. "Nadine, I wouldn't count on that. I don't even know how to control it." And I can't count on it. It has already failed me once.

She shrugs. "I believe in you."

Sighing, I turn away from all of them and head off toward Gus.

As I draw closer I see that he's sitting, legs dangling, on the edge of a long overhang. Down below is a massive city. The towers are thin thrusting fingers that break an ominous black sky with silver gilding. Below, pods zip along in midair without the aid of hover-ways, and people walk through glass tubes. They look like Aristocrats, all Modified and Altered and Primped.

They even wear the same Neo-Baroque style of clothing. But the city is not like Evanescence. There is no dome here, and a wall is built around the building in the center of the city, not around the city as a whole. In lieu of a security wall, the city has a massive body of glinting black water that stretches in every direction.

"Wow, this place is crazy," I whisper.

Gus looks over his shoulder and forces a smile.

I try to return the smile. "Hey."

"Hey."

"Can I sit?"

He turns back to the city and nods. As I sit down and edge closer to the opening, he says, "So, this is what humanity would have looked like had it not destroyed itself."

I cock my head. "Is it?"

"I've seen pictures of futuristic cities. Those buildings have that same look to them."

I glance down at the people again. "A different city, but the people are exactly the same." Why would Dad make the center of his game this place? Why not an ideal Utopia like what he would have wanted? A model of a city as a "good" humanity might have made it?

"People don't change, Elle. The places we live might, but we're fundamentally always the same destructive force we've always been."

I think about that for a moment. "Utopia on the outside, an implosive, self-destructive entity on the inside. It's not an onion at all; this game is the earth as it should have been. This is the molten core, Hell."

Gus tips his head. "You think they're as bad as that?"

I frown. "No, probably not. I mean, I guess I'm just trying to find answers where there aren't any."

After a moment of silence, Gus says, "Hey Elle?"

"Yeah?"

"This might end badly."

I lift my hand and feign interest in my cuticles. "I know."

"We might not live through this."

I close my eyes and nod.

"I want to see you," he says in a rush. "Outside. At home."

I bite my lip to keep from smiling. I want to see him, too. I want to be with Gus here and there. But then I realize that here is not like there. Our entire world is different, made restrictive by Aristocratic rules. Even if I see Gus in Real World, there's no guarantee that we could be together. In fact, I know we can't. I drop my hand to my knee and squeeze the flesh there. In Real World, these legs don't exist. *I* don't exist. I have no rights, I have no freedom. I couldn't see him if I wanted to; I'm still a prisoner. Gus doesn't deserve that kind of disappointment. And frankly, neither do I.

I take a deep rattling breath. "No." One word. It feels like a death sentence. I refuse to open my eyes. I can't see his face.

"Is-Is there someone else?"

I shake my head. "No, Gus. Nobody but you. Only you…" *Ever.* "I just…I can't. We can't." *Stop with the words.* "No. The answer is no."

I hear his exhale, can almost taste the argumentative air that overcomes him, but he doesn't speak. He just stares at me, hard and long. I can feel his disappointment, as thick and choking as dragon's breath clogging the air. Eventually, he gets to his feet. "If that's what you want," he says. "Then you can have it. You can have anything you want…even if it's not within reason."

I bite the inside of my lip, determined not to cry.

He steps away from me, as if the distance might heal the wound. "We'd better go. The Knights will catch up soon and we're already going to be dealing with enough of those when we get to where we are heading."

I chance a glance at him. His face is implacable. "Where's that?"

He points in the direction of the wall around the tallest building in the middle of the city.

A grimace fights its way across my face. "How did I know you were going to say that?"

"How are we going to get there?" Opus demands.

I spin around. I hadn't noticed he and the others had come to stand behind us. I feel my cheeks warm and hope that they weren't there to hear me turn Gus down.

Disappointment temporarily sidetracked by a new challenge, Gus's eyes light up and he points into a corner where a number of pods like the ones outside are parked in a small lot. "Who's up for a little flying?"

I shake my head. "Oh no."

He playfully pouts, letting me know that he's willing to forgive me for not wanting to see him outside of the game. "Why not?"

"It's stealing." I say, but he's already walking toward the nearest pod.

"It's not stealing, it's borrowing," he reasons. "Besides, this is why I'm here. At times like this, you need a good thief."

Gus parks the pod in an alley just underneath one of the glass walkways. Above, the Aristocrats are too busy with their daily frivolities to notice five airsick Naturals creep out onto the street. One of them catches my eye, making me pause. It's Quentin Cyr, lovely as always, but nothing compared to my Gus. He's with Carsai Sheldon. They're kissing. I guess she found her cheat code.

"Good for you," I whisper to her.

"That's disgusting," I hear Gus say beside me. He's staring up at them, his eyes and mouth pinched tight in disgust and anger.

"I'm going to vomit."

I smirk at him. "It's what she wanted from the game," I reason.

He turns that expression on me, and for a long moment I see something wrestling inside him. He turns away. "Doesn't make it right."

Confused, I follow after him. Why does he care what Carsai gets in the game? Maybe he knows her. It would make sense—they're both Elite.

We crouch beneath a couple of metal storage containers for a long time, waiting for our stomachs to settle from Gus's badly executed flight into the city.

"Next time, I drive," Morden grumbles.

Gus shrugs. "Give me some credit, that wasn't bad for my first time."

"Would you two shut up, you're gonna get us caught," Opus hisses.

We begin watching the road and the flow of foot traffic. After the sixth person has walked by, I draw back. "Have you noticed that the only people on the streets are all wearing those blue uniforms?"

Gus nods.

"What are those?" Nadine asks.

"Looks like some kind of service uniform? Maybe those are workers?" Opus offers.

Gus and I glance at each other and both say "androids" at the same time.

He grins and looks down the road. "If this is modeled after home, that would mean that everything on the ground level is robotic. Which means these people passing us aren't people but androids in service uniforms."

"Right," I add. "So does that mean you're thinking disguise?"

He nods. "That's exactly what I mean."

We trail in single file, Gus in the lead, then me, then Morden, Nadine, and Opus. The uniforms are stiff and smell of machine oil, but that only helps to mask our identities.

"Mord," I hear Nadine whisper behind me. "I don't think robots swagger like that."

"I don't think they look as pretty as you, either," Morden replies.

Nadine giggles.

Gus turns. "Can you take this seriously, please?"

Morden harrumphs. "I can't take anybody seriously, 'specially you with that stupid pair of goggles on."

Gus reaches up and pushes the goggles up onto his forehead, his eyes revealing just how annoyed he is. "Shut up or I'll shoot you."

Morden doesn't say anything.

"He sure showed you," I hear Opus say.

Morden maintains his silence.

We keep walking along the wall. High above us, Knights are stationed at regular intervals, looking hauntingly similar to the security droids back home. Except here, there's no G-Chip to tell one not to shoot me. In fact, I'm fairly certain they *want* to shoot me. These things hold a grudge. Gus and I killed a few measly Knights, and they are dead set on revenge. Why else would they have followed us across the whole of Nexis?

We keep walking, stiff and jerky, looking for a door. We go around once, twice. Gus's pace begins to slow, uncertain.

He lowers his head and speaks so low that only I can hear him. "There's no way in. What should we do?"

I lower my own head. "I don't know."

"Try digging a hole?" Morden suggests from behind. Apparently he can hear us.

I can almost imagine Gus rolling his eyes behind those idiotic goggles, but he doesn't humor Morden with an answer. He just glances at the wall. "There has to be some way in," he whispers.

I wrack my brain, trying to think of ways to open doors. I've learned of many here in Nexis. Keys, pads with special codes, secret words. "Maybe it's pressure or heat sensitive? Like the storage closets at home?"

Gus shifts his head, his gaze going to the wall just a foot to our left. "You think?"

I wince, my nerves on edge. "Well, it can't be as simple as 'Open Sesame,' can it? Try?"

Biting his lip, Gus reaches out. His fingers skim the blank wall, brushing a rivet. And then the sirens go off, a loud keening whine that refuses to die or take a breath. The noise is accompanied by a flashing white strobe light that seems to emanate from the very sky.

"Oops," Gus whispers.

It's as though the Knights were just waiting for us to make a wrong move. They pour out of every alley, every street and crevice, appearing in windows and on top of rooftops, spilling out like a biblical plague and surrounding the entire circumference of the wall. We back up against the wall and hold our breath, but they don't fire on us. They seem frozen in some kind of defensive position.

"Don't move. No one move," Gus whispers.

"What do we do?" Nadine whispers.

To my far right I see Opus throw up his hands. "Dag nab it, you bunch of brats, this is not how I wanted to die," he yells. Almost as soon as he speaks, the shots come. A hundred laser strikes that fry him to black and brittle.

For a moment, I can't see. I can only smell the putrid stink of burned flesh and ether, can only hear Nadine's surprised yelp and the distinct *shink* of The Reaper. I blink, trying to orient myself, trying to see so that I might fight or flee, but no one fires on us again. When I can see, I refuse to look, though a massive soot mark haunts the area at the corner of my eye.

There's a second flash that seems to reflect back at the Knights, through the cracks of the crevices in the road and up the wall. The Knights lift their hands, shielding their eyes as familiar strands of code explode forth. Numbers, letters, and symbols seep from under the wall and cascade across everything like a ghostly holographic projection.

Behind me, the steel bulkhead grows hot against my back. And then it moves. An inch at first, making me jump, and then it suddenly buckles inward with a hiss.

The earth bucks, and we all tumble backward. Backward and down a long incline, head over heels, grabbing out and calling for one another in the darkness. And then we hit bottom. I hear Morden's groan of pain first, then Nadine's soft grunts as she struggles to get to her feet.

Gus's fingers find my shaking hand. "You okay?"

"No," I whimper, my throat tight with oncoming hysterics. "They killed him."

He drags me to my feet and wraps his arms around me. "I know," he whispers into my hair. There's something raw in his voice, a tenderness that lets me know that he feels Opus's death as keenly as I do. "But," he says, raising his voice so the others can hear him, "it's just a game. Don't forget that he's not really dead, he's just not playing with us anymore."

"Which means he might as well be dead to us," Morden retorts, voice angry.

"Just think of it like he just moved far away," Gus says. "He was going to leave us anyway." When he's met with silence he adds, "Look, you can't let this get you down. They're trying to demoralize us. But we can't fall apart now. We've come too far. We can still win."

Biting my lip to keep it from trembling, I blink tears out of my eyes and step away, forcing the pain of loss back into a corner of my mind. "He's right."

Nadine's voice says, "You're enabling again."

I close my mouth and frown. "Just because I happen to truly agree doesn't mean I'm enabling. I want to get out of here as much as you do. And I want to win. That's why we're here, isn't it? That's why Opus just died."

For a long moment, no one speaks. Then Morden says, "Where in the blue blazes are we anyway? Does someone have a light?"

"Yeah, I—" I begin, but Gus stays my hand.

"No, not yet," he says.

"What?"

He tugs my arm. "Let's get a little bit away from here."

Still aware of Nadine and Morden judging my acceptance of everything Gus says without question, I confront him, because it makes no sense to stumble around in the darkness. "Why?"

Gus lowers his voice, barbing it in a way that tells me he's aware of my sudden self-consciousness, and it annoys him. "Because what's left of Opus's body didn't disappear when The Reaper appeared. And I'm pretty sure he fell down here with us. I don't want to see it, do you?"

I shake my head, ashamed for even doubting him. I trust Gus. He's smart, and he'd never do anything to harm me or his friends. That's why I accept what he says so easily. There's nothing wrong with that.

I knit my brows, though I know he can't see me. "How will

we keep from getting separated?" And nearly as soon as I say it, I feel the threads. I can sense the three threads trailing away from my body, one to Gus, one to my left, and another behind me. I let out a long exhale, grateful. "The threads are here," I whisper, my relief obvious in my tone. "Nadine, take three steps to your right. Morden, walk straight ahead; you should find each other."

I hear them bump into each other and Morden says, "Well hello, stranger."

"Good, now both of you come forward."

A moment later, a hand brushes my arm. I take it, feeling the delicate smoothness of Nadine's thin fingers. Taking a deep breath, I steady my own shaking nerves so that I can be strong. She said she had faith in me to get them out alive; I have to live up to her expectation. "Okay, let's go."

Gus at point, we walk forward. "Be careful where you step. The ground is uneven here."

I try blinking to adjust my eyes, but the darkness is absolute. It smells of deep earth and decay. The air tastes like something musty and cool. There's a claustrophobic closeness here, something that makes me feel that there are things standing close by. It's eerily silent, only the sound of our breathing and our feet scuffing along on the bare dirt. This place feels closed in, as if we're in a small box. "Where are we?"

"Inside," Gus says hesitantly. "I think."

"H-How'd we get in?" Nadine asks, her voice wavering for the first time since I've known her. She's scared. But of course she is, death does that. Real or not, she just lost a friend. We all did.

Morden sighs. "Opus. Did you see the way that code just came spilling out of his body? Almost as if The Reaper released it or something."

Without meaning it, my fingers tighten around Gus's hand. "I know that code," I say softly. "I wrote it myself."

No one responds to me. For a moment, I wonder if perhaps I didn't speak loud enough for anyone to hear. When I feel Gus's thumb gently stroke the back of my hand I know they've heard me, but no one knows what to say. What could they say? A moment later, his voice breaks the uncomfortable silence. "There's a wall."

As he leads us along the wall, I reach out and touch it. It's rough, cold, and damp. Grains from each block rub away on my fingers, and the cracked mortar in between crumbles at the touch. I can feel bare, hairy roots and dried bits of leaf. "It's a building?"

"Dunno," Gus says. "I feel an opening. Give me the light, it should be safe now."

I drop Nadine's hand and reach into the pocket of the utility overalls I'm wearing. I picked them for their deep pockets—a place to store the contents of the small pack I was wearing when we hastily escaped the Fief of Lau. I hand him the flashlight, and he snaps it on.

Half blinded, I look around. We're all bumped, bruised, and caked with dirt, but no one seems to be too badly hurt from our tumble. I can see little in the small circle of light encasing us. What I see is what I already know. Naked earth, ancient walls, complete entombing darkness.

Gus shines the light down the break in the wall. It reflects off another wall at the far end.

"A dead end?" Morden says. "Who'd bother building that?"

"No," I reply. "Look at the way the light doesn't reflect off that one side wall—there's a turn down there."

Nadine says, "Should we go down it?"

I glance at her. Eyes red and dark trails where her tears left muddy tracks down her pale face, she looks like the darkness has half possessed her. I bite my lip and look to Gus; he must have lost his goggles in the tumble, and there's a bloody gash over his eyebrow. He frowns and flashes the light around some more. There are more openings farther down and in the other direction.

He lets out a heavy, uncertain breath. "We'll have to go into one at some point."

Morden takes a step toward the opening. "Better now than never, right? I want as much distance between me and all those Knights as possible."

I reach out and take Nadine's hand once more. "You all right?"

She squeezes back. "Yeah, it's just a shock." She smiles, bitter. "Least he died being defiant and sassy. I'm sure he wouldn't have accepted it any other way. Still, he just went so…easy."

I turn my head away, not wanting her to see my uncertain expression. There's an unsaid accusation in her voice. Maybe it's really there, maybe it's imagined. I barely helped with the dragon, and I couldn't do anything to help Opus back at the wall; the threads didn't come. They're here now, but what about when I need them again? Will I let someone else die? Will I let them down again? I don't want her faith; it's too much of a burden.

Besides the lack of threads, the image of that code haunts me, making my fingers clench around Nadine's as if I could deny my role in Opus's strange fate. Why my code? What's it doing here? Maybe it's just a fluke—one project that somehow got tangled in with all of Dad's other projects. Still, every breath burns ominous, and my stomach feels sour.

I creep after Morden and Gus as they move down the long passage. It's the type of place where I feel creeping is warranted. We can see now, so I know there isn't anything standing close by, but it still feels like there is. "Anybody else have the feeling like we're being watched?"

I feel Nadine's body shift as she examines the darkness

behind us. "More like being followed."

"Try not to think about it," Gus says. There's uneasiness in his face and body. There's no crazy-as-a-fox smile on his face, and that worries me. The stakes are too high now to smile, even to grin, in challenge.

We move on, corridor after corridor, sometimes right, some-times left, sometimes backtracking when we hit a dead end. We go until my shoulders ache from the tension and my eyes burn with trying to see into the shadows. My skin itches and prickles, sensing touches and phantom breaths that don't exist.

When I hear a yelp out of Morden and he disappears as if the very earth has swallowed him, the shock makes both me and Nadine scream in fright. The shriek echoes far and wide, going on and on and on for what seems like forever.

A moment later, Nadine comes to her senses, runs past Gus, and skids to her knees at the mouth of a huge pit. "Mord?"

A grunt replies.

I get to my hands and knees beside her and motion for Gus to shine the flashlight down the pit. "Are you all right?"

He glances around and grimaces at the grinning skeleton of an unfortunate soul who found one of the spikes at the bottom. "Well, I'm better than that guy." He kicks at the shards of a shattered spike at his feet. "Good thing I've got buns of steel."

I let out a relieved chuckle as Gus kneels next to me. "Any ideas on how to get him out?"

I scratch my head, my dirt-caked fingernails finding all manner of tangles. "Rope?"

"That would work if I had my pack, but it's still tied to the vivacycle back in the Fief of Lau."

I chew my nail as Gus sweeps the flashlight around the pit, examining the edge and the respective drop.

"No handholds," he says. "Nothing to stand on."

A flash of silver lances across the shaft of light. "Wait," Nadine yelps, grabbing his hand and almost making him drop the flashlight. "What's that?" She swings his hand back around and focuses it on the fine line.

Gus's brows scrunch. "Is that…"

They trace the light back up the line, back over the edge of the pit and to me. It's wrapped around my wrist. "Thread," Nadine breathes, relieved.

An idea occurs to me then. Excited, I yell down to Morden. "Keep hold of the thread."

"Thread? What thread?" Morden begins running his hands along his body.

I scramble in the dirt, trying to grasp the fine thread of spider silk that leads from me to Morden.

"Oh," I hear him say. "That thread. Okay. Now what?"

When I've got it in hand, I stand and hand Gus an expanse of it. "Just hold on." Gus twines the thread around his arm, spins so that it's around his body, then braces himself as he slowly begins to back up. I help him, pulling as hard as I can, and Nadine scrambles forward and joins in. Together, we haul Morden back over the mouth of the pit.

When he's out he shakes feeling back into his arm, and Nadine fusses over him. "Man, that stuff's as fine as fishing line."

Gus begins raveling it into a tight little ball. "Yeah, but it's useful."

We bypass the pit by going down another passage and continue on.

chapter thirty-seven

POST-AMERICAN DATE: 6/24/232

LONGITUDINAL TIMESTAMP: 1:18 P.M.

LOCATION: FREE ZONE, CENTRAL DOMINION; NEXIS

When I materialize back in the Central Dominion, it's like being smothered. The dry mouth returns, the prickling of my skin makes me want to crawl out of my flesh, and the darkness is dizzying. For a moment, I can't breathe and when I finally can, it's a choking gasp of a breath.

Light appears as Gus materializes in front of me. He continues forward, step unbroken.

"Hang on," I croak.

He turns around and gives me a questioning look, his expression both asking why I want him to stop and wondering if I'm all right.

"I-I think I know what this is," I say, my voice laced with dread.

Nadine comes up beside me and puts her hand on my shoulder. "What?"

"I didn't think about it yesterday, but…" I pause, hating the thought. Knowing makes being here so much worse. "I think it's a labyrinth." Meems, after I explained it to her, thought as much, and all the signs point to it.

"Labyrinth?" Morden repeats. "What's that?"

Gus's grim face appears behind him. "It's not good."

Nadine says, "Not good how?"

"Like wander around until we die of thirst not good. A labyrinth is a maze, Nadine. A really big one." Gus turns away from us. "So big and confusing that people aren't meant to come out of them alive."

"Oh swell," Morden mutters. "I should have just impaled myself in that pit."

I roll my eyes. "There's got to be a way out."

"Yeah," Morden says. "Death."

Nadine suddenly bursts out crying. "I don't want to die here," she howls, her voice carrying through the labyrinth so that it echoes back. *Die here. Die here. Die here.*

I move forward and try to console her. "It's all right, Nadine. No one's going to die."

She shoves me away. "Opus is dead. He's gone, can't ever see us again." Her gaze flicks to Morden and back to me. "I can't be taken away from you. This is my life." She's backing away now, frantic and scared, shaking her head. Her outline is growing faint in the dark light. "We're all going to die. You brought us here to die."

To die. To die. To die. The walls mock.

Confused as to why I'm apparently the one she suddenly blames, I say, "What? Wait a second—"

"Just-just stay away from me." She turns and runs.

"Wait, Nadine." *Nadine. Nadine. Nadine.*

Gus grabs my hand. "Come on, we can't lose her." I shake my head, denying the hideous whispers of the cavern above. We run in the direction Nadine fled, Morden hot on our heels.

I follow her sobbing echoes and whimpers as she stumbles and scuffs about in the dark.

"Nadine!"

I hear something then, a noise that none of us could make. A deep primal braying noise that chain-echoes around the massive subterranean cavern like a steam locomotive.

I go still. "W-What was that?"

Gus shoves me forward, urging me to continue. "Not good. We have to find her."

I rush forward. "Nadine. Wait. Please." I call again, more frantic than ever. I strain to hear her.

But it's no good, I can't hear her anymore. Not over me and our rushed pursuit, not over the thing that's now awake and moving in the darkness. I reach out with numb fingers, trying to find her thread in the confusing tangle of Gus's and Morden's wrapped about my clammy skin. *There.* I yank at it and it glitters down a hall to the left.

Pursuit now renewed, I plummet after her. I continue running, pressing on and down corridors, searching, following the thread. I hear her sobbing again.

We're so close. I try to command the threads, to pull up more, to command the one in my hand to yank her back toward me. Nothing listens to me.

But the thing, whatever it is, is closer. I hear it grunting along, and then it bellows again.

She screams. A terrified, surprised exhalation that trails off into bursts of painful yelps and screeches and moans and pleas. Then it's just a long whine and then a whimper. The line grows slick in my hand. I refuse to look at the blood dripping down the line, turning the silver thread red.

It has her now, is traveling with her. She's still alive. Though by the distressed noise that Morden seems to be making at her crimson trail, not for long.

On and on we go, the thread never going slack, always yanking us, only a few turns behind Nadine's captor-killer. I can hear it grunting, breathing heavy. I feel its heavy footfalls *thump-thumping* against the hollow earth. When we are running down a parallel corridor to the one it's traversing, I can smell its fetid stink, like rotting flesh, can see its outline high above. Massive and tall, with a misshapen head and broad angular horns. My blood is ice and I'm covered in cold sweat. I have little hope for Nadine, but I have to try. She had faith in me. I let her down. *You led us all here to die.*

When the line finally goes slack, I slow, uncertain.

"It stopped," I whisper.

Morden steps forward and slaps his armor into place, holding up his gun. "Well, good. Let's kill the bastard." He charges forward.

Gus and I exchange glances. If he knows what a labyrinth is, maybe he also knows what's inside the labyrinth. He mouths a word to me. A word that looks suspiciously like "minotaur."

"We may not be able to defeat it," Gus whispers, trying not to let Morden hear.

"I know, but—"

"What are you two doing?" Morden demands.

Gus taps his defensive button. I follow. We charge after Morden.

Nadine was right. She did die here. Nadine lies slumped against a broad door. Morden, Gus, and I sweep into the open area, guns raised and ready to fire, but the monster who attacked is nowhere in sight. It could have disappeared down any number of the dozens of outlets leading into this circular clearing.

When Morden realizes he's not going to get a fight, he holsters his gun and squats down beside Nadine. I look away when he rolls her over. I don't want to see how badly broken she is. I can't look upon those dead staring eyes, accusing me of not protecting her with a power I don't even understand.

Where is this power anyway? Have I used it up? Why aren't my threads coming to help me fight off my attackers and save my friends like so many other times? Do the threads only work on the Knights?

The Reaper appears, and I close my eyes. *Shink.*

As the lights flash across my closed lids, I hear Morden sob. I feel so numb. Numb and lost. I open my eyes. From where Nadine's body lies decapitated and broken, another code pours forth. Out and over the walls and up a central shaft leading into the dark distance.

Her dead eyes draw mine back to her, accusing. *You brought us all here to die.*

Tears begin to well, and I bury my palms against my eyes. "It's all my fault."

Gus's arm slips across my shoulder and brings me close, sheltering me in his strength. "It's *not* your fault."

I shake my head, denying him. "She trusted me to keep her safe. Now she's gone."

Gus's hand tightens on my shoulder as he draws me toe to toe with him. His finger hooks under my chin, making me look into his hard, determined face. "Then that was *her* mistake. You're not God, Elle, and it was unfair for any of us to have saddled you with the responsibility of keeping us safe. We're a team, we're one another's responsibility." He looks away. "No one person should ever have to feel like they're responsible for the whole."

Swallowing, I nod—if only to please him, but deep down, her words gnaw at me. Logically, I know that Nadine's fear and pain at losing Opus must have eaten at her, not only here, but in

Real World. She must have realized that our time here is reliant only on our avatars' ability to stay alive. She must have realized how, like me, she doesn't want to lose what she has here. All that hit home and ate at her so that when she came back, she was so close to snapping she blamed the most convenient person. She'd considered my power the strongest, and I'd proven a good guardian up until yesterday, so she'd always relied on me. When that power failed—when I failed—I became the convenient person to blame. But she chose this game, this company, this quest. She chose it knowing the consequences, and she was smart enough to know it was foolish to rely on the threads. And, in the end, it was her own sudden, inexplicable hysteria that killed her. So, really, she's just as much to blame as I am. Still…I can't help feeling like I let my friend down.

We let Morden take the time he needs. When he's done, he wipes his eyes with the back of his arm and stands over Nadine's body. "You stupid woman," he breathes. "I thought you were stronger than this."

Gus puts his hand on Morden's shoulder. "Don't blame her. People forget who they are in times like this."

Morden slumps his shoulders. "If she'd just stayed quiet, it wouldn't have found us. She killed herself."

Gus glances over Morden's shoulder, finds my eyes. "I know," he says. And the words say, "You should know that, too," because he thinks I'm also smarter than this. I look away from him.

They begin dragging Nadine's body away from the door. Why she hasn't disintegrated, I don't know. I wish she had, then I wouldn't have to see what I've done. As they roll her all the way to the side, her foot bangs against the door, and it opens.

"The door's unlocked," Gus says, moving forward and pressing his hand against the dented and bloodstained plastic. Inside is a small room.

Morden peeks inside. "A magic box," he mutters. "Delightful."

Gus steps inside then comes out again, dragging the flashlight up the length of the shaft the doors lead into. "It's an aerovator."

chapter thirty-eight

The doors slide open with a *ding ding*. The light of the hall beyond the aerovator is blinding. Wanting the open, clean promise of the world beyond, I raise my revolver and step out.

We're in a long empty hall. To either side the walls are bare of all ornamentation, showing only their defensive skeleton. Steel sheets, welded seams, and rivets. White paint. White tiles. White squares of sterile blue-gray light glaring down from the featureless ceiling.

"Something smells fishy," Morden whispers as he steps forward. In a moment, his defensive armor is back on, and his gun is in his hand.

Having never cancelled my own armor, I follow after him, revolver at ready. Gus keeps his back to mine, covering my rear.

We're halfway down the hall before the first door hisses open to my left. From within comes a Knight. For a long moment, he stares at us. I don't know if he's surprised to see us or perhaps wonders if we're friend or foe.

Most definitely foe. I take aim and shoot him between the eyes before he can come to the proper conclusion.

The resounding *bam* of my gun brings more Knights oozing through doors like the swarm of beetles they resemble. I brace myself, hoping the world will slow, hoping the threads will drop out of space and time to allow me to manipulate them, but they don't.

"Run," Gus yells.

And I do. I run because my life now depends on it.

We shoot through the door at the end of the hall and blaze down another hall just like it. It leads to a massive chamber filled with banks of computers and flashing holo-screens.

I can hear the rubber on Morden's soles squeak against the floor as he skids to a halt and drops off from my right. "Go ahead, I'll try to hold them off," he yells.

I spin around. "What? No."

Gus grabs my arm and drags me along with him. "Come on."

"No." I fight against him, but he's stronger than me. He drags me around a corner. "Gus, we can't leave him."

He tugs me harder, his eyes intense. "We have to. He's buying us time."

"He'll get himself killed." As if on cue, the door explodes inward, and I can hear the Knights marching into the chamber, their numbers growing exponentially as their boots echo off the high ceiling.

Morden's voice echoes above them all. "I am the Devil, and I am taking all you Goddamned bastards to hell."

Shots ring out. *Bang. Bang. Bang.* Glass shatters, a CPU explodes. There's a low hum as laser rifles recharge. *Bang. Shink. Bang. Shink.* The shots keep going. Morden is still alive.

We keep running.

Kaboom. Bang. Shink.

We keep running.

The hall before us illuminates as we run, the motion sensors lighting the way. White light on white metal walls. Metal walls lined with panels and numbers and blinking lights.

Shink. Bang.

My heart pounds fracture lines into my ribs. My blood courses like a river against my ears. Gus's lungs heave beside me. The air is too hot and dry. I'm going to choke. I'm going to throw up. I don't dare. I keep running.

There's a door ahead. Closed.

Shink.

Silence. Feet behind us.

Morden is dead.

We keep running, fear more powerful than loss. The feet continue to thunder after us.

A blast of white-hot electric energy snakes along the crevices in the walls. The code follows.

The door blasts open. We careen through it. It slams shut behind us, cutting off the Knights, but we keep going anyway. It's only a matter of time before they catch up.

Through another corridor, down a flight of steps, turn to the left, another corridor.

And then, far ahead, we see another door, and we slow. And then we stop.

For eternity, the silence of the insular white hall is filled with the echoing sound of desperate breathing, the breathing of the half drowned just pulled up into the light.

When my lungs stop burning. I straighten and swallow. My eyes find Gus's. His expression is dark, telling me he understands exactly what this means.

Another door. Another death.

If the pattern holds true, we won't be able to get through

unless another blood sacrifice is made, unless another code is released. But which one of us holds the code?

We stare at each other, long and hard, a silent battle waging between us. I know what I have to do. He has to accept it. I'm the side quest, the attaché picked up to aid him on his journey. He is the Quester. It's his job to get inside the Chamber on the other side of the door. I slap my wrist, disengaging my armor.

Gus does the same. "Elle," he begins, his tone argumentative.

I don't give him the chance to say anything else. I step forward and I kiss him, hard. I put all my love for Gus into that kiss. I want him to know how very much this has meant to me. My fingers tighten on the revolver in my hand, steeling for what they must do.

A gunshot resounds between us. Gus's lips yank away from mine as if someone were tearing at him from behind. I look around wildly, trying to find who is attacking us.

Gus lets out a coughed breath, drawing my eyes back. "Circuits, that hurt," he gasps. He holds up a bloody hand and stares at it with teary wonder.

For a long moment, my brain either can't, or won't, compute what I'm seeing. Blood blooming from a wound just under his rib cage. Gus holding the gun in his other hand. He shot himself. He shot himself before I could do the same thing.

He moves to take a step, but tumbles over, his body bumping hard against the wall and collapsing to the floor.

I drop my own gun as my body spasms downward with him, my hands going to the bleeding wound, wanting to stem the flow.

"Are you insane?" I scream, the horror of what just happened overtaking all good sense.

Gus turns his eyes away from his hand and looks at me like he can't quite believe what he's done, either. Then his expression changes to something grim. "Yeah. Yeah, I think I must be."

"Holy Hell, Gus, what possessed you?" The tears are falling now, the reality of what's happening sinking into my very marrow, making it quake with fear.

"I-It had to be done," he says simply. "I knew it had to be done."

"No," I wail. "You can't die. This is your quest. You need to get up, Gus."

Gus forces a smile, showing me bloodstained teeth, and feebly shakes his head. "No, Elle." His voice is a pained rasp. "I can't f-feel my legs."

It's then that I notice the smudge of blood down the wall behind him. He shot right through himself. Right through his spine. There's no way he's going to live.

"I won't accept that," I scream, anger now filling me. "We can't have come all this way for nothing—not for you to shoot yourself like an idiot."

"It needed to be done." His voice is too reasonable, too weak.

"I needed to do it. I'm the one who's supposed to die next," I rail.

"No. You're the one who needs to go on," he gasps. "This was never my quest, it's yours."

I whip my head back and forth, spraying tears across my face. "No. No. I'm just a side quest. I'm the one who should have died—like the others. You need me to help you get in the Chamber, that's what you said."

His eyes find mine and hold them. I want to say there is strength in those eyes, determination to live. But all I see is resignation, and even that seems to be fading to something dull. When he speaks, his words are halting and difficult. "No," he says, his face smiling gently. "Remember when I said I found something the Knights wanted? It was you. I found you. They wanted you. They wanted to stop you." He heaves a labored breath, the blood rattling in his throat. "It was never my quest to bring anything *out* of the Anansi Chamber. It was to bring something in. You. *The child needs to go to her chamber*, the Oracle said. *Bring the Spider Child to her Chamber and all will be right in the world.* That's what she said and that's what I did." He pauses to take a few more breaths, each heave sending more blood welling between my trembling fingers. He reaches out and touches my cheek. "*You* were my quest."

I stare down at the insurmountable amount of blood, the tears coming harder.

I feel Gus's fingers through my hair, weak and uncertain. He tries to tip my head up so that I see his face, but I fight him. I won't meet his dying eyes.

He whispers, as if trying to make this less terrible for me. "This is your destiny, your quest."

I refuse to look at him. I just sob. "I don't want it to be." My voice comes out high and whiny, barely making any sense. "I don't want this. I can't do this without you."

His fingers tighten in my hair, forcing me to look at him. "You have to," he growls. The effort makes him cough, and blood dribbles down his chin.

"Shhh," I say. "Don't talk, you're making it worse." I reach out and touch his face, streaking blood across his cheek. "Please, don't do this. Don't leave me."

"It's already done."

I can hear the pounding of feet now. The Knights are drawing closer.

He releases my face. "This is my choice." One hand finds mine, buried hard against his wound, and pulls it away. He holds my hand out, reaching toward the distant door at the end of the hall. "Don't let it be in vain. Do it for the greater good. Be Robin Hood."

I stare at the door. I blink and stare at my bloody outstretched fingers, at his hand seizing my wrist. *Assess the situation; look at who is being affected and who is gaining from your endeavor.* If I just sit here and weep, if I let the Knights come along and kill me, everyone—Opus, Nadine, Morden, and Guster will have died for nothing, and the Knights will win. I don't know what's in that Chamber, but I have to bring it out, give it to the world.

I look back at him. He smiles for me as he raises his gun. "I've got your back."

Knowing I have to do this, I lean forward and I kiss Gus one last time. I kiss him sweetly, but the sweetness is tainted by metallic blood and whistled breathing.

I wobble to my feet and stand there, swaying. I am beyond numb. I feel like I did right after the accident back in Real World. Without legs. Without hope or any meaning to my life. I feel sick. I feel like screaming and wailing and pounding on something. I want to fall back to my knees and sit beside Gus, drinking him in for the last few precious moments of his insane and wonderful life. Worst of all, I don't feel anything at all.

I turn away from Gus and take a step toward the door.

One by one, leaden legs make a slow advance.

I try to focus through my tears, try to breathe evenly, but it doesn't work. I'm falling apart. The shock of loving him has already taken hold.

"Elle," Gus calls.

My heart jumps into my throat. For a moment, I can't acknowledge him, but then I force myself to turn toward him.

He smiles at me, carefree and wonderful as always. "I love you."

I turn away and I run, because if I don't run *from* Gus I'll run *to* Gus. I'll throw my arms around him and wait with him until the Knights end it all.

And they come soon enough.

And it ends far too fast.

Bam. Bam. Bam. Shink. Shink. Shink.

Shink.

With a cry of anguish, I throw myself upon the door. Slamming against it and thrusting out my bloody hands, smearing Gus's death against the pure mocking white of their panels. The code explodes across the door, complicated and confused. The protocol is as familiar as my lost lover. I remember this code well. It's the last one I solved before Dad died. It had taken me nearly six months to solve it. Dad had been so proud. His message had said, "I love you." Just like Gus's last words.

The doors hiss open. I collapse inward. They close.

Instant regret closes in on me. I regret coming here. I regret playing this game. Falling in love. The pain is so intense I can't breathe, and I just want it to go away. I realize I'll never see Gus. Never again. And I regret not allowing him to find me in Real World, not exchanging those few simple words needed to do so while he sat there dying on the other side of the door.

I reach into my pocket and pull out the jump stone—the broken promise—and hold it close to my chest. I cry.

I cry for a very, very long time. Deep down, I know I'm being stupid, lying curled into a tight little ball sobbing and whimpering. But I can't help it. Gus is dead. Everyone is dead. They died for me, so that I may recognize a destiny I didn't even know was my own.

And here I am. I'm in the Anansi Chamber, and it's totally empty. Nothing is happening. What am I supposed to do here?

A bitter scoff escapes my trembling lips. "That's it then," I growl to no one in particular. "Everyone died. For this?" Absolutely nothing. There was no point to it at all.

I exhale and sit up, pulling the cap and blinders away.

"Is everything okay? You're early."

Meems's face swims before me. A sight that makes my heart leap with joy. Someone who is real and will never leave me.

I throw my arms around her and I hold her, shaking. I cry for real now, my sorrow at ending my game so great that I'm not sure I'll ever truly recover.

Unsent Letters to Delia

Dee,

This might be the last letter I write you for a long time. I simply don't have the will to do it anymore. What's the point of me talking to you every day? It's a fantasy, an illusion I tell myself to make me feel like you still think of me when I know you don't.

Your letters stopped coming a long time ago.

It's been almost a year, after all. I only hope that you've found your place in this awful world. Maybe you're engaged to someone wonderful. Maybe you look just like one of the Aristocrats now. Perhaps you've been placed in a good job by Central Staffing. Maybe you play the game.

Just, don't fall in love in there, Dee, whatever you do. Love. It's the most beautiful thing in all the world, there's nothing to describe it, nothing to surpass it. It's truly a gift. But that just makes it worse when it's gone. All it does is make you stupid. So very stupid.

I could have seen him in this world, you know? I could maybe have grasped that. But I was so worried about being good enough for him, and worried about the danger to him, that I didn't do it. I'm glad I saved him from danger, I don't regret that, as it shows how much I really do love him. But I'm so ashamed of myself for denying him on any level because of my legs. I love Gus, and I know he loves me with all his heart, wouldn't pause for an instant if he saw what I really look like in this world.

Perhaps my choice means I don't deserve him. Perhaps I deserve this heartache. But you? I know you don't deserve this pain, Dee. That's why I can't talk to you for a while. Perhaps someday I'll be able to write you without my depression showing through, but not now. I wish you all the luck and so much love.

—Ella

part six:

ELLA PERSEVERES

chapter thirty-nine

"*Someone's at the door.*" Startled by the voice in my head, I look up from my flex-bracelet. I've been staring at the same complicated puzzle my father left me for hours, unthinking and numb.

I miss Gus and the game. But what's the point of going back? He's gone. And I don't see how the quest could continue, so I'd have to start another game. I'm not sure I want to do that. Not yet, anyway. Who knows what will happen this time? I connect with Tasha. *"Who is it?"*

"Master Simon."

"Uncle Simon?" A flash of excitement bubbles up at the idea of seeing Uncle Simon again. But then it dies. He's not here for me. I'm dead. So, why *is* he here? *"What's he doing here?"*

Tasha doesn't humor the rhetorical question. Instead, she says, *"Shall I let him in?"*

"He must be here to see Katrina." Probably to talk about Bastian and Sadie's engagement. *"You should let her know he's here."*

"Neither Mistress Katrina nor Sadie are present. I would not have addressed you otherwise."

"Oh." I should have realized that, but I haven't been thinking straight recently. I need to get my head out of the clouds and start focusing on the here and now. Gus is gone. The game is over, and I'll never see him again. I need to accept that.

What should I do? Let him in? Then what? Talk to him? But I'm dead. Should I just ignore him? That would be better for him, right? To not have to deal with the ghost of his niece... Wait a second, what am I thinking? This is Uncle Simon. He'd be delighted to see me, dead or not. And he can get me out. He can save me. But then I remember what Katrina said about reporting me and being killed. I can't involve Uncle Simon—whoever Katrina works for could go after him, too. *"Tell him no one is home. To come back later."*

A moment later Tasha pings back in. *"He insists that he is here to see you. That if I don't let him in, he'll override my system."*

"What?" I gasp aloud. *"He knows I'm here?"*

"Shall I let him in?"

He knows I'm alive? And that I'm here? When did he figure it out? Is he here to rescue me? I take a deep breath, mentally preparing myself. *"Okay, let him in."*

A few minutes later, Uncle Simon steps into the room. He's as handsome and tall as I remember him, dressed in an immaculate butter yellow and canary gold doublet and tan trousers. He steps over the threshold, his glittering golden shoes catching the late morning light of the synthetic sky.

I steel myself, trying not to grin stupidly. I want to run at him and throw my arms around him, but obviously that's a physical impossibility. I'll have to wait for him to come and embrace me, so I just try my best to look good. I square my shoulders and lift my chin, determined not to be judged as a lesser Ella despite losing a good third of myself. I am more than just my physical body and certainly more than a ghost.

But when I meet Uncle Simon's eyes, I know he sees me as more than a ghost. Not a ghost at all. There's no horror, no happiness, no realization. Nothing. "Hello Ellani."

My mouth opens, but no words come out. How can he be acting so normal, like nothing is different? Like I wasn't dead to him for the past year, like this isn't a wonderful, tearful reunion. Unless... I swallow and, when I speak, the words are tight. "You knew this whole time?"

He lowers his gaze in acquiescence.

My chest is hitching, searching for enough air. I'm suddenly hot. Hot and cold and in desperate need of something. A scream maybe? "But, but..." I don't know the words, don't know what to say. I'm not sure I fully understand.

He waits, patiently standing and looking at me as if it's no big thing to see me in my mutilated state which, of course, only upsets me more. He knew I was alive. He knew I'd been handicapped. He didn't come to see me. He didn't take me in. He didn't save me even though I was captive and being starved to death. All that I can say, all that I can manage out of all the thoughts floating in my head and bursting in my chest, is, "Why?"

Uncle Simon takes a deep breath. When he lets it out, his spine seems to cave a little bit. He glances at the chair. "May I?"

I just stare at him. I stare hard at him, because if I even blink I'll burst into tears.

He sits. Adjusts his coat. Leans forward and places his elbows on his knees. He looks me over a few times, stares at the floor. I grip my half thighs, trying to keep myself from squirming. I bite my tongue, resisting the urge to scream at him, to demand answers. Worse, I have no words at all.

Eventually, he says, "I'm sure you would like a clean

explanation for all of this, Ella."

I say nothing, I only wait.

"After all," he glances around the room, "none of this seems to make any sense. But…" He lifts his Custom green eyes and stares into mine. "I want you to know, above everything, that I do love you. And this entire charade was done to keep you safe."

I laugh at him, a tight breathy thing that borders on hysteria. My outburst ruffles him, making his face unhinge into blatant indignation. When I've chuckled myself to breathlessness I shake my head and wipe my eyes. "Safe?"

He lets out a breathy growl, obviously looking for patience. "Yes."

"With Katrina?"

He nods. "With Katrina."

"Do you have any idea what she's been doing to me?" I demand. "That I'm a prisoner? That she cut me off from everyone? That she's been starving me? That she refuses to let me get treatment for my legs?"

Uncle Simon doesn't look away. "Yes. I know."

I feel myself droop. I wasn't expecting that. Granted, I wasn't expecting any of this, but not that in particular. He knowingly let Katrina do this to me. My Uncle Simon, my flesh and blood, who I thought loved me. "How could you?" The words shake as they come out. I ball my fist, commanding my voice to sound more strong and confident. "How could you even say you love me? That you want to keep me safe?"

Uncle Simon sits back and is quiet for a long moment, his eyes stern, his body calm. He's looking at me in that same way he used to just stare at Bastian when he was having a tantrum. He says, "You were never in any real danger, Ella."

I feel my jaw unhinge in shock. How could being starved to death not mean danger?

"I watched your vitals. I spoke with Meems and Katrina." He glances toward Tasha's lens at the corner of the room. "I watched you. Daily. Hourly sometimes." He folds his hands in his lap. "I made adjustments to your diet, added supplements. I wouldn't have endangered you. Not really. And when it came time for you to take the next step, I made it possible for you."

My mind races down a thousand paths. He spoke with Meems? I glance at her. She has her blank mechanical face on. "Meems?"

"She won't respond to you," Uncle Simon says. "I've got her on power reserve."

"What? She doesn't have that kind of program."

Uncle Simon's lips twitch. "She does now. I upgraded her while you were incapacitated. It was necessary."

I blink at him. For some reason, this angers me more than anything else up until this point. "You had no right to do that to her—to change her against her will."

Uncle Simon scoffs. "Of course I do. She's just an android. A robot. She's nothing but mechanical parts and circuits. She's not a person. She has no rights."

I grip the arms of my chair, wishing I could leap forward and scratch his eyes out. "I'm a person. What happened to my rights? Why did I get locked up and held against my will?"

"Oh yes," Uncle Simon says with a wave of his hand and a roll of his eyes. "Let's let Ella run around Evanescence so everyone can see she's not really dead like she should be. That sounds like a fine idea."

"That's the point," I hiss. "I shouldn't be dead."

Sighing, he drops his head back and, when he speaks, his voice sounds tired. "No. No, Ella, you should be dead. You really should."

Petulant, I prod, even though his voice and body tell me he's annoyed with me. So what? I don't care what he thinks anymore. "Why? So you can take Dad's wealth? So you can steal all the fame and glory for yourself? I know that's what you always wanted."

Uncle Simon's eyes cut toward me, low and dangerous. "So I could keep you safe. So I didn't have to stand the loss of yet another person I loved."

"By forcing everyone else around to think I'm dead?"

"Yes," he growls. "That's what it took."

I try to puzzle it out, to understand how he could seem so logical and calm. But I can't. All I see is betrayal and confusion. A person who has done what he has done to me should seem crazy, right? But he doesn't. He seems so straight and earnest. I almost half believe that he did all of this out of love. But I can't. "I can't believe you. I don't understand."

He sits back again. "I don't expect you to, Ella. But..." He takes a breath, "I'll try my best to explain. I just..." He pauses. "It's so complicated, I don't even know where to start with you."

I purse my lips. "You can start with why you faked my death. Why you made poor Delia have to endure that. And..." Oh my sparks, I don't even want to think. "Does Bastian know I'm alive?"

He shakes his head. "No. The fewer people who knew, the better. Though I think he suspects."

A wave of relief washes through me. At least someone isn't evil. Even poor Meems was used in Uncle Simon's diabolical plot.

"I tried thinking of everything," Uncle Simon is saying. "But it all pointed to the fact that you had to die. I needed them to truly believe you were dead."

I blink. "They?"

"G-Corp. President Cyr, specifically."

I cock my head. "Why would you want them to think I was dead?"

He rubs his temple, glances at the pictures of my parents on the workstation. "So they wouldn't try to kill you again. So that they wouldn't actually succeed next time they tried."

"What?" I whisper. G-Corp? Trying to kill me? But why?

Uncle Simon forces a smile, but it's more like a grimace. "You see," he says, trying to sound light, "I should have started somewhere else. Now you're confused."

I pinch the bridge of my nose. "I'd be confused no matter what."

"What do you understand?"

"That you're operating under some delusion that G-Corp is trying to kill me."

He snorts. "I'm glad you have such faith in me, Ella."

I hold out my hands. "Not much to work with here."

He nods. "Point taken." He runs his fingers through his hair. "G-Corp isn't *trying* to kill you. They *did* kill you. At least, that's what I am trying to make them believe."

I roll my eyes. "Why?" I demand. "Why would they want to kill me? It doesn't make sense."

"So that you couldn't continue on with your mother's work," he says very plainly. "That's why they killed her. That's why they killed your father, and why, very obviously, they tried to kill you, too." Seeing that he has my attention now, he continues. "Your mother didn't kill herself, Ella. She was killed. A droid came into this very house and shot her between the eyes with a pulse weapon. That pod accident that killed your father and did this…" He points at my stumps. "To you, was not a sensor malfunction— at least not an accidental one. That pod was meant to crash. You weren't just collateral damage. G-Corp doesn't off brilliant minds for no reason. You're dangerous, Ellani, dangerous like your parents. Perhaps more so because you've got both of them in your veins and twice the reason to carry their torch."

I blink at him, certain he's gone mad. "Making video games?"

He grins, his eyes bright and full of fire. "Starting revolutions."

For a long moment, the word hangs in the air. It's as if he expects some great revelation on my part. But the room just feels stale and cloying. I close my eyes, trying to keep my sanity because one of us has to. "Uncle Simon, the only thing revolutionary about my parents was their relationship. And maybe, just maybe, if you stretch it, Nexis. But, honestly…" I lose my steam. I just don't have the energy to try and lay the path straight for him. I'm so tired. And I have no idea how to combat such monumental madness.

Uncle Simon's grin fades to a wistful smile. "You're so much like your mother. She was so skeptical. But the passion? You get that from Warren."

I wring my hands, suddenly more sensitive to Uncle Simon at the understanding that my father wasn't only just mine. And neither was my mother. I remember Uncle Simon crying at her funeral, and I know he would have cried all the harder for my father. Could this be some crazy man's attempt at keeping his last remaining relative alive? Is it possible that he's made up this whole G-Corp conspiracy thing to explain why their deaths happened? When I look at it like that, I feel bad for Uncle Simon. "I've met mom. In the game," I say, as if that could somehow ease the pain. "She's the Oracle. Was she like that in real life?"

Uncle Simon lifts a surprised brow. "Yes," he says. "She was. She had a powerful personality, but she had a weakness for you and your father. He always made her laugh, as though his very existence were a joke. And you…" He pauses to exhale and shake his head. "She always had such plans for you."

"Plans?"

He smiles to himself and casts a furtive sidelong glance at the bank of computers. "Do you know who and what your mother was?"

I feel my shoulders tighten and lift with sudden unease. "Cleo Drexel. She was a Programmer."

He stands and moves toward the window where he stares out at the wasteland for a long time. "Cadence is always blue. Adagio is always yellow."

I nod, now certain he's lost his marbles.

He glances over his shoulder, his face grave. "Why do you think Adagio is yellow?"

I think about this for a moment. "I don't know. I've never really thought about it."

He turns away. "The dome is broken. The air they breathe in Adagio is no different than the air the Disfavored breathe out in the wasteland. Well, breathed."

I flex my brow. "Breathed?"

"Most of them are dead, I think. Some kind of malfunction. The city began killing them. So they fled. They came here to Evanescence, and they went to Selestia."

"Selestia?"

"It's the other city Adagio is linked to. The tunnels go across Post-America, linking each of us in a chain that runs from sea to sea. As Cadence and Adagio are our sisters, so Evanescence and Selestia are Adagio's sisters."

I stare at Uncle Simon. "I never knew that."

He shrugs. "Why would or should you? It's not as though we have open trade or communication with our sisters. They are as mysterious to us as I'm sure we are to them. Your mother was amazed when she first learned of life inside Evanescence.

Actually, I think appalled is a better word."

"Wait," I squeak. "You mean Mom didn't grow up here? She's from someplace else?"

Uncle Simon points out toward Adagio. "She's from there. They came through the tunnels when the dome cracked. At first the old President Cyr didn't want to let them in, but they camped against the Undergate for months. While he didn't let them in, he forced his son, the man who is now our current President, to involve himself with a humanitarian effort to help the people on the other side of the gate. Still had to look good on The Broadcast, you know? Anyway, it's said our President Cyr met and fell in love with Lady Cyr while working in those tunnels. When his father died and our President Cyr took control of G-Corp, his very first act was to open the gate to the refugees from Adagio. Most of them were quickly integrated into society, your mother included."

I slump in my chair. If I had legs they would be weak. "So she's not from here. She's from there." Should I believe him? With all the nonsense he's spouted so far? "How'd she meet Dad?"

"Your mother was a Programmer, like your father. They worked together. Nexis is your mother's brainchild."

"What?" I breathe. "I thought it was Dad's."

He shakes his head, cutting me off. "No. It was hers; she just died—was killed—before she was able to complete it." He moves away from the window and throws himself back into his chair in the manner of a man who is bone-tired of everything. "It was her life's wish that the game be completed, so—diligent as ever—Warren took up the mantle." There's a brief pause, a slight tinge of bitterness in his words, but he covers them with a smile. "He quickly realized he needed help, of course. Even with my help neither of us was a match for your mother's brain. It took us the better part of your life to complete the game."

I rock my head from side to side, not wanting to believe but somehow understanding that all of this makes perfect sense.

"Now that your father is dead, it's my job to make sure your mother's wishes are fulfilled."

I narrow my eyes at him. "Why? Why not just let it go?"

He looks away, his expression distant. "Your mother was such a spectacular person. She was a Natural but never bent to the pressures of her own society or ours. She was unapologetically herself, strong-willed and rebellious. She was ravishing and enchanting in a way that made everyone around her love her."

I suddenly feel pity for my Uncle Simon. I know that expression and that tone of voice. Katrina was the same when talking about Dad. "You loved her, didn't you?"

He smiles sadly. "Love isn't quite the word. I'd say inspired. She was brilliant in her vision of the world and of Naturals. She's the reason I adopted Bastian. Did you know that? More than anything, I wanted to be part of her vision of the future. I wanted to work with her. But she only ever worked with Warren. He *understood* her. That was her reasoning. I suppose it took me much longer to mentally get to where she and Warren stood. Of course, I blame that on Lady Cyr. Your parents were handpicked to develop Nexis, did you know that? Out of all the Programmers in Evanescence, the only two to receive the grant to research and develop a breakthrough game. You know, until that game came out, I was the foremost Programmer in VR, and your father never would have completed the game without me." There's dark pride in his voice and more jealousy.

"You feel shortchanged because you weren't selected?"

He nods. "Shouldn't I be? I mean, in the end, I helped develop that game. Did anyone give me a Civil Enrichment Award? Do I see a single credit from the royalties? It should have been me from the beginning, not Warren."

Swallowing, I rub my hands together and glance at Meems. It's good to have her in the room, even if she can't do anything. I lick my lips, uncertain if I want to know. "So, my captivity *is* about the royalties."

"No," he spits. "I don't care about wealth. I don't care about fame. What I want is to be part of the vision."

"What do you mean, *vision*?"

Uncle Simon's eyes wander up and around the room in a vast arc, examining my prison. "It's not much different in here from when this was your mother's workroom. Did you know it was hers before your father's?"

I shake my head.

"She liked to work from home, so that she could be with you. She wanted you with her all the time." He scoffs to himself. "She sometimes joked that you understood things far more clearly than even she did. *A child's mind*, she'd say, *is the best mind of all*."

I fidget. I don't know where he's going with this conversation. I just know he's starting to make me a little uncomfortable. "Uncle Simon," I say haltingly, "why did you come here today?"

He lifts his eyes and stares at me. In the depth of those eyes is the desperate determination of a madman. "I've been watching you play the game, Ella. We all have."

We? My blood runs cold and my heart begins to thunder, making a lump form in my throat. "What do you mean?" I croak.

He stands and comes toward me. The chair responds to my nerves and begins to back away, but he grabs the armrests and keeps it still. He falls to his knees before me and grabs my hands. I try to struggle, tugging away and kicking with my useless stumps, frightened and confused by what he wants with me.

He wrestles my hands into stillness and leans in until we're face to face. "Why did you stop playing?"

"I-I don't know," I say, my voice breathy and panicked. "I just didn't want to play anymore. I didn't see the point." It's half true. Tears are prickling my eyes. "Why bother with the Chamber? Everyone is dead, and I don't know what to do."

"Did you even try?"

I shake my head, somehow feeling ashamed though I don't understand why. The tears slide down my cheeks, slow and painful. I look away. "I didn't want to."

Uncle Simon sits back on his heels and stares at me, his face intense in how ponderous it seems, as though I'm as complex a puzzle as the one loaded onto my flex-bracelet. "Why did you start playing in the first place?"

Wiping at my tears, I look down, embarrassed. I don't want to tell him that I wanted to be closer to my father. Instead I say, "I-I wanted legs."

"And you got those in the game."

I nod.

He crosses his arms over his knees, his countenance that of someone who is ready to have a long, drawn-out discussion with a petulant child. "What made you stay?"

I bite my lips together. There's no way I'm telling Uncle Simon about Guster. He'd probably laugh at me.

"Ah, I see," he says, his voice quiet and knowing.

"See what?" I demand.

He begins patting his pockets. "I have something for you." I watch him, suspicious-eyed, as he draws out a small data disk and hands it to me.

I examine the disk, a tiny silver sliver encased in a hard plastic shell. "What's this?"

"Read it."

I slip the disk into my flex-bracelet. A moment later a title flashes across the screen. *The Collected Sonnets of William Shakespeare.* Unable to believe what I'm seeing, I scroll down.

Sonnet 1

From fairest creatures we desire increase,
That thereby beauty's rose might never die,
But as the riper should by time decease,
His tender heir might bear his memory:
But thou, contracted to thine own bright eyes,
Feed'st thy light'st flame with self-substantial fuel,
Making a famine where abundance lies,
Thyself thy foe, to thy sweet self too cruel.
Thou that art now the world's fresh ornament
And only herald to the gaudy spring,
Within thine own bud buriest thy content
And, tender churl, makest waste in niggarding.
Pity the world, or else this glutton be,
To eat the world's due, by the grave and thee.

Fresh tears sting my eyes as I come to the last passage. "Where did you get this?" I squeak.

"Where do you think?"

I shake my head.

"He came to me, looking for you. He wanted to give them to you himself, but he says you refused to agree to meet him here in Real World." Uncle Simon lifts sympathetic eyes to mine. "Why?"

I look off toward the window, wishing I could dissolve into a puff of smoke, leave everything behind. "It wouldn't have worked out here. I'm a different person in the game; we both are." My fingers wander to my stumps, touching them like I did when I first lost my legs—reassuring me that it's a truth I can't deny. The small gesture isn't lost on my uncle.

"I see." As he reaches out and puts a hand over mine, he

lets out a long sigh. "Ella, it's no coincidence that you ended up going into that game. It's no accident that you ended up on the quest that you did. Your mother and father made that game for *you*, Ellani; the whole thing was designed just to house your one simple quest."

I lift my eyes to Meems again, desperate to know he's lying. "Meems?" I whimper.

"Go ahead, Meems," Uncle Simon says.

A moment later, Meems's body relaxes out of its rigid pose. I meet her eyes. She will have been listening, even though she's been in power save. "It's true?"

She lowers her head.

"So," I say, "that's why you wanted me to play it so bad."

"Besides it being part of my new programming, it was what your father wanted for you," she reasons. "I would have encouraged you anyway."

Hurt, I look away.

"I wanted to tell you everything," Meems reasons. "But I could not. It is not in my programming."

I scowl at her. "You've undermined your programming in the past. What about not reporting my hacking?"

Uncle Simon clears his throat. "I removed that protocol from Meems's chip. She retained the memory that it was wrong, but had been programmed to allow it."

"Why would you encourage her to let me break the law?"

"For the same reason I did all of this."

I flex my brow. "You said you did this because G-Corp was trying to kill me."

"I faked your death because of that, yes. But all of this? Katrina, the imprisonment, the starvation, the withholding of prosthetics, continually reprogramming your G-Chip, Meems's chasis, the game. All of that was training. We needed you to grow as a Programmer, to embrace the Trickster's mentality. Your mother and father did the same, albeit in their own way."

I think of Dad's puzzles.

"Of course, Warren was too soft with you. Cleo wouldn't have approved of him humoring your foolish notions of being a Designer. You're a Programmer, Ella; you needed to embrace that."

"Why? What's the point? If G-Corp thinks I'm dead, I'll never be a Programmer."

"It was necessary for you to progress to the final level of the game."

"But," I argue. "I don't understand. What's the point of me getting into the Anansi Chamber?"

Uncle Simon smiles. "Anansi," he repeats softly. "I haven't heard that name in such a long time."

I pull my hands free and demand that the chair back away from him. He lets me go, making no effort to come after me this time. He seems sober now, subdued by that one word.

"What is Anansi?" I demand, my voice breaking.

"Anansi meant everything to your mother. She put it in that game, wanted you to have it. She considered it your inheritance."

"That doesn't tell me anything about *what* it is," I reason.

"A concept," he says simply. Then, seeing that I don't understand, he says, "In its simplest form, Anansi is a spider, a spider that teaches a lesson. More complex, Anansi became a virus to prove to the Aristocracy that they are not as invincible as they think they are. We rely so much on technology, but what we don't realize is that our technology has taken on a mind of its own—has the capability to destroy us." He casts a meaningful glance at Meems, who hunches her shoulders. "Our technology is what destroyed us in the Bio-Nuclear War. It's what made us build walls against one another in the first place, and it keeps us addicted to it even still. We just don't learn. When your mother came from Adagio, she tried to tell them, she tried to make them see. It was her role as Anansi to open their eyes, but no one believed her. They just forced the chip into her mind, made her conform to their reliance on technology. But your mother was smart. She was a Trickster to the bone. She knew how to use the technology they loved so much to make them see their own folly, but she died before she could carry out her mission. It's up to you now."

Despite my fear of Uncle Simon in his current state, the chair has drifted back to him, responding to my intrigue. I'm curious about my mother and my so-called inheritance. "What does the virus do?"

"It stops it," he says smiling. "Stops everything. Kills it all." At my horrified expression, he adds, "It's only for a minute. She insisted on that after what happened in Adagio."

I frown. "Then what?"

He shakes his head as if disappointed. "Then nothing. It's only meant to show them how vulnerable they are, how they rely too much on their own technology, even to protect that same technology. It's a warning against a greater threat. And, with hope, the harbinger of a new age. A better one."

"And that's Anansi? The one that's in the game?"

"The whole of the game is built to hide and protect an underlying protocol: a quest designed to break through the antiviral programs and firewalls that the G-System has built to protect itself and release the Anansi Virus into the system."

I blink. "A protocol that I was meant to carry out?"

He nods. "You've been trained from a very young age to counteract and deprogram the antiviral protocols. That's what all those puzzles your father always gave you were."

"But," I reason, not wanting to believe that I could be part of such a diabolical plan—that my own parents had basically programmed me like a tool from my birth, that all my hardships over the past year were nothing but Uncle Simon sharpening me for the final blow. "Wouldn't I have noticed I was fighting viruses? I mean, antiviral code is distinct. I'd notice it in the coding."

Simon shakes his head. "That is what took the longest. Creating the game to cover the virus was the easy part. It was hiding the true aspect of the quest from you that was the most difficult part. Your father knew you'd discover what they were. He had to make absolutely certain that you'd never suspect, so he asked you to decode the programs ahead of time and then imbedded them in the avatars of other Tricksters. He knew they'd find you in the game; your mother had programmed it that way. It was another lesson, you see, a way for you to learn that there are others like you out there." He points to the window.

Everything makes horrible sense. I can clearly see why G-Corp would want me dead. If President Cyr suspected what my mother and father had been doing, he'd eliminate them. And just to be certain the virus was never released? Kill me—the avatar who the virus was meant to piggyback—before I even started playing.

But I wasn't killed. Uncle Simon saved me, hid me. Forced me to go into the game by giving me Katrina, and not giving me legs, and programming my android to encourage me to play. And once I was in? Continually torturing me and subjecting me to solitude so that I sought relief and companionship, daily.

The game did what it was programmed to do. The Tricksters found me, encouraged me to go on the quest to the Anansi Chamber, supported me when I needed it. But I was the driving force—the one who discovered the quilt and how to crack it, wrote the program to interpret the data, killed all the Knights.

And when it came to actually getting into the Chamber, or

rather, the G-System? Dad hid the codes in my companions. In the end, the only function the other members of my group had was to die and release codes that I wrote. Codes that broke down walls, opened doors, and stopped Knights. Firewalls and antiviral programs. The Knights never wanted revenge; they wanted to destroy me—because I was a virus waiting to happen.

Uncle Simon continues speaking. "He shouldn't have worried so much about hiding everything from you; you were so cross-eyed in love with that boy, you wouldn't have known an antivirus if you tripped over it. He made getting you to play the quest far simpler than we thought. I knew he would."

I feel my face go hot with embarrassment, and then dread tightens my stomach. I knew he was too good to be true. "Oh no, Gus, he isn't…" I swallow, barely able to get the horrible thought formed into words. "He isn't part of the game, is he? Something developed to distract me?"

Simon stares at me for a long cold moment before saying, "No. He's a real person."

I grip the armrests, trying to keep myself from shaking. "But you had him go in with the distinct intent of distracting me? He lied?"

Simon smiles. "Ah, to be in love." He shakes his head. "No Ella. The Oracle is the one who assigned him to you, implanted the last virus in his avatar. She picked all of them. Though, I must say, she outdid herself with him. His Naturalist sympathies and inclination for you made him perfect for your team. To him, all he did was play a game and fall in love with a young woman who is too much like her mother. The fool didn't have a chance. I feel bad for him, actually, to be denied the ability to meet you in Real World."

I knit my brows and look away, heat stinging my eyes. I never wanted to hurt Gus. "It was for the best."

"What if it doesn't have to be?"

I glare at him, suspicious. "What do you mean?"

"I told you, we have to finish your mother's wish. Your work in that chamber isn't done." He looks over his shoulder. "Meems, I brought a case with me when I arrived. Would you go retrieve it for me?"

Meems nods and moves out of the room.

"What was that about?"

He smiles. "You'll see."

Frustrated, I lean back in my chair and close my eyes, trying to puzzle out this very confusing encounter. "So Guster and the others were bystanders to the game?"

"Yes."

"And I'm dead to everyone but you and Katrina and Sadie?"

"Correct."

I bite my lip. "So that stuff about Katrina and Dad."

Uncle Simon frowns. "That was true. She should not have told you about that. She shouldn't have talked to you at all."

I glare at him. "I needed answers from somewhere. And I thought—I thought…" My voice dies. I don't know what I thought anymore.

He smirks. "You thought she was the bad guy."

"Isn't she?"

He shrugs. "I hired Katrina to be your guardian specifically because she hated you and wouldn't question what I had planned for you. I paid her well, agreed to let her daughter marry my son, I gave her this house—which she always wanted. In return, she kept her mouth shut and let me do my work."

I stare at him for a long moment. "I believe I just might hate you now."

He finally looks away from me. "That hurts, Ella. Hearing you say that…after all I've done to keep you safe from G-Corp. But…"

He takes a deep breath. "I knew what I was getting into when I started this charade, so I have to say, I'm not surprised. I don't ask your forgiveness. I just ask that you make an effort to understand where I was coming from."

I look away. That logical, conniving part of my genetic makeup completely understands, even tips its hat to Uncle Simon's brilliance. The other part, the sensitive, caring part that is the Ellani I prefer to be is just hurt—hurt beyond forgiveness.

Finally, Meems returns with a large case and puts it on the bed.

"Ah, here we are." Uncle Simon stands and moves to the bed where he punches in a code. The case pops open with a pneumatic hiss, and he reaches in. What he draws forth makes my lungs seize in my chest.

He chuckles. "I thought your eyes would bug out, just like that." He holds the cybernetic leg up for my examination. "Well?"

chapter forty

I glance from Uncle Simon's face to the leg in his hands and then back to his face, overwhelmed and confused. "I-I don't understand."

He says, "They are yours, if you want them."

Hysteric laughter bubbles up in my throat, but it gets stuck behind a lump of emotion, and all that comes out is a choked sob.

Simon moves toward me with the leg. "I had them specially designed for you. Your mother would have strangled me otherwise if she were alive." He holds it out for me to examine. It's not my leg. My leg could only be reproduced by nanites and stem cells, but it's the relative size and shape of one of my real legs. It will pass.

"These are, of course, only temporary. After we take care of everything here, I can have proper ones cultured for you."

Tears sting my eyes again. "I finally have legs," I whisper. "I have legs, but what's the point?" I wanted legs so that I could see Guster. But he's gone. He died before I could know who he was and how to find him here in Real World.

"The point is…" Uncle Simon pulls back the leg emphatical-ly. "That you still have a chance to get what you want, *if* you do what you're expected to do."

I reach up and rub my temples, my frustration and confusion making my world spin over on itself. He's showing his evil-genius side again. "You want me to be a tool, you mean?"

Uncle Simon closes the case. The locks click back in place, trapping the legs away from me. "I will make a deal with you. Anansi is your inheritance, and I will not rest until you've fully embraced it. You go back in that game and finish what your mother intended you to do. You fulfill your role as the spider and make the wrongdoers see their folly. You do this for me, you can have the legs. I'll dismiss Katrina. I'll set up a new identity for you and transfer every credit that is rightfully yours into your accounts. You'll have to Modify your face to throw them off, but that's small change for what you're being offered. You can have a brand-new life."

I scowl at him. "Now that I know the truth and I've been so conveniently trained, what's to stop me from doing that, anyway?"

Uncle Simon's grin is flawless. "I'll also give you the identity of the boy. That is something that no amount of hacking will reveal."

My brain is reeling out of control. It all seems too good to be true. I can have legs. I can have Gus. I can be free. I can have all of that, and all I have to do is plant a simple little virus. But still, it's a virus…being introduced into the very arteries of Evanescence. Would releasing the virus make me the criminal that's pulsing through my veins? "Are you certain it's not going to do any harm? The virus?"

He tucks his chin, grim. "You can't tell me that after everything you've seen and been through that you wouldn't like the Aristocrats to learn a little lesson. Don't you want them to see how idiotic they are? Don't you want them to realize how wrong it was to destroy our beautiful world in favor of constant advancement?"

He has a point. Does coming on my own to the same decision my parents did make me their tool? Does carrying out my inheritance make me a tool if I really want to do it?

I glance at Meems. "What do you think?"

She clutches her hands together in front of her. "I cannot deny that this is what your father wanted."

"I didn't ask what he wanted, I asked what you *think*."

She looks a little startled at my adamant tone. "I think," she says slowly, as if the words are foreign to her, "I think that I would be happy if you were happier. If doing this will give you the things that will make you smile once more, then you should do it."

I could have legs, freedom, Gus. And maybe Evanescence will become better after this. Perhaps I can help build a better world. Be a Designer after all, and it wouldn't hurt to do something that Dad wanted me to do in the process. That's what I wanted when I started this whole thing, wasn't it? To be close to Dad, honor his memory—complete his legacy. Now I can do that while starting my own. "Okay," I breathe. "I'll do it."

chapter forty-one

As I manifest into my avatar, the striking pain of grief overwhelms me once more. In Real World I've had time to recover from my losses, but here they are fresh all over again. I roll onto my side and stare at my hands, still sticky with Guster's blood, the jump stone stuck to one palm.

Guster is gone. Broken promise.

Get up.

He's not really dead. Do what you came here to do and you can see him.

Can I? Is the boy I'll meet in Real World anything like the one I knew here?

Even if he isn't, don't let it all be in vain. You didn't let him die so that you could mope for the rest of your life.

Meems's words float up out of the confused thoughts in my head. *You are still here. Make him proud of you, Ella. Be strong. Do not let this beat you. You must persevere.* Her words had been about my father, but that doesn't make them any less potent when it comes to Guster. I have to persevere. I have to be something. I have to make my father and Guster proud. I have to deserve their love. I have to make myself proud. I have to love myself. I have to fulfill my inheritance, continue with Dad's legacy. I have to be Anansi, be Robin Hood. I have to help make a positive change. Be a Designer for the future. I must persevere.

I wipe my face with the backs of my bloodstained hands. I'm still crying. I'm not sure I can stop. It all feels too fresh and, to top it off, I have everything I've just learned from Uncle Simon to process as well. I could sit here and mope for days with the amount of crying I need to do. But I will keep going. I struggle to my feet and look around the Anansi Chamber, searching for some indication of what I should do.

When I first fell to the floor here, it had seemed that the Chamber was completely empty, but now I see that I was wrong. There is something, though it's not what I thought it would be.

It's a massive hollow cylinder stretching up and down for as far as the eye can see. Along the perimeter, I can see lights twinkling and flashing. All along the inside of the cylinder are threads—a massive spider web connecting one thing to everything else, and along the silver threads the flashes travel back and forth.

It's like a brain with glinting synapses, a vast network communicating at lightning speed. Ahead of me is a narrow walkway that leads out over the vast emptiness below. On a small landing at the center there hovers a familiar site.

The last of my father's puzzles.

Biting my trembling lips, I step forward.

The puzzle is not like I remember it. I've stared at it every day for months, trying to puzzle out the code so that I can write a decoding program to unravel the strands and reveal the message. Now, as I look at it, I don't just see the fiber-optic strings. I see the silken spider's threads. I see the threads like I always do when I really need them. And I know and understand them in that mysterious way I always seem to when it matters most. I reach out and touch the backlit data-command board mounted just beneath the puzzle.

I see the threads. I know the intricate knots. I know these threads as the strings pulling the program along. Understand them as a Programmer should. That's all they've ever been, just programming.

And I know how to unravel the code and design a new one.

My fingers fly over the keyboard, knowing exactly where to go and what to write; they are well-practiced from my time working on Frankie. It's a long, complicated program, but my body and mind are operating in a time and a place that don't adhere to relative reality. It's like I can hear them whispering: Opus telling me where to put this backslash and that colon, Nadine showing me how one protocol interacts and overlays another, Morden telling me the secrets of what I can't see.

I feel my mother's breath on the back of my neck, silently urging me to reach out and take what she's offering—an instrument to bring about change. I remember my father's words, always telling me how special I am, sharing his vision with me—showing me the building blocks of a better world.

I am preprogrammed, acting on impulse, dumping a vast memory into a whirling pool and somehow bringing order to it. Building a complex web. I am the spider. This is my venomous bite. I will make them see their folly.

Guster's hands guide mine, deft and sure. When my finger hits the enter button, it's his command to execute, the absolute desire to stand before him once more overruling every other thought.

I am Ellani Drexel. I am a Natural Programmer and Designer. I will stand proudly for who, and what, I am. I will understand that I am worthy of love, no matter my color or creed. I will work for a world that can see this as clearly as I can.

And then it happens. The puzzle unravels and bursts apart like a glimmering flower—a lotus more beautiful and perfect than those on the pools in the Fief of Lau.

In the middle of that vast flower, my father stands smiling at me. His holographic image is a sight that makes my heart ache even more, makes the slow tear quicken. I reach out to him, knowing he's intangible, but wanting to touch him still.

"Dad," I whisper. "I made it. I did it."

He smiles and nods at me. Then he folds his arms over himself, his body transforming into that of a golden bird. He rises high in the chamber, screams aloud, then bursts into flame and ash, making me gasp with horror. But as he tumbles downward, his ashes disappear in a slow shower of gently falling crystalline rain. In his place comes the message. From above and below, the threads wind and twirl inward, crisscrossing in a woven pattern that forms a single almighty word.

Persevere.

Almost as quickly as I can read it, it disappears, blasting apart in a thousand different directions only to slingshot back inward, as if drawn by some magnetic force. The threads come at me. Go through me. The first through my hand. Another through my hip. And then my shoulder and my chest, and then so many that I can't tell where they are coming from or where they are going. It's like being attacked by millions of long needles. There's so much pain, but I don't cry out. It's too quick. I can only draw a breath of utter surprise.

A nd then it's over.

Fingers numb and shaking, I reach up and pull off the blinders.

"Is it done?" Uncle Simon asks, his voice anxious and his eyes bright with excitement.

Swallowing hard, I nod my head. "Y-Yeah, I think so."

"Well played."

Well played. I've planted a virus in the Main Frame—planted seeds of hope. What will the Aristocrats do after this little hiccup? What change will come? I'll have to be there to help. Which means that it's time for this spider to descend from her secluded hiding spot. "A-Am I free now? C-Can I have my legs?"

Uncle Simon smiles, warm and bright. "Of course you can. You deserve them."

I exhale a nervous laugh. "Thank you." Tears start falling unbidden from my eyes. I can't tell if they are tears of joy or terror of what's to come. I have a whole life ahead of me. A life where I will be unapologetically me and, hopefully, make change. Meems comes over and lifts me from the chair.

I cry silently as she carries me to the bed and pulls my modified half pants off, revealing my stumps. I continue crying as Uncle Simon opens up a medical bag and begins attaching my new legs. When he uses the numbing spray, it stings a little, but then I can't feel anything as he and Meems work to attach the leg to my stump, mending together nerves, muscles, bone, tendon, and flesh with synthetics.

I stand in the bathroom and stare at myself in the mirror. Now that I can stand, albeit a little uncertainly, I can finally see my face. I look older than the Ellani of my memories. My hair is longer, my cheekbones more prominent, my expression more somber and reserved. I look, more than ever, like my mother; the only thing separating my face from hers is the scar on my forehead.

I try to measure the time that has passed since I last thought about a birthday. It had been in the pod the night of the accident. I'd wanted a Mod for my upcoming birthday. I got a Mod. One that changed my entire life. And now, this face will go, too. I'll have to Modify myself and be someone new. In order to survive. Still, I just managed to learn to love this face, to appreciate the features my mother gave to me, to function without being Modified… And now, it's being forced on me. It seems so cruel. But I need to live.

"Tasha, what's today?"

"July 3rd of the year 232."

I blink at myself. I'll be eighteen in a few days. No wonder I look older and more reserved. I've been shut up in here for a whole year.

Uncle Simon comes to stand in the doorway. He stares at me, arms crossed. I'm painfully aware of the fact that I haven't yet put any pants on. I feel a little awkward, but his eyes are on my face, and he doesn't seem to notice my indecency; his mind is somewhere else.

"How do they fit?"

I shift my weight back and forth. My stumps feel tender, but the prosthetics are well fitted and padded. "I'm surprised I can stand so easily."

He nods. "With the amount of sitting up you do, your abdominal muscles are strong. The circuitry attached to the legs keeps them wired directly into your neural interface, so they should re-act with the same speed and precision of true appendages. You'll just have to worry about slight atrophy of the gluteal and thigh muscles, so don't do too much bending over or squatting until you've gotten them toned again."

I nod. "I'm not too worried about that. Meems made sure I exercised."

Uncle Simon smiles to himself. "I always kept Meems abreast of my plans for you. She knew that I wanted to eventually restore you as a citizen and give you back your whole body. So she must have been preparing you."

I reach down and touch the synthetic skin encasing the cybernetic leg. The only thing to indicate that the leg is not truly flesh is the band where it attaches to my leg. It's even warm, made more human by micro circuitry that heats the silicone inside. "Thank you," I say quietly. It feels like I shouldn't be saying such a thing to him, that he took my life away from me and I shouldn't thank him for finally giving it back. But, at the same time, if he hadn't done all this to me, I wouldn't be the girl standing in front of this mirror. In fact, I'd most likely be dead. So really, I can't hate him, can I?

"You've earned it. You must think I'm a cad, letting your parents train you like they did and then keeping you here and striking that bargain with you, but I truly believe in what they were working for."

I stare at myself again. "I think I want the same thing. Maybe even more. So, that doesn't make me a tool, does it?" I turn back to him with a smile. "And our deal was equally beneficial, right?"

He nods.

I turn away again. "Fulfilling their dream is only a stepping stone to my own dream." I smile at myself. "There's a lot to look forward to. A whole future filled with possibility."

Meems appears behind Uncle Simon with a large garment bag in her hand. I lift a brow. "What's that?"

"It's your birthday present," Uncle Simon says.

I slip past him and watch as Meems lays the bag on the bed and opens it. Inside is a vibrant red dress. Meems lifts it and turns it one way and then the other, letting the light glitter off the nano-fabric that looks so soft and vivid it might be liquid fire. It reminds me of the firebird that Dad became in the Anansi Chamber.

I look to Uncle Simon. "What's that for?"

He grins. "You can't go to a ball in your underwear, Ellani. Even your mother wasn't that rebellious."

"A ball?"

"G-Corp is holding a ball tonight."

I swallow hard. "And you mean for me to go?"

He nods.

"But now that I've planted the virus, won't they come after me? Kill me, too?"

Uncle Simon looks serious. "It's a possibility. If they can trace it back to you."

I reach out and touch the dress, certain that this has to be a dream—or a nightmare. I can't decide which. The dress feels like water slipping between my fingers. Whatever kind of fabric it is, it must be a brand-new development of the textiles department. I should be happy. I have legs, I can be free, and I can find Guster. But my nerves are all in a twist, and I'm suddenly terrified of again trying to become one with the world that shunned me. "So, if they want me dead, why am I going to their ball?"

Uncle Simon bows low. "Your prince awaits. I did promise."

Excitement punches me in the stomach, making me feel giddily nauseous. "He's going to be there?"

"I guarantee it."

Remembering Gus is an Elite in Real World, I frown. I probably don't have a chance at all with him. Even if I am technically

as rich as they are, his social circle wouldn't approve of him being with a Natural—because, even if I change my face, I won't
look like the Aristocrats. I refuse. But he did say that he wanted
to be with me here, and he *did* come looking for me. And after
tonight, the world will change—technology will be shunned, and
that which is natural will become beautiful again. "Does he know
I'm coming?"

"Doubt it."

I try to even out my suddenly ecstatic breathing. "But I'm
supposed to be dead. Won't that arouse suspicion?"

Uncle Simon grins as he reaches into the side pocket of his
doublet and pulls out a familiar headband. It has been repaired
since the last time I saw it.

I gasp. "My holo-mask."

He holds it out to me. "I assume you see what I have in
mind?"

chapter forty-two

POST-AMERICAN DATE: 7/3/232

LONGITUDINAL TIMESTAMP: 8:00 P.M.

LOCATION: DOME 5: EVANESCENCE

The pod skims to a halt outside of the Bella Adona, the massive main building of the Cyr estate. It's a boxy golden building that towers above every other structure in Evanescence and houses the whole of G-Corp conglomerate's most prized possessions, including the Cyr family and G-System's main terminal.

I stare at the leviathan that makes up the heart of our city. It reminds me of the massive building in the middle of Central Dominion. "Here?" I say with a shiver. "Why?"

"It's Master Quentin's birthday today, and the ball is being held in his honor," Uncle Simon reflects. "It was his decision to have the party here."

I scrunch my nose. In some not-so-distant past, the old Ella would have been tickled pink at the idea of stepping into Quentin's home, but thoughts of him don't stir anything inside anymore. I take note of the hundreds of security droids stationed along the building's perimeter, looking like frightening gunmetal-gray gargoyles frozen against the delicate lawns and gardens that the holo-screens project around the building.

I follow Uncle Simon as he gets out of the pod. "Simon Drexel, plus one."

We wait as the android usher checks the list and then scans each of us in turn. As the scan of my chip doesn't prompt any kind of alert, I let out a breath I didn't know I'd been holding. The false identification I programmed over my own is holding true.

Uncle Simon offers me his arm, and we follow the android escort down the red carpet and through the nano-glass doors of Bella Adona. He leads us through a richly appointed main hall, empty save the security droids and the aerovators, but still managing to speak volumes of its richness through simple grandiosity and the materials that were used to build it. White marble covers the floor. The columns and walls are covered in rich carvings, scrollwork, and gold leafing. There are marble statues stationed at either side of the aerovator, their classic, full-bodied subjects looking just as out of place here as I feel.

The aerovator shoots upward and pings to a halt on the topmost floor. As the doors slide open they reveal a penthouse encased in nano-glass. The inside of the Cyr mansion is just as opulent and beautiful as the main foyer downstairs, except here there is antique furniture and pieces of lost and forgotten artwork from ages past displayed in suspension chambers.

Everywhere, set among the lost relics of humanity, are the Aristocrats. They, themselves like their own pieces of artwork— designed to complement the creativity of their ancestors. Swallowing, I tighten my grasp on my uncle's arm.

"What if someone recognizes me?" I whisper.

He pats my hand reassuringly. "Trust me, they won't. Not with that ingenious little device you've invented for yourself.

Even if they did, what could they do? The virus has already been planted and is working as we speak. At eleven o'clock, we'll have a complete blackout, and they will have more on their hands than a dead girl who snuck into a ball."

I nod, giddy with excitement at the prospect of all of Evanescence deciding to reevaluate its way of life.

As we're announced—my uncle under his proper name and me under the name I put on my chip earlier, Charlotte Webb—I scan the crowd.

"Charlotte Webb?" Uncle Simon asks.

I smirk, my eyes still searching. "She's a literary character. Another spider."

He nods to himself. "I like it. It wouldn't be right to take Anansi, would it? That was your mother's code name. You, little spider, should have your own code name."

I turn my head and blink, sheepish. "I'm sorry, what?"

He scrunches his brow, annoyed that I'm not paying attention. "Who are you looking for?"

I lower my head, a little ashamed that I'm being so obvious. "Delia."

He frowns. "Avoid her if you see her."

"Why?" But I don't need his explanation. Her laugh, that lovely falsity that is the Modification, cuts through the crowd, stirring memories both treasured and painful.

My eyes find her the next moment. She's changed. Everything about her has changed. Her hair is different. It's blue and spiky with white tips, her eyes are the same shade of blue, the pupil a narrow black slit, and her eyebrows short slots on the edge of a forehead that has been implanted to look more bulbous, the skin around it dotted with bright yellow and jet black. Her cheeks and the bones over her temple are more angular. She still looks like a bird, though which one, I don't know.

"Oh circuits," I breathe, my heart sinking. "What did she do?"

Uncle Simon shakes his head, his face sad.

Frowning, I watch Delia. She says something, and the girl beside her laughs and kisses her in the same friendly manner that I once did. In the manner of best friends. As Delia's new friend turns, I catch my breath. She and Delia have matching Modifications, something that's common for close female friends in the Aristocracy, though her pallet is green. To my surprise, their outfits look very familiar. They're both dresses that I designed, dresses I sold to save Meems's chasis.

I pause, outraged. "Carsai? But they hate each other. How could she?"

"Don't make a spectacle of yourself, dear." Uncle Simon tugs my arm, reminding me that we're still on the red carpet, too obvious to everyone in the room. I trudge after him, allowing him to guide me behind a large painting of a cottage in a garden filled with flowers. As we draw closer the image seems to blur into delicate brushstrokes.

Uncle Simon notices my interest in the painting. "Impressionism. Things aren't always what they seem from a distance. This one is a Monet. It used to be quite valuable in the old world."

I peek around the gilt golden frame and find Delia again, my chest tight. "I just don't get it. Why are they friends?"

Plopping himself down on a brocade armchair that creaks under his weight, Uncle Simon reaches for a half finished glass of wine that some flighty Aristocrat abandoned on a side table. "Best leave her to the wolves; she's a lost cause now." As he lifts it, the glass leaves an ugly gray-white ring on the polished surface of the wood. Uncle Simon notices and touches the ring. "It's only a matter of time before they understand the atrocity they've become. The game was meant to make them see, but the privileged never open their eyes. It's only when things get hard and frightening that they begin to realize. The Disfavored are much more malleable; it only took a few months of your father's game for them to realize what they're missing."

"But she was my best friend," I whisper.

He sighs, as if frustrated that I don't want to listen to his tirade. "And she lost you," he reasons. "What do you expect it was like for her when she realized her only other kindred reject was never coming back? How outcast do you think she felt? Abandoned by you and by society?"

I bite my lip. "I never thought about it that way. Poor Delia, being forced to conform just so she didn't stick out so bad." Suddenly I'm ten times happier that I planted the Anansi Virus. In the new world, it will be better for Naturals. The Aristocrats will treasure anything not tainted by technology.

Uncle Simon scoffs. "Poor Delia." He downs the remaining wine in a single gulp. "Don't cry too hard over her. She's found her happy place now. Just look at her, have you ever seen such a happy little sheep?"

I watch Delia interact with Carsai and her cronies. One would never be able to tell that Carsai had once hated Delia, that she and those other girls spurned her. And Delia does look happy. Absolutely giddy that, a few hundred thousand credits and months of painful surgery later, she's finally accepted. Any sign of my old best friend is gone.

Maybe she doesn't need my revolution after all. I turn away and sit in a chair matching my uncle's. "I suppose it would be stupid to try and talk to her."

"Very. You're dead. Be dead."

I take a deep breath and let it out. "So, I'm here. Now what?"

He waves his hand at me, dismissive. "You're young and beautiful, go have fun. This is a ball, after all."

I blink at him. "What about Guster?"

"What about him?"

Slight panic mounts in my voice. "You promised I could see him."

He smiles at me. "Oh, you'll see him. By the end of the night, if neither of you has figured the other's identity, I'll point him out to you." He gives me a little wink.

I grimace. "Gee, thanks a bunch."

chapter forty-three

POST-AMERICAN DATE: 7/3/232

LONGITUDINAL TIMESTAMP: 9:14 P.M.

LOCATION: DOME 5: EVANESCENCE

For a long time, I simply stand and watch. Not many people notice me. It had been an easy decision to design my holo-mask to project Nadine's face. Even though I have to hide behind a mask, Guster would know Nadine's face. Plus, Nadine is pretty enough that she doesn't stand out too badly; she looks almost Custom. It's a fairly decent likeness. I don't look entirely like her, my hair is still that curly brown, but it's good enough.

I stare out one of the nano-windows. I get a full 360 degree view of Evanescence from here. Nothing but the city and the inside of the dome. We're too high, too far from the walls, to see the Disfavored or the wastelands from here. I would have once found this view beautiful, but now I long for trees and cloudy blue sky.

"What would you think of all this, Nadine? Of what I've chosen to become and what I've done?" I whisper against the nano-window. I think that Nadine would approve of my positive vision of the future. I try to imagine what she'd say to me right this moment, but all I can think of are her last words. *You brought us here to die.*

Annoyed by the somber thought, I put my glass down on the railing and try reexamining the crowd. Guster is here somewhere. Inspecting each person in turn, I methodically go over the people standing in chatting throngs, their eyes lazily following the people on the dance floor.

Half of the dancers are androids. They, like the musicians in the corner, are programmed to entertain the guests and make anyone who wants to dance feel less like a spectacle. They're domestic androids, made to look like Custom Aristocrats, but if you watch them long enough you can tell they aren't human. They never make mistakes or sweat or breathe heavy. And they never laugh.

I see Sadie and Bastian dancing together. For once, Bastian actually looks happy. Zane Boyd is in the corner with some Elite girl wearing a too low-cut dress. I look away, for some reason not wanting to see if he notices just how close she's inching toward him.

Spying a service android weaving through the crowd, I step off the landing and go after her. When I catch up with her, I grab a plate of fruit and shove a grape in my mouth. I bite into it, eager to feel something alive, to taste something good, but it seems bitter and mealy to me. Grimacing, I force myself to swallow it.

It tastes better in Nexis. Now that I've tasted the truth, nothing will ever be the same. Delia's laugh cuts the crowd once more, this time close. Startled, I glance around. She and Carsai are right behind me, watching me. Carsai points in my direction, whispers something, and Delia starts cackling again. She says something back.

They're making fun of me? The Delia I knew would have

never made fun of someone who was a Natural. But she's not the Delia I know anymore. I calmly place the plate down on the android's hover-tray and turn back toward them, watching and standing there as they make an obvious display of enjoyment at my expense.

As they whisper and giggle, I'm struck by how much they look and sound like a particular little animal that once roamed outside a town we visited in Nexis, a town called Myst. They were bell-shaped creatures with leathery wings and bulbous appendages on their faces. Even the eyes of those little monsters look like those of Delia and Carsai. They were foolish-looking things, clumsy and awkward. I feel a smile crack my annoyance and, before I can help myself, a laugh bubbles forth.

The two of them stop talking then, both their mouths open in abject horror as I point at them and laugh myself breathless. Delia and Carsai, thoroughly embarrassed by something they don't even understand, hustle themselves away from interested gazes. Still chuckling to myself, I turn back to the hover-tray and pick up my plate once more. I take another grape and chew it, all the while grinning. Somehow, this one tastes sweeter.

Spirits now unaccountably high, I prowl the crowd, my mind interpreting the overindulgent people around me into characters in Nexis. Here this monster, there that monster. I wonder if Mom and Dad did that on purpose, showing me more truths.

And then I see a monster who was once the beauty among the beasts.

In among his crowd of horribly Modified monsters is Quentin Cyr. He's lovely in the way of Aristocrats, the new Mods he has received since I last saw him making him outshine all around him. But he's not as pretty as I remember him. In fact, he seems desperate. Now, instead of seeing someone who naturally rises above the crowd, I see someone constantly needing acceptance from those around him, someone who must always feel that he is just a little bit ahead of everyone else. Why did I ever really care what he thought when it seems he's so much more worried about what everyone else thinks of him? How sad to be that desperate and unable to handle rejection.

I remember the conversation so long ago in the last few moments I had with Dad. They're insecure. How insecure must Quentin be to do such things to himself? I glance at his Dolls. How awful to make others suffer along with you.

Cocking my head, I smile to myself, the new Anansi part of me wondering, *How would you receive a rejection, Quentin Cyr?* Should I make him see? Can I? I have to try. I have to make him understand that he isn't the sun and stars.

I begin walking toward the boy who once mattered so much in my world. It's a long shot, I know, but I'm feeling lucky. Tonight, I have legs. Tonight, I will find Guster. Tonight, the world is going to turn upside down for these people, and maybe then they will see just how silly they really are...and after that? Infinite possibilities. I could walk on air.

Instead of waiting for Quentin to get up and judge me along with all the other girls, I prance up the carpet and stop right in front of him, completely throwing social grace to the wind. He looks down at me, glances from side to side as if uncertain what to do with me, and then looks down at me again. "What are you...doing?" It's the first time I've ever heard his voice. Surprisingly, it's very deep. Lacing the deepness is a sort of amusement and confusion mixed together. I can't help but wonder if it's his natural voice or a Mod.

I shrug and simply say, "Standing."

His smooth brows knit, causing the spiral pattern on his forehead to crimp, and a slight crinkle forms at the edge of his mouth. "You can't stand there, you're blocking my view."

I glance over my shoulder. "Of what? There's nothing of interest for you over there."

He cocks his head, the crinkle around his mouth rising into an amused smirk. "And you fancy yourself more interesting to look at?"

I wave a dismissive hand. "I don't really care what you think."

He's silent for a long moment. "You remind me of someone. A dead girl."

Grinning, I plant my fists on my hips. "Perhaps I've been reborn?"

He leans back, his perfect face thoughtful and his eyes bright. "Interesting."

After a long moment of silence, I cant my head to one side, expectant. "Well?"

A brow lifts. "Well what?" There's that amusement in his voice again.

High off adrenaline and pride in my own Natural body, I smirk. "Aren't you going to say something more intelligent than 'interesting'?"

He frowns. "Like what?"

I brush a piece of normal, wonderful brown hair out of my normal, wonderful gray eyes; he'll see my eyes as blue. "Oh, I don't know. You think of something. I can't imagine the heir to G-Corp is ever short on words. Seems like someone like you should know exactly what to say to everyone. Even me."

Quentin's eyes go a little wide with surprise, the diamond lashes flashing in the recessed lights and his iridescent irises glimmering dual rainbows. Slowly, as if he has forgotten how, he smiles at me. Not the normal bored sneer that he bestows upon his confidants, but an actual, genuine smile. Perfect straight white teeth. I don't think I've ever seen Quentin smile and mean it. "I believe you render me speechless."

I pout, though inside I'm laughing. This is fun. I was always so scared of this boy and his judgment, but now that I don't care, being in his presence is even more enthralling. "Really? Shame. There are no Mods for that, are there?"

The grin broadens and he lifts his hand, half hiding a chuckle. Then he says, almost endearingly, "You're perfect."

Confused, I straighten and blink. "Pardon?"

Standing, he rushes down the stairs at me. I take a nervous step back, worried that I've overstepped my bounds and am about to be punished, but he stops short of me and circles me instead. I bristle at the gesture, but I force my fists not to ball up and my tension not to show in my bare shoulders.

Once he has circled me once, he stops before me and stares down into my eyes. Up close, I can see how every inch of his skin has been delicately inlaid with intricate swirling designs, how each muscle has been augmented to stand out just so, how each bone has been filed or bolstered to give him a chiseled planar appearance, how every hair gleams like a string of starlight, every breath smells of freshly crushed mint, and his body gives off a faint hint of pheromone. So many Mods and Alts. Nothing about him is real, and it makes my stomach turn.

"You're very brave," he's saying to me. "It makes you shine like the sun." Reaching out, he offers me his hand, the whirling designs on his palms glinting in the light. "Will you do me the honor of dancing with me?"

I stare at his outstretched hand, confused. This wasn't what I wanted. I hadn't intended to win him over. That was a desire from a different life, a different Ellani. I want him to see his folly, not feel like he's being rewarded. I look away from the hand, from him, and my eyes fall on the cluster of monsters gathered around his chair.

Back when I first saw them, I had thought they were lovely

Dolls, creatures who complemented Quentin's beauty like mythical stars clustered around the invisible moon. Now, I feel bad for them. I know that they are slaves to his whims. I know that he forces Alterations and Modifications on them, destroying their Natural beauty.

What he has done to them is not lovely. It is an atrocity of human nature, cruel and unusual punishment for merely being who they are. Yet they endure. Though they are as monstrous as sideshow freaks in the carnivals in the encyclopedia, they hold their heads up high and bear it with a certain mark of pride in their own human ability to persevere.

My eyes fall on the tallest, the proudest, the ugliest. Shadow. The last time I saw Shadow he ruined a perfectly good evening at a ball. But that seems so far away, a tiny pebble in a road upheaved by seismic activity. I've killed a dragon. Shadow doesn't scare me anymore. "I'll dance with him, not you."

Quentin sucks in a gasp and blinks. "But he's a—"

"A Doll? Yes, I know," I say, simple as can be. *And how much of a blow is this to your ego, Quentin Cyr?* "And I'm a Natural. Or haven't you noticed? I want to dance with him."

"But." Quentin seems at a loss. "Why?"

I smile at him. "Why not? Haven't you taught your Dolls how to dance?"

Quentin shakes his head, indignant. "Of course they can dance, but they're just—"

"And I'm just me," I say with a shrug. *I am a Trickster.* My smile deepens. *I will show you your folly. You won't be rewarded for your wrongs.* "I'll dance with him and no one else."

Quentin frowns and, for a second, I think he's going to throw a tantrum. But then he turns from me and makes a brisk hand gesture at Shadow. "Do as she wishes. She can have anything she wants."

Shadow bows deeply and comes toward me. As I watch him, something tickles the back of my head. Something about his movement or his expression excites me. Of course I'm excited; I'm going to dance with the devil of this world. I'm going to shame Quentin by favoring an unworthy Doll over him. He steps flush with me. He's tall, like Gus, and just as big.

I offer my hand before he has a chance to be the gentleman. Grunting slightly, as if a little put off by my gesture, he takes my hand and builds a fortress around me with his body.

And then, we begin to tango.

chapter forty-four

POST-AMERICAN DATE: 7/3/232

LONGITUDINAL TIMESTAMP: 9:29 P.M.

LOCATION: DOME 5: EVANESCENCE

After a few steps, he leans close to me. "I'm not so sure Nadine would approve of you using her face in such a manner, Elle."

Startled by both his words and his voice, I trip over my own two feet and stumble into his chest. He takes the chance to lock his arms around me, keeping me from taking hasty steps backward. I stare at him, confused and horrified, as he drags my leaden body across the dance floor, keeping up some semblance of decorum.

This monster has his voice. This monster knows who I am. This monster knows Nadine. And, yes, beneath all those Alterations and Modifications, this monster looks a little bit like *he* does. "Gus?" I squeak.

He keeps his head up as he thrusts his hip into me, prompting me to lose the mannequin routine and dance. "Surprised?"

I clop disgracefully through a few steps, trying to find my

place in the song and a world that has just turned on its head. Gus is here in front of me. Gus is Shadow. Gus totally made me cry the last time I saw him in person. Is Gus the same person here as he is in Nexis? He certainly doesn't look the same, but then, technically, neither do I.

He drops me into a dip, making me linger arched against his body. When he snaps me back up, he drags me close, pasting us together. As we tango across the bare floor, his leg slips between mine in a way that lets me know he at least feels the same way about me as Nexis Gus does.

I suddenly feel awkward with all these people watching us. "Gus," I breathe.

He snaps me away from him, drags me back, trapping me in his inhuman arms. "Are you surprised?" he whispers, his voice like fire on the back of my neck. He spins me the other way, giving me a moment of reprieve.

We collide again. "No," I say. "I'm not surprised in the way you think I am."

His false brow lifts in mockery, pulling at knit-together skin. "And how do you know what I think?"

I step back into the solid cage of his arms, pressing into him, accepting and refusing him as the dance demands, flaunting my Natural body while taunting his false one. He has that expression in his eyes again. The wild one that used to scare me when I met it at school. On this unnatural face, it has a harsh, frightening quality. On Gus's true face it was the expression that told me that I was the only thing he was paying attention to. Now I see them both and understand the fearsome man behind them.

"How do you know it's me?" I wonder.

His lips curve into what I think is a smile, though with his Mod-ravaged face it looks more like a snarl. "You forget that I saw this mask before, Elle. Only you'd be smart enough to create such a marvelous thing."

I toss my leg up in perfect time with the music. How wondrous it is to dance again. I let out a chirp of laughter. "Last time I checked, you didn't seem to think it was such a marvelous thing."

His eyes go sad, the Alterations making the expression so much more desperate than anything Gus could ever conjure. "I'm sorry."

A few moments go by, the song ends and another, slower one starts. He pulls me close, hugging me to him like a lost part of his soul. He presses his face into my hair and begins to speak so low that only I could possibly hear him.

"At first, I hated you," he whispers, his voice a desperate, raw thing. "You had, from the first day you came to Paramount, represented something ideological and great to me. You were a Natural, beautiful and smart, yet you were part of their world. You were like a breath of hope. A promise that all was not lost. I cherished every moment I got to see you, even if it was only at a distance." He's lost in a dream, when the dark memory crashes in, making his voice bitter and harsh. "But then, that mask," he growls. He turns away, his face disgusted.

For a long moment, his grip on me tightens, as if he's fighting to keep me with him even though I'm making no effort to go. He shakes his head and loosens his grip. His words spill out in a blur of emotion. "You wore that horrible thing. It made you look like them, covered up what you were. And it made me so angry with you. At first I hated you for it. Hated you for wanting to be like them, for being weak like they were. But then, when you stopped coming to school, I began to fear that I had been too cruel with you, that I had frightened you with the monster that I was, scared you away with my righteous anger. And then you were dead. I immersed myself in the game. It was the only happiness I had left." He pauses and looks at me, his face soft with affection.

He reaches out and puts a beastly hand on my cheek in such an accepting way that I know I can die happy knowing that he might be the only man in the world to ever love me.

"And then one day, you were there," he continues. "I didn't understand why or how. I just realized that you were with me again. Alive and just as Natural and beautiful as I remember you the first day I saw you. You hadn't Modified or Altered yourself even though I knew that in the game, you were easily able to. I wondered if perhaps that mask hadn't been some kind of farcical joke on your part, that you truly loved yourself for who you were. Either that or you had understood my message to you and knew that you were perfect without any Alteration or Modification. That was my hope, that you already knew that I needed and wanted you, and you'd come to be with me. Whatever your reason for finding me in the game, I vowed not to lose you again. So this time, I spoke to you."

I feel tears of happiness prickle my eyes, but I blink them away. It wouldn't do for either of us if I began crying. I don't want him to get in trouble for disturbing a lady with his hideous features. I hold him tighter, wishing above all else that I could just melt into his decimated body and cleanse him of what that terrible Quentin has done to him. I understand that Game Gus had the real body that this Doll should have had, that it was his wish—like it was mine—to have his true body back. He was so handsome, so strong a Natural. And now he's this—a slave Doll to an egomaniac.

I'd love Guster no matter what he looked like, but I have to know. "What happened, Gus? Why are you like this—with Quentin?"

He glances back toward where Quentin is sitting. He's half paying attention to a conversation, half watching both of us. I know it's us he's watching. I've spent enough of my life keeping tabs on who or what he's watching to know, but I've never seen that expression on his face before. Is he...jealous?

"I have an older brother," Gus says quietly. "Max. Quite some time ago, he got the scratch lung."

I glance up into his eyes. "What's that?"

"It's a common respiratory disease that affects the Disfavored. It's a result of the bad air quality. It's easily treated but, because so few of the Disfavored can afford the necessary health care, it's often fatal."

Gus looks down, his eyes sad again. "I loved my brother more than anything. Our dad died when we were little, and my mom worked so hard just to make ends meet. I wanted to help him in some way. So I dropped out of school and started looking for work, but everyone said I was too young and too scrawny to do the kind of manual labor necessary to raise the credits for his treatment. One day I saw a sign advertising for Doll applicants." He pauses and shakes his head, scoffing bitterly. "I had never seen a Doll before, never knew what they did. But the sign said that the salary was more than enough to cover the cost of my brother's treatments. Enough even for my mom to get us out of the ghetto. So I applied."

I cock my head, examining his expression. He looks distant, almost wistful, as his eyes trail toward his master.

"The Doll House accepted me. They accept everyone. All I had to do was wait for an Aristocrat to adopt me. Quent wanted me the moment he saw me. I still don't really know why. You know the rumors, I'm sure."

I nod, an awkward blush creeping up my neck.

"It's not like that with us," he says quickly. "It's like...I don't know, he needed a friend or something. After his parents adopted me for him, I moved in with them, became just like a family member. For a long time, that's what we were. Brothers. We became so close that it was like we were the other person. And I got paid. My brother started undergoing treatment, and my mother got a job working as a teacher in a better part of the block."

"That doesn't sound so bad," I reflect.

He purses his lips. "No, it wasn't. As we got older, Quent's father started talking about Moding and Alting. At the time, I was Quent's only Doll, so when the time came, I got the Mod before him. I was terrified of it. The other Aristocrats frightened me. I didn't want to look like them. But I knew that if I left, my brother would die, and my mother wouldn't be able to stay living in the area they'd moved to. Plus, I didn't want to leave Quent. So," he breathes, "I underwent the Mod."

I reach out and run my hands over the ridges in his shoulders. He's had some kind of implants, making them look almost reptilian. "It was brave of you."

He shakes his head. "I remember the first one. It was a cheek job, to make his face look more chiseled, because his father thought he still looked too boyish at eleven, too much like a cherub. It hurt so bad. I was bruised and swollen for days. All I did was cry. Eventually, Lady Cyr sent me home just to comfort me. He…" He pauses and draws a breath. "Max wouldn't even look at me. He was disgusted by what I'd done. He said he'd rather die than have a little brother who pranced around with Aristocrats and let them play with him like a little doll. He beat me until I couldn't breathe then threw me out of the house. My mother didn't say a word the entire time."

I stay quiet, knowing that this moment is too raw for me to speak. I don't know what to say. I'm too shocked to speak. I always knew Gus had it hard in Real World; I could tell by the expression he sometimes got in his eyes and by the way tension seemed to drain away from him the moment he stepped into the game.

His fingers begin absently stroking my back, as if the touch of my body brings him comfort. "I don't remember much after that. Quent told me that he found me curled up, half dead on the doorstep the next morning. He'd been the one to carry me in and treat my wounds. He wouldn't let anyone near me. He cried for me, told me he was sorry for what happened, swore that he'd demand another Doll and wouldn't let them touch me again. I made him promise to make sure that when I died, I didn't look at all like who I really was."

My head snaps up. "What?"

He gives me a sidelong glance. "Does that surprise you? It surprised him, too, when I said it. I didn't want to be who I was anymore. I didn't want to be that weak boy who gave up the world to save the person he loved most only to have that love spurned in return. I didn't want to be part of that family any more. I wanted to be part of Quent's." His eyes wander back toward the group of Dolls and Quentin. "And I am."

"So," I say. "You like being Modified and Altered?"

He shrugs. "When I was younger, I thought that changing my skin would change who I was, but I'm still the same person inside. I can't change that. I've had a lot of time to do some soul-searching. I don't like what I've done to myself—not because it made me lose my family, but because it made me lose myself. When I look in the mirror I don't really know who I am anymore. I can't find myself among all the implants and pigments. But in order to find myself again, I have to accept that I've done this to myself—that the choice is part of who I am."

I touch his face. "You're there. I see you."

He puts his hand on mine, trapping my fingers close to him. "And I see you."

We dance like that for a long time, lost in each other's eyes. Eventually, I say, "Have you ever seen him since then? Max? Or your mother?"

He shakes his head. "They made it clear what they thought of me, though they seem to appreciate the credits. They never send them back."

My step falters again. "You still give them your salary?"

He shrugs. "You think it's stupid of me? I have nothing else to do with it. The Cyrs take care of all my needs. As much as Mom and Max may hate me, I still love them. She's still my mother, and he's still my brother. Besides, Max's treatments are lifelong; if I withdrew my financial support, he'd die. I don't want to carry his death on my back, even if he did try to do the same to me."

My chest swells and I can't help smiling at him, despite the inappropriateness of the moment. I didn't think it was possible, but I think I just fell even more in love with Gus. Pulling him tight, I bury my face in his neck. The bulges and ridges of his implants feel foreign to me, but the heat and scent of him do not. He's still Gus. I still love him. He's better than I remember.

chapter forty-five

I'm vaguely aware of a slight commotion occurring in the room, though the dance floor is shoved into the corner, and it's hard to see what's going on around all the art displays and the clutter of furniture. I notice Quentin's mother cut across the floor.

You can tell Lady Cyr from every other woman in the room because she's the final piece of the Cyr puzzle. All three are like marble statues, cut to perfection, and decorated with silver glitter and tinsel and celestial light. They're just *different*. It must be some kind of special Mod that only the Cyr family can utilize.

She moves across the dance floor, sluicing dancers to the side as efficiently as the prow of an ocean schooner. Gus swings me out of the way of Quentin's mother as she makes a very deliberate beeline to her son. Gus's attention shifts toward Quentin, and his steps slow until he stops entirely and stares up at Quentin. Lady Cyr is crouched over her son, speaking to him in rushed words that don't seem to please him at all. His face contorts in a manner I've never seen before, different than the scowl he gave me last year.

I glance up at Gus, whose face appears just as disturbed, but he doesn't seem to notice I'm even there. Lady Cyr turns prettily and flounces back down the landing, retracing her steps back over the dance floor and dissolving into the crowd. Quentin turns to Gus, who in turn cocks his head, his brow concerned. Quentin leans back and whispers something to Zane Boyd, who I hadn't noticed was even standing there. Zane nods and reaches over Quentin's shoulder, slipping something into the breast pocket of his jacket.

Quentin stands and comes toward us. Grasping my elbow, Gus draws me backward. For a moment I think he's trying to escape from Quentin, who looks wildly intent, but then I realize he's backing us into a small alcove where a hover-tray piled with dirty dishes is waiting to be loaded onto the service aerovator. Quentin glances behind him before joining us.

"What's wrong?" Gus asks, his voice urgent and tight.

Quentin frowns as he keeps one eye on the room. "My father wants to do a birthday toast at eleven. I need to stay here."

Gus makes a low growling noise at the back of his throat, then he draws a quick breath. "Give it to me, I'll do it."

Quentin's head whips around. "What? No, you can't,"

Gus steps forward, coming inappropriately close to Quentin. With the darkness subduing the difference between beauty and beastliness, the two of them standing so close brings out the distinct similarities of their bodies. Both are nearly the same height and build, and both have the same basic augmented facial features. Gus slips his hand into Quentin's breast pocket, removing whatever Zane had left there, and whispers into Quentin's ear. "Watch me."

He draws back before Quentin can make a move to reclaim whatever Gus took. He opens his mouth to argue with Gus, but Gus slips to one side and places a hand on his shoulder. Quentin gives him a desperate expression, but Gus ignores it, looking instead to me. "Take care of him for me, would you? With that, Gus steps back into the open service aerovator. As the doors slide closed, cutting off the harsh florescent light from within, Quentin and I are left in complete darkness.

"Well," he says softly, "looks like I'm going to get that dance after all."

I turn to him, too bewildered at first to speak, then I find my voice. "What the heck just happened?"

His hand finds mine in the darkness and tugs it toward him. "Nothing you need to worry about, Ella. Let him do his job."

I feel my jaw fall open as he begins backing toward the dance floor. "You-You know who I am?"

He glances behind him, making certain he's not going to back into any of the swirling couples, then he grins. "Sure." As he spins into the rotating crowd, he pulls me toward him and puts his free hand on my waist.

"But," I breathe, unable to compute what's going on, "how?"

He gives me a nervous sidelong glance, as if he's a little afraid of making complete eye contact with me. "Best not to look too talkative, people might get suspicious. I have a reputation to uphold, you know."

I scowl up at him. "*You're* the one who asked to dance with *me*, Quentin."

He tries to suppress a smile. "It's Quent," he corrects, "and I asked to dance, not talk. Everyone knows I'm the broody silent type — you'll ruin my image."

I suck in my lips and bite down on them, trying to suppress my annoyance. "It's a stupid image to want to uphold," I mutter.

"Not when you don't want people in your business. It's the perfect image for someone who wants to be left alone."

I look up into his eyes, challenging him, but what I find there surprises me into lowering my proverbial sword. Quentin is staring at me with the same kind of intensity that Gus does, that combination of awe and reverence that has an unhinging quality. I remember what Gus just said: *we became so close that it was like we were the other person.* How alike are they? I look away, confused. "What's Gus doing?" I ask, trying to keep my lips from moving.

He twirls me in a circle. "Oh, nothing too crazy. Just starting a rebellion."

My step falters but Quentin's arms tighten, deftly keeping me upright and spinning.

Not daring to look at him, I stare at his chest. "What?" I hiss.

He pulls me closer, pressing us together so that he can speak without anyone seeing or hearing. "You're not the only Trickster, Ella. Not the first, or last, or the only of your kind."

Eyes wide, I attempt to look up at him, but he keeps me pulled close, his jaw preventing me from moving my head. As we spin, I catch sight of Carsai and Delia standing on the edge of the dance floor, their birdlike faces flushed with indignant horror that I'm dancing with Quentin. I smile to myself, amused by how much they care and how much I don't. Quentin's not the god I thought he was; he's just a lost boy. One with a surprising array of secrets, but he's still a monster. He still destroyed the man I love, and it was his family that killed my parents and tried to kill me.

It doesn't matter to me that Gus doesn't blame him, even loves him like a brother. I will never forgive him.

spend more time dancing with Quentin than I did with Gus. That's fine, because I know that as soon as he releases me I'm going to be inundated with jealous harpies demanding to know what, exactly, I—a Natural—think I'm doing dancing with Quentin. The music abruptly dies in the middle of a waltz. Quentin pauses, shifting his arm so that he can glance at his flex-bracelet. "That time already," he breathes, looking to me.

"What time?"

He twists his wrist, letting me see the time. 10:57, almost eleven. Almost time for the virus to kick in. "Almost time for lights-out."

I feel my mouth form into a stupid little *O*. "You know?"

His fingers splay against the small of my back, guiding me toward the platform. His father is standing there already, his arm around Lady Cyr. Quentin nudges me off to the left, close to where the service aerovator and the rest of his Dolls are all standing like little toy soldiers. "Stay here."

I open my mouth to argue, but a hand clamps on my shoulder. I spin with a yelp, but it's only Gus. "Gus," I breathe and throw myself into his arms. "What the heck have you—"

"Shhh." He puts his fingers to my lips and nods toward where all the guests are piling onto the dance floor. "It's time for the birthday toast."

The lights dim around the room, blanketing the robots, who are standing in shadow among the relics of old, and spotlights focus on the landing where Quentin and his parents are standing. They shine, the three of them, beacons stationed at the tallest point in all of Evanescence. It makes me sick to my stomach.

"Ladies and gentlemen," President Cyr begins. "Today is my son's nineteenth birthday."

A cheer rises up in the crowd, followed by thunderous applause that quickly turns to a moment of silence and then shrieks as the spotlight and every other light in the city wink out.

Gus's hands tighten around me, as if he's afraid I'm going to disappear with everyone else. Around us the darkness is absolute, punctured only by the fiber-optic glint of skin Alterations, the faint glow of Argence, the light of flex-bracelets, and the glowing red eyes of the security droids—who, like all robots, run on energy cells.

"Calm down, calm down, everyone." President Cyr is yelling, but I doubt many can hear him. The people are in a panic. I can hear feet stampeding here and there, glass breaking.

Suddenly something lances through my skull. Gasping, I double over against Gus, but he seems struck with the same pain. By the intensified level of screaming and yelling, I think everyone does. It hurts so bad, making me feel like my head is going to explode, but then it dies away, leaving a dull thudding headache.

Gus's hands find my face. "Elle?" he asks, his voice tight with pain.

"What was that?" I whimper.

"I-I don't know." His voice is low and concerned.

Suddenly, over the panicked crowd, I hear someone laughing, cackling really. I recognize the laugh. "Fools," he screams, still laughing. "All of you are fools. They thought I didn't see, they thought I wasn't good enough. But I see better than any of them, any of you. And I'm superior to them. I've done what they could not. You're ruined. Ruined."

With that, the shooting begins.

In the panicked jostle of bodies and the deafening cacophony of terror and demise, I lose my orientation. I think I can hear Gus; I don't know. His hands went missing, but I move toward where I think he is anyway, calling for him. I don't know what's going on.

"Gus," I yell.

"Elle. Over here."

I run toward his voice and trip over something, landing hard on my jaw. I scramble to untangle from what I'm now feeling is a body, bloody across the neck and face. Horrified, I stumble backward, my heel catching something else. I collide with another body, this one upright and too sure on its feet to be human. I glance up just in time to feel massive hands clamp around my throat.

It picks me up and throws me, making me collide with a railing where I melt down into a puddle of confusion and pain. I lie there for a moment, unable to move, because the pain in my back is too much. Then it dawns on me. That was a robot; I could tell by how cold the hands were. But, its eyes didn't glow—it was a domestic android.

I spin around, trying to find the floor and get my feet underneath me. I crouch there, terrified. I can see the red eyes of the security droids. I can see the room, blindingly lit up for milliseconds at a time as flashes of their laser guns go off. I see the bodies going down, the blood spilling.

And then I understand. The robots have all gone mad. They're killing their human masters.

There's a cluster of them near the aerovators, their fire concentrated in one area. An area where all the humans in the room have congregated, seeking escape. Except the aerovator doors aren't opening. There's no electricity. There's no escape.

"Ella." Gus's voice is harsh and determined in my ear. I glance up, searching for him. I can see his shape looming over me in the darkness, the fiber-optic cords in his flesh glowing dully, can feel his hands clutching at me.

I grasp his wrists, letting him pull me up into his arms and fold me into the comfort of his familiar scent. We crouch low, tiptoeing around the landing, trying not to attract attention. Something swipes at us from one direction, there's a burst of laser gunfire, and whatever it was falls to my right.

I hear screaming on the landing.

"Circuits," he growls. He pushes a hand against my back. "Go, toward the service aerovator."

"But—"

"Go," he hisses. There's another burst of light and I can see in the flash that the boy standing beside me isn't Gus at all, but Quentin. He turns and sprints up the steps.

The light blinks out, hiding my horror. I had thought Quentin was Gus. Why? I stumble in the direction he indicated, trying to understand how and what went wrong in my brain, but I can't. I crash into a hover-tray, making a loud clatter. The next moment, more hands are upon me. These are synthetic, reaching at me, punching at me. I struggle to free myself, but the onslaught is too much, making me fall to my knees because I'm already off-balance. The hands follow.

I roll, trying to avoid the crouching android. My hands fall on something cold and flat. My brain registers that it's a knife as I bring it up and stab it right into the android's neck. I heave against him, kicking him off-balance as hydraulic fluid sprays out of what would, in a human, be a vital artery. I roll to my feet, knife in hand and ready for the next attacker.

The lights flash back on, blinding all of us for precious moments. I hear Uncle Simon laughing again. "I'm better than all of them. I did what no one else could. Do you see it now?"

As my vision clears I feel my stomach roll over. Bile rises to my throat and I double over, sickened by what I see. Everywhere, Aristocrats are strewn over the floor, their blood soaking into the industrial carpet, seeping along the dance floor. The air is thick with the smell of burned flesh. The people near the aerovators are screaming behind a pile of bodies, their fists slamming against the glass.

The aerovators should be reading the G-Chips, should be letting people escape, but they aren't. The people are trapped at the mercy of robots that aren't programmed to kill their masters. The robots should have shut down. All of them are programmed to go offline with a single defense word uttered through the Internetwork. Somehow, the G-Chips aren't communicating with the network at all.

Someone grabs my arm, hauling me to one side. I lift my knife and slash before I can think. Gus, the real one, leaps away from me, narrowly escaping being gutted. He gives me a dark annoyed look, made more horrible by the Modifications on his face. Horrified, I drop the knife. Shaking his head, he shoves me in one direction, covering me as I run toward the service aerovator, shooting at oncoming robots with a gun I didn't realize he was carrying.

They've all got guns—all of the Dolls. They've set up a defensive perimeter, cutting off a small group of Aristocrats from the robots. As I pass the landing I can see President Cyr's body, lying among a group of robots. They tear at him like rabid animals, obliterating him. I turn away, sickened again, and skid under a table one of the Dolls is crouching behind. Hands grab at me, hustling me to the back toward where the Aristocrats are gathered. I turn, searching for Gus, but I don't see him.

I end up in a small group of shell-shocked women and men, Quentin and his mother among them. One of his Dolls has removed his own uniform jacket and now has it pressed against Quentin's shoulder. I can see blood dribbling down his arm.

"What happened?" I demand of Lady Cyr. She doesn't look up; she's too preoccupied with tearing at her dress.

The Doll gives me a cursory glance. "Something went wrong

with the virus."

My stomach turns to lead. "The virus?"

"Went wrong?" Uncle Simon repeats, his voice that of a madman. I whip my head around, searching for him. He and Bastian have both been bound and are now being held at gunpoint by two of Quentin's Aristocrat friends. "It went exactly as I planned. I'll tell you what went wrong." His mad green eyes are on me now, only me, as if I'm the one these words are meant for. "What went wrong was that we didn't just bomb one another into extinction during the war. What went wrong is that you, the ancestors of the very terrorists who started the war, just don't think big enough. What went wrong was that I wasn't the one who was asked to do this in the first place. Well, who tricked the Tricksters now? I did it right."

Out of the corner of my eye, I see Lady Cyr get to her feet. She drops the strands of fabric she's been ripping off the hem of her dress into the Doll's lap and calmly walks toward my uncle. She crouches before him. "Simon, are you telling me that this is your doing?"

He grins madly, pinkish drool dribbling from his lips. I realize now that he's been beaten to near unconsciousness, probably to get him subdued and bound. "I changed the program, Kitsune. You all had such high ideals, but they were never extreme enough. What's a power outage going to prove? What's a couple of angry Disfavored armed with antique guns going to do? You were all too scared. Too afraid after what happened in Adagio. But I wasn't." His head wobbles to one side, and his eyes search out mine. "You want change?" He coughs, spattering blood onto Lady Cyr's white dress. It dribbles to the floor, repulsed by the anti-stain nanotechnology woven into the fabric. "You gotta make change."

I swallow, horrified. This isn't the change I wanted. I didn't want death and destruction. I wanted growth.

Lady Cyr reaches down and grabs a fistful of his hair, hauling him a few inches off the floor and wrenching his face to the side, making him see into her steely eyes—eyes of an avenging angel. "What did you do? What did the program do?"

He grins again, blood showing between his teeth. "I have done what you should have asked me to do in the first place. Why didn't you ask me to program the game? I'm just as good as they were. Better. You'll all burn to ash; it's the only way. Cleanse this filthy earth." His eyes flutter backward, revealing bloodshot whites.

She shakes him. "Simon. Simon, damn you, don't you pass out on me." But Uncle Simon is out cold. She lets his head drop to the floor and begins weeping.

Quentin grunts as he gets to his feet and shuffles toward his mother. The Doll has tied off his wound and fashioned a sling for him out of the strands of Lady Cyr's gown. Quentin stops above his mother, a bloodstained ivory tower, and reaches under his shirt. He pulls out his own revolver, the same kind I used in the game, and aims it downward.

"Permission to take out the trash?" His voice is dark, emotionless, his eyes predatory in a way I never dreamed Quentin's eyes could be.

Bastian's eyes widen in terror. There's only the slightest nod from Lady Cyr, something that comes before I can fully process what is going on.

"No," I scream and lunge forward, but my word is lost as Quentin's finger clenches on the trigger, releasing one pointblank round into my uncle's skull. *Bam.* And all my answers are gone.

Quentin turns the gun to rest between Bastian's hateful eyes.

"No," I scream again, managing to stumble to my feet and throw myself between them. I grasp onto Bastian, practically squeezing the life out of him. "No. Don't you dare,"

I feel the gun at the back of my skull, still warm.

"Get out of the way, Ellani," is Quentin's cold reply.

I shake my head, hold tighter to Bastian.

Quentin cocks the gun. Bastian holds his breath. "Move."

I glance over my shoulder, meet Quentin's diamond-hard eyes. "I won't. He's all I have left. You'll have to kill me to get to him."

Quentin stares at me for a very long moment. His eyes are hollow and hard, a prince without his dynasty. I glare at him, hateful. Despite the noise and everything going on around us, it's as if it's just him and me. Finally he tucks the gun back into his waistband and turns away, leaving us kneeling in my uncle's oozing brain.

"E-Ella?" It takes a long moment for me to register what Bastian's saying and even longer for me to turn from Quentin. I draw away, and we look at each other for the first time in over a year.

A blast sends glass and foul-smelling wind whipping across the dance floor. Bastian draws his eyes away and looks across the room. The doors of the aerovators have been blown from the inside out, making the bodies and few remaining survivors topple backward, half burying the security droids. From within people are pouring out. Disfavored.

Quentin steps back into the corner of my vision, his eyes fixed across the room. "What a crappy time to start a rebellion," he mutters. He makes a militant hand gesture at the Dolls defending us. "Get everyone out of here."

Before I realize what's going on, there's a mass heave toward the service aerovator. I grab Bastian's wrist and drag him along with me. Everyone's back on their feet, panicking as more guns are turned on them. It seems the newcomers haven't yet realized that the droids are shooting at everyone, not just them.

There are Dolls defending the aerovator. They're reaching into the crowd, pulling out people by their hands and shoving them into the tiny box. It won't hold everyone. But I don't need to worry; Gus is already in there, his body thrown against the weighted doors, keeping them open. He, at least, is safe.

Someone grabs my free hand and drags me forward. It's Zane Boyd. He pulls my arm up, volunteering me and demanding that I be saved at the same time. A Doll grabs me, shoves me in. Bastian follows behind, practically falling on top of me as we go. Gus smiles at me, tired and sad. I wriggle into the corner by the Doll tinkering with the control panel and wait, listening to the whimpers of the forever broken.

I see a familiar face floating in the crowd. "Sadie," I scream. My fellow ward turns huge, frightened eyes on me, her expression confused. She doesn't seem to recognize me, but she reaches out anyway, as if trusting that because I know her name I might save her. I move to get up, but Bastian is on his feet before me, clambering forward and reaching out for her.

At the door, Zane seems to notice Bastian's focus, because he grabs Sadie and shoves her into the aerovator. She stumbles forward and wraps her trembling arms around Bastian. Still bound, he presses his face into her hair and comforts her as best he can. "It's okay, it's okay." Even though we both know it's not.

A few more bodies jettison past me before Gus cries out. "We can't fit any more."

"Just one more." I hear Zane on the other side. "My mother. And my brother, where's my brother? Someone find them."

A moment later, Quentin appears beside Zane. "Is Mom in there?"

"No."

The gunfire draws closer, old-fashioned bullets ping against the metal furnishings. One makes it into the aerovator where it ricochets and then slugs someone in the back. They fall, shoving bodies against me, separating me from Bastian.

"We don't have time," Gus screams, "We have to go."

"Not without her." I can see white reflected off the polished chrome frame of the aerovator. Quentin's moving away, searching, yelling for his mother.

Gus swears. "Stop him."

Zane grabs Quentin by the back of the collar. "I'll find her." He tosses him backward so that he topples into Gus. Gus's body folds inward, bear-hugging Quentin as they both collapse on the Doll beside me. For a moment, there's a frenzy of limbs and grunts and cries before Quentin leaps to his feet and launches himself forward, but the door slams shut in his face. He hurdles against it and sticks there for a brief moment before taking a step back, fire in his eyes.

With a curse, he punches the door, making the whole aerovator shake, and leaving a dent. He leans down and grabs Guster's collar, hauling him to his feet. "Open the door," he demands, insane with grief.

Guster grabs Quentin's hand, already bloody and bruising from punching the door, and eases it away from him. "It's too late."

Almost on cue, the gunshots and screams reach a horrifying crescendo. And then it's silent. Too silent. A moment later there's a pocket of rapid gunfire, maybe a body moving in the heap, and then it's silent again.

Quentin reels away from Guster and slams his back against the doors. He does it again and again, until he collapses beside me and begins to sob.

"Got it," breathes the Doll.

I blink at him. I hadn't even realized he'd gotten up and

resumed his work on the control panel. He pulls a wire that sparks and spits, making him draw his hand back with a grunt, but he goes back to it, wincing. The aerovator clicks, and then suddenly we're going down.

"Go to the basement, Sid," Gus says. "There's a service tunnel they don't know about."

The Doll named Sid nods.

It's a long, slow descent. I assume the aerovator is working on auxiliary power, or maybe it doesn't realize it has anyone inside so it's on energy-saving mode. Or maybe it just feels like eternity.

Gus crouches beside Quentin and pulls him into his arms. Wanting to avoid the little bit of pity I have for Quentin, I look around the aerovator. Delia and Carsai are there, along with maybe two dozen other people. Everyone else was mercilessly slaughtered; the G-Chips no longer work, the robots have run amok, the Disfavored have somehow infiltrated the dome. The Aristocrats are being massacred. Evanescence will never be the same. All of it is because I played a stupid game and chose to plant a virus. All because I wanted to build a better world. But this isn't progress. This is destruction. Because of me.

Meems's words are suddenly in my mind. *From what I can see of humans, you often destroy wonderful things in the pursuit of something that your delusions make you think is more wonderful.*

I'm so stupid. Why couldn't I see what I was doing? Tears suddenly burst forth, and I let sorrow wrack me until my body is so confused by the shakes and the sobs that it doesn't know what to do, so it just seizes up, keeping me from breathing.

"Hey," Gus whispers, coming to his knees and reaching out to me. "What's wrong? Are you hurt?"

Clinging to him, I sob into his shoulder. "It's all my fault."

He cradles my head. "What? No, it's not your fault. Why would you think that?"

I shake my head and pull away. "It is." I insist. "It was the G-Game. The Anansi Chamber. It-It did something to the Main Frame. P-Planted a virus." I try to explain, gasping against my hitching voice.

Gus sits back and leans against the door beside Quentin. Quentin's own constitution seems to have grown hard and distant in the time it took me to put two and two together. Quentin is the one who speaks. "We know."

I blink at him, tears still spilling. "W-What?"

He lifts his eyes, the irises amber now that the sparkle has gone out around them. There's a bitter sneer on his face. "You heard me," he growls.

Gus reaches over and puts a hand on Quentin's arm. "Don't blame her, Quent." But Quentin flinches away and struggles to his feet, off-balance, because he still has one arm in a sling. The aerovator hits the ground floor and the door slides open.

Quentin looks at the Aristocrats huddled into the back of the aerovator. When we first piled in, it seemed there wasn't even enough room to breathe, but now there's a good distance between us and them, as though they've all managed to shrink on the ride down. Their eyes are on us, terrified and confused.

"Get out of here," Quentin demands. "All of you. And take that as well." He gestures to the body.

No one dares disobey him. With his mother and father dead, Quentin is now the new President Cyr of Evanescence. They file out, dragging the dead man along with them, and stand huddled in the stark, gray tunnel, leaving only Gus and Sid.

Quentin looks at them. "You, too."

Gus straightens and opens his mouth, ready to argue, but Quentin lifts a hand and dismisses him again. Gus closes his mouth and glances down at me, worry in his eyes. When Gus and Sid are standing in the hall with the other Aristocrats, Quentin punches the manual button to close the door. I get to my feet and scramble away from him, frightened by what he might do to me. I completely destroyed his world—caused the death of his parents, friends, and most of his Dolls.

He turns around and stares at me long and hard. He has a gun hidden under the loose tails of his shirt, though I don't doubt that he's strong enough to beat me to death before Gus manages to get the door open.

Uncertain of what to say or do to prevent him from killing me, I swallow hard. Finally, I just say, "I don't blame you. I deserve it."

His brows lift in surprise, and he laughs bitterly, shaking his head. In the next moment, he launches himself at me, his one good hand most likely broken as it is, clamping around my neck, pinning me against the aerovator wall, a warning restraint more than pain. My first instinct is to kick him in the groin, but I know that will only make him angrier in the long run, and will most likely just prolong my own death. I'd rather die swiftly.

I feel more tears welling over my eyelids. Hysterical tears of fear and self-loathing. I'm ashamed that I'm crying. I can't even die with dignity. "I-I didn't know what I was doing." I whimper. "I thought it was just a little virus to cause a blackout. I swear I didn't know what he'd done to it. I didn't want this. If I had known, I swear I never would have planted it."

"Stop it."

"I never would have even played that stupid ga—"

Quentin's grip tightens on my neck, making my words seize in my throat.

Seeing that he has my attention again, he eases up and steps close to me. So close that our noses are touching. "Listen to me,

Ella," he whispers, his voice a dangerous purr and his breath too clean and refreshing to herald death. "Don't you dare blame yourself for what happened tonight. Yes, you played the game. Yes, you planted the virus that caused all of this. But you are only one piece in this movement. We've all been betrayed."

I stare into his eyes, eyes that have found their color again, but the diamond has gone dark and smoky. I can't compute what he's saying or doing, but I nod. I don't want him to kill me.

He continues speaking. "We all have a part to play in this. My mother, your parents, you and I, Guster and Zane, and the rest of the resistance. If you need to blame someone for everything that went wrong tonight, blame Simon. The virus *was* only supposed to cause a blackout. A blackout that would allow the Disfavored rebels to infiltrate the city, get through a door to Bella Adona that was conveniently left open, and make a point by killing my father. The system wasn't supposed to go down for as long as it did, it wasn't supposed to make the robots go mad, and it wasn't supposed to fry the G-Chips. All that was Simon's doing. Do you understand?"

I nod again, understanding that Guster must have disappeared to open the door for the rebels. He and Quentin and Lady Cyr had planned the rebellion. Had been ready to escape through the service aerovator, but no one had accounted for how horrible the virus truly was. I look up into his hard eyes, and my lips tremble as I speak. "K-Kill your father?"

The skin under his eyes pinches. "Oh, don't look at me like that," he growls. "He did this to me. Do you know what it's like to have this forced on you? Do you have any idea what he did to my mother?"

I shake my head, not understanding what he's talking about. A moment of silence ticks by as I search for some way of derailing his anger. "C-Can we fix it?"

Quentin's hand slips slightly on my neck as he draws far enough away to look off to the side, truly thinking about my question. "I don't know," he says finally, his voice calm again. Then he turns back to me, his face intent. "But I don't know if I want to. His methods were extreme, but perhaps what Simon did was for the best."

A crazy laugh garbles up my throat. "They died today, Quentin. Your mother and father. All those people. Don't you care?"

Quentin's hand tightens on my throat again as his whole body sweeps flush with mine, pinning me vertical. He stares into my eyes. "I'll say this once. My mother meant the world to me. She was more important than you'll ever know," he hisses. He blinks, his face confused. "Do I honestly look like I'm happy my mother and Zane and all those people are dead?"

He may have plotted the death of his father, but he'd cried genuine tears for his mother. His mother, who planned that assassination with him. His father had done terrible things to him and his mother. What could he have done? What could the wife and son of the President have endured to make them plot to kill the city's most beloved man? I shake my head.

His thumb arches up and gently presses itself into the soft flesh under my jaw, making my head go still. He stares into my eyes again; this time there's something vulnerable there. "Good," he says quietly, too intimately. "I would hate for someone—especially you—to think I'm heartless. I'm just..." He pauses, searching for the right word, his face going softer and more exposed, revealing the boy that he is. "Trying to figure this out. All that death. It's hard to think anything good might come out of it."

I swallow. "I only wanted something good. I didn't want to hurt anyone. I'm so sorry."

He looks back at me and smiles a smile that could melt anyone's fear, his fingers brushing along my throat. "I know." Then he kisses me.

Quentin's kiss is a memory torn forth from the back of my mind and set forth for intense examination. First that moment in the dark of the room upstairs where I thought he was Gus, and now this. His lips, the way he kisses me, the arch of his body against mine, the way his fingers linger on my neck—never a threat at all—is the same way Gus kisses me. Not the Gus outside the door, because I haven't kissed that Gus, and his lips wouldn't feel the same anymore—they're too badly destroyed—but the Gus I know from Nexis. It's the kind of kiss that I can't refuse, because there's a kind of love and emotion in that kiss that we both seem to recognize, so I don't refuse. I kiss him back.

Eventually, he pulls away; the desperation in our bodies is too much to let it go on. Quentin stumbles backward, staring at me like he doesn't quite realize what just happened. I can feel the heat on my cheeks, can feel the drying track marks of tears, hydraulic fluid, and blood itchy on my hot skin. He looks away, his own face redder than I thought possible for someone with skin as unreal as his.

He runs a hand through his hair. "I'm, uh, I'm sorry. I shouldn't have done that."

I reach up and touch my lips, confused. "Who played that game?" I whisper, my voice barely audible.

He looks away.

I repeat myself, my voice growing louder with confusion. "Who played that game, Quentin?"

He turns and punches the button. The doors open again. Gus rushes in as Quentin rushes out, and he takes me into his arms. "Are you okay? Did he hurt you?"

I scrunch my brow, searching for Quentin beyond. "No, he

didn't hurt me," I say, my voice relaying disbelief. Scared the crap out of me, sure, but he didn't hurt me. Even when he had his hands around my neck, he was aware of my body enough to know the difference between what controlled and what hurt. That kind of knowledge only comes with knowing someone *very* well. I'm not entirely convinced that Quentin, volatile and confused as he is, *could* hurt me.

chapter forty-six

POST-AMERICAN DATE: 7/4/232

LONGITUDINAL TIMESTAMP: 1:20 A.M.

LOCATION: DOME 5: EVANESCENCE

Sid's cat-like eyes scan the console before him. We're in a small utility closet just beyond a door leading onto the ground level of Evanescence. "Looks like they've breached gates A, C, and D. There's no telling how many of the Disfavored have come through."

Quentin shifts on his feet, his face contemplative. "We need to get out of here."

Gus nods in agreement.

"What?" I gasp. "We can't leave."

Gus glances down at me and then at Quentin. Quentin gives a curt nod before turning back to watch Sid navigate the command board. Gus's fingers grasp around my upper arm and lead me a distance away from where the other Aristocrats have clustered nervously around Quentin.

When he gets far enough away that no one can hear him, he says, "We have to leave the city."

My eyes go wide. "No." He shushes me, his eyes searching

beyond my head, looking to see if anyone heard. I attempt to lower my voice, but my panic is clear. "What do you mean, leave? You can't leave. We have to fix this."

Gus puts his hands on my shoulders, whether it's to shut me up or steady my suddenly gelatinous legs, I don't know. "I know, but we can't stay here. It's too dangerous."

Shaking my head, I pull away from him. "No. No, I won't. Where would we go, Gus? It's death out there, you *know* that."

"No more out there than in here. Besides, we wouldn't go to the wasteland," he reassures. "Quent can get us into the Undertunnels. We can go to Cadence."

"Cadence?" The blue dome. Our sister city. Only one of many supposed domed cities spanning Post-America. A city that is inhabited by people who have genetic ancestors and a Pre-Dome history similar to ours, but that might be the only thing we have in common. I try to think of what it must have been like for my mother when she came to Evanescence from Adagio and had to integrate herself into a new culture. Uncle Simon said they forced the G-Chip on her.

I think about what Quentin had said about President Cyr having done terrible things to his mother. What if he forced that on her, too? What if, unlike my mother, Lady Cyr's Mods and Alts had been forced on her? If Lady Cyr was from the outside then she would have been a Naturalist too, right? Did that mean she'd wanted Quentin to be a Natural like me? Did that mean that she'd taught Quentin Natural values, made him not want to Mod and Alt himself? Had he been forced to Mod and Alt himself despite how he felt? What would that be like, to go to bed loving who you are only to wake up with completely new skin that you hated?

What if we go to Cadence and that happens to all of us? I don't know what that would be like, having something so monumental forced upon me. "We don't know anything about Cadence."

Gus's hands slip off my shoulders. "It has to be safer than here."

I look up at the cement ceiling. "I don't understand. We could regain control of the robots. Quentin is President now—he can change the rules, he can let the Disfavored live inside the dome. He can change things to be right. Why do we have to leave?"

Gus shakes his head, his eyes sad. "I'm not sure you understand the reality of what's going on here. For one, we won't be able to get the robots back. The G-Chips are fried and with the amount of droids out there, regaining control of the Mainframe is impossible. Besides, to the Disfavored, this is a take-over—a changing of regimes. It wasn't supposed to get this far. The electricity was only supposed to be down for a minute, the rebels were supposed to infiltrate and cause a ruckus. The security droids were supposed to cut them down in an instant. It was only meant to shake things up, to cause a commotion that would, hopefully, let Lady Cyr step into the President's position. Putting her in the position as President would have meant new hope for us. But…"

I look away, feeling bitter. I had that hope, too. "But it got out of hand," I finish for him.

He gives a curt nod. "Without the security droids to help control the Disfavored they'll be impossible to reason with. They've taken this opportunity and run with it. We won't regain control of the city—they'll kill us all."

"But you helped them get in," I reason. Then I remember what Uncle Simon said about the game. "You gave them the Gaming Houses—helped them realize they should rebel. You're on their side."

Gus scoffs bitterly, his eyes shifting to the Aristocrats once more. "We also represent that which they hate. Do you honestly think they'll let Quent and the others live? No, I have to go, if only to make sure they get out of here safely, especially Quent."

I scowl. "Who cares what happens to that monster?"

Inhuman, Modified eyes level on me and peg me with an icy glare. "Why do I get the feeling you don't like him?"

"He killed my parents," I reason, trying to make myself reject the notion that he might have played the game.

The icy glare goes wide. "What? Quentin had nothing to do with that."

"He's a Cyr."

"He's his mother's son, not his father's, and Lady Cyr was your mother's best friend," he growls. His eyes find Quentin, and he keeps his gaze fixed on his friend as he says, "They were part of the same revolution. Do you honestly think Lady Cyr or Quent would have anything to do with your parents' deaths?"

I look away from him. "I don't know anything anymore. No one is who I thought they were." A long silence passes. I scan the Aristocrats clustered around Quentin. Some are watching him, others are watching me. They had to have heard me, about being responsible for the virus. They know that Quentin talked alone with me. I wonder what they suspect. I wonder if they blame me. I look for Delia and Sadie and Bastian. I'm still wearing the mask. Do they realize who I am yet? Would they forgive what I've done? Forgive me for making them lose this world they loved so much? I rub my foot against the floor trying to cope, to let everything sink in. "So you're just going to drag these poor people away with you?"

"We're saving them, Elle. If you don't want to come, then don't. You can test your luck against the Disfavored. You're still a Natural after all; maybe you'll be able to blend in. As for the rest of us…" His eyes sweep the others, making a deliberate point.

"We're not that lucky."

I suddenly remember Gus telling me the story of his brother Max. How Max had been so disgusted that his little brother had been Modified that he'd nearly beaten him to death. The Disfavored hate the Aristocracy, perhaps more than the Aristocracy hate the Disfavored.

And why shouldn't they? The Aristocracy lived in the safety of the domes while radiation and pollution cut down the unlucky Disfavored. Because the Aristocracy had such advanced technology and the convenience of a robotic working class, they enjoyed leisure and comfort while the Disfavored worked themselves to the bone every day just to put horrible food on their tables.

I remember the gruel that Meems fed me before I hacked and reprogrammed Tasha, and a rock forms in my stomach. "They'll kill them all, won't they?" I say quietly. "Out of sheer hatred and resentment."

Gus doesn't look at me. "Most likely. The Disfavored are a hard, unforgiving people, forged by the broken wasteland they were left to rot in."

I bite my lip. The world has so many problems, how could I have ever hoped to build anything good out of this mess? I drop my shoulders. "Isn't there anything we can do to fix this?"

"Perhaps, but it will take a lot of time. We at least need to get someplace safe to regroup and figure things out. We can't do that here."

"There's no telling if they'll even let us through the Undergate at Cadence. We could be stuck in the tunnel until we die of starvation. And even if we do get in, there's no telling what it will be like."

"It's better to not know what's going to happen than to be certain you'll die. We don't know what it's like there. They might help us." Gus forces a smile. "Come on, Elle, it could be like being on a quest in Nexis all over again. You never had any problems fitting in there. You're more versatile than you give yourself credit for."

"That was a game. A game my parents designed *specifically* for me to play," I remind darkly. "There's no Oracle to guide us, there's no spider's silk, and there's no waking up."

He shrugs. "Guess that's why the Pre-Domites believed in life after death. It's reassuring to think there's something else beyond all this. Something to die for." He plants a hand on mine. "Come with us. I just found you again; I don't want to say good-bye so soon. Fixing this disaster will be easier if we stay together."

I look away from him. I honestly don't know what to do. I want to be with Gus, but I'm also responsible for what happened here in Evanescence. Leaving it now, even with the intent to eventually return, doesn't seem right. I wish I could ask Meems for help deciding. "Oh my sparks, Meems."

"What?"

"Meems." I say more urgently. I pull away and glance around. "I need to find her. I have to make sure she's all right." I take a desperate few steps toward the door leading topside before Gus grabs my arm.

"Hang on. Tell me what's going on."

"Meems," I say, my voice growing more desperate. I put a hand to my forehead. "Oh, how could I have forgotten about her? I'll never forgive myself. Please, Gus, we have to go get her. I can't leave her to the Disfavored. Who knows what they'll do to her."

Gus frowns and looks back toward the crowd. His gaze meets Quentin's, who has been watching us for I don't know how long. I look to him as well, pleading. Quentin glances back at the people gathered behind him, then at Sid, then at the screen before him. And then he nods.

"**M**ake sure they follow you to the Undertunnel," Quentin is saying to Sid. "If any of the others are alive, they will meet us down there. We can get food and supplies out of the cache when we get there."

We're standing just on the edge of the Cyr complex, the group of us hidden by a three-way collection of holo-glass screens projecting the gardens that don't exist. I try to catch Quentin's eye, trying to ask that pressing question, "Who played the game?" without using words, but he avoids meeting my eyes at all costs.

Gus squeezes my hand. "Are you all right?"

I squeeze his. "Yeah."

"You're acting weird."

I look up at him. "Am I? How can you tell?"

He gives me an "oh please" expression. "I can read you like a book, Elle."

Elle. That's what game Gus called me. And this is game Gus's body, destroyed as it is, and this boy talks to me about Nexis, knew Nadine's face. How could I wonder who played the game? Still, that kiss… "I'm just worried about Meems is all," I lie. Then, wanting to change the subject, I ask, "How close are you two? You and Quentin?"

He shrugs. "Very close. Like brothers."

"I don't know what it's like to have a sibling." For whatever reason, I glance back at Sadie. She looks so much like she has lost a part of herself. Most likely Katrina died back in Bella Adona and probably all of her friends, considering that she's standing only with an awkward-looking, still bound Bastian. Did she love her friends like sisters? Like how I felt about Delia? I look to Delia who is huddled close to Carsai. Is Carsai Delia's new sister? The idea makes my stomach hurt.

Gus says, "We've been companions for twelve years. He and I have a lot in common."

Like the same kissing style? I shake my head, rejecting what Quentin did and the feelings he raised in the aerovator. Nothing good will come of this confusion. The bottom line is that, in real life, Gus and Quentin are two very different people. I like Gus—love him. I don't even like Quentin. Bottom line. I squeeze Gus's hand, affirming our history and the feelings it brings me. "I'm glad I found you out here in Real World."

He smiles at me. "Me, too. Not just a game anymore, is it?"

That's all the answer I need.

Quentin walks over, his eyes still trained on Sid as he leads the Aristocrats through the deserted street. We stayed underground until most of the overhead commotion stopped. There are bodies, robot and human alike, strewn all over the place. Now that we're out in the open, I can still hear gunshots in the distance, and I'm not so avid to continue.

"How long are they going to keep fighting?" I ask.

"They can't go on forever," Quentin whispers. "By this time tomorrow, all of the power cells in the robots will have died."

"That's if they don't remember to recharge," I add, my voice morbid.

Quentin looks a little disgruntled at that. "Well, let's hope that's not the case."

"What about the rebels?" Gus asks.

Quentin shrugs, his left eye twitching in pain as the gesture pulls at his wound. Gus grimaces and reaches for Quentin. "We need to take care of your wounds."

Quentin steps away from him. "Not now. Let's do what we have to do and rendezvous with the others." He reaches down and pulls out a revolver. "Here." He shoves it into my hand.

I examine the revolver, still warm from being pressed against his skin. I've seen it so many times in Nexis, used it so frequently, that it's like an appendage. I never thought I'd see it again. "I," I start. "I don't know how to use a gun." I look up into Quentin's eyes, but he glances away.

He reaches out and takes the gun that Gus offers as a replacement, then pulls me off to the side, lowering his voice so Gus can't hear him. "You remember asking why you knew how to use a gun in Nexis?"

I don't respond. I'm too busy staring at him in confusion. How does he know something so specific about the game?

He continues speaking. "You knew for the same reason I knew. Proficiency with weaponry was hardwired into your head."

"What?" I breathe.

He looks down, checks the ammunition. "Your mother and my mother. They both programmed us to be exactly as they needed us to be, Ella."

I look back down at the revolver. I remember what Uncle Simon had said about my parents training me. Is it possible that my mother uploaded certain proclivities into my subconscious? It makes a horrible kind of sense. But, if proficiency with a firearm is one, what are the others?

Part of me wants to tell myself that I can't do this, but another part knows I can't afford self-doubt. I need to get to my house. I need to get Meems. I have no way of knowing if she is all right or if she went mad like the other androids. She could be hiding behind the door, waiting to strangle me. But I have to know. If she's all right then I'm not leaving without her. She's all I have left.

I release the safety on the gun and look up. "Okay, let's do this."

We snake through the city, running shadow to shadow, guns upraised and at ready as if this is part of Nexis and we're just on another playing field. Except this is real. If any of us get shot there's no second life. But the streets are quiet, filled only with the moans of the dying and the trickle of blood and hydraulic fluid rushing down the pavement. The scent of singed flesh and the metallic tinge of blood and oil hang heavy in the air. Everywhere I look, there is a body. As expected, there are more dead Aristocrats and Disfavored than robots. Many Aristocrats are in their nightclothes, their bodies shattered from having been thrown out a window by some trusted domestic android.

We can see flashes from above—pods zipping on the hover-way, glass shattering and raining down from above, people screaming. But it's all above. Down here on the ground, where the robots and the machines made our lives so simple, it's quiet. They, like the Disfavored, have opted to climb up in the world.

We reach my housing block without incident. My building doesn't look good. I didn't really expect it to; we lived so close to the wall, and our housing unit is so near to ground level. All the windows have been shot out, the holo-screen for the back garden is shattered, and the front door is ajar. The Disfavored have already been here. I run forward, "Meems," I scream.

"Ella!" That's Quentin.

I can hear them pursuing after me as I slip thought the door and run through the front hall. Most of the lights have been shot out, the art broken to pieces. There's one light on at the very top of the stairwell, across from my room. "Meems?" I call again as I take the stairs two at a time.

As I pass the second landing, I hear a door hiss open behind me. I whip around, expecting Meems, but all I see is the gun in the Disfavored's hand and a flash as he releases a round in my direction.

Behind the Disfavored, Gus's gun is up and firing back, his reflexes inhuman, but not before a shot gets me in the leg. The circuits in the prosthetic limb sizzle as the laser fries them. My whole leg goes stone still, and I tip to one side, tumbling down the steps.

"Elle." Quentin grabs my arm, hauling me up, before I can really gain momentum and hurt myself. Despite his wound, he grits his teeth and lifts me into his arms, carrying me the rest of the way, Gus at point—kicking down doors and scanning rooms before we pass. As we reach the top landing, Quentin lets me down.

Gus crowds him, yanking up my dress, desperate to find my injury. When he sees my damaged leg his hands go still and he stares, eyes wide and disbelieving. Not at the wound, but at the band where the prosthetic meets the flesh.

I hunch my shoulders, feeling sheepish. "Guess you know where that mod chip went."

He drops his hands and lets out a long slow breath. "Guess so."

Seeing that Gus isn't going to tend to my wound, Quentin squats down and puts his hand on my bare skin—the part that's still there—and examines my leg under the harsh glow of the one remaining light in my house. "It doesn't look too bad. We can change out some of the circuitry; that should fix it. Do you have a soldering iron and some extra parts?"

I nod, happy that he seems to know how to handle this. "There should be some extra parts in the case." I'd forgotten Quentin was actually intelligent. Or maybe I never even realized it. He'd always just been eye candy, the attractive boy in school. But he *was* attending the most prestigious school in Evanescence. I scoff. "I always thought you got into Paramount because you were the President's son."

He smiles to himself and shakes his head. "It's good to know those engineering classes are paying off. Where's the case, Elle?"

I frown at him. Elle, huh? And engineering? It doesn't mean anything; Gus went to the same classes as Quentin. They're both trained as Engineers. And Gus must have talked about what he did in the game with Quentin. He must call me Elle outside the game. It only seems natural. It makes perfect sense, Quentin must know everything about what Gus and I did in the game. I blush a little, hoping Gus hasn't told him *everything*, but if he's so specific as to mention my confusion at knowing how to use a firearm, I doubt he excluded much. "In the lower storage facility."

He nods to Gus, who is still staring at my injured leg, and heads back down the stairs.

I tip to the side and try peeking around the doorframe, hoping I can see if Meems is inside.

"Here," Gus grunts. Stepping forward, he drags me to my feet and puts my arm over his shoulders. He helps me into the room where I stop cold.

Meems is on the floor. Dead. She looks like someone threw her into a trash compactor and then the shredder. I wouldn't even recognize her save the torn uniform and the color of those lifeless blue eyes.

"Meems," I whisper, the strength suddenly gone from my whole body. I collapse against Gus, and he lets me down gently.

"Holy Hell," he whispers. "What the heck happened here?"

Holy hell indeed. My eyes linger on the desk and the bank of servers. They've been completely destroyed. There's holo-glass and chips and wires all over the floor, sparks winking in and out, glinting off exposed silicone disks.

I swallow hard. "Can I have a minute?"

"Uh, yeah, take all the time you need." Gus leaves me on the floor where I stare for a very long time at nothing in particular and everything all at once. Numb.

Something twitches in the darkness, clanking gently against the glass. It's Meems. "Meems," I yelp crawling toward the largest chunk of her body. The skin of her chasis has been torn and two of her limbs thrown away from her body, the wires and plasticky sinew still attached. I look into the mush of synthetic muscle, stainless steel bones, ball joints, and hoses, searching for a sign of life, determined that I didn't just imagine movement. I shake her. "Meems?"

Her head ticks in my direction, and an eyelid flaps over one cracked glass eye. "E-e-e-e," her mechanical voice hiccups and skips, "ah-ah-ah."

"Shhh," I whisper, rocking her. "It's okay, I'm going to fix you. You'll be all right."

Erratic, her hand twitches at my side, the wild fingers grasping before the limb shoots up between us, knocking me backward.

"N-n-n-oooo," she wails.

I scramble back to her. "It's okay, it's okay. I'm here. It'll be okay." I grab her clawing hand and hold it to my face, hoping she can sense the warmth of my skin. I want her to know I'm here, want her to feel how very much I love her. "Meems," I whisper. "We'll be okay. I'm going to fix you, hold on." I pivot toward the door. "Quentin, hurry up."

Her head jerks back and forth, back and forth, all the while the wires disconnecting and spitting against the rug. Death throes. "Har-har-harit-t-tant-st-sts. D-Die."

"No," I wail in protest, clutching her hand. "No. You're going to live. We're both going to live. I love you too much to let you die."

Her head stops jerking, and she looks at me again. "L-l-luuhh?"

I nod and touch her face with my free hand. "Yes, love. I love you, Meems."

The muscles around her mouth twitch upward, trying to smile for me. "Meems-loves-Meems-loves-" Her hand opens on my cheek. "Loves, Eh-eh-la-ah-ahhh-ni-ni-ni."

I smile back at her, tears falling. Then her hand slips away, and she spasms one last time. "Meems," I shriek. "Meeeemmms-ss."

But she doesn't respond. Desperate and determined as a madwoman, tears blurring my vision and fingers shaking, I wrench through her biomass, ripping out wires, tossing handfuls of it off to the side. It's just a body. The real Meems, the Meems I love, is deep inside. When my hand closes over the tiny little chip that encloses Meems's personality program and memory bank, I let out a sigh and start laughing, hysterical. I laugh so hard that I begin sobbing again.

I pull the burned chip free and hold it to my chest, letting the ichor of Meems's insides drip down my arms as I cry for my surrogate mother and rock myself through the pain of all this horror and loss.

The chip is fried. Meems is gone. I will never be able to bring her back. As I look around the room, taking in the destroyed console, I see the shattered frames that once housed my parents' smiling faces, and I hear the devastation outside the walls of my own home.

This is my inheritance, another lesson, another truth.

At its root, this destruction isn't from technology. It's from humans. Technology is our tool. We made it, and we control it. And this is the consequence of using tools we don't understand.

While I've learned to love the beauty of the natural world, there is still unforgiveable ugliness inside nature's most prolific creature: the human. That's something I never focused on enough. How much of my fear of my own internal destroyer drove me to plant that virus? Was I only seeing the things I feared in myself reflected in those around me? Am I a self-fulfilling prophecy?

It's not just a matter of making humans love the beauty of their bodies and the world around them. It's also a matter of making them love the beauty inside themselves and others. I understand that now, though I have no idea what to do next.

chapter forty-seven

Light flickers against my drawn eyelids. Despite the din outside of our housing block, I hear a strange new sound. Something like a low, persistent hiss. A dragon's hissing exhale. I open my eyes and blink against the new gray-white light. All around me the shattered nano-glass is coming to life with static—each piece like its own tiny sheet. The holo-screens have popped up, some lopsided and others distorted, because their projectors have been knocked off their stands. Everywhere it's fuzzy black and white, and the hissing noise is deafening.

With a bright white flash, the screens clear, revealing a pair of hands fidgeting with a lens, adjusting it for clarity. It's the same image in all the screens, hundreds of pairs of hands reaching out. I tip my head, trying to make out the picture in the largest of the screens. The hands draw away in the next moment, and there's a face of a woman. Me. No, my mother. She smiles demurely into the camera and dances away for an instant before the image moves once again to her sitting with a small child.

"Do something for the video." The voice behind the camera is my father's.

My mother grins and laughs a little, like this is a game. "What do you want us to do?"

"Sing for us," Dad commands.

My mother waves her hand in dismissal. "No, I'm a terrible singer."

"Your voice is lovely." Dad's words are warm and serious, laced with the same kind of tone Gus uses on me. "Come on, Cleo. Please sing for me?"

Mom rolls her eyes and fights her laughter as she fidgets. "Okay, okay."

She turns to the small child and tucks her legs underneath her, giving the child her full attention. There's affection in her eyes, something I've only ever wished for in a mother. "Okay, Ella, we're going to sing for Daddy. You ready?"

The child looks up at the camera, and I realize belatedly that it's me. That chubby, curly-haired thing is me, and I'm with my parents. Swaying, I grin at the camera; I'm so young I can barely hold myself upright.

My mother holds out her hands, drawing the attention of my child-self back to her. I'm mesmerized by her—by those beautiful outstretched hands. And then my mother begins to sing.

"The itsy-bitsy spider went up the water spout." As she sings she makes complicated hand gestures, upward and finger-to-finger in a way that makes the child on the screen giggle and scream with delight. *"Down came the rain and washed the spider out."* Her fingers wriggle down and crash against the carpet. My child-self flaps her arms in approval. *"Out came the sun and dried up all the rain."* The fingers move above her head and form a circle. My child-self claps in admiration, making my mother's gray eyes smile as she moves to make the final finger-to-finger

gesture again. *"And the itsy-bitsy spider went up the spout again."*

The screens go white, the brightness casting a ghostly pallor over the decimated remains of Meems. In the background my mother's song repeats itself. As she sings, another video starts. It's the video in the last code my father gave me—a magnificent golden bird, perched on a lotus, unfurling its wings, taking flight, and then bursting into flames. As the ash rains down, tiny silver threads begin weaving back and forth across the screen until I can read one single word. *Persevere.* From the ashes at the bottom of the screen, a tiny sprout begins to grow.

Fresh tears sting my eyes as the plant grows strong, blooms, and from its petals springs the bird once more. Only to take flight and burn up all over again.

Gus bursts in through the door, startling me. For a moment he takes in the screens on the floor and then he glances up to me, crying again. He lets out a long, slow breath, his eyes showing the pain he feels for me—with me. "Come here." He holds his arms open as I struggle to my feet and hobble toward him, my feet crunching over broken circuitry and shattering nano-glass into dust. He folds me into his arms and holds me for a long moment.

The reel of my mother singing starts up again.

"The itsy-bitsy spider…"

"You need to see this," he whispers into my hair as he turns me away from the room and toward where Quentin is standing staring through the frame where the hall window used to be. Even here the bird continues its cyclical death, and the word "persevere" litters the hall floor.

"What is it?" I ask.

Quentin glances over his shoulder. "It's a phoenix."

Phoenix. I've read about those. A creature that rises from its own ashes. A beauty born from destruction. That was my father's hope, that's why he watched the Disfavored. Because they kept trying, despite the odds. My father's very last message to me—ringing true, even after the destruction of the Anansi Virus.

As I come to stand beside Quentin, my eyes go wide with wonder. *"Down came the rain…"* Written across the sky, across every building face, across the hovering holo-screens, and the billboards, and the windows of every building, are my father's word to me. *Persevere.*

Standing here, I can hear the echo of my mother's beautiful natural voice blaring from every speaker in the city. *"Out came the sun…"*

The phoenix bursts upward, stretching toward the sky.

I lean in to Gus and smile to myself. "Gus?" I whisper.

I may have destroyed the world, but I shouldn't fear the destroyer inside.

He tightens his arm around my waist. "Hmm?"

Because sometimes you have to destroy in order to create.

"I know what I have to do."

And sometimes the most beautiful things can rise from the ugliest of ashes.

"And the itsy-bitsy spider crawled up the spout again."

acknowledgments

First, of course, is my mother, who raised me to believe I could be anything if I tried hard enough, was the first to tell me that I had talent as a writer, and then later sat and listened to me gush about my pieces for hours without complaining. Mom, you're my hero and my greatest supporter, and I'll love you forever!

Abby, you started me on this crazy writing path by convincing me to write a *Dragon Ball Z/Digimon* mash-up fan fiction—it was pretty silly, but I found my core through that stack of papers, and I'll treasure that story always.

Tamora Pierce, I don't know if I would have discovered my love of the book without you. You're the first author I read whose work I could not put down. Your books drove me to sit down and write beyond fan fiction with a friend and opened a hundred-thousand worlds to my mind.

My fans deserve a giant bow. You, ladies and gentlemen, keep authors sane and on track. There is no way for any author to express her thanks for your insatiable appetites except give you more, and I promise to do just that.

My Beta-Readers, you keep me from making a fool of myself before the literary gods with my constant homophone confusions and unfathomable addiction to dues ex machina. Thank you for always taking that last-minute look and for reading the same story ten times over every session I edit.

Stella Price, I owe you a lot for being my first writer friend, guiding me into the industry, inviting me to cons, and urging me to pitch the woman who became my agent.

Speaking of agents, Louise Fury, you're in here, too. We've had a long, hard road as an author/agent duo, but we're finally here! Thanks so much for sticking with me and believing in my work!

Liz Pelletier, you saw potential where so many editors did not. Nexis is a dynamic and challenging book, but you dove in with both feet and never looked back. Thank you for the opportunity to make my dreams come true.

My lovely publicity team and the other fantastic people who work at Entangled, you guys rock!

Finally, I would like to thank the friends and family who have stuck by me throughout my writing career. Being part of a creative person's life isn't always easy—we keep weird hours, we fall off the face of the earth for months, we obsess about projects and don't shut up about them, we share ourselves with so many people that we often don't have enough left for those who are closest to us, and we aren't always present because our minds are literally someplace else. Our priorities aren't always straight, and that makes loving us hard. I lost some people I never thought I would lose while on this path and it only makes those who have stood by me even more precious to me. Thank you all so much!

thief of lies
BY BRENDA DRAKE (coming 1/5/2016)

When a leather-clad hottie disappears into thin air at the library, he leaves only a book behind—a book of world libraries. With that, Gia Kearns stumbles upon the world of the Mystik, where there is magic, the ability to travel through "gateway" books to other libraries...and Arik, a Sentinel charged with protecting humans from malovolent creatures. There are also those who long to destroy both worlds, and Gia will to choose between her heart and her head, between Arik's world and her own, before both are destroyed.

forget tomorrow
BY PINTIP DUNN

The epic love story of Obsidian as told by its hero, Daemon Black! I knew the moment Katy Swartz moved in next door, there was going to be trouble. And trouble's the last thing I need, since I'm not exactly from around here. My people arrived on Earth from Lux, a planet thirteen billion light years away. But Kat is getting to me in ways no one else has, and I can't stop myself from wanting her. But falling for Katy—a human—won't just place her in danger. It could get us all killed, and that's one thing I'll never let happen...